HEART OF DESIRE

11.11.11 REDUX

HEART OF DESIRE

11.11.11 REDUX

KATE ROBINSON

TOOTIE-DO PRESS

LOS ANGELES
REDWOOD HIGHWAY 101
SAN DIEGO
AJO

This book is a work of fiction. Any references to real people, events, establishments, organizations, or locales are intended only to give the fiction a sense of reality and authenticity and are used fictitiously. All other characters, and all incidents and dialogue, are drawn from the author's imagination and their resemblance, if any, to real-life counterparts is entirely coincidental.

TOOTIE-DO PRESS
LOS ANGELES :: REDWOOD HIGHWAY 101 :: SAN DIEGO :: AJO

Cover design by Clarissa Yeo, Yocla Book Cover Designs
Interior design by Starstone Editorial
Author photo by Joe DiBuduo
Tootie-Do Press logo photo by Kate Robinson

ISBN 979-8-218-05300-0

FOR ALL SENTIENT BEINGS

"What is hovering in the sky above the White House and the halls of power in Washington, D.C. besides global warming, political intrigue, and secret love trysts? Kate Robinson leads readers on a journey of switchbacks and blind views to *Heart of Desire's* riveting, thought-provoking conclusion."

::: Carl Hitchens
Author of *Sitting with Warrior*

"Writing of the prologue and first chapters commands attention . . . may be closer to the truth than any of us know . . . I think this writer did an excellent job . . . has thought [the story line] through carefully and hints at complications with extraterrestrials that stretch the imagination. The writer makes even unlikely scenes between [humans] and extraterrestrials believable . . . The writing is good. The grammar is excellent. The narration, dialogue and tension are high . . . The reader immediately likes the characters and roots for them."

::: Anonymous Judge
Arizona Authors Association 2006 Literary Competition
Unpublished Novel category

"Well written . . . movie script adaptable. Gripping style . . . Chapter 7 reminded me of Hunter Thompson's 'Gonzo' journalism, i.e. 'Fear & Loathing' – Kate Robinson is a talented and imaginative writer!"

::: Rev. Robert Hanzel
Aquarian Church of Universal Service

"The fifth revolution will come when we have spent the stores of coal and oil that have been accumulating in the earth during hundreds of millions of years."

::: SIR CHARLES GALTON DARWIN, 1952

"In the counsels of Government, we must guard against the acquisition of unwarranted influence, whether sought or unsought, by the Military Industrial Complex. The potential for the disastrous rise of misplaced power exists, and will persist . . . Only an alert and knowledgeable citizenry can compel the proper meshing of the huge industrial and military machinery of defense with our peaceful methods and goals so that security and liberty may prosper together."

::: PRESIDENT DWIGHT D. EISENHOWER, 1961

"There [is] an inner government in the United States, a centralized state, far more powerful than anything else, for whom the enemy is not simply the Communists, but everything else, its own press, its own judiciary, its own Congress, foreign and friendly governments . . . it does not function necessarily for the benefit of the Republic but rather for its own ends . . ."

::: NEIL SHEEHAN, 1971

"When the solution to the UFO problem comes, I believe that it will prove to be not merely the next small step in the march of science, but a mighty and totally unexpected leap."

::: J. ALLEN HYNEK, 1972

"*What are the elite media . . . first of all, they are major, very profitable corporations . . . most of them are linked to or outright owned by much bigger corporations, i.e. General Electric, Westinghouse, and so on. They are . . . at the top of the power structure of the private economy, which is a tyrannical structure. Corporations are basically tyrannies, hierarchic, controlled from above.*"

::: Noam Chomsky, 1997

"*Others are engaging even in an eco-type of terrorism whereby they can alter the climate, set off earthquakes, volcanoes remotely through the use of electromagnetic waves. So there are plenty of ingenious minds out there that are at work finding ways in which they can wreak terror upon other nations.*"

::: Secretary of Defense William Cohen, 1997

"*One of the saddest lessons of history is this: If we've been bamboozled long enough, we tend to reject any evidence of the bamboozle. We're no longer interested in finding out the truth . . . Once you give a charlatan power over you, you almost never get it back.*"

::: Carl Sagan, 1997

"*The world today stands on the brink of a confluence three major, global crises: peak oil, global warming and the imminent collapse of the global banking system. All of these are inter-related, and have greed as their ultimate cause.*"

::: Emanuel Sferios, 2006

"The desires of the heart are as crooked as corkscrews . . ."

::: W.H. Auden, "Death's Echo"

::: Prologue

"The irony of human life is that our very desire results in suffering."

::: Judith Simmer-Brown, *Dakini's Warm Breath*

Teresa Vaughn looked up from the softcover novel and glanced down at eight-month-old Mikka, pleased with the baby's contented play. Her attention soon wavered back to the tragic story, so real and yet so insubstantial, like the bubble dissolving on the surface of her spearmint tea.

A few pages later, the silent room jarred the fortyish mother from her book. Mikka was absent from her usual place beside the basket of toys on the braided rug. Tess's chest contracted. She gazed around the kitchen and jumped up from the ladderback chair, spilling the cobalt-glazed mug in a clanging tumble from tabletop to rug to hardwood floor. It spun and inched to a stop against the love-worn plush lion that Mikka was teething on.

"Mikka? Mikka!" She didn't go . . . did she?

Her voice grew louder each time she called the baby's name. She rattled the kitchen doorknob. Securely locked. She dashed from the kitchen and sprinted in circles throughout the lower level of her hand-built house, a log and stone cottage adrift on a high desert prairie. In the spacious living room and office area, she rummaged behind furniture and piles of colorful floor cushions, flipping light switches and snapping lamps on, one with so much psychic force that the bulb burned out.

She screwed up her face in thought while she trotted up the carpeted pine stairwell to the second story. Mikka liked to crawl up stairs, though she'd never gone all the way to the second floor before. Tess began to repeat her search as if second nature. Mikka was absent from the master bedroom at the top of the stairs. With a little prayer, she pictured the baby safe in her room at the end of the hall.

No joy. Some old-fashioned wooden toys lay scattered below bright storage modules bursting with toys and picture books. Standing for a moment over Mikka's empty crib, Tess balled her hand into a fist and pressed it over her heart. An instant later, she took a step backward, turned abruptly, and strode from the room.

"Mikka-ah," she called a hundredth time, her voice vibrating with the rhythm of her footsteps.

She turned and jogged down the short hallway, her long hair swinging across her back. Pushing a half-closed door open with a thud, she peered inside at an empty clawfoot bathtub illuminated by the hallway light. Her cheeks rounded with a relieved sigh as she inhaled the lingering lilac scent of Mikka's evening bubble bath.

Tess retraced her steps down the hall and stairway and called again, her voice rising. "Mikka!"

She paused at the massive front door and flipped another light switch, arching her back and flexing a trim bicep to unfasten bolt and security chain. She burst through the door with another loud thud, the brass hinges squawking. Her eyes darted again around the screened porch that wrapped around the front of the house, and underneath the weathered wicker chaise lounge, rocker, and side table.

When a happy squeal pealed from outside, Tess held her breath and kicked the screen door open. Her baby sat in a flowerbed, one chubby fist partially crammed into her mouth, the other hand extended toward Tess. A large Luna moth fluttered from the shadows and lit upon the tip of Mikka's tiny forefinger.

She marveled at the sight until the moth spiraled into the darkness. Then she scooped Mikka into her arms and held her close, a tight smile softening her frazzled expression. She kissed the baby's cheeks, bounced her, and smoothed her yellow and pink flowered dress and leggings in little nervous pats.

"Goodness, Mikka."

"Pre."

"How did you get out of the house? The doors were locked!"

"Pre," the baby repeated. "Pre-pre."

"That's a pretty moth. Pret-ty mo-th." She lowered her face level with Mikka's and elongated the syllables.

"Pree ma. Pree pree ma," the baby chortled again, her auburn curls and golden skin glowing under the yellow porch light.

Relieved, she placed her forehead against Mikka's and they each grinned at the one-eyed, cyclops view of the other.

"How do you leave one place and end up in another, Meekers? You can't even walk yet. This is the third time . . . you scared the daylights out of me again."

Mikka wiggled with delight, crowing a happy squeal that rose to the stars. She suddenly straightened her back and turned a sober face toward the ranch gate at the driveway's end, fastened with chain and padlock to a stout post.

Tess followed Mikka's gaze, her heart dropping, but she saw only a shadow cast across the frosty ground, a play of light caused by clouds crossing the moon.

::: CHAPTER 1

PRESIDENT HARRIS CANTRELL HENRY
AUGUST 2009

President Harris Cantrell Henry sighed and turned to watch the street. After a brief visit with his ailing mother in an assisted living facility—his real mother, not the woman who pushed her aside to help his dad raise him—he found himself hurtling toward the Des Moines International Airport in yet another black bulletproof Mercedes. He prayed that Myrtle Davis Henry would fully recover and make it through his term in office. He'd always reveled in her enthusiastic support and sometimes secretly doubted his power to achieve his goals without her.

The broad sycamore trees lining the boulevard seemed to fly past the tinted windows. He admired the lush setting near the Governor's mansion in the heart of downtown Des Moines, a garden city at the confluence of two rivers. The clouds gathering over the gilded dome of the state capitol building reminded him of his possible loss. His early separation from Myrtle as an infant, a situation he didn't question until his university years, would make losing her permanently even more poignant.

But Myrtle was gaining strength, so he shouldn't worry about losing her, not yet. But a real loss crossed his mind. The day felt almost identical to that drizzly, overcast morning nearly a year before when his campaign manager deposited Tess Vaughn on a commercial flight after their final night together. He'd never strayed before—he felt content with First Lady Merrill Webster Henry and found no fault with her—but his world tilted when Tess walked away. Despite his stellar relationship with Merrill and their twins Delaney and Leigh, despite all they'd worked together to achieve when he'd emerged victor at the Democratic National Convention, Tess had attracted him. She put him in touch with something different in himself, something he'd never experienced before. A vital, creative aspect that lay hidden in his heart like a single wildflower blooming in the concrete heart of a city. He'd given Tess up reluctantly, felt her absence even as he and his family strolled along the inaugural parade route on Pennsylvania Avenue under the stern eye of the U.S. Capitol dome.

For a moment, he allowed himself to visualize Tess in the last photo he shot of her, that half-crooked smile lighting up her angular olive face and wide-set brown eyes, the outline of her breasts visible under flowing silk.

Then he turned his disciplined mind back to business. U.S. oil extraction had increased with systematic fracking but caused earthquakes and polluted groundwater; the threat of domestic terrorism popped out like a pox here and there; the economy still lay in shambles, and no one could predict or control the weather. By coincidence, he hoped, not only was arctic ice melting at an unprecedented rate, the Earth's axis tilt was increasing and its magnetic field had destabilized over the past few months. Would the result be a normal migration of magnetic poles or a disastrous polar shift?

He mulled over these contradictions as the Mercedes slowed to a stop. The driver, a Secret Service agent, and a second agent riding shotgun briskly stepped from the Mercedes and ushered him outside. The Service detail dispensed with the typical motorcycle escort to avoid unwanted attention on this trip. He'd slipped into Des Moines quietly and would slip back out again unnoticed.

A senior aide appeared at his side. "Mr. President, the latest NIHSA environmental report. Urgent and needs immediate review." The bespectacled young man placed new scientific data, safely shielded in its classified folder inside a locked and coded valise, into his hand while his Secret Service detail hustled him from the auto and into an unmarked military chopper. Probably some ploy to appease public grousing about global warming by "the Agency," he thought, using his nickname for the National Intelligence Homeland Security Agency (NIHSA), the recently combined NSA, FBI, CIA, and Homeland Security.

He sighed. Alternative media speculated often about the dire consequences of global warming. Amateur astronomers and armchair scientists as well as seasoned professionals documented Earth changes daily in blogs and chat rooms around the world. Yet the latest celebrity scandal or baby bump received far more popular mainstream news coverage. To his dismay, NIHSA insisted that mainstream media downplay climatic events. Even trusted venues like National Geographic and NPR discussed Earth tilt and magnetic field ramifications in a measured, rational bent that made dire consequences seem remote. Conservative pundits mocked legitimate scientists and foundations while cleverly spinning data to their own ends.

He hated the subterfuge, but he understood it. He'd reluctantly conceded it was not necessary to create undue anxiety about the gradual inundation of coastal cities. America's coasts were clobbered regularly by record-breaking hurricanes during the regular spring, summer, and fall hurricane seasons of the new millennium, but also at random as weather patterns became even more chaotic. It didn't require an advanced degree from an elite university to see where the combination of violent supercell storms and polar ice melt would lead. Not to mention the rise of atmospheric CO2, and the Earth tilt, rotation, and magnetic field irregularities that aggravated climate anomalies. Every industrial nation in the world except the US and China signed the well-reasoned multinational agreements recognizing global warming. Only the two corporate empires, a capitalist democracy and a capitalist communist bloc, had held out, unwilling to stop profiting until doomsday arrived. President Henry vowed to change that, and soon.

He soared northeast to meet Merrill and their entourage in Chicago, shepherded by another somber Secret Service detail. After completing their late morning speaking engagement in Chi-town, they boarded Air Force One at O'Hare International to conclude a post-election policy jaunt that sliced through the Midwest to the upper East coast. Normally he felt energized while meshing with the grand cogs and gears of his political machine. But today he wished they could simply relax. Wander downtown, stop for a bite at one of Chicago's famous pizzerias, and soak up some blues in old dives on the South Side as he and Merrill used to do when they studied at the University of Chicago campus.

Rushed again from military chopper to Air Force One, his day was far from over. Valise in hand, he geared up for an afternoon policy briefing as they soared to Cleveland.

Merrill Henry smiled over reading glasses at him, pushing a lock of honey-colored hair behind a dainty, honey-colored ear. "Hey, sweetie. How's Myrtle?"

"Better. She's stronger. The blood tests are good. Her doctors are optimistic. Should have a few good years left if she continues to improve. She laughed about our invitation to live at the White House."

"I'm glad." Merrill smiled warmly at him and resumed reading.

A moment later, Merrill gazed around and jabbed him in the ribs with a long, slender finger as he absorbed a policy paper. "Is there a mechanical problem? Shouldn't we be in the air, Harr?" She tapped her favorite stainless-steel mechanical pencil against a cabin window.

Generally, Air Force One taxied for takeoff immediately after the phalanx of Secret Service agents whisked the government servants and journalists aboard. This time the plane continued to perch near the brand-new VIP terminal, a marvel of geodesic angles and bulletproof glass. He looked up from the front page of The New York

Times and nodded at Chief of Staff Lody Ramirez, a trim, youthful man with a full head of wavy, dark hair sitting nearby with favored media representatives. Ramirez conferred with the black-suited Secret Service agent who stood with crossed arms at a discreet distance from the entourage.

"They're a bit behind schedule—according to the crew, an unexpected electrical anomaly cropped up," the agent advised Ramirez after returning from the cockpit.

Ramirez turned to him. "Mr. President, they've got a handle on the situation, but the flight crew will have to repeat the pre-flight routine. It will be about twenty minutes before we take off."

"Thank you, Lody." He yawned and checked his watch. "A nap'll do me some good." He kissed Merrill on one cheek and excused himself. "Conference room in fifteen."

He emerged from one of his famous power naps in the private cabin as promised exactly fifteen minutes later. The staff rose and followed him into the Air Force One conference room. Vice President Gaphurst Allen and his wife Ashara joined the conference via monitor from Air Force Two, where the couple and their staff preceded his entourage to Cleveland from Washington, D.C. and awaited clearance to land.

A lively appraisal of issues that a recent poll deemed most pressing ensued: economy, environment, and terrorism. "Gloom, doom, and the apocalypse," he reminded them.

"We've got our work cut out for us," Gap agreed from the monitor.

Associate Attorney General Baxter Chopps jotted notes on a legal pad and Ramirez typed nimbly into an envelope-thin laptop across the table from Henry and the First Lady.

So skillful and finely tuned was the jet's ascent from the flight line that the passengers took no more notice of it than the gradual acceleration of a fine automobile on a motorway.

When Henry gazed at his watch approximately thirty minutes later, Ramirez took the cue. "Take five, ladies and gentlemen."

Henry stood and pulled up one leg behind him and then the other in runner's stretches. Running in place for two minutes, he circled the small room several times before sinking back into his leather chair.

Meanwhile, the briefing trailed into Beltway gossip. He flashed one of his trademark smiles when Ashara took center stage on the monitor and started to clown around, puffing her cheeks and belly out in imitation of pompous and fabulously wealthy Senator C. Clelland Collins. Holding a hand toward the conference monitor, she rubbed her thumb and fingertips together. "I fully support environmental concerns *and* the health of the American economy," she boasted in a fake baritone voice.

"Hear ye, hear ye." Bax stood in front of the conference monitor and puffed his cheeks and belly out, waddling in a circle and polishing his nails on his lapel.

Lody's insane giggle trilled through the cabin, putting everyone in stitches. Lody crouched to the floor and imitated a lizard doing head bobs and push-ups, making fun of the recent tabloid reports that Collins and his family were in cahoots with extraterrestrial human-reptilian hybrids.

Henry left his presidential cares behind to lean back and chuckle at Ashara's and Bax's antics and Lody's giggle. He encouraged light-hearted banter in his administration and his daily vitamin was at least one belly laugh per meeting. Usually his staff wasn't this silly but the tough election and the even tougher national and international issues they faced made them susceptible to letting off steam in a childish way. Barely five months into the administration's first year, violent opposition from Collins' so-called Moral Right movement and constant monitoring by NIHSA was taking its toll.

His smile faded as he checked his watch again. Though sometimes a laughable buffoon, Republican Senator Collins of Iowa—Triple C, he liked to call the man—was truly powerful and the bane of his political existence long before he'd ascended to the presidency. His long-time best friend Drew Forrest, the impeccable investigative reporter, had dug into rumors about the Collins family since Henry cut his teeth in law school. Drew's latest book rocked DC, but like he said, people in

Foggy Bottom had short memories and there was always more muck to rake. Drew was now unearthing strange new odds and ends.

"Let's begin again, team," Ramirez coached. All eyes on the monitor image from Air Force Two turned to Henry as he pulled his valise from his lap, hefted it to the conference table, deftly keyed his code into the digital lock, and extracted the thick blue binder stamped CLASSIFIED in bold, red letters.

Merrill shifted in her seat, questions reflected in her cat-like brown eyes.

"An environmental study sanctioned and interpreted by NIHSA. We've got a bigger problem than we thought." He licked his thumb and shuffled through the pages, held with old-fashioned brass fasteners at the top, until he came to the final narrative summary.

"Is this meant for review by everyone here?" Gap's face became sober on the conference screen, collapsing from a boyish grin to what Ashara called his doctor look.

"Yes, everyone aboard Air Force One and Air Force Two is privy to what I'll present now. We'll discuss the more sensitive, 'need to know' aspects at the next Cabinet meeting." He cleared his throat and raised his head as though posing for a television broadcast. "The gist in fifty words or less: Earth's axis tilt has changed by seven percent over the past year, two percentage points more than the normal variable of one to five percent. Added to the planet's magnetic field weakening by ten percent over the past 150 years, the result might be an upcoming field revers—"

A sudden glimmer in his peripheral vision piqued his curiosity. He glanced across the table at the conference monitor, affixed like a flat screen television to a wall divider.

"Is that static interference . . . ?" Static was a problem with the specially encrypted video linkage between Air Force One and Air Force Two. Everyone followed his gaze. Twin translucent forms shimmered from the monitor and firmed in consistency.

He blinked. Another electrical anomaly, a malfunction caused by the screen's holographic capability? The tall figures emerging from it had to be an optical illusion. Perhaps he'd stared at the screen too long.

As the figures continued to materialize in front of him, he tried to stand and shout. But he barely managed to blink his eyes. His heart started to pound and he imagined in cartoon-like images that his jaw sagged and his eyes bugged out on sticks. Who in the hell were these black-suited gentlemen? They weren't the beefy Secret Service or NIHSA agent types. Definitely not holograms either, a feature rumored to be gleaned from reverse engineering of an extraterrestrial craft stored in Nevada's Area 51. Holograms were rarely used with the conference video screens aboard Air Force One and Two due to interference with terrestrial navigational systems.

He tried to peer through a window to see if anything was happening outside but couldn't turn his head. Were they on the ground? He couldn't recall whether they'd taken flight or not.

He tried to speak and to motion to Merrill, but managed only to jiggle his lower lip in the tiniest of motions. Beads of sweat trickled down his forehead. His arms tingled with an odd electric current and his legs felt like over-inflated balloons about to pop. At least he could move his eyes, which darted in a blur from Merrill to Ramirez to his other colleagues around the conference table, and finally back to the lanky men in front of him.

The handsome blond men stared at him with intense yet vacant eyes. His body relaxed a bit. Finally, he uttered a few words that bubbled out as if he spoke underwater. "What's going on here?"

Mr. Henry, excuse our intrusion. We are reviewers. We will review your instructions.

Their detached, mechanical voices manifested, to his consternation, inside his head. But his own fleeting thoughts felt garbled. *Can they read my mind? Is it possible to block my thoughts? How do I control this situation?*

The pair moved in odd synchronized motions as they edged closer to him.

He tried to thrust his foot out and trip them, but his leg barely twitched. *Holy crap*, he thought.

A contradiction in terms, the pair responded, casting a curious look at one another.

Their response answered one of his questions—the pair were definitely clairvoyant. He tried to grip the arms of his seat, but his hands refused to budge. His thoughts began to sputter out and he did his best to make them gruff. *You're dealing with the President of the United States!* He added a few more phrases, protesting, threatening, and finally whining. The men did not respond. And everyone he could glimpse onboard Air Force One and on the monitor from Air Force Two appeared frozen in place.

He trembled with the effort to open his eyes wider. He stared hard at the pair's faces, which wavered like mirages and then became translucent for a split second.

He almost shit his pants. *Crapola.*

One guy cocked his head. *Excrement?*

Henry blinked and looked again. Textured brown amphibian hide and bright eyes like yellow ice surfaced behind the Miami tans and sky blue eyes. *Good Lord.* Had the tabloids gotten the wildhair story about Senator C. Clelland Collins right? Drew Forrest had found something strange about two of Collins's staff members right before the election but couldn't quite pin it down at the time . . . Henry stopped in mid-thought, reminding himself that the strange men read or heard his thoughts just as he read or heard theirs.

The pair pulled devices about the length of ballpoint pens and about the thickness of relay running batons from their breast pockets, positioned the devices between thumbs and ring fingers, and aimed them at Henry.

He couldn't hide his surprise. *Whatinthehell? What kind of bad sci-fi movie is this?* He half-expected Tommy Lee Jones and Will Smith to burst into the cabin.

Though the devices emitted no noise or light, he felt suddenly tranquilized and he heard the men's hypnotic directives as though no other truth existed.

We are concerned, one "said" in an officious tone.

The other beastie boy chided him in the same mechanical

cadence. *We are disappointed at the digressions from NIHSA policy made by you, your cabinet, and members of your administration. The new climatic conditions are essential to the alignment of our power structure. These conditions are not to be interfered with in any way.*

Power structure? Extraterrestrial directives? The pair, the ETs, Henry thought of them now, began talking about taking "mind prints."

We will check on your progress periodically, the first ET thought tersely.

Henry tried to grimace. *Why do I feel reassured?*

They looked at him again with quizzical expressions, apparently confused by his sarcasm. Henry tried to glare at them, instinctively realizing they'd embedded their instructions in his mind.

Apprehension filled his gut with a big cold lump.

The scene in front of him flashed faster and faster into a blur, a video chip stream on fast forward. The tiny data chips were rumored to be either a straightforward gift of ET technology or another NIHSA reverse-engineered device. The new chips were presented to the public in the form of chipped credit and debit cards holding basic account and ID information. But Henry learned of the advanced chips in his first NIHSA briefing, how these were used in the bowels of the intel agency to hold massive gigs of info, including holographic images and films of suspected terrorists and other clandestine activity. These could be contained in small gemstones and worn as jewelry, making them almost impossible to track.

The ETs disappeared in a quick dissolve as enigmatically as they'd appeared. Henry felt his body relax and he twitched once when full bodily sensation surged through his nervous system.

His wife and his colleagues stirred as if awaking from a deep sleep. The press pool seemed especially confused when Henry personally rose to check on them and the Secret Service detail outside the conference room. He gazed around without comment at the dozen or so personnel and staggered back to sink into the leather upholstery of his chair. Lody Ramirez looked stunned. Merrill began primping, pushing her bangs across her forehead as though she'd mussed her hair. Chopps frowned at him, looking perplexed. Across from Henry, the faces of National Security Advisor Howard Raineville and his perky black senior aide, Terry T., as she liked to be called, were split by the wide grins they sported during the playful interlude prior to Henry's introduction of the NIHSA report.

He reached out to pick up the report, but it was no longer on the table in front of him.

No one aboard Air Force Two noticed his confusion. Onscreen, Vice President Allen pulled his hand away from Ashara's shoulder and loosened his signature sky blue tie. He responded to the viewpoint she'd voiced before the interruption about the preservation of disappearing public lands. "Yeah, you're right, Ash," he said, not missing a beat.

Merrill cocked her head at Gap and Ashara's images, simultaneously business-like and girlish. "We've got to do more than that. You're both too soft on environment," she told them.

Ashara cast a frown at the conference screen. "What? Environment equals politics these days."

"What's the matter, Mr. President?" Allen shot a sharp look at him via the screen.

Henry opened his mouth to reply. No sound emerged. Merrill handed him a bottle of purified water. He slugged down half of it, then tried to speak again.

"Cat's got my tongue," he joked, transforming his lower Midwestern drawl into a parody of his veep's New England accent.

In a sudden burst of energy, the groups on both aircraft began to engage in a sobering argument about the environmental terrorism that had erupted recently, replacing suicide bombings by foreign terrorists. No one paid any more attention to Henry's ongoing struggle to readjust. He leaned back and sniffed the air. A subtle and peculiar odor hung over him, the scent of a kitchen match doused in a beer can. He rubbed a sore spot on the back of his skull next to his right ear and checked his watch again. His skin crawled and he almost shivered involuntarily. Nearly an hour had passed.

Henry pushed the incident out of his mind because there was no other way to get through the day's final public appearance.

⁘

In another generic-looking though luxurious room in a Philadelphia hotel, after his sixth identical speech in three days, President Henry tossed and turned through the night. A subtle, almost chronic headache had nagged at him since the flight from Chicago to Cleveland.

"Honey?" Merrill winced when he turned a bedside light on and grabbed his valise from the side table, snapping it open in an almost savage gesture.

"The classified report is gone again. It disappeared twice before on Air Force One."

Merrill propped herself on one elbow. "Harris, are you okay? What are you talking about?"

"The report disappeared during our meeting on the way to Chicago, reappeared in the valise after we left Chicago, and then disappeared when I made a mental note to discuss it again on our flight to Philly. At first I didn't quite get it, but now I remember."

"Harr—are you sure you're not dreaming?" She patted the bed beside her. "Get some rest, honey. Let's talk about this in the morning."

"You're right," he conceded, crawling back in the warm cocoon of bedclothes and snuggling closer to his level-headed mate. The room faded as he drifted into exhausted sleep.

⁘

President Henry came to with a start.

"Harris, wake up." Merrill pointed the television remote at the flat screen television on the wall opposite the bed and raised the volume. "What in the world is this?"

He yawned and tried to focus. A spear of sunlight shone between the slightly parted drapes on the other side of the room. Onscreen, two morning show newscasters railed at one another over a curved walnut desk about the hour's delay in air traffic at O'Hare International Airport and the closed VIP terminal, one dismissing "The Air Force One luncheon party" as a reason for both, and the other decrying the decadent and self-absorbed Henry administration. No one dared mention race, but the administration attracted every other criticism possible and the race issue simmered beneath the situation like an invisible toxin.

He looked at his wife square in the eyes. She didn't remember anything, did she? Perplexed, he struggled to find the words needed to explain his experience. But she probably wouldn't buy it. "Lord have mercy, Baby. What the media won't dream of next. The Moral Right must be on the warpath again. Supplies are brought aboard Air Force One in advance of our arrival. And we boarded after lunch that day."

She gazed at him quizzically. "Honey, this just doesn't make sense."

Despite a non-existent luncheon party, the media bombarded the airwaves with shots of flustered air traffic controllers and livid politicians grousing about Air Force One impeding air traffic. Most convincing were the interviews of angry passengers who'd queued up outside the cordoned VIP terminal while their flights were delayed. Supposedly, this was a much bigger boondoggle than the expensive haircut Bill Clinton scheduled aboard Air Force One years before.

He pulled the remote from Merrill's hand and turned off the television. "Well," he said, puffing his cheeks out, "sounds like this will come off as our people's word against the media. Actually, my word against . . . whose policy? Would the goddamn Agency offer me classified information on a need to know basis and then intimidate me about it? Because that's what they seem to be doing."

Rock-steady Merrill gave him one of her penetrating gazes. "Harris, whatever are you talking about? Are you keeping something from me?"

He took a deep breath and explained what he remembered about his contact with extraterrestrials. "I'm not sure I recall everything that happened even though I was the main course, so to speak."

Amused and skeptical at first, Merrill quickly recognized he was telling the truth, or maybe she felt he believed he was. "I don't know what to make of it," she said. "I have a feeling we're going to find out more when we least need to deal with it."

He didn't try to discuss the classified report with his staff on the last leg of the speaking tour. He wished he could dismiss the incident as a crazy dream. Though he knew better, he rationalized briefly that the incident was an off-the-wall plot by Washington's Moral Right faction to bully him about his affair with Tess. Or did it have something to do with the Moral Right downplaying legitimate environmental concerns as God's divine will? The thought of parleying again with the Moral Right on either a real or unreal issue added insult to injury—somehow that entire day reminded him of Tess, and he didn't need any more emotional agitation. He'd been reamed repeatedly by the Moral Right about an alleged dalliance he'd manufactured to divert attention from Tess. Though Merrill suspected it was a sham story, she thought it a maneuver to deflect attention from something else too, but she wouldn't have guessed an affair. She would have thought of "the experience." When he dug past his guilt about Tess, he took illogical comfort in knowing the affair was far more serious than a fling, and that the personal issue paled in comparison to this new situation, a matter of national security. No, of international security. He would just have to rock and roll with the punches.

Like Merrill, everyone else aboard Air Force One and Two had little recollection of what Henry came to call "the event." Two months passed before he got a better grip on his recall, and two more passed again before Merrill and the cabinet began to connect all the dots he'd understood almost from the moment the two ETs faded away.

Finally, he summoned enough courage to continue their low-key briefings about the extraterrestrial hand in Earth affairs. The possibility of full disclosure loomed before him, a controversy never mentioned in the President's Daily Brief and one he'd always wanted to tackle. He knew those shape-shifting lizards with the beach boy identity fields, whatever they were, would be far peskier than the prudish Moral Right hypocrites and the bigoted naysayers who secretly didn't like having a progressive, multi-racial family in the White House.

"We're getting a better picture about what happened that day on Air Force One and Air Force Two," he said to Merrill as they snuggled in the family quarters late one night after a White House dinner, "but our story doesn't have much clout. This administration isn't much more than a flea biting a big dog. But Baby, before my term in office ends, someone's gonna have a gigantic itch to scratch."

::: Chapter 2

Tess Vaughn

Tess fingered the photo—really a short video—in an oversized electronic frame on her mantel. Harris had shot it during their final happy visit in Arizona together. Her long chestnut hair and the delicately embroidered yellow silk floated all around her like a dream, saguaro cacti topped with cup-like white flowers standing sentry in the background.

Was her affair with Senator Harris Cantrell Henry a fairy tale dream or a star-crossed tragedy? Once she birthed Mikka, she never felt certain what to call it. For the moment, she recalled the ordinary Sunday that changed her life forever as a crazy fluke. She'd taken one of her early morning jogs from her brother's north Phoenix condo toward a ridge marking the division between middle-class homes and the voluptuous estates near Dreamy Draw. Bored, she'd veered from the street into a mountain park to run a hilly trail and break the monotony of running along level asphalt. As she crested a hill brightened by the spring sunrise, she literally ran into a group of joggers with attitude.

"Halt!" A man in black athletic wear with a shaved head appeared from nowhere and shouted at her. He reached under his jacket, stepped forward with a menacing stare, and motioned her back. Feeling threatened, she slowed her pace. There were lots of nutty people floating around Phoenix.

"He said halt, chickie!" Another almost identical guy swung around and positioned himself behind her. A third and a fourth hemmed her in from the sides.

She tried to stop her forward motion, terrified of the joggers' intentions. Her feet grazed a stone, launching her, an unintentional missile, at the tall, mocha-skinned male jogger dressed in white.

The bald man snarled and leapt between the jogger and her in a flying tackle. The jogger thrust long-fingered hands out to catch her as the grimacing bald man arched his body to butt her backward, grounding her in a dusty heap. In one smooth, athletic move, the jogger disentangled her from the sputtering tackler and helped her to her feet. He motioned to the men in black to stand back, but they scowled at him and remained around her, hounds poised for the kill.

"I'm so sorry, miss. Are you all right?" The jogger tilted his head and gazed at her.

Speechless, she nodded and dusted her rear end off. Was she looking into the famous turquoise eyes of . . . ?

Senator Harris Cantrell Henry, the Democratic candidate for President of the United States of America, flashed his famous, disarming grin. "Good morning, I'm afraid our manners are lacking," he drawled, his voice sweetly husky. "I'm Harris Henry. No relation to Patrick." His eyes lit up at his own joke. "Nor Henry Harrison." His grin widened. "Please call me Harris. Who are you, pretty lady?"

She shrank back, afraid of the Secret Service agents. "Uh, T, Tess. Vau . . . Teresa Vaughn."

"Don't be frightened. The agents are here to protect me." Henry smiled again. "Do you live around here?"

She shook her head as he glanced up and down her body. The man was sizing her up!

"I'd like to make this up to you. Now that you've fallen for me, would you care to join me for brunch?"

Every American regarded this presidential candidate as a family guy, outgoing and sometimes mildly flirtatious, but Henry had winked at her. *What a dweeb!* She opened her mouth to ask him why her legs and breasts interested him more than her face, but all that came out was gobsmacked agreement. She wanted to kick herself, but rationalized her weakness as journalist instinct. Here stood a grand opportunity, even though she'd sworn to retire permanently from the business.

"Excuse my confusion. I. Um, I'd be honored, sir." She froze and squinted into the sun, not sure how to exit. She resisted the urge to cover her sweaty, burning cheeks with her hands, feeling like she blushed with every inch of her body. At least she'd worn loose shorts and a T-shirt rather than revealing spandex.

Baldy and the other three Secret Service agents arched their eyebrows above their sunglasses in disbelief. They strutted like a flock of flustered roosters in a knot around her, one with a hand hovering near what was probably a weapon concealed under his armpit. Another lifted his wrist to his face and started muttering into his sleeve. Agents number five and six, also decked out in sports clothes, sprinted up the hill she had just crested, panting and waving their arms.

"How'd *she* get through?" one of them growled through clenched teeth.

Henry scattered them away with a grin and wave of his hand. He pulled a pen and an embossed ivory business card from his navy blue waist pack and jotted something on the back. Later, Tess would stash the card with other mementoes, but at that moment, she clenched it in a sweaty, unmanicured hand.

Henry turned back to his agents. "Let's hit it, boys," he ordered, and started jogging back in the direction he came from.

She turned and jogged back to her brother's condo in a daze. Was she losing it? Even a chance of a lifetime might not be worth the stress it might create. She still felt exhausted after her decade of investigative reporting. But her love of good writing and the unanswered questions she might ask the presidential candidate made her old journalist mind-engine rumble to life. If she wanted to kick-start an independent freelance career, an interview with Henry was a stellar opportunity. At the very least, the one-in-a-million meeting in the mountain park would amuse family and friends. She'd be crazy not to accept the invitation. Would *anyone* refuse to socialize with Harris Henry for an hour?

There wasn't much time to consider the situation—after she showered and dressed, she had only minutes to make the appointment. She didn't want to share the tantalizing tidbit with her brother just yet. After the brunch, when the story was juicier, she'd spin the yarn. She figured she'd have to stand on her head to make Paul believe it.

How does a regular person like me have brunch with a potential president of the United States?

She and Senator Henry dined at the Biltmore in a vine-covered private bungalow far from the prying eyes of the public. There was still no real privacy to speak of, with Secret Service and staff people swarming all over, but then, she didn't expect it. As the minor guest of an important public servant, she was stricken virtually speechless, an unusual condition for a seasoned journalist. Most of her thoughts revolved around wondering what Mr. Henry told his people about her, or how he justified her presence at his table.

She reconsidered her feelings about him over brunch, finding she liked his easy style. The Henrys did seem genuinely interested in the country, in citizens' lives, and in making bad things better. She had concerns about his biggest campaign contributors, the wickedly wealthy who'd gained their fortunes in questionable corporate manipulation. And she definitely felt leery about the way he'd come on to her.

Apparently, many people, not just women, found Mr. Henry or the aura of power about him fascinating. She hadn't considered him particularly attractive before she met him—he was appealing in a boy-next-door way, but not her type. She was in for another surprise as she sat across a roomy dining table sharing fresh berries, yogurt, and croissants. She felt her blood heat, finding him both mentally and physically provocative. The shock of silver and charcoal hair she'd thought old looking in media photos seemed, in person, a perfect complement to the hypnotic turquoise eyes that sparkled mischievously from a square-chinned mocha face. He was buff, more muscled than he seemed in photos and on television. And the accent! Lower Midwest – Upper South twangs might sound nasal to some, but she heard his voice flow like honey.

Starstruck and jittery, she barely opened her mouth at first. Aware of her butterflies, Mr. Henry led the conversation into light, airy avenues—weather, recent movies, and comments about the attractive room. She buttoned her lip and listened.

Finally, they both opened up.

"You know, I've always been fascinated by the Southwest. I always wanted to live here but got involved early on in Iowa politics," he said.

"Have you explored the history of Arizona Territory?" she asked. "It's a fascinating tale."

Henry talked at length about the establishment of Arizona Territory after miners discovered gold near Prescott, Arizona's territorial capital. He discussed articulately the state's economic development and water dilemma, tribal gaming and sovereignty. He even understood the linguistic origins of some tribal languages.

"I'm stunned by your extensive knowledge about our state," she said, realizing her time with him was drawing to an end. She didn't ask many questions and her feature might never be written. Perhaps this was the cosmic answer to starting a freelance career, that she shouldn't bother.

Henry leaned forward and gazed at her warmly. "Thank you, Miss Vaughn. You'll give me your contact info, won't you? We can talk again. I've enjoyed this so much."

She giggled, taken aback. She snapped her mouth shut, not believing she heard the girlish trill coming from her own mouth. "You're kidding."

"No-o—I'm serious." Senator Henry reached for her hand, poised with butter knife in midair.

Her hand collided with his and the dab of blueberry jam on the knife plopped into her lap.

"Why would someone like you want to talk with someone like me? I mean . . ." Her voice trailed to a squeak. She blushed, swallowed air, cleared her throat and regrouped, searching her lap under the table with her free hand for the errant blob of jam.

"You mean despite your role as a journalist," he said gently. "I didn't know that when I invited you to brunch. I appreciate you telling me that."

"Need another vote?" She winked, imitating him, hoping to seem mischievous.

Henry rolled his head back and his honeyed laugh tickled her in the solar plexus. "One after another, darlin'."

After a bit more chitchat, Mr. Henry excused himself to attend to other matters. The bald Secret Service agent who'd tackled her, now smartly dressed in a black suit and silk tie, escorted her outside to the little pickup truck that now seemed tacky in the rarified resort atmosphere.

As she drove herself back to Paul's, she engaged herself in a stern mental lecture—Mr. Henry's flattering attention was only an interview; at the very best; they shared some polite conversation made to pass the time. She wouldn't see him again. She felt a twinge of regret, and then corrected herself. *Why* would she want to see him again? A man in public office with a gorgeous wife and two kids. Who needed that? She could hear her grandmother's voice declaring, *Why, the very idea!*

Despite her devotion to single life—or maybe because of it—she continued to fantasize about Harris Henry, safe in the knowledge he was out of her reach. She started writing a feature story even though she hadn't drawn much out of him. The unfinished piece morphed into a human interest story that could only reaffirm his supporters' interest in him or perhaps draw a few fence sitters onto his side, and she'd ultimately let it languish in her computer.

May 9, 2008

For some reason I can't quite articulate, I haven't told anyone about my encounter with you in April, as though revealing my secret would dilute its power. I've always been a private person, and my dicey attraction for you makes me feel more guarded. I know I should resist you, that the responsibility for saying no lies with me.

Your sincere demeanor at brunch almost canceled your coming on like a train wreck of a gigolo. I was charmed by you despite the way you looked me over when we met, probably because you flaunted more than your physical self. You have a razor-sharp mind and the way to my heart lies through my mind—I'm a pushover for articulate, intelligent conversation. On the other hand, your status as a senator and a potential president are propelling me past my better instincts, I'm ashamed to admit.

My attraction to you feels so different from my old flames, the high school and college crushes, and the adult relationships that never really took off during my career. I think of these men now as if they're beads strung on the necklace of my life: the colorful rock and roll musician who loved his white powder more than any woman, the budding war reporter consumed by the adrenaline of his life, the sensitive and romantic but equally dark and brooding portrait painter, and finally, the water quality specialist and environmental activist, practical, earnest, lively, but not particularly loving and giving.

At the bottom line, I've not experienced a fully satisfactory relationship and to this day, I relish my independence more than I relish relationships. Not that it matters. Why would we want to have an impossible relationship?

Six weeks later, the phone rang in her Tucson condo. "Yes, this is Teresa Vaughn," she responded briskly to the business-like voice, a travel agent notifying her of an airline reservation in her name at Sky Harbor International Airport, and lodging reserved in a San Francisco bed and breakfast.

"Booked by whom?" she asked, annoyed at Senator Henry's presumption that she'd accept the anonymous invitation. Who else could it be?

"I'm sorry; we're unable to reveal that information."

"May I speak to your supervisor?"

"Of course. Hold, please."

But the agent's supervisor also steadfastly refused—or was unable—to reveal the source of the booking, even though Tess tried to discreetly offer a modest bribe, delicately referring to it as a deposit.

So she bit at Senator Henry's lure, penciling the bookings into her calendar, curious about what might happen next. Perhaps she'd do the feature anyway, a series on his campaign.

But she arrived in San Francisco to find a bouquet of lilies and a silky, diaphanous gown in a suite of designer rooms, and later, the same at each destination. The flowers and dress became essential props for each rendezvous. Harris liked her nude and barefoot under the gowns, and called her his Desert Rose, and—her favorite—Mariposa Lily.

After the first passionate rendezvous, they'd repeated the process more than a dozen times as she headed for San Antonio, Tallahassee, St. Louis, and other locations recognizable to any American. Whenever Merrill and the Henry twins couldn't travel with him on the campaign trail, he installed her behind the scenes.

"It may be difficult being involved with me," he'd drawled before he made love to her the first time. His words were matter-of-fact and spoken with a straight face.

"I know," she'd simply replied. She had no reason to think otherwise and fighting it was futile. She struggled to maintain mental and emotional detachment after that steamy first night and the others that followed. She pretended she was but one of Henry's conquests in a sordid snarl only the powerful, wealthy, or famous dared entertain. That fantasy helped to distance her emotions.

She imagined Barbara Walters interviewing her. Baba Wawa would lean forward, cup her chin in her hands, and cast a knowing look. *Tess, did you feel used by this powerful married man?*

Not really. She truly cared for him, harboring none of the youthful illusions that someone like Bill Clinton's young Monica must have struggled with during their brief affair. Tess had no agenda or aspiration except to enjoy Henry. Always self-contained, independent, and relationship-shy after her series of interesting but scattered boyfriends, she'd learned to develop definite boundaries she had never moved beyond.

Tess, did you ever feel guilty? No, but sometimes she felt, ironically, that she'd contributed to Merrill Henry's "captivity." Everyone knew that Merrill Webster Henry, with her degrees in law and international politics, could easily have forged a successful career in her own right, maybe even outrun her own husband for President. Even so, the twenty-first century American public still expected candidates' wives to play subordinate roles to their husbands. Merrill abandoned her promising career to support Harris and he'd repaid her with . . . well, if not abuse by having an affair, then benign neglect. Tess felt some female kinship by engaging in what she understood as their mutual humiliation. To tolerate her subordination, Merrill must have found Senator Harris Henry and his presidential aspirations enchanting. But the couple claimed to be happily married and truly appeared to be, despite Henry's fascination with her.

July 17, 2008

I'm long past my initial nervousness and denial about our "torrid affair," as it would be looked upon if discovered, and I'm more focused now on how we share the secrets of our hearts.

We've become true friends, enjoying one another's minds, bodies, and spirits without clinging expectation.

The one thing I most appreciate about you, Harris, is that you've never offered less than honesty. It helps too that I've never expected more than you could give. And we really do have much in common. Not in a tangible sense, for our lives are very different. Your life as a small-town boy turned urban sophisticate is career-driven and goal-focused. I was born a city girl, earning scholarships and then degrees in journalism and communications, climbing to the middle rungs of the career ladder with my quest for truth and my passion for writing. But lately I've begun to go in the opposite direction, longing for the simplicity of a life in the country, even if it's a bit hand-to-mouth. At our core, we strange bedfellows share a desire to help all beings live in harmony while we figure out how to live in harmony ourselves . . .

What I find most touching about you, though I don't say this openly, is the fear that you cover with bravado. Your life as one of two minority candidates with a chance of winning the White House isn't simple nor is the network of power that presidential candidates negotiate. It's one thing to hear about your trials and tribulations in the media, and another to get the scoop from you. It's fashionable and easy for your detractors to condemn you, to brush you off as just another hapless politician in a multiracial skin. The way you brush away your clouds of anxiety with jokes and laughter while under such vicious scrutiny is remarkable.

After competing candidates dropped like flies in the Republican and Democratic primaries, the Progressive Left as well as the Moral Right yammered through the remainder of the campaign year about corporate conspiracies and corporate support of candidates. What Henry shared with her before he gained the nomination chilled her more than his detractors' accusations. She'd heard the general story before, but it seemed more sinister coming from the mouth of a potential world leader.

Henry spoke about international bankers and agendas implemented decades, if not centuries ago. His narrative contained a story within a story, a tale of an outside influence that extended into the dim recesses of almost prehistoric memory, an extraterrestrial civilization hinted at in ancient texts, basically the stuff of many woo-woo internet sites.

She listened to him, perplexed, more concerned with soothing his fears than with absorbing everything he said. In spite of his strange commentary, Henry seemed lucid enough. Sometimes she asked herself if maybe the campaign stress loosened his screws, and she wondered if maybe she didn't need hers tightened for hanging out with him.

At the last, he said his opposition was harassing him, perhaps warning him in a peculiar way. "Maybe I should let you go, Tess. I'm seeing myself coming and going, literally."

She felt startled by this take on their imminent breakup, something she wanted too but for different reasons. "You mean doubles?"

"Yeah. Someone appeared as me at least twice in Washington recently, minor public affairs, but still . . . Drew Forrest is looking into it . . ." He seemed reluctant to elaborate, as though naming the devil might cause a manifestation. He offered no more about the doubles, but mentioned how Washington, D.C. was "crawling with intel." Then he connected that with cryptic comments about "oil deficits" and "extraterrestrial agendas" and "technology wars."

Was all this strange talk a symptom of instability? Was he coming unglued because of his—their—infidelity and the havoc it might play in his personal life and for his presidential aspirations? Did trying to please everyone under intense political scrutiny and racial animosity send him over the edge? Though the country was far more racially tolerant now than in their respective childhoods, this derision had certainly reared its ugly head again in a multitude of ways.

Probably all this exacted a terrible pressure.

In the midst of her investigative career, she might have regarded his far-out claims like juicy steaks. But no more. She shook her head and steered the conversation back to the break-up.

"I agree, but for completely different reasons. I'm total jeopardy for your campaign," she replied. Did he even consider his wife and kids as a reason to "let her go?" She opened her mouth to remark about this omission, then stopped. No point in going there because their relationship was ending one way or another.

Harris pulled closer, stroking her hair and kissing her eyelids. "Maybe not right now," he said, as if appeasing her, "but soon."

"It has to be soon," she replied.

His eyes softened, and he looked visibly shaken with her resolve. She'd held back tears, but not the heaving sigh that rose from her soul. She gazed into his deep oceanic eyes. "You're doing the right thing, Harris. I've let you and your family down by agreeing to spend time with you."

Henry pulled away slightly, perturbed at her ability to shoulder the blame. Clearly, he wanted to take the lead. She couldn't pretend to be as reluctant or as attached as she might be in a normal love affair, if there was such an animal. At any rate, the affair had to end. Even if Henry was single, if he was going loopy, she certainly didn't need to hang around.

She locked eyes with Henry. "We knew at the outset we were fated to renounce our relationship," she said softly.

He stared at her for a long time until his eyes filled with tears. He leaned toward her again, kissing her forehead, each eye, the tip of her nose. "Yes, I suppose we did know, didn't we?"

The poignant pre-breakup session was not without pain, yet not heartbreaking either. But she received another phone call from a travel agency confirming airfare. They spent two more nights together a few weeks later. Tess felt spooked and distracted while hanging around Henry's Mississippi River stomping ground, right outside his birth town in Iowa. After his campaign commitments, the pair sat outside an old but charming brick farmhouse owned by one of his old school chums, splashing around in a Jacuzzi near a private pool while the Secret Service and the owner's security men milled around outside the high brick wall.

Tess vowed to keep the visit on a platonic level, and assumed Harris would too, because he'd told her he only wanted to make sure she was okay. She tried to resurrect her feature article, to approach their last meeting as a professional journalist. She'd been in the process of quizzing him about his Democratic Party platform, hoping to flesh out her abandoned feature about him when he'd taken her by surprise and initiated lovemaking in the hot tub. He poured his body over hers, rubbing his hips rhythmically against hers, giggling and whispering love words in his honeyed accent.

"Want my willy, Lily?" He teased her like a schoolboy with his prankish wordplay.

"Come pick my posies, hillbilly," she retorted, among other silly things, matching his language. They carried on like teenagers, giggling and toying with each other until Tess finally led him on a merry dripping chase through the old-fashioned verandah and into the suite. It was the last time they would make love.

October 14, 2008

Yesterday I rushed to the pharmacy for a home pregnancy test. I've played with the idea of dropping a hint about the pregnancy in person, and I seriously considered an abortion, and telling you so. But every time I hear your voice, I can't do it—not the abortion nor the telling. I shudder to think of the broiling publicity if anyone finds out. Which leads me to wonder again how the Secret Service thinks of me, and about my hope you're right that they appraise me as a temporary distraction. The old Service veterans had many more problems with both W and Clinton, you claim, but what if a disgruntled or retired agent writes a tell-all book or drops hints to a journalist?

We were supposed to be finished, but you beg me to meet you again. And no matter how much I want this relationship to end before it causes more heartbreak for us and our families, I know that every time you bid me, that I'll come hither. I'm heartsick that I'm so easily controlled.

And Senator Henry did buy her presence again. She worried

herself sick before the trip that reporters would discover them, though she hid her fears behind her new façade of not caring any more. They rendezvoused one last time for a precious hour after Harris made a campaign speech in Flagstaff, Arizona, a week before his triumph at the Democratic Convention in Denver.

She held her emotions back as she visited with him in the guise of a journalist, warm yet neutral. She glanced around the hotel sitting room at the oil paintings of the San Francisco Peaks and the nearby Grand Canyon. "Flagstaff is too small for this, Harris. I shouldn't be here," she told him.

He played the flirt and winked at her. "Don't worry, Sugar, you're just another member of the press. The media—the rest of the media—will focus on someone else they think I'm seeing." He exaggerated his drawl, knowing she liked the way it rolled into her ears. "I leak phony clues." He displayed a wavery smile.

"I love my privacy . . . I really love my privacy . . ."

She felt momentarily guilty about her self-serving attitude. Perhaps this married man would miss her more than she would miss him. "Will you be okay?"

"Tess," he said, only it sounded like *Taz*; "Now that I'm close to the White House, I have mixed feelings. I'm exhilarated for the opportunity to improve the world. On the other hand, I'm a puppet, a controlled man. You know American politics. Old Triple C and worse are sniffing around my doorway. All the usual stresses along with others most people wouldn't believe. Doubles. Shape-shifting ET types. I'm apprehensive. It will only get worse if I'm elected."

"Triple C, I understand. Doubles I get. Shape-shifting ET types? I'm sorry, Harris . . . what can I say?"

He looked at her with pleading eyes. He said nothing more.

How creepy! He really did seem to be losing it. His anxiety and weird new obsession with ETs seeped like cold water into her bones. She grasped the antagonism between the Dems and Repubs, the Progressive Left and the Moral Right, Whites, Blacks, Jews, and Asians, who all ganged up on Hispanics, and especially upon recent immigrants and undocumented immigrants. She understood the super-conservative Collins family political schemes, not to mention the conundrums of the oiled-up, washed-out economy and global warming, but she really didn't want to follow the murky, Fortean thread of Henry's revelations.

It wasn't as if she didn't believe the stories about extraterrestrials, but she felt uncomfortable with the topic and didn't want to figure out why. She briefly touched the tiny swell above her pubic mound. *Maybe that's why*, she thought.

Not only would she avoid sharing Henry's strange revelations, she couldn't and wouldn't tell him about her condition. The relationship was clearly over and no one needed any further complications, pregnancy or no pregnancy.

So she rubbed his shoulders instead, fighting her dark emotions with busy fingers.

Harris eased into her hands, relaxing with a sigh. When she was done, he reached into his trousers' pocket. "If something happens to me, to any of us in my campaign, would you find a reporter who can be trusted and give them this? It's safe with you," he said softly, fastening the lovely platinum necklace with a glowing opal around her neck. Her favorite stone.

She raised her eyebrows. "A reporter? What's the significance?"

"It holds a nano chip, somehow melded into the stone. Like the ones set into credit cards, but smaller, transparent."

"What's a nano chip? What's on it?"

"New technology not yet released to the public. When the time is right, you'll know how to play it. You can project it anywhere. As for the data . . . there are some strange things happening . . . this stuff is pretty far out, but . . . well, my old campaign manager Ramirez and my old friend Drew seem to be on to something . . ."

Tess hesitated for a moment. She'd idolized Forrest when she was starting her career. The world-class investigative reporter had everything she'd aspired to be.

She gently pulled the necklace back over her head and pressed it into his palm, closing his fingers around it. She lay one cheek against his.

"Farewell, old friend," she murmured.

Senator Harris Henry pulled away, touched his chest over his heart, and pointed at Tess, mist in his eyes.

:::CHAPTER 3

TESS VAUGHN

Six months after their breakup, Tess figured life couldn't get much better. How many people in a country of 300 million people get to kick back on a chaise lounge in their yards and stargaze any time they felt like it? Besides daydreaming about her new life, she reflected on her emotional state since she and Harris had parted. She recalled a reflective journal entry she'd composed just days before, almost word for word:

> April 19, 2009
>
> There is no doubt in my mind that that you and I did the right thing. Whether you were going crazy or the stuff you mention is real, I prefer to disappear into the quiet channels of my own life.
>
> I still miss you—or is it the excitement of travel and clandestine meetings I really miss? Our romantic trysts were heady stuff.
>
> At least thinking about you doesn't make me feel sad any more. When I think of you, I feel warm inside and consider you

> a dear old friend. I've felt a marked sense of relief as my life has returned to normal despite the intimacy gap. Of course, facing motherhood alone isn't exactly normal, but I embrace my new solitude with enthusiasm, no, treasure it, in fact.

She rubbed her bulging belly, vowing to nurture herself even more after the baby's arrival. Daily concerns would never tie her down; she envisioned creative outings and nature walks, and attending concerts, author readings, and art shows.

That she didn't want Harris to know—couldn't let him know—about the baby, niggled at her from time to time. But when she imagined what a zoo her life would turn into if the media got wind of the issue, she let her discomfort go. She worried more about publicity than child support even though peak oil and real estate prices spawned by corporate greed made ends harder to meet, especially in a low-wage, right-to-work state like Arizona. But she'd managed to ease through her fortieth birthday and was wending her way through personal and national disasters with minimum stress. Her modest, paid-for home on twenty acres in a semi-rural county was tucked away from national politics and prying eyes.

The sky above Tess started to come alive with a Lyrid meteor shower, a celestial gathering of rock fragments that zoomed around the sky like speeding fireflies. Harris had introduced her to fireflies in Iowa, what he'd called lightning bugs.

She sighed. Did it again, hadn't she? So many things reminded her of Harris. She often wondered if the baby would look like her, him, or both of them. *Perhaps him more than me*, she often concluded, because his black and Native American genes and her mother's Mexican blood might overrun the creamy skin she'd inherited from her father's Welsh forebears. On the other hand, Harris had Irish blood too, and said his father had ginger hair before it grayed to silver. Together, their melting pot gene pool could produce a child with almost any conceivable hair, skin, and eye color.

She startled when a meteorite sizzled through the air not far above her head, the bright burning tail so close to the ground that it must have fallen nearby. She counted fifteen more "shooting stars" in the next half minute, easy arcing meteorites like lines of light tracing through the stars. Then another shot over her, causing her body to tingle with delight. A spectacle even better than fireworks, an otherworldly gift from the heavens. She closed her eyes and imagined tiny shooting stars raining down on her by the thousands, penetrating her body as pinpoint blessings.

When she ended her visualization and opened her eyes, she felt as if she stood on some swift, dark island in outer space. She rose and walked away from the lounge chair, tilting her face upward, wanting to soar into the heavens. She loved the drifty feeling, the mental whooshing through space with moons and planets, meteors and stars. What a grand ride.

The waxing moon, setting behind a mountain ridge in front of her, cast a sudden, bright ray of light. For a micro-instant, she stood illuminated in a moonbeam and she laughed aloud. Might this magical night bring a special blessing to her child?

The next morning Tess awakened from a sweet dream in which she'd floated away over the earth through sandalwood scented forests and flower-strewn meadows, landing to mingle with scores of beautiful creatures—elk, bison, big cats, birds of prey, butterflies. The only odd thing about the dream was its emphasis on eyes: shimmering, bejeweled insect eyes, the greenish glow of predator eyes peering from moonlit forests, and the dark, moist eyes of grazing animals glittering in sunlight. Her heart contracted with sadness for these creatures, all at serious risk between natural circumstances and man's environmental abuse.

In the shower, she blasted herself with hot water, scrubbing away sleep and sadness with her favorite coconut crème wash. While lathering her body into a delicious froth, her fingertips brushed across something bumpy on the inside of her left elbow. She rubbed soapsuds away from the spot and leaned around the shower curtain into a pool of sunlight. Three tiny raised bumps the color and consistency of a pencil eraser were grouped in a triangle at the outside edge of her elbow fold. If she had but one, even two, she'd think the slightly raised protrusions were insect or spider bites. But three in an evenly spaced pattern?

After breakfast Tess Googled insect bites, skin disorders, anything that might yield a clue to the mystery, but didn't find anything that matched her bumps. She decided to forget about it and moved on to more mundane Saturday routines, cleaning the kitchen and bathroom, opening the press of homemade paper crafted from leaves and flower petals to see what she'd created this time, and when all her tasks were complete, she daydreamed over a new short story at her computer.

The marks faded as the hours passed. She decided to let herself believe some bug bit her three times and coincidentally made an equilateral triangle on her arm. Maybe the bumps were an allergic reaction. In the last glow of light before dusk, she searched in the gramma grass and wildflowers for the meteorite she thought hit ground, but she couldn't find a metallic stone that looked as if it had rained from the sky nor a telltale impact crater.

Spring turned quickly into summer in the central Arizona highlands. Tess savored her country life and when she wasn't busy with newborn Mikka, she chipped away at her creative writing projects and her journaling. She continued to speak to Harris in her journal entries, saying what she could not express to him otherwise.

July 14, 2009

Apparently your ruse worked, because not a single reporter approached me after I fled Tucson for Yavapai County, and not a single one appeared when Mikka was born. True to my word, I've never told my family, not even Paul or any of my closest friends, about the identity of Mikka's father. I made up a lame story about messing around with a guy I dated briefly during my affair with you, one who took off to Costa Rica with a broken heart when he rightly suspected me of two-timing him whenever I disappeared on one of our rendezvous. At my age, single

> motherhood is more a privilege than a problem. No one cares about paternity—my mom and dad are simply glad to have a late grandchild, even more so because of Paul's sexual orientation as a gay man.
>
> After the birth of our beautiful golden child, a perfect composite of you and me, I sometimes feel a gnawing sense of guilt about Mikka's fatherlessness. This big secret, her paternity, wells up through the seam of my days and nights, a stain impossible to wash away. I see you daily in Mikka's face, her shell-like ears identical to yours, and the tiny but long fingers and toes shaped just like yours too. This discomfort grows into an uneasy silence that laps and worries at me like cold water seeping into a sinking ship.

If someone discovered the secret, what would happen to her and Mikka? How could she bail out of her emotional fears and move forward?

::: CHAPTER 4

PRESIDENT HARRIS CANTRELL HENRY
11.11.2011 9:00 A.M.–10:55 A.M.

President Harris Cantrell Henry spread his fingers across the top of the podium and faced the media at the biannual presidential press briefing, unaware the same journalists would report his demise that evening.

According to fans of Mayan history, an energetic event beginning that morning at midnight would usher the Earth into a new reality that would culminate on December 21, 2012, the final day of the Mayan calendar. That is, if a majority of souls on Earth chose to climb through the much-hyped window of positive opportunity on November 11, 2011 into higher consciousness. But who believed in the end of the world or prophecies of sweeping change predicted for a particular day? Harris Cantrell Henry figured that human misery simply cycled and recycled. But his controversial bill was surfacing now, so maybe he ought to give the legend a spin.

Henry sipped from a bottle of purified water, reminding himself to soften his accent, a combination of his father's flat Midwestern tone and his mother's soft Kentucky twang. Make his "ings" sing, as his granddad used to say. It suddenly dawned on him that a possible strategy to control the discussion of his controversial environmental bill would be to cut bait and allow some questions first, then move into the actual briefing. Press Secretary Daniel Morehouse would be livid. He stifled a grin at the thought of Morehouse spinning like a chubby Tasmanian devil around the pressroom.

"Good to see you, ladies and gentlemen," Henry said brightly, offering his engaging smile and waiting for the laughter to die down. "As you're well aware, normal press briefing protocol calls for the President to open with remarks about the most important pending legislation or world event. Today we are faced with pressing national legislation based upon unprecedented global climatic events. On that note, I open the floor to whatever questions you may have first, before I proceed."

A few faces appeared bemused in response to his lighthearted banter, but no one offered any resistance to the change of protocol. A rangy young fellow, a newbie sitting next to Dondra Sontag, a veteran reporter with the New York Times, waved his hand wildly.

"Yes, sir."

"No new taxes?" His grin looked half-playful, half-serious.

Congress implemented a new 1% federal sales tax during the troubling budget confrontations after his election, but income taxes remained static, and corporations still weren't taxed at rates comparable to the middle class. Henry opened his palms upward. "No new taxes. Not yet."

The young man winked and sat down. Dondra Sontag, a rabbity, gray-haired woman in a navy blue power suit frowned at him and waved a pencil in the air. "Mr. President, more mass graves were excavated this week on the Gulf coast. What are you doing about it?"

"Ms. Sontag, Secretary of State Wickersham and Idaho's Senator Ty Voegtlin are heading the committee that will join UN Representative Charlie Ammerman on a fact-finding mission. They will meet with all governors, senators, and representatives of Gulf coast states, a consortium of relief organizations, including the International Red Cross and Doctors Without Borders, as well as human rights organizations like Amnesty International and Witness for Peace, who wish to assess political aspects of the high death rate during Hurricane Tyrell—

Dondra looked him in the eye and interrupted. "How much money are you prepared to spend, Mr. President?"

He choked back an impulse to spill the whole pot of beans about Earth's ongoing axis shift, surely responsible, along with the rise in carbon dioxide levels, for the increase in superstorm disasters. "I've pledged an additional thirty million dollars for data gathering, in addition to sixty million for the military operation quelling the most recent rebel uprising in the Delta."

The Mississippi Delta. He'd never dreamed he'd ever speak about such things.

The reporters seemed pleased with his response, and a positive energy subtly swept the room. He predicted they'd bat environmental concerns around at this point, considering the controversy surrounding the U.S. global warming bill.

Dondra scribbled notes on a white legal pad, a satisfied smile spreading in slow degrees across her narrow face.

Russ Snodgrass, a veteran reporter and op-ed writer with the Washington Post, caught his eye. Russ's rumpled and loosened necktie dangled over a paunchy belly.

"Mr. President, the borders for the UN-mandated Palestinian state were finalized only weeks ago, and Israeli refugees in the former Gaza strip and other Muslim sectors stream into Israel. What role will the U.S. play in the organization of Palestinian government?"

No doubt the Agency would monitor the region. And keep it stirred up so that the U.S. military would have a continuing presence there. His personal concerns lay with both Israeli and Palestinian refugees, their numbers and plight unmatched since Pakistan split from India in the 1940s.

"That has not been decided. A record number of UN troops are supervising the operation, dubbed Exodus II by the media—you, ladies and gentlemen."

He paused for a burst of soft laughter. "U.S. troops already stationed in the Persian Gulf will be deployed via Navy carriers, if the United Nations needs assistance. Miraculously, there aren't any reported casualties of violence yet, but scores of heart attacks and stress-related physical reactions are creating an urgent need for more medical personnel and supplies."

Another reporter he had never noticed before, an elegant, thoughtful-looking fellow with an olive complexion and baby blue yarmulke, motioned with his reading glasses. "Our nation is a traditional ally of Israel. How will our government continue to support both Israeli and Palestinian concerns?"

The reporters' questions came faster and faster. Henry prayed for fortitude.

"As you're aware, the United States government is fully cooperating with the international community in this era of unprecedented change for Israel and Palestine. Our nation's compassionate support of both Israelis and Palestinians is synchronous with UN policy," he said firmly, hoping this wouldn't become a big lie in the months to come.

He took another deep breath. Here came the second big story of the week. Every hand in the house went up.

"Mr. President, what will U.S. involvement be in Peru and Nigeria?"

Peru was broiling in its own juices after the assassination of their chief executive in a cunning coup engineered by a rebel group consisting of reorganized veteran Shining Path rebels and Nigerian Muslim fundamentalists, first-time allies in an international operation. The flow of news from both countries was restricted, but intelligence suggested that rebel bands controlling a small oil field recently discovered in Peru had also secured a major Niger delta outfit with great bloodshed, and were wrenching control of the cocaine market from northern South America into the U.S. and Europe.

Henry visibly hesitated for a moment, stalling by taking a long swig of distilled water and checking his watch. At least this question had a straightforward answer, even if he didn't want to deal with it.

NIHSA would damn well do whatever it took to keep drug money and oil flowing. Despite public opposition to perennial war, the Agency stirred up enough false patriotism to create an uneasy acceptance of ongoing conflict in the Middle East as the popular uprising in Tunisia and Egypt spread like wildfire through most Muslim nations earlier in the year. No country was immune to their youth taking to the streets in this era of diminishing opportunity, and the uprisings were beginning to spread into the Western hemisphere in both North and South America.

By now it should be obvious to Americans that the hotbeds of armed conflict or popular unrest all have oil or oil exploration at their roots. And drugs. Baghdad had no major drug problems until the U.S. invaded and intel interests flooded Iraq with heroin. The same thing happened everywhere American imperialism reared its ugly head. Intelligence, big money, and the oil conglomerate destroyed cultures. Henry hoped to put a stop to this monstrous, corrupt corporate machine somehow.

He threw his shoulders back and glanced pseudo-confidently over the press room. How did the White House press secretary manage his press gaggles day after day?

"At this point, Nigeria's situation does not critically affect us and we will continue to monitor it. The uprising has severed communication between the legitimate Peruvian government and the outside, and as you know, the Peruvian president was murdered. The free world must respond, like it or not. The Pentagon is conferring with our allies and reluctantly considering a strike in Lima before the Thanksgiving weekend is over. This move is not popular either with me or with the American public, especially following American deaths in the Middle East since the invasion of Afghanistan, Iraq, and Syria. It will be tough to redeploy active troops into another region, even to help friends. The agony of the situation will continue to be felt in the field and at home."

Almost everyone in the cramped press room stirred in their seats. Henry expected follow-up questions, but there were none. He predicted the topic would move to Russia. The Russians still pounded on Chechnya, Ukraine, and Georgia. And NIHSA had a hand in it, no doubt. Always the curse of oil—

"Mr. President, what do you say to the loose-lipped threats by Russia about a military assault in independent eastern Europe?"

His attention snapped back to the question. "Despite the perennially weak Russian economy, the Russians are feelin' their oats, aren't they? I suppose they'll wait until after the 2014 Winter Olympics." He cut loose with his natural accent and dropped -ing, teasing the reporters into scattered laughter. Did any president ever show as much humor as he did in these press conferences?

Henry waited another moment to let the laughter die down. "Let's see what happens. We'll respond when something other than rumors fly."

A mouse-like voice squeaked from a large, formidable lady. "Mr. President, is there any progress in determining who is responsible for the attempted bombings of the two obelisks?'"

He didn't feel like grappling with this question, either. Or the dozen connected questions subsequently fired off like missiles. The media had buzzed the past few weeks with "Tales of the Two Obelisks." Western freemasonry appeared to be under attack by Muslim extremists bent on preserving pure Egyptian freemasonry. But the Moral Right media, backed by the Agency, promoted it as another Islamic Jihad against Christianity and the free world.

"According to intelligence, Aziz Ala' al din, the estranged son of a minor Saudi royal and a distant cousin of Osama bin Laden, as you recall, remains in seclusion in his heavily guarded villa in southern France, as he did after the first bombing attempt on the obelisks during the opening year of this administration. NIHSA is evaluating intelligence concerning his movements."

The ultra-conservative Masonic faction of the Moral Right was howling for Ala' al din's head and demanded sanctions against France despite neither France nor the Saudi having any clear tie to the current Al Queda nemesis, Mu'tazz bin Rashad, bin Laden's self-appointed successor.

Sweat poured from his armpits and he briefly tugged the front of his damp, clingy silk shirt away from his ribs. Give 'em the real me again, he thought. "At least we're eatin' French fries again. That ole freedom fry thing after 9-11 got on my last nerve."

The laughter skimming the room turned discreetly to coughing and then silence. Some of the high-powered, Moral Right-aligned reporters glared fiercely at President Henry. One well-heeled reporter finally cut to the chase.

"Mr. President, how do you respond to reports from the liberal media that C. Clelland Collins is involved in the Obelisk bombings?"

He held his breath and refrained from banging his head on the podium. He'd rather tiptoe through a mined oilfield than publicly express any honest opinion about Triple C. The kingpin of the Moral Right movement, Collins was perhaps one of the most powerful players in both U.S. and world politics.

"Sir, I believe that topic has been thoroughly digested. Until a congressional hearing proves or disproves any connection, there's no point in rehashing the alleged matter. The gentleman is innocent until proven guilty. And he certainly hasn't been indicted for anything."

The reporter's smug, self-satisfied look left him relieved that he'd dumped bullshit down the right hole.

He hoped to hell no one wanted to talk about China, a complicated and sensitive topic. Things improved slightly for ethnic groups in the Republic of China after the fierce and mostly unpublicized protests before, during, and after 2008 Olympics, resulting in the fourteenth Dalai Lama's poignant January 2011 ambassadorial trip to Tibet. But the happy event was followed by a sudden Chinese nuclear test just days before the North Korean Valentine's Day nuclear debacle. Fortunately, China wasn't much of a player on network news since, except in surpassing by double the U.S. appetite for dwindling petroleum supplies.

"Mr. President!" Bud Wilkens, a robust international wire services reporter with longish hair who looked like he'd be more comfortable in shorts and Birkenstock sandals than his cheap suit, stood and waved a notebook of recycled paper over his head. "SR 1447 on Global Warming?"

Ah, at last. The real reason for the press briefing, bless Bud's organic heart.

"Unusual global weather patterns have every nation on edge. Global warming is one of my gravest concerns and it should be one of the nation's gravest concerns. I will do everything humanly possible to pass this bill and bring its precepts to fruition."

He absorbed the electric undercurrent that filled the room. A voice like a deep gong issued from the back row. "Many people perceive this legislation as self-defeating. Do you see this bill as a revolutionary turning point in energy policy, Mr. President?"

"This legislation is revolutionary and unprecedented in the United States. Less stringent measures, such as stiff "user fees" on petroleum products have failed to bring about the desired results." He tilted his chin up in his best gesture of paternal patience and braced himself for his presentation of SR 1477 and the press reaction.

"SR 1477 is a comprehensive bill that will foster healing of Earth's environmental ills as petroleum-fueled engines are phased out of production and their use in vehicles banned in the United States of America. Ford Motors produced 64-mile per gallon engines in Europe in 2010, despite dragging their corporate feet here at home because of American public and corporate apathy about surpassing the 40-mile-per-gallon mark. This limit, as you may be aware, is the product of oil industry propaganda. Brazil implemented a no-gasoline engine policy last year, and when we do as well, the rest of the world will follow our lead."

The room became quiet while everyone assessed his honest words. Hands snapped up. He nodded at an average-looking Joe.

"Dave Magden, Associated Press. Mr. President, please outline the details of this bill."

"Yes, sir. The proposed initial reduction in gasoline engine manufacture will begin in January 2012, two months from now, culminating in their obsolescence by January 2015. Owners of gasoline-powered vehicles will be required to either relinquish them or retrofit them for alternative fuels and methods of propulsion by the end of 2012. Oil consortiums will be required to devote 50 percent of their yearly profits during this three-year period to continue intensive research, and the production and implementation of alternate energy technologies. While great strides—"

"Sir, excuse me," Dave shouted over the buzz of reporters' asides to one another, "what are the subsidies?"

He cleared his throat. "Yes. There will be subsidies offered for both engine conversion and purchase of new alternative vehicles; however, because of the long-term economic slowdown since 2008, and the sheer numbers of citizens this proposal will affect, the subsidies are minimal—$3,000 for each taxpayer owning a single vehicle or $1,000 for each vehicle for taxpayers with multiple vehicles. Special tax breaks will be offered to taxpayers in the position to give up private vehicles entirely and depend solely upon mass transit, bicycles, and their own two feet. "

Dave batted another question at him. "What prevents foreign manufacturers from stepping up to the plate?"

"We'll ban imports, if necessary. If Brazil can do so, so can we. However, not too many countries other than the US manufacture gas guzzlers."

A wave of chuckles swept the room. The reporter nodded as others frantically waved fingers and pens at Henry, who re-entered his narrative at the point of interruption. "While great strides have been made in the development of solar and wind energy alternatives, construction of corn-derived ethanol plants, implementing cellulosic ethanol production, and the increased use of methane and gasified biomass, as well as a greater use of hydrogen fuel, the oil industry remains a viable and powerful player in our world economy. Petroleum is used for much more than producing energy or propelling vehicles. The production of crop-based corn ethanol at home has contributed to food shortages abroad. Corn ethanol is not a viable fuel because it deprives people of nourishment; I'm also calling for legislation that will place serious limitations on corn ethanol production. As things stand right now, we're headed toward wars and possibly even nuclear wars over food scarcity issues."

Henry nodded at a young woman with a masculine haircut. "Mr. President, it's clear that zero-emission ethanol plants are as detrimental to the environment as petroleum. Not to mention devastating to the food markets and the underlying cause of some food deficits beginning to span the globe. Will carbon emission standards be lowered in factories to facilitate the change to all hybrids and electrics?"

"Good questions. As far as fuel needs go, we must abandon ethanol and concentrate on dependable renewable energy sources such as solar, wind, and ocean wave. There has been a great deal of progress in harnessing these energy sources since the energy mandates of 2009. Hemp farming is another alternative that would provide fuel and many other needed products. It's high time we embraced a new paradigm for commerce, industry, and our personal energy needs."

Murmurs swept the room. Most reporters appeared delighted at his strong stand. A few faces reflected sober questions, and two or three smirked with disdain. Henry scanned the faces and called on an older man wearing a FOX television network nametag.

"Mr. President, how do you propose to address mass transit subsidies in our major cities? What about people who need private transportation?—hybrid cars, electrics, and especially the new solar electric thermals are still out of the reach of most Americans!"

He forged ahead with the planned answers his staff had rehearsed with him. "Not only must we end our dependence on foreign oil, we must end our dependence upon petroleum, period. Full stop. The fossil fuel era must end. I realize this stand is not popular in the oilfields of the Middle East or the fracking fields of North America. Nor is it popular with foreign or domestic petroleum markets, the myriad of manufacturing concerns ranging from pharmaceuticals to plastics, nor with automakers that must retrofit their facilities with new labs and new technology or expand existing manufacture of hybrid, electric, hydrogen and solar alternatives to the gasoline engine. We must also solve electric infrastructure problems to handle increasing numbers of electric vehicles. There is no way to approach complex, multiple issues without reducing our energy consumption, period. The petroleum crunch is affecting all business endeavors . . . agriculture, technology and manufacturing. A massive restructuring of industry is not only necessary, it is clearly inevitable. There will be a hugely uncomfortable transition period while we shift from petroleum-based technology to renewables. Because the world economy has depended upon petroleum for over a century, we must expect great obstacles during this transition. A billion-dollar fund will be created to assist businesses and individuals through this transition. Many citizens and corporate enterprises in this nation will be temporarily inconvenienced and even hurt by the change—"

The same reporter jumped to his feet. "And if the bill is not passed by Congress and the Senate, Mr. President?"

"I'll encourage a redraft and go for the gusto again."

The room exploded in a raucous uproar. Hands snapped up like whips.

"Before I answer more questions, let me say this, ladies and gentlemen. We must tighten our belts and pull together. While our nation has done much to end our reliance upon oil in the past decade, it is not enough. We must do more and do it now. Right here at home, growing numbers of working poor labor endlessly at survival level. Our unemployment rates have risen well past official figures in many states. It doesn't take a statistician to understand how the collection and presentation of data can be manipulated. While we've cleared some hurdles in supplying health care to masses of people who were previously uninsured, bringing the economy back to a vibrant state through a massive change in our industry and infrastructure must also happen. The situation is even more critical in non-industrial nations, some of which have been in political and financial turmoil for several years. We cannot do any less than restructure our lives in the same way that emerging industrial countries move forward by integrating new technologies with the old. Ending our reliance upon oil will decrease environmental and social ills caused by the petroleum era. I can only hope it is not too late."

The Associated Press reporter seethed with questions. "Mr. President, an energy platform that caps greenhouse gas emissions started in 2008, and aims to cut them 15 percent or more by 2020; we've eliminated $3 billion in subsidies to oil companies over the past three years, we've got corporations selling the right to emit greenhouse gases and using their proceeds to fund alternative energy; we've frozen electricity demand and raised fuel economy standards to 50 mpg for 2015; and drafted a new global warming treaty that includes developing nations. Those are significant changes in the fight against global warming. Aren't you jumping ahead of yourself with your radical personal demands, Mr. President?"

"Uh." He held his hand up and began to speak, but reporters continued shouting questions over each other.

"Mr. President, Mr. President, Mr. President!"

Henry mopped his sweaty brow and attempted to answer several questions in one condensed narrative. The group quieted by slow degrees as most media representatives concentrated upon recording his answers.

When he finished speaking, the briefing dissolved in a swirl of related questions: "What about agriculture? What about pesticides and fertilizers made from petroleum? How do you propose to replace the corporate farming infrastructure with a local organic farming model?"

After his answers, Joe Rankin, a baldheaded UPI regular with big ears, sneered at him. "Why don't you ask seven billion people to stop eating for a year or two while we figure this out?"

He ignored Rankin, navigating his way through the morass of follow-up questions, answering sincerely when he could, skimming past a few with skillful non-answers or pure political spin. He hoped his old Henry charisma would bring the tension in the room back to a dull buzz. At the bottom line, things had happened or were scheduled to happen. The nation was stuck in a holding pattern of reaction to past, present, and possible future events. This was the perfect time to get the environmental show on the road—and soon enough, he hoped, disclosure of the secret extraterrestrial agenda.

Hands waved wildly again as new pandemonium broke out in the pressroom. The media hyenas sniffed and howled as the briefing ended and the Secret Service formed a wall around him. Henry sucked in his gut and squared his shoulders, attempting to appear presidential as he exited the press room.

:::CHAPTER 5

PRESIDENT HARRIS CANTRELL HENRY
11.11.2011: 11 A.M.–3:02 P.M.

President Harris Cantrell Henry's face relaxed into a neutral expression as he strode from the press room through the West Wing toward the Oval Office. The Secret Service detail scrambled behind him, trying to keep up with his long gait.

"Too little, too late," he groused softly to himself. "Should have drafted SR 1477 during my first year in office."

He had to admit that the opposition was too powerful in the past. But both corporate entities and citizens now saw the writing on the environmental wall. Or did they? His mind drifted back to the ET directive he'd received on Air Force One shortly after the election: *The new climatic conditions are essential to the alignment of our power structure.* He hadn't heard from those shape-shifting beings since, though his briefings, staff research, and Drew Forrest's investigations revealed some uncomfortable things about them.

He slouched at his desk no more than five minutes when the intercom buzzed for what seemed like the hundredth time. He held his throbbing head between his hands after punching yet another blinking button that connected him to every problem in the world, it seemed.

"Yes, Dottie."

"Mr. President, your scheduled conference call is waiting on the video monitor, line one," she said.

Without comment, he reached for the monitor, keyed in his code, and joined Langley and DoD in a round robin on military strategy in Peru. Pentagon toughs and NIHSA spooks had streamed in and out of the White House situation room and the Oval Office over the past few days in case troops were mobilized into Peru or if someone discovered whatever cave bin Rashid resided in on the other side of the world.

He continued browsing through drafts of legislation and speeches as he talked, grunting uh-huh when appropriate, crossing his arms in a body English message to the military and NIHSA officials that, like it or not, their protocols would have to include his expertise. In fact, the Agency could take a flying fuck, he figured.

West Wing morale was sinking lower than a grasshopper's knees. For over a year, the cabinet scrambled from one crisis to another, and everyone looked forward with relief to every weekend, and especially to the upcoming Thanksgiving holiday. If the U.S. military was deployed to Peru soon, it would ruin the holiday, a dismal ending to a dismal month. If he spent one more weekend in the stuffy situation room and the conference room next door with a bunch of stressed-out politicos, spooks, and soldiers, he just might go over the edge.

In spite of the looming military crisis, he couldn't stop obsessing about his environmental bill and his plan for UFO disclosure. After three years of research by his aides, it was clear that an extraterrestrial invasion was humanity's greatest threat, next to the ongoing environmental crisis. Peru was small potatoes in comparison. In fact, the UFO enigma was the elephant in the room that no one ever talked about.

Determined to solve the mystery once and for all, he'd first asked Associate Attorney General Baxter Chopps, an old college pal, to dig into the dark corners of UFO policy during the early weeks of his administration. Gibb, his Sci-Tech advisor, hated the subject but reluctantly brought in top UFO researchers and some egghead scientists for briefings. Like Bill Clinton, Henry favored individual briefings over cabinet meetings. Less distracting, and these allowed for discrete development of individual opinions. Solo briefings also deflected public curiosity that full cabinet meetings on controversial matters created. But leaks about the briefings, especially after a key advisor to the Secretary of Defense attended one, fueled gossip on Capitol Hill about Henry's style. Ratings dropped, but would come back up soon if he played his cards right.

Bax hit many walls while ferreting out classified information that federal agencies had gathered in previous decades about publicized UFO cases like Roswell. Finally, after months of head banging and staff resignations, he received some mysterious digital files courtesy of groups interested in full government disclosure about UFOs. Bax revealed that the group who e-mailed the encrypted files called themselves "The Library."

Henry imagined a disenchanted network of spiritual intellectuals shining light into the shadows of the world. If this network truly existed, then his bid for full disclosure might have a glimmer of hope. After waiting several months to hear from The Library again, the administration tried to make contact but as the months passed, nothing else surfaced.

Almost every time he thought of Bax, Bax showed up for a chat. He wasn't disappointed this time. Bax strolled into the office just as he disconnected the DoD and Langley video conference call. Henry waved Bax toward a chair. "Keep in touch, boys," he muttered toward the videophone monitor as the screen faded, "we'll get this straight."

Yank my chain whenever.

Bax nodded at Henry, dragged the JFK rocking chair to the enormous desk, and plopped down a dog-eared stack of files.

"Harris—Mr. President, we've got a problem. Two problems."

"Number one."

"It's Drew."

Henry's already sober face tightened.

Bax stared at the files on his desk for moment, and then gazed into Henry's eyes. "I'm sorry to have to tell you this—DC police found his body moments ago in a garden at the Georgetown Hilton."

He felt his mouth tighten and his face cloud over. "The Agency? Or Collins's people?"

"Either/or, as far as I'm concerned. There's probably a connection between the two. Isn't any clear cause of death and the case is still in police jurisdiction, but I have no doubt the Agency will take over soon. I just got off the phone with the Langley division."

"What's their take on it?"

"Drew's book on environment. That's the whitewash, anyway. It's actually his latest project, I'm sure. Not long before the call came in, he texted me about a video. You were still in the pressroom. He mentioned an anonymous source, and that it would blow the lid right off suppression of disclosure. He said he was on his way to bring it to you."

"Whew." Henry stood and walked to a window, hands on his hips. He stared outside for a long time without really seeing anything. Then he squared his shoulders, returned to his desk and leveled steely eyes at Bax. "What now?"

Bax hesitated. "I'm not sure."

"You mentioned two problems."

Bax held one palm over the files on Henry's desk. "The files you asked for. Not all cases pertain to close encounters. A few documents confirm the transfer of secret technology to the old CIA, including the first mention in writing of reverse-engineering from ET technology." Bax opened an expanding file and pulled out a thin paper-clipped pile of yellowed documents. "Of course, I'm not having anything to do with . . . space material . . . any more. These files need to go to Lody."

Henry strode back to the desk and sat down with a grim grin on his face. "Son of a bitch. I figured you were onto *something* big. Before the conference call, I got a phone call from Langley myself. Special Ops. Jiminez, the director's assistant, told me in so many words—off the record, of course—that I'd better zip my lips. Hinted I'm in hot water up and his tub's fillin' up, too. Ran the usual intel line about experiments in mind control and weather-control technology—'everyone's doing it and we've gotta keep up, damn it, surpass the sons-of-bitches in our understanding', he said. DoD isn't waterin' roses, either—they bristled earlier about my 'dogs' sniffing around. Same tired line about 'we have little existing information about UFO intrusions into terrestrial airspace.' Their screwing around with the ionosphere and whatnot is applicable to national defense, in their limited minds. Might help the terror wars, you never know."

Bax shot the President an empathetic look, but fear soon clouded his eyes. "Since I hit bottom at NORAD, my aides are running those checks you ordered on the Air Force ET situation, and the potential mind-control and harassment activities by HAARP."

HAARP, the High Frequency Active Auroral Research Program in Gakona, Alaska, a high power transmitter facility, bothered Henry as much as the UFO question when he took office. Ostensibly just a harmless scientific endeavor aimed at advancing knowledge of the physical and electrical properties of the Earth's ionosphere, the bulk of the project's research focused on how the ionosphere affected U.S. military and civilian communication and navigation systems.

Every time the HAARP antenna array was operational, there were weather anomalies inside and outside the country, followed by civilian and foreign complaints about weird weather and suspected electronic surveillance. Scientists involved claimed there was no classified research done at the facility, that HAARP couldn't affect weather and had negligible effects on living beings and the environment.

"Damn it, Bax, they roll over and play dead when I spell U-F-O or H-A-A-R-P. This ET thing's biting my butt. There's gonna be more calls about it and soon. Maybe worse. I don't want to repeat my experience on Air Force One. You were there, even if you don't remember it—"

"Don't know if I'm lucky or unlucky on that one," Bax replied.

"It'll come to you sometime, Baxie. Anyway, you've been briefed, heard the stories. Even before NIHSA, the spooks terrorized people when they were close to uncovering secrets. Remember the one about the mind-twisting suits who visited a civilian scientist a few years back after his contract at Area 51 ended? Or the Major from the CIA remote viewing program they raked over the coals years ago? How 'bout the slew of new directed-energy harassment suits by anti-mind control and environmental activists—these people are brave, but the Agency will continue to kick their butts unless we act. Do they really need a repression cherry on top of their shit sundae?"

Bax grimaced. "It's already pretty much happened to us . . . especially to you, Mr. President."

"Without as much drama, I suppose. I'd like to know how much of this is contrived bullshit. What's real? Is the Agency *really* in charge, or are the strings getting pulled from out there?" Henry waved his hand at the ceiling, meaning space. "Hell, I wouldn't blame you for backing down because of Drew. But what's this crazy video? What could possibly be on it to cause his death?" His angry expression melted into tears, revealing his grief.

Bax rubbed his palms together as if brushing his question off. "I saved the worst for last, Harris. Someone gave Drew Forrest a video of Senator Collins, who seems to be in the process of morphing into a reptilian ET. An aide e-mailed a copy on the encrypted circuit while Drew called. I wish it was a big joke." Bax pulled an enlarged still frame from a file and placed it in front of Henry.

He stared at the photo. The face of a lizard was superimposed over Collins's face, exactly what he'd seen aboard Air Force One. "Get the video downloaded into my security computer ASAP. We'll review it at the 3:30 cabinet meeting."

Bax nodded. "You sure this is what you saw? I have trouble absorbing the incident . . . I'm sure the Agency will have their internet flunkies post it and debunk it. But I sent it for a preliminary analysis through Gibbs' people before I came in." He pulled a thick analysis packet from an accordion file. "The analysts think the transformation is real, not a video program special effect. They said they'd never seen anything like it. They'll have to study it further for full confirmation."

Henry's heart did a little triple leap in his already tight chest.

"Seems everything we've ever suspected is true. And this might be their way of warning us again. Damn, Bax . . ."

They fell silent, grappling with the enormous implications.

"We're practically sleeping with the enemy," he said after a moment. "It makes sense now, the manipulation of global warming, and the HAARP 'research,' allowing the Moral Right to completely disregard climatic and environmental science."

Bax nearly wrung his hands with dismay. "They've got the Agency, Harr, I'm sure of it. Look at Drew. This secret took him out. Maybe the ETs even gave him the video as an excuse to whack him."

"Anybody else know?"

Bax tightened his lips for a moment. "My wife. Sorry. Couldn't keep it from her, you know how Colleen is. She was petrified about the implications of our research long before Drew died this morning. She keeps buying new prepaid cell phones every few days to make sure no one's listening to us."

"I wouldn't expect you to keep this from your spouse. Maybe you should try buying a couple of those new scrambling gizmos for your phones . . . Damn it, Bax, we gotta keep our heads. This video thing stinks, but we still have some wiggle room. Lody's on target. We're armed with the facts—more facts than ever before. Let's call a Congressional investigation, pull some disclosure documents into Federal court. How can a few shape-shifting lizards and their Agency lackeys fight a concerted effort by all three branches of government?"

"We can't control NIHSA with facts. Or dreams of the Founding Fathers, Harr. The Langley division's laughing at us—they're not going to just let us . . . you might be . . ." Bax left his fears unsaid, shivering at the implications.

Henry started to say there was no choice but to go for disclosure, but he let it slide. The Agency made the Big Chopper wonder whom they'd bite next. He'd seen similar situations several times during his political career. Some public servants were willing to sacrifice themselves for a higher cause and others preferred a long, peaceful life.

"Bax, help me get Collins in here, fast. We need to talk."

With a reluctant nod, Bax pulled the rocking chair to its original position, strode to the door, and let himself out.

Bax's fear stuck in his craw, a sinking goddamn feeling that made it hard to breathe. He grabbed the files, stuffed them into a valise, changed the combination lock, and slid the valise into a fireproof safe he'd installed himself in a section of floor-to-ceiling bookshelf behind his desk over the last long holiday weekend. It was quite a chore to keep the Secret Service and his staff distracted while he worked, but those high school shop classes his practical father insisted he take finally came in handy.

He reached into his desk for a bottle of Tylenol and choked a couple down with a swig of fancy bottled water in blue glass. He slumped into his chair and stared across the Oval Office. God, how he wished he could talk to Tess. When push came to shove, he'd always loved spilling his heart to that gal. Her hackles were slow to rise and she seemed to know just what to say or what to do before he knew it himself. True, he'd worried her with his talk about extraterrestrials, and it wasn't fair of him to expect her loyalty. He wagered she would have supported him through thick and thin if he'd been single. Well, and if she'd accepted his proof of the details she labeled his "crazy talk."

Henry doodled in the margins of a legal pad, making one of his "maps" of the issue, accompanied by a deep, heartfelt sigh he hoped no one heard. The face of the Moral Right newsman who'd asked about C. Clelland Collins sprang into mind like one of those whack-a-moles in a children's arcade game. After the Obelisk bombings on Halloween, New Yorkers and Bostonians returned in short order to business as usual. But NIHSA goaded the media to stir the rest of the country into a frenzy. Even so, a large transfer of funds from a small Buena Park, California branch of Bank of America, funneled through a Swiss bank to two locations, Riyadh and Jerusalem, remained back page news. The transfers only came to light when a senior teller stumbled upon a stray document that missed the shredder just days before her retirement.

Now the Moral Right faction of the Agency was busy minimizing the fallout. The Collins family, including Senator C. Clelland Collins, Jr. and his son CCC III, waved reporters away after the discovery. Just as they'd done two years before on publication day of Drew Forrest's triumphal investigative book on the Collins's and bin Rashid's extensive family business connections, knotted in a snarl of drugs, illicit sex, and nuclear weapon components. Forrest took a lot of flak for the book, and Henry had asked him to dig further into the government/ET connection.

Henry brought his fist down hard on the desk. He'd been steamed when the mainstream press clammed up after the publication of Drew's book. Someone upstairs must have issued a blanket warning about the topic. Unfortunately, the Forrest Report went largely unread by the aliterate voting public. The Collins's family image shone like pure gold because many Americans identified with their phony pioneering hubris. A Collins had run most of Iowa since statehood and ironically, Iowa was his old stomping ground too. The Collins family wasn't about to yield an inch, certainly not to the more progressive Forrest Report readers or to the Henry administration.

He had no doubt that the District coroner would hastily declare Drew a heart attack victim, a common diagnosis after the Agency brought someone down. If this situation spun the Agency's way, the only people left to rally Henry's cause would be diehard government conspiracy buffs and alternative media reporters. He sighed again. And he'd probably experience the worst-case scenario: the Moral Right would spread rumors, blaming him for his best friend's murder. He felt responsible already, having personally asked Drew to investigate the extraterrestrial question.

Henry pressed an intercom button. Dottie's generally reassuring voice answered in a monotone. "Yes, Mr. President?

"Is Mr. Ramirez on his way? I need to see him immediately."

"Sir, his ETA is five minutes."

"Send him in when he arrives. Thank you, Dottie."

Henry leaned back in his chair and mopped his forehead with a tissue. He forced himself to re-analyze the more mundane elements of the press briefing and the video conference call between fielding routine phone messages and periodic staff updates. He regretted leaving some details of his bill under-covered or left unsaid at the briefing, despite the many good but uncomfortable questions.

His thoughts whirled around his head, the voices and images becoming louder and louder. How could he order these in any rational sequence? He gripped his head and squirmed in his chair, mentally shuffling from rock to hard place and back. Why did he chew himself up over this? What the hell did he expect? He'd endured the veiled racial slurs tossed at him during his entire political career. He pushed himself mercilessly to overcome his angry reactions to racist hecklers. Then not a goddamn month after the election without a major crisis, two attempted terrorist attacks, ongoing financial crisis, multiple natural disasters, and now, Drew's murder.

Goddamn the Agency. He'd originally considered the major problems in the country as stemming from NIHSA's darkest inner echelon. No matter who he appointed to lead the super-agency, it seemed to take on a life of its own, challenging the intended balance of the three branches of U.S. government As Bax and Lody pointed out as New Politics 101: the Agency wasn't just NIHSA, federal law enforcement. Their power rolled from NIHSA and the Pentagon elite laterally into another elite group of corporate and Wall Street players, oil and energy people and banksters who pulled the nation's strings. Drew and Bax had finally painted a clearer picture of who pulled *their* strings.

Another buzz from the intercom jangled his last nerve. He punched the intercom button so hard that the handset flew off the console.

"Yes?"

"Mr. President, the Director of Sierra Club on line two, audio only."

He reached across the line of telephones sprawling along the far edge of his desk to an old-fashioned beige ten-line hardwired phone, trying to compose himself. He'd have to assume that Drew's death was not yet publicized.

"Hey Morris, I appreciate your call. We're on the same page about Dr. Resek's death."

"Mr. President, how can we secure safety for our nation's ecologists and microbiologists?"

"There's a definite pattern to the deaths and I'm glad you tell it like it is, Mo. But be careful."

Worse than the public's trip down "da Nile" about Senator Collins, maybe even worse than Drew's murder, was the alarming assassination of environmental scientists. The nation had lost one or two a year since Al Gore's Oscar win mobilized the American public and the world to fight global warming. Houston, Minneapolis, Omaha, Miami—it didn't matter where these researchers lived—if they supported global warming theory *and* extreme methods of dealing with it, they came up dead, drowned in swimming pools or found stiff in their beds. Hardly anyone in the mainstream press asked questions about the so-called suicides, heart attack victims, and accidental overdoses.

But now there was Drew. Might be hard to whitewash his death.

Henry's lower lip quivered. "My cabinet and I have a briefing this afternoon to discuss the problem. On one hand, we have the Moral Right embracing climate denial and environmental degradation as economic stimulus and a precursor for the Rapture. On the other, we have rich adventurers seeking new home worlds to settle. Somewhere in between, we have those who continue profit from degrading the Earth no matter what. I'm calling for the organization of a Congressional committee to investigate, if they don't do so themselves and soon."

"Mr. President, we can't thank you enough. I'm concerned—it's not hard to notice that every environmental success seems to be followed by a weather crisis."

"Yes, and it's keeping people in a perpetual state of turmoil." Allowing tighter government control, or neglect, whichever worked best, Henry thought. No doubt those friggin' ET lizards are at the bottom of it.

"Keep a low profile, Mo. Davis at the Interior will be in touch with you when we get this ball rolling."

How he wanted to talk to Morris about Drew, but it would have to wait until his cabinet devised some talking strategy.

"I will, Mr. President. Thank you for your time."

"You bet. We'll talk again soon."

Henry placed the handset back into the receiver and sighed. How else but ending dependency on petroleum could we save the planet and ourselves? Clearly the wetland droughts and desert floods, more frequent Midwestern earthquakes, as well as the expected California quakes (moderate ones so far, fortunately) and the violent tornadoes, hurricanes, and rogue snowstorms swirling all over the damn place were not coincidental to the petroleum-based economy. Even before the newly discovered axis tilt, icebergs appeared in New Zealand waters for the seventh year in a row as arctic ice shelves collapsed and shriveled into a ghost of their former size. Amphibian species were disappearing in the tropics and polar bears drowning in the Arctic, reduced to the lowest numbers ever recorded. The beleaguered Yellowstone buffalo, their gene pool declared too small for recovery, vacated Montana for cooler climes in Canada. Starfish were losing their limbs and turning to goo on the West coast. Fish off the coast of Japan had high levels of radiation and this would affect U.S. West coast fisheries in years ahead. Whole species of bats simply vanished in heavily populated Eastern seaboard areas. Honeybees disappeared from hives faster than breeders nursed new colonies to health, disturbed by pesticides and attacked by an exotic fungal fiber-producing disease, Morgellons. Any crop dependent upon honeybees was in danger of becoming a luxury, and food prices climbed everywhere. The only thing keeping U.S. citizens from rioting at grocery stores and gas stations was the sense of community spawned by the quest to overcome global warming on the left hand side, and the promise of religious solutions and smaller government from the right. The division was getting tense as the two opposing viewpoints began to tangle on the streets. Gun ownership proliferated everywhere, accompanied by lax self-defense laws. New states' rights agendas were challenging Federal authority, and people were especially vocal about the 2nd Amendment right to bear arms .

Still, human politics often changed in a heartbeat. But damage to the Earth and its beings would not disappear without definite change in human behavior, behaviors that were far less obvious than gun worship. How could anyone miss the space shuttle photos on the internet documenting the earth's frail atmosphere and visible environmental damage? Behind the scenes, the space shuttle and new space station crew also spotted myriad UFOs hovering around the planet, probably to observe the chaos, and from what he'd heard in his private briefings, NASA continued to play their hand close to their chest, controlled by NIHSA. Henry's researchers speculated that some UFOS taking positions around Earth were ETs interested in taking advantage of the extinction of Earth life, and others, he hoped might be standing by to assist human interests. Able to avoid close observation with their advanced stealth technology, both types reportedly hovered in a celestial game of cat and mouse. The craft were often not reported in the United States, although leaks sometimes reached alternative news sources. NIHSA played mum and continued to spin misinformation, citing national security issues. There was no real proof of UFOS, they claimed.

Henry sighed again. Banning petroleum powered engines and winding down the fossil fuel industry was the only answer to the Earth's environmental and political woes. But could he realistically give full UFO disclosure on the heels of supporting this ban without literally losing his head?

Maybe not. Henry found himself staring out the window again. The partly cloudy sky took on the heavy gray pallor typical of DC in November. His mood dropped another notch, the dense afternoon lending itself to morbid self-examination. Dark skies always made him forget his accomplishments, the legacy he'd tried to set in motion despite his personal weaknesses and outer obstacles.

Three dark birds eased into his line of sight. They flew in unison, away from him, wheeling out of range, disappearing one after the other. Two birds, then one flying alone, and finally an empty, overcast sky framed by golden brocade drapes.

The intercom buzzed. "Mr. President, Mr. Ramirez is on his way in."

Lody entered as he toyed with a letter at the bottom of his inbox. The envelope was stapled to it, with a sticky note memo initialed by the aide who'd opened it. "Woo-woo," Bax cautioned with a big smiley and his initials on the sticky beside the aide's. Seems a couple of New Age ministers from Arizona found his name in their Bible Code—a resurgence of interest in the code was soaring—and they cautioned him too, sans smiley. Apparently, he'd find himself chased through the desert, dead, or both . . .

Normally he'd laugh at the prospect, but wasn't this the case already, metaphorically speaking?

"This is tough, Lody. I'm sure Bax has briefed you. You're in his hotseat now."

"Yes, sir." Ramirez cast his unwavering, honest expression at Henry.

"Then you've heard about Drew. The cabinet will convene soon and we'll discuss that matter as well." Henry's eyes moistened as he picked up the letter and shook it. "Quite an interesting letter. Bax fielded this one. From some amateur investigators. Bible Code enthusiasts." He read the contents to Ramirez. It also explained that the Bible Code suggested possible use of scalar waves to steer Hurricane Katrina, Cyclone Nargis, and subsequent monster storms like the recent sonofabitch Tyrell that ravaged the Atlantic seaboard and the Gulf coast yet again.

"Lody, why do you suppose NIHSA and our own armed forces use secret technology to subject their own countrymen to such horrors unless there's some hugely compelling reason—such as extraterrestrials wanting Earth?"

"I can't think of any other reason sir, unless there's some application to protect Earth from the same. A real global security agenda, although I don't how you separate the real thing from the propaganda."

Henry tossed the letter back in the basket and glanced at the desk clock. Nearly 3:00 p.m. The cabinet meeting was set for 3:30, enough time for a quick workout in the gym or upstairs in the family quarters. Working up a sweat in fifteen minutes and showering in cold water would make him feel alive and appear refreshed at the meeting. Hell, even national leaders on a doomed Earth in the 11-11-11 window should exercise.

He forced his chin up and his body out of the chair. "Make some phone calls, will you, Lody? See what you can find out about Drew."

Clapping Ramirez on the shoulder, he escorted him into the reception area. He excused himself with Dottie and staff, who still plucked away at keyboards in the outer office.

Careful to make his voice smooth, authoritative, he said, "Thank you, ladies and gentlemen. I'll see some of you in the Cabinet room in thirty minutes."

"Don't fall through that triple-eleven window, Mr. President," one of the clerks joked.

Dottie glanced up from her work with a wooden look. "Mr. President, do you need me after the meeting?"

Lately, Dottie scared him and he stayed as far from her as possible. He considered replacing her but couldn't figure out any good reason that would satisfy a possible media ruckus. He couldn't remember the day she'd changed, become a caricature of herself. She started moving in a subtle, mechanical way as if powered by batteries, her emotional repertoire flat. Did anyone else notice? Dottie wasn't the only person in the White House who had changed. His scientific advisors told him about some rumored technology, some crazy cloning technique that sounded like pulp science fiction. Just like this bizarre story of humanoid lizards taking over the world.

"Take some time for yourself, Dottie," he said, avoiding her gaze.

The rest of the staff stared at their desks, avoiding his gaze. Everyone knew he'd return for the cabinet meeting, and afterward, a meeting with the Chairwoman of the Intergovernmental Panel on Climate Change, another of a thousand coalitions concerned with increased global poverty and starvation, drinking-water shortages, infectious disease, and vanishing species.

He hesitated and impulsively returned to his desk. He reached for a videophone, then pulled his Blackberry from his pocket and entered a speed-dial number.

"Senator Collins' office, how may I help you?"

"Miss Rees?" This is the President. I'd like to invite Senator Collins to the Oval Office for a chat. I have two engagements this afternoon, but we can talk over dinner."

Whether the Senator would respond and what to say if he did were big question marks hanging in the air.

"Senator Collins is in a meeting, sir, but I'll give him your message shortly."

"Thank you, Miss Rees. Please ask him to respond to the message personally."

"I'll do my best, Mr. President."

The perennial Secret Service detail trailed behind him outside the office. Two agents kept their distance, muttering into their sleeves, exchanging his movement specifics with detail headquarters.

He passed a couple of janitorial people in the corridor. "Mr. President, good afternoon, sir." The short, rotund cleaning woman's equally round face creased into a smile, and her lanky male coworker turned off a vacuum sweeper, nodding in deference.

"Good evening—thank you for your work." He offered the pair a jaunty salute and forced himself to smile back. As he neared the East Wing elevator corridor, he felt the day's heaviness evaporate. His body tension melted away in anticipation of his workout.

Suddenly, a peculiar hum edged into one ear and filled his throbbing head, the same sensation he'd heard *and* felt in Air Force One during the so-called luncheon party. But it felt softer, subtler, and more painful this time. He shook his head. He must be imagining it because he'd revisited the incident so many times.

But denial didn't work. He began to lurch like a California earthquake. A piercing light stabbed his eyeballs and a crushing pain shot from his cranium downward into his left shoulder. The faint but distinctive noise of paper rustling surrounded him. His body rose from the floor, throbbing with a sensation of contraction and expansion. He stared up at the ornate hallway ceiling through a greenish haze.

The rustling noises crescendoed into a chopping sound whose vibration pushed him through a body-sized tunnel. He seemed to fall into a dream with four-fingered hands plucking at him from all directions. Then he plummeted into deep darkness, completely disconnected.

:::CHAPTER 6

TESS VAUGHN

Tess dropped her hand from the radio tuner, her heart surging in a swirl of grief, relief, and disbelief. She muted the special report for a moment, then regained composure and turned the volume back on, snorting at the mention of a lone gunman. A classic assassination story line grown thin, transparent, ludicrous.

". . . According to NIHSA spokesperson David T. Russell, the alleged gunman's motive is unclear," the familiar National Public Radio commentator noted. "The case appears to involve a mix of celebrity obsession and political delusion. An unconfirmed field operative report suggests the agency has seized the suspect's laptop, including files with a rambling narrative about the danger of imbalance between the executive, judicial, and legislative branches of government. Jason Ming Orlando, an Idaho native, refers to himself a 'cosmic patriot' and a 'hero who saved his country from an evil, renegade president.' Upon his arrest, Orlando stated that he received a directive to assassinate President Harris Henry on 11-11-11 from a galactic council who, in his words, 'visit me each full moon to discuss Earth affairs.'"

Tess blanched, recalling Harris's mention of ETs and UFOs during their last few hours together. She shook the feeling off by focusing on the commentary: *Harris Cantrell Henry, distinguished as the first multiracial President in U.S. history, was shot two weeks before the anniversary of President John Fitzgerald Kennedy's death, evoking the nation's painful memories of November 1963.*

As the report concluded, the commentator segued into a human interest story, noting that Henry's charisma and sex appeal were often compared to that of Presidents William Jefferson Clinton and John Fitzgerald Kennedy. Harris had kindled the same strong emotions in people as both former presidents. Charisma or race or both? Tess mused. Ironically, Kennedy was Henry's as well as Clinton's childhood idol, and Henry's only regret was that he wasn't old enough to meet JFK before the president died. During a high school computer class, Henry said he'd created a fake PR photo of himself shaking Kennedy's hand in the White House, one he framed and kept in his bedroom to remind him of his goals. Tess liked thinking of Harris as the ambitious teenager.

She wasn't quite old enough to recall the day Kennedy had fallen in Dallas. She'd asked her parents to relate their memories of the dismal day. Some older Vaughn cousins, her great uncle's kids, told her about their school principal's somber visit to their Tucson classrooms. The enormity of the event swept through the school and the heart of the nation like a lightning bolt, they said. Something cold surged through Tess as she listened to their narrative—and now, to this one—making her skin crawl with goose bumps.

Tess reached out with a shaky hand and reduced the radio volume. She was stunned yet not surprised at the announcement. She pulled the pick-up off Highway 89 onto the wide shoulder where a passing lane opened, and fumbled in the glove box for a stick of the incense she used to scent the truck. She climbed over the console and stepped out of the truck's passenger side, then lit the incense. Holding back her tears, she cupped her hand around the stick and offered it to earth and sky. The tendril of smoke wafted into the air like a gnarled wraith.

Her mind wavered from the incense and her prayer, and focused on the boundless hills beyond the highway, an energy that still overpowered everything manmade. Gazing at the natural beauty peeled away the gravity of her heart to its tender, secret center.

Vehicles whizzed past, their occupants gazing quizzically at her as she recalled the synchronicity that crossed her life with a president's.

Suddenly, a speeding truck ripped across the rumble strip bordering the shoulder. Jarred by the ear-splitting whir of the truck tires, Tess realized the incense was burning a fraction of an inch from her fingers. She stubbed the ember into the dirt and prayed again, calling upon the light to receive the friend of her heart. She appealed also for Mikka's safety. Not quite three years old, Mikka had never met her father and now she never would.

A tear trailed down each of her cheeks. Tess shivered in the cold wind, wondering what spooks might bite her in the days ahead. She climbed back into the truck and continued driving from Prescott into northwest Yavapai County. Traffic started to slow down. Tess chafed and frowned at the line of vehicles ahead and behind her in the rearview mirror, the SUVs, over-powered pickup trucks and scattered hybrid cars idling around her silently like little flying saucers. She watched other drivers press radio buttons and chat to their passengers or on their Bluetooths, no doubt digesting the radio report that would change their lives forever.

Tess closed her eyes for a moment and tried to focus on her breath. She gazed again past rooftops and over ranch fences, seeking comfort in nature. Stands of ponderosa pine and granite boulders thinned out to scattered junipers and piñon pines in the stretch of undeveloped state land. Below the treeline in the far distance lay an open range of curly gramma grass, sere under a sullen, gunmetal sky. A ring of low purple mountains pricked azure patches in the hazy clouds at the eastern and western horizons. The air was thick with dust and some auto exhaust—over ten years of serious drought and fifteen years of uncontrolled growth and the state of Arizona still hadn't opened emission control centers in Yavapai County. Bereft of the native pronghorn antelope and bald eagles that now leaped and soared mainly upon civic logos, the high desert valley hosted rush hour traffic and manufactured houses like boxy mushrooms that popped up on almost every available acre surrounding the big parcels of state land.

Tess glanced in the rearview mirror and her red-rimmed eyes stared back at her. A blaring horn snapped her back to reality as traffic began to surge forward again. She gripped the steering wheel harder, not wanting to confront her generally confused feelings about Harris.

Grief caught in her throat like a stray bone and she let herself wail once, swallowing the sound into a rasping sob. She grasped for another rational thought to bury her emotion.

She turned up the radio volume. A new voice detailed President Harris's final day. He'd attended a press briefing in the late morning, followed by several hours of routine meetings, then signed documents and fielded phone calls. A gunman apparently accosted the president and a Secret Service detail in the late afternoon as he made his way toward the East Wing to freshen up in the White House family quarters before a cabinet meeting. Somehow the killer had penetrated many levels of security, a statistical improbability. The pair of Secret Service agents tailing President Henry were temporarily overcome, but left unhurt. Shocking. And his friend Drew Forrest was found dead earlier that day, his death now overshadowed by the President's . . .

A conspiracy of massive proportions. A coup. Tess imagined the resulting Congressional hearing, a sham Henry Report. There would be no connection allowed between the deaths of the two friends. The official story would not compute, though a majority of the American public would swallow it hook, line and sinker. And the ones who didn't? Most would forget about it in a month or two. Life spun on and new entertainment always appeared in Washington.

The rest of the afternoon played out in a loopy blur. Tess went to pick up Mikka from a play date with the Perez family, her closest neighbors. Mikka ran to the door beaming, her usual bouncy self.

"I can't believe this is happening," Darcy Perez said when she opened the door for Tess, searching her face. "You look tired."

"Bizarre news," Tess agreed. "I'm exhausted." She and Darcy chatted over tea in the kitchen, sharing their thoughts about the President's mysterious death, sandwiched between their kids' interruptions.

Darcy recalled Tess's status as a former investigative reporter and prodded her for opinions about the assassination. Tess felt like an imposter, considering Mikka's ancestry. But what else could she do but pretend?

Tess did a little jig on her doorstep with Mikka in her arms when they finally arrived home. She'd forgotten to leave the back light on and fumbled with the key in the twilight. The cold wind picked up, whirling through the dusk like a malevolent spirit. She literally breathed a sigh of relief when she unlocked the back door and flooded the kitchen with light. She held Mikka close, unwilling to put her down. She wanted so badly to talk to her little daughter about Harris, but as bright as Mikka was, she was far too young to absorb his death.

Mikka wrapped her legs around Tess's waist, and with two plastic bags of groceries dangling from one hand, Tess lumbered past the big century plant stalk displayed in an antique copper pot. Her hand-painted gourd ornaments shivered on its branches, jolted by the vibration of her heavy footsteps on the hardwood floor. She detested seeing any type of Christmas decoration before Thanksgiving, but in this case, she'd left them up since the previous year. Southwestern style decorating was less garish and Christmassy than tinsel and red bows and she enjoyed the Native symbols on the gourds.

When Tess reached the antique maple desk that her great-grandmother willed to her at Mikka's age, she jabbed at the answering machine. It held a breathy request for a return call from an old friend, Jim. A reporter for the Phoenix Gazette, he'd blurted something almost unintelligible about working for him.

She dropped the grocery bags to the worn Persian rug beneath her feet and shifted Mikka to one hip to dig for her cell phone in her jacket pocket. Dead again. She picked up the landline receiver and speed-dialed Jim's number.

"Yo," Jim answered, true to his brisk character.

"Hey Jim, Tess."

"Tess. How you be, girl?" His voice crackled at Tess's end.

She stifled an urge to tell him about Harris, their baby. "A little befuddled. Life's strange, as usual. What's up?"

"Surely the big news has leaked all the way into your mountain lair by now. The Henry thing would be my assignment, but I'm flat on my back with the flu. So's half the office. Lou's shitting bricks. We're short several reporters. Agencies have freelancers booked for weeks. No way will Lou settle for picking up wire stories. He asked about you. I know the daily isn't your idea of writers' heaven."

"Whoa. You mean you want me to go to Washington? For the Gazette? Get outta here."

"For reals. I'm begging. I owe Lou a favor—I need some brownie points."

"No shit." She was no stranger to Jim's shenanigans. The last she'd heard, Jim directed an Air Force colonel to the men's restroom when asked for directions to the office of the executive publisher.

"Pretty please? With a cherry on top?"

"I stay home with Mikka as much as possible . . . Oh, wow."

"Is that a good wow, Teresa? This is great stuff, girl. Career reviving . . . don't you need the dough? Lou liked the specials you did right after you left the Weekly. You never know where opportunity leads. . . " Jim stretched his last syllables out in a singsong voice.

"Oh God, please don't beg me. I've retired from the media biz."

DC was the last place in the world she wanted to be, but the attraction outshone the danger. Maybe she'd learn more about the assassination. She could gauge if anyone suspected anything about Mikka. Maybe learn more about what chewed on Harris the last time they met too.

Friendship and curiosity overwhelmed her. "It is an opportunity," she admitted, changing her mind in midstream. Harris's funeral was scheduled in three days. Just three short days and she'd fade back into the safety of her quiet life, armed with new knowledge, in case it affected Mikka. It wouldn't hurt to add the probably unnecessary entry on her résumé. It also didn't hurt to be flexible in the rough economy—rural Arizona was a hard place to make a living.

Jim's boss, Lou Crouch, had offered her a plum reporting job and later, an editorial position, but she didn't have the stomach for the constant deadlines or life in metropolitan Phoenix. She'd reported for Old Pueblo Weekly for a few years, a popular Tucson alternative investigative paper, rising to the challenge of reporting with her introverted personality. She'd managed to win a local media award for a hard-hitting series on local environmental issues. The next logical career move was joining one of the Phoenix or Tucson dailies, but she grew tired of the stress and fled Tucson for a quieter country life shortly before Mikka turned her world around. She loved her laid-back life in the mountains and poking around at odd jobs—cleaning houses, setting up events with a caterer friend, digital photography, nature art projects like making her own paper and binding it into handmade journals. She started writing some picture book manuscripts, inspired by reading the stacks of books that Mikka demanded at bedtime. She discovered that making up stories was much more fun than reporting real ones.

"Pleasepleaseplease. I'll give you a *bone-us*," Jim crowed in a cartoon voice.

"Forget your bonus, Jimbo. I remember what *that* is . . . Okay, a good wow." She rolled her eyes at the ceiling, not believing she was actually saying it.

"Lou'll meet you on Van Buren, in front of the downtown office. Give him a call before you leave. He'll keep your truck in the parking garage."

She sighed. "You owe me big. Really big."

"Whatever, my lady. We'll figure that out. Hurry, I'm wasted," he croaked.

"With wings on. Catch you when I get back. Keep those germs to yourself." She faked a light tone, but her heart threatened to spiral into a black hole again.

Jim signed off as usual, a hasty ciao punctuated by the dial tone.

She turned on lamps and lights in the kitchen and dining area, then went upstairs to the master bedroom. She set Mikka down on her queen-sized bed with another big sigh, handing her a Sharpie marker and a sketchpad, forbidden goods on her handmade star quilt. She grabbed a garment bag and a couple of basic black career outfits stashed in the closet, sighing again at their uniform appearance. They'd have to do. Her Indian jewelry, the squash blossom necklace and the bolo belt her folks gifted to her at her U of A graduation, would brighten any outfit up. She made a quick run through the master bathroom, filling up a cosmetic tote with essentials and a blow dryer. Another rummage through Mikka's room filled her little pink overnight bag.

She hated the thought of leaving Mikka for a few days, especially after Darcy swore she'd seen an odd black car lurking around their lane the week before. She reasoned that the cars her neighbors spotted were spying for Harris. Maybe things would settle down now.

Anyway, Mikka and the Perez kids spent the morning and afternoon playing and Darcy would take Mikka any time. Mikka loved imitating four-year-old Ana and five-year-old Ray-Ray. Darcy's husband Ramon wouldn't mind feeding and watering her animals—a horse, two llamas, a small flock of chickens and a trio of cats—when he tended his own livestock. In one fell swoop, her dear friends would cover all her bases.

The groceries. She sighed again and she turned to go downstairs and stash the food in the fridge.

"Looks like microwave for us tonight, kiddo."

"'Roni 'n' cheese?" Mikka inquired. She didn't look up from her sketch of Tess's mare, Mulan. She'd captured the animal's essence and made the stylized horse's head nearly move on the page. Proud of her talent, Tess didn't want Mikka to know her skill was unusual, or to let anyone exploit her.

"You've got a kid's meal tonight. Kiss my tandoori chicken goodbye," she joked. "Hey, that's quite a picture, Meeks. Mulan would be proud."

"Thank you, Mama. 'Roni 'n' cheese do it for me!" Mikka grinned, tore her picture from the sketchpad and handed it to Tess. Her little face settled into a dreamy expression, and she began a new sketch. Within a minute, a line drawing of seven horses galloping in a windstorm began to emerge.

Tess watched her, transfixed, until a series of thumps sounded from an outside wall. Her heart skipped a beat. She startled and Mikka gazed up at her with round eyes. She picked Mikka up, dark thoughts leaking into her fragile good cheer. Was somebody trying to get in? She pictured government agents stuffing them into that dark sedan.

She suddenly realized the sound's source. The TV antenna wire rattled in the wind outside the living room downstairs. She left Mikka to her drawing and made house rounds, securing every window and door. She raised a shutter panel and peered out a dark living room window where the wire slapped the wall and gazed over the valley toward Mingus Mountain, the largest, most distant mountain facing the scattered houses in her rural neighborhood. She tensed suddenly, catching a glimmer of movement from the corner of her eye. That shadow down the lane, nearly out of sight—did her imagination turn a tree or a boulder into the gleam of a vehicle?

A chill surged from her tailbone to her shoulder blades. She let the panel close again and hurried back upstairs and to Mikka, questioning again the wisdom of leaving her behind. But was Mikka any safer at home? Ramon was an ex-Marine and Darcy had grown up on a remote ranch, she reasoned. They were tough, no strangers to defending their turf. Their pair of shepherds and the big, woofing Rottweiler never let anyone get close to their rancheria. Mikka would be in good hands. Anyway, it was easy to imagine things on a windy, spooky evening, she told herself. She shuddered and shut her eyes against her negative thoughts.

When she took Mikka back to Darcy, she saw nothing unusual along the half-mile lane to the Perez house.

Darcy met her at the gate. "Get back, Ranger, Danger. Hush, Rad!" Darcy pulled at the shepherds' collars, shoving the Rottweiler back with her hiking boot. "Tess, this is wonderful, you going to DC!" Her friend gushed on, bestowing celebrity status on her.

Tess nodded grimly. She shook off Darcy's words and focused on Mikka instead. Darcy carried the sleepy toddler into Ana's room and lay her down on a ruffled twin bed. Tess peeled off Mikka's puffy nylon jacket and pulled the Disney character comforter up to her chin, restraining herself from covering her daughter with kisses or bursting into tears. When Darcy left the room, Tess paused in the doorway, listening to the girls' soft, uneven breathing. As she turned to leave, Mikka rolled over abruptly and uttered a little sigh.

:::CHAPTER 7

HARRIS HENRY

Huge, bulging black eyes floated toward President Harris Cantrell Henry and hovered inches from his face. He swiveled his neck to look away. Somehow those eyes rotated his aching head back from the blank wall and locked onto his eyes with magnetic ferocity.

Henry made another conscious effort to glance away. Beads of sweat sprouted from his forehead and cheekbones, but his gaze snapped right back to those terrible eyes.

You won't remember this.

A chill shot through his spine. Someone was talking to him inside his own friggin' head again. Those damned shape-shifting lizard reviewers who'd visited him some months before on Air Force One?

You will not remember anything.

The hair on the back of his neck pricked up. His second experience with telepathy, and it still jolted the shit out of him.

Like hell, he thought. *I remember those lizards and I'm damn well gonna remember you.*

Henry's guts turned watery when he tried to focus through the haze. He could barely make out a single form bent over him, a narrow, gray face and exceptionally large almond-shaped black eyes. A peculiar iridescent glow emanated from them at particular angles, like large insect eyes caught in the sun.

If he'd been prone to religious fervor, he'd think he'd gazed into the eyes of God or the Devil. He stared into them again, suspecting what he'd heard was true, that ET abductees described those big black eyes as goggles or covers that protected vulnerable eyes. Still, they glowed hypnotically with life and purpose.

Henry's heart almost burst from his chest when he tried to move again, pushing against the sticky sensation, like swimming upstream in molasses. Sleep paralysis? He'd awakened thinking he'd fallen asleep in the back seat of a limo, nested in soft leather, cozy and womb-like, but found himself strapped to this narrow, metal platform suspended at the edge of a drab, semicircular room.

Henry closed his eyes and tried to recall the sequence of events that brought him here. He remembered striding down a White House hallway, his mind churning out mental "to-dos" for his afternoon meetings.

The creature somehow forced his eyes open and recaptured his gaze, making him irresistibly sleepy again. He felt like a goofy cartoon character with eyelids propped open by sticks. All he could see for the next few minutes was a play of light and shadows caused by the twitch of his eyelids. When he finally managed to raise one eyelid to half-mast, figures swam above him as if he were peering through thick, frosted glass.

He found that if didn't try to force his will on the situation, his surroundings came into clearer focus. At least he didn't hurt, well, everything except his neck and head hurt, but he'd had chronic headaches for months. As he thought this, his entire body throbbed subtly with a massage-like undulation and he began to feel pretty good.

A pale hand with four spidery digits rose beside an oversized head positioned near Henry's feet. The creature held a short wand of metal or shiny plastic with a globular end on top. Henry squinted at the variety of shimmery colors moving like northern lights inside the globe, but everything else still looked swimmy. Watching the changing flow of light soothed him. He began to like his placid, motionless position—how long had it been since he vegged out in comfort like this?

The creature continued to channel superfluous telepathic commands. Superfluous, because Henry found he involuntarily responded to the wand's glow. The simultaneous telepathic commands made by the creature seemed unnecessary. Perhaps it thought humans felt more comfortable when addressed in their native tongue. It sounded contrived and mechanical, more like a computerized voice than anything real.

Without warning, the little bastard jerked him right out of his reverie. Holograms somehow appeared in the small space between the table he reclined on and the one nearby. Various three-dimensional scenes began to unfold in front of him. Assaulted by images of a dying Earth, the creature seemed to be accusing him of destroying the fragile planet through his complicity as a world leader. He puzzled over that for a moment, realizing he'd been told not to interfere with climate change.

He tried to shout, to stop the devilish picture show, but the creature just cocked its head as though showing deep interest. He wondered if the being projected this perception, because it had little facial musculature capable of expressing emotion and seemed to convey its curiosity telepathically.

The creature proceeded to turn up the emotional heat and observed his agony like a scientist observing wildlife. Worse, he thought, like a scat researcher probing an animal dropping.

The holographic images took on a personal note. Henry watched his wife and children starving, wasting to skin and bones until disease finally took them. Healthy friends and acquaintances dissolved like wraiths, ravaged by exotic diseases. Millions of people burned alive, screaming to ash in huge fires spewing across continents. He tried to close his eyes, to block his mind, rationalizing the visions as a test of his compassionate reaction to a possible future reality. His gut surged, knowing this path probable if greed and technology continued to outpace spiritual awareness. Suddenly he felt enraged by the creature's manipulation and grieved by the solemn truth. Anger gave him the impetus to flex the muscles of his neck. His head wobbled from side to side.

The creature cocked his head in interest again. *You are uncomfortable?*

Henry tried his damndest to keep his mind blank. *Hell yes,* he sputtered, glaring up at those eyes with murder in his heart.

He *would* get out of this . . . somehow. He'd listened to his advisers' reports about extraterrestrial abductions, and he now accepted that his fellow Americans operated under laughable naiveté about who *really* ruled the world.

Since the incident on Air Force One, his dreams were peppered with images of human faces melting into reptilian masks. Often he would awaken and feel threatened, unable to shake the notion that someone or something watched him much of the time. Overworked and sleep deprived, he sometimes felt an insatiable urge to escape into sex and medication. Yes, he admitted to regressing into some collegiate behavior, mostly to catch some sleep. All he needed to do was touch base with a cousin and his medicine chest. He'd kept a low profile, except the time Merrill found him locked inside Lincoln's bedroom. That was some good shit. The Secret Service paraded a double at a State dinner that night. Livid, Merrill moved into a guest bedroom for several weeks until she too admitted that the pressure of the office had become severe.

Now his fears stared him in the face and all he could do was stare right back. His gut began to clench in the preliminary of a sob. The little motherfucker had him exactly where it wanted him. He nearly screamed with the zenith of his discomfort. The wand glowed purple, waved in front of his face again.

Don't worry. You will not remember this, the creature assured him once again.

Shit yes, I will remember this! He prayed he would and desperately tried to grasp at his only real sensation, the emotional discomfort. Typical of human males, he wanted to vent it physically, explode from the table like a superhero and kick that walking stick to shreds.

His fuming suddenly dissolved as abruptly as it started. The creature, his Watcher, Henry began to think of *him*, because the gray being displayed an aura of male authority, slid a panel out of the platform underneath the exam table. Four long, knobby fingers quivered over a tray suspended from the ceiling, covered with an array of unfamiliar instruments. The Watcher chose several, laid them aside, and picked up what looked vaguely like a computer mouse with a tendril of illuminated fibers, passing it back and forth over the selected tools.

He tried to speak again. All he managed was a grunt and a moan, but he could sure as hell *think* out loud. *Hey buddy, looks like it's time for a tune-up. Hope I'm not the tunee.*

The Watcher's mind remained smooth as a lake on a windless day while his emotions jumped from fear and rage to jokey pleading like some clown in a drunk tank. Next time the Watcher pointed that wand at him, he'd probably slobber his love and devotion to an extraterrestrial life form.

You won't remember any pain, the Watcher assured him.

Henry tried to speak aloud, but his mouth suddenly felt sticky and full of something, like when he gobbled raw cookie dough when his stepmother baked at holidays during his childhood. Almost lost in that sweet sensation he fought to focus upon the pain and outrage that lay beneath his forced tranquility. *What the hell? What other pain? Fuck you and your pain!*

The Watcher placed a dull sphere the size of a b-b on the tip of a long needle threaded into a syringe-like contraption. The Watcher approached him warily, as if it understood he could cause serious damage if he rose from the exam table.

He continued to respond, venting months of tension into his thoughts. *What do you mean I won't remember any pain? What the hell! I'm the President of the United States of America. The most powerful country on*

Earth, goddamn it. You won't get away with this!

He raged on until his Watcher's twin stepped into his field of vision. The identical creature held another infernal wand in front of his face. The first Watcher lay a hand on Henry's. It felt like bony marshmallow, a hint of warmth emanating from the fingertips. He'd expected something cool and harder, like the armature of an insect.

Distracted by the touch, his body relaxed involuntarily. That is, until the second Watcher made a deft movement under his nose. Pain flared from his upper nostril into his cranium and stabbed into his brain. No doubt the bastard had implanted that little sphere into him.

This will aid our communication.

Your communication! You have no right!

We have every right.

Who the hell gave you this right?

The Draco-Orion Federation.

His mind went blank for a split-second, then churned into overdrive. Draco? As in dragon? Those Reviewers? Maybe it *was* true, what the UFO researchers suggested. The reptilian race of extraterrestrials claimed Earth as their territory and the human race as their livestock.

Henry suddenly noticed the presence of other people. Small hooded things that moved mechanically led dazed people into the room. Of all races and sizes, the humans wore a variety of clothing, business wear, nightwear, jeans and t-shirts. A few were nude. Some had blank looks; others gaped at the room with disbelief, but most appeared terrified.

Until that moment, he thought he lay in a private cubicle, but the room seemed to expand as the number of humans and ETs increased. A subtle hissing sound wafted across the room as the walls pulled back and more platforms emerged from the floor. He panicked, picturing himself trapped inside of a living, growing cell, an intelligent organism that would never let him go.

His Watchers continued playing with their infernal devices. He still felt the pinch in his sinuses when one of them placed a cup over his genitals. *Hells bells, I'm nude. The emperor is wearing no fucking clothes.*

Two Watchers stared at him, eyes gleaming.

Henry caught a glimpse of something blue out of the corner of his left eye and strained to turn his head a fraction of an inch. A tall male dressed in flight helmet and blue jumpsuit stood in a corner, really a rounded space between two panels of screens with large keyboards bearing unusual symbols etched into triangular keys. This human looked like a USAF airman, except that his jumpsuit bore a patch with a winged serpent-like dragon rather than Old Glory.

His eyes met the soldier's for a moment. Did he imagine that the man's eyes turned golden with vertical pupils, his skin sleek and scaled, just like the Reviewers who'd appeared on Air Force One? He tried to focus again. No, he didn't imagine it. The soldier's face seemed more human than reptilian, but the fine scales gleamed in the soft light, the Caucasian skin tone an amalgam of pearly-pink scales with heavier reddish-tan tones slashing across his high cheekbones. Was this creature one of the hybrid star people that abductees described? Or was this exactly the same brand of shape-shifting lizard he'd encountered before?

When his vision inevitably blurred and he struggled to focus on the soldier a third time in order to ask him who he was—what he was—and why he was there, the face morphed into a normal human face. A mist oozed from the walls and into the center of the room, spreading overhead.

He wasn't sure how much later he found himself dressing in his rumpled business suit, led by a Watcher taller than the others to a group of humans, real humans, huddled against a curved wall. A sense of timelessness pervaded everything—had this interlude taken minutes, hours, days, or weeks? A pounding headache extended from his sinuses to the base of his skull. When he put the palms of both hands to his face to rub the discomfort away, he found blood caked around his right nostril and upper lip. Gingerly exploring farther, he located a tender spot behind his right ear, the same area that stayed sore for days after his Air Force One encounter with the Reviewers.

An itchy spot at the back of his neck alerted him that either he or his captors had put his undershirt back on wrong side out and the tag was sticking up.

He lined up behind many other abductees outside a thick industrial door capable of admitting heavy construction equipment. He had the distinct impression the crowd stood in an underground bunker. Damp air flowed across his face, alternating warm and cool currents. He gazed at the attractive woman standing before him, sheathed in a sparkling cocktail dress and coiffed with equally sparkly ornaments in her upswept hair. Her expensive and extensive makeup looked smudgy around the eyes, and one of her polished nail tips was missing.

"Woo-hoo, Nathan will never believe what happened tonight!" She threw her head back and giggled profusely, her breath tinged with tobacco and peppermint liqueur.

No one responded to her exclamation. When he turned to look behind him, a man in tartan plaid pajamas eyed him back, but most people seemed locked in a trance or deeply absorbed in their own thoughts. When he strained to gaze past the woozy socialite and over the heads of people before him, he thought he saw human guards dressed in unmarked blue jumpsuits. More lizards in human identity fields? A chill coiled in his gut and twisted up his spine like a big, hungry snake. The U.S. military, or some part of it, anyway, was in cahoots with extraterrestrial races.

We're all in deep hot lava, he recalled his twins saying when they were small.

He wasn't sure how his sudden burst of courage emerged. He'd make a break to God knows where, but wondered why, conscious of the consequences. Why endanger whatever life he had left? On the other hand, did he have anything to lose? He was beginning to realize that when he'd disappeared, the news headlines must have described his demise. He was already dead in the eyes of the world . . .

Voices rose behind him, no doubt belonging to the guards in blue. "To the right, XV2, another one running tonight. Get a Gray responder. Radio the next corridor. I'm circling around to nab him from behind. XV3 out."

Henry heard XV2 copy the command. A flash of light—a laser?—zinged past him like a paper-thin lightning bolt. The area lit up for an instant, causing him to jump at his own shadow when it lurched in front of him. At the end of the corridor, a high tunnel lit with dim pinkish lights, a large paved area extended far beyond the tunnel and seemed to be outdoors. His ankles and thighs ached with the exertion of running on the slight incline. If they were underground, maybe it wasn't at great depth. Maybe the large door where the abductees gathered covered an elevator shaft leading to a location deeper underground. Rumors abounded about military installations so top secret even presidents weren't privy to their locations or purposes.

The guard's heavy footfalls drew closer, gaining on him. He tore through the end of the tunnel, taking deep gulps of air that seemed almost fresh. Gathered like wadded satin in front of him was a dark sky brushed with stars and a light haze. He sensed both a limitless horizon and a contained, virtual reality. He tried to sprint faster.

"Damned astral mover . . . Halt!" The guard sounded more amused than frustrated. He pulled a device from his belt and barked into it. "Secure perimeters eight and nine, I repeat, secure perimeters eight and nine! Enforce bilocation and elimination of astral mover."

Another bolt of light flashed past his torso. He imagined himself with a crispy, laser-fried center. Amused or not, the guard wasn't messing around. The guy had no reason to, he chided himself.

Henry continued sprinting across what looked in the twilight like an asphalt tarmac. The uneven surface was easier to run on than the concrete ramp. He'd done this routine in airfields around the world countless times under more dignified circumstances. Suddenly, huge dark objects loomed out of the darkness several hundred yards ahead. He'd expected planes or choppers, but these machines looked heavier and squatter. Earth moving equipment?

He tripped on something and landed sprawling against a low wall. His throbbing head met solid block with an audible thud. The end of the line. He froze and played dead. But several sets of legs in light-colored camouflage with feet shod in high, laced black boots rushed past in the other direction, toward the guards.

He cowered and rolled his body parallel to the wall. Shots, sizzles, lights, shouts, grunts, thumps and bangs tumbled around in a cartoon-like cloud of confusion. Within seconds, sirens wailed, so loud they almost drowned out the drama playing out on top of him.

Henry grasped the wall and dragged himself up, panting. A tall, lean, muscular soldier with a grim face motioned him back down.

"Get back, sir. Keep your head down," he shouted. "This isn't over yet."

A friend? He stared at the soldier for a moment, not able to see colors clearly in the murky light. The warrior wore a light camouflage jumpsuit uniform, matching helmet, and backpack. In one hand, he held an odd-looking laser weapon similar to the ones the guards zinged at him. His other hand fingered a round glassy object like a grenade. More of the glassy things dangled from his webbed belt. A curious emblem glowed on the soldier's left shoulder. Triangular with rounded corners, it held an inverted V with a group of stars above and a comet or a shooting star arcing across it. He squinted to make out the bold black letters of the name tag below the insignia: Hanzel, R.

Henry leapt up and beat it over the wall as the soldier began lobbing the glassy orbs at figures and shapes rushing toward them. While scuttling like a crab toward the big, hulking shapes, the zinging of lasers and the peculiar sound of vaporizing explosions echoed behind him. This sucked, as his twins would say. He had no experience on the killing fields, and definitely not in any high-tech conflict. For years, he'd mused why a war record rather than a spiritual bent should be a prerequisite of high office.

Henry sucked in a deep breath of smoky air, trying to calm his pounding heart. He turned and ran back to redeem the young warrior inside him. Scattered forms dropped and sprawled everywhere. The air steamed with the smell of burnt flesh. His soul jerked backward even as his body leaned forward . . . perhaps his responsibility should be to his office? His Secret Service agents would have shielded him with their bodies if they'd been here, spirited him away from the conflict. Were the soldiers in camouflage a rescue team who discovered his whereabouts?

He dropped to his knees. What he witnessed kept him on his knees and held him transfixed. It was one thing to hear about these things, and another to actually see them. If only Merrill, Bax, and Lody were here! At the beginning of his administration, he'd set Associate Deputy Attorney General Baxter Chopps to digging after the answers to two questions: Who killed Kennedy and are there UFOs?

Living proof of a massive cover-up stood right in front of this captive audience of one, the 44th President of the United States of America. A cover-up scamming Earth citizens of their evolutionary birthright. A cover-up plaguing presidents since Truman. One that surely killed Kennedy, disgraced Clinton, controlled Bush 2, and was now trying to kill me.

An onion-shaped vehicle nearly thirty feet across rose from the pavement, spinning like a child's top. Its landing gear retracted like the legs of a mechanical insect. A soft glow emanated from it. He wasn't sure if he actually heard a pleasant hum over the ensuing chaos, but he definitely felt it, a soothing vibration in his belly, as sweet as a woman's bedroom touch.

The UFO wobbled gently only two yards above the ground, like a leaf suspended in a slight breeze. Circular rows of colored lights underneath the craft flashed one after the other in a dazzling, pulsating ring. Then the craft vanished, disappearing like someone hit a cloaking switch.

A muffled explosion suddenly shook the ground, a burst he might not have noticed if he were running. Startled, he turned to see more figures curling like small, gray commas on the ground. A tidal wave of eerie silence rushed at him followed by a pall of smoke that swept across the landing field.

Another explosion zipped through the air with the force of a thousand lightning bolts. High over his head, a crack ripped through the wall of the structure. It zigzagged downward with a peculiar rending sound, forming a door-like cavity several hundred yards in front of him. The real sky, sprinkled liberally with stars, shone through. It *was* an artificial underground environment.

President Harris Cantrell Henry seized the moment and ran like he'd never run before, slipping through the crack without looking back.

::: CHAPTER 8

TESS VAUGHN

By the time Tess reached Phoenix, she longed to call it a day. Lou rushed her in a company SUV to Sky Harbor for a redeye to Dulles International Airport, reciting rapid-fire instructions along I-10 and into the terminal.

"We always have enough AP stuff. Do a human interest slant. And clever photos—Jim says you're pretty good with 35-milimeter film as well as digital, and don't forget to work in black and white. Nice, old-fashioned touch . . ."

She focused on the nasal drone of Lou's voice but his words barely registered as she stared through an exhausted haze at the list he'd prepared for her. Whenever he gave her that penetrating, sideways look of his, she tried to look alive.

Tess barely had a half-night's rest before the three-day whirlwind of work, literally running around DC to attend press conferences, and interviewing or attempting to interview various public figures. She longed to get her hands on Vice President Gaphurst Allen, but he proved unreachable except for the televised press conference crawling with celebrity journalists the day after his swearing-in ceremony. Allen briefly expressed his deep sorrow and his commitment to the Henry administration platform from his desk at the Oval Office, and afterward, White House aides and the Secret Service whisked him away. Media hounds were denied access to him ever since.

She whipped through several "man on the street" interviews and photographed anything worthwhile. A shot of a mysterious black-clad woman viewing the President's casket in the Capitol Rotunda turned out well. Some thought the woman was Amber Wheaton, Harris's imaginary student paramour, disguised in a wig, gloves, sunglasses, and voluminous hat. A journalist or photographer, or both, would surely score Pulitzers, and some claimed her photo was clearly in the running. Her cautious side hoped not, afraid of exposing Mikka, and she even toyed with the idea of reporting under a pseudonym. She simply wanted to do decent work, and that mostly in the hopes of learning more about Harris's demise or disappearance without undue publicity. But the other side dared her to relate her *real* connection to President Henry. Wouldn't that rock America?!

Every evening Tess whipped up a new post from her journal notes for her trademark "new journalism" blog, delivered with photos via e-dropbox to Phoenix from the Gazette's super-thin laptop or their new iPhone before she collapsed into the hard hotel room bed. The mattress reminded her of the last night she spent with Harris on a similar, unforgiving bed. She brushed her sad thoughts away before she slept, stabbing a forefinger at the television remote, often staring at the ever-changing images while muting the sound.

On the night before the funeral, she stared at the CNN scroll rolling past her burning, unfocused eyes, until a screen-sized image of Harris nearly jumped out of the television at her. A sob rolled from her chest, the first she'd allowed herself since the day of the assassination. She knew her emotion wasn't all about Harris. She now ached more for her former equanimity than she did for him. Truthfully, she wasn't learning much and her questions only led to more anxious questions.

Every second led inexorably to the inevitable climax of Henry's funeral, the assignment Tess dreaded most. She'd already faced the seventy-two-hour public viewing in the Capitol rotunda. She felt numb when she entered the historic gallery and gazed at his ashen face. But there was little time to linger and she focused upon the streams of people paying their last respects, shuffling through the tedious wait under gray and drizzling skies. A few displayed genuine sadness and many more seemed curious, grasping at a chance to participate in the national drama.

On the morning of the funeral, a riderless horse and caisson made the short final journey to the White House. Mercifully, Tess rode with an entourage of assorted press vans that followed the procession. She rolled the window down to inhale the somewhat fresh air and to listen to the crowds. Although the streets boiled with people clad in dark woolens and furs, they were mostly silent, the engine sounds obscuring any quiet conversations. The crowds were not as dense as the crushes that gathered for Kennedy, nor did they express as much sorrow. Someone carried a digital banner with a breathtaking photo of Earth from space, with a scrolling message— "HCH cared." A few carried digital banners and homemade placards with racially divisive stuff that had circulated since his campaign for President, or politically conservative slogans about "Dirty Harry" or "Hapless Harris" that celebrated his demise. Others wished a similar fate to his party. Tess had no quarrel with the free expression of opinion, but it seemed gauche to advertise it during this period of mourning. She shrugged it off—America would always be the land of the free and the home of poor taste.

Adults and children alike peered between the cast iron bars fencing the White House lawn at the stream of expensive automobiles entering the northwest appointment gate on Pennsylvania Avenue. The press vans funneled through security at the East Executive Avenue appointment gate, then wheeled around through the extensive grounds at the rear of the White House. Streams of mourners and press converged from two directions into yet another security kiosk near the

West Wing at one edge of the Rose Garden.

Harris worshiped at a large Methodist church in downtown DC, and many citizens thought it odd services wouldn't be held there or at the National Cathedral, where religious affairs of state generally occurred. The President loved the Rose Garden, and First Lady Merrill Henry insisted the funeral be held there after the media railed about the odd choice. Weddings were performed there when flowers bloomed during the spring, summer and early fall, but an off-season public funeral? November certainly wasn't rose season, though the area would be filled with potted greenhouse roses, at least, the press conceded. Tess recalled that Harris had never mentioned the Rose Garden to her. She'd even read somewhere that his administration hosted fewer Rose Garden events there than other administrations.

As Tess stepped from the media van, a chill ran up her spine. In her bones she felt Mrs. Henry was trying to convey something symbolic about Henry's death—the political "rose garden strategy" of holding important discussions inside the White House as opposed to traveling throughout the country or debating an issue in Congress.

Tess gazed over the crowd as the Rose Garden lawn gradually filled with reporters and elite mourners. A military band played some somber but suitably soothing music. She'd never seen an open casket funeral before and bit an already ragged fingernail at the thought of looking at Harris again. She half-expected a funeral pyre on White House grounds, so adamant was Harris about the subject of cremation when they'd talked about everything from politics to death. Strangely, Merrill Henry said he'd requested an open casket public viewing at the funeral in addition to the customary closed casket viewing at the Capitol Rotunda. Mrs. Henry's insistence caused a stir, and she was apparently unmoved when pressured by the public, media, and government figures to reconsider on both accounts. The nation would watch him being put to rest before his cremation. Odd as well that there would be no presidential gravesite and that his ashes would be distributed privately at an undisclosed location.

A brass instrument fanfare echoed through the gathering. Four snappy young honor guards, one from each armed service, bore the weight of President Harris Cantrell Henry and his casket to the shade of a white canopy draped with black velvet ribbons and garlands of roses in every possible hue. They rocked the casket from their shoulders, setting it reverently on a marble stand. The presidential canopy rested like a small shrine in front of three wide tiers of hundreds of white wooden rental chairs filled with well-heeled people, the red-carpeted aisles trimmed with more garlands of roses and black velvet ropes.

Tess stood in front of her chair at the far right of the proceedings in an area slightly behind and to one side of the invited guests, cordoned off for press under a trio of canopies bordered with black velvet ropes sans the flower flourishes. Except for the television cameras allowed a closer position, the press viewed the funeral canopy from an angle that irritated many photographers.

Tess scanned the scene from the press area toward the mourners. Then she shut her eyes, wincing at the tinge of anguish rising from her heart. When she opened them, she searched the crowd for the woman in black. Was she here, the woman she'd photographed at the Capitol, dressed perhaps in another disguise?

Reporters and cameramen muttered, shuffled, and scribbled furiously around her. Somewhere, an infant began wailing. A rotund white-haired woman wearing multicolored reading glasses next to her yanked at the press ID around her neck and sputtered, "Gawd, please shut the kid up."

"You got that right," agreed the pimply, redheaded stringbean next to her, a pencil tucked behind one pink ear.

Tess tuned both out, feeling more annoyed with them than the baby. She drank in the scene again—press, mourners, and funeral canopy. Tears welled up in her eyes. She hated herself for wishing she and Harris had had a normal relationship and the way this filled her body with a tingly longing. Grief and confusion collided in her chest. What would happen to the nation? To Mikka?

A sudden flash of déjà vu replaced her grief with a sense of unreality. In a dream she'd awakened from that morning, the corpse winced when the honor guards' white-gloved hands deftly opened the upper lid of the elegant casket. Harris turned his head a millimeter and squinted to get a bead at onlookers. Her astonishment in the dream soared several notches higher when she noted a well-built man standing near the speakers' podium. His resemblance to President Henry was remarkable, a virtual double. She hadn't been able to place him in her dream, not being well-versed on the Washington scene in either fantasy or reality. Henry's look-alike wore heavy black sunglasses, the opaque lenses making it impossible to track his eyes. Several times during the dream service, Tess distinctly felt the double gazing at her.

The honor guard opened the casket, but Tess didn't want to see Harris's face again. *Even if it wasn't really him.* She startled at that thought, and excused it as another stage of her grief—denial. She fitted her old Pentax with a long lens and aimed the camera at the scene, but resisted focusing on the corpse. It seemed rude, staring at the body of a dead world leader displayed like a museum piece, even from a distance through a camera viewfinder. But looking was irresistible, like gawking at a car wreck, especially after her dream. She lowered the lens and focused on the casket instead. But she raised it millimeter by millimeter. When the lens reached the body, it seemed . . . different. Another thought assaulted her and sent a tingle up her spine. Was the corpse a mannequin?

Her heart froze. She turned and scanned faces around the lawn with the camera. The press corps murmured among themselves and the funeral guests absorbed the scene without fanfare, many dabbing at their eyes. She aimed the camera at the casket again and focused on Harris's face. His bronze face had paled in death. His upper lip and visible cheek seemed freshly shaved. The incongruity of his narrow but sensuous full-lipped mouth struck her as normal. His mouth looked just right, but the ear seemed off. It was the right size, the right shape . . . yet something subtle about it was all wrong. She'd heard somewhere about the difficulties museum and movie mannequin makers encountered in creating exact replicas of ears.

Another sudden chill enveloped her. She recalled Harris talking about doubles on their last night together. "I see myself coming and going, literally," he'd said. Was that it, the message of her dream? The double—Henry's possible replacement, his assassination?

The new President of the United States of America, Gaphurst Allen, clad in his perennial gray suit and sky blue tie, stood in the dream where he was standing at the funeral, his arm around his wife, Ashara. But the dream double, some person who was a ringer for Henry and had stood to Allen's left and slightly behind him, was not there. Allen appeared insignificant both in her dream and in reality, the way that vice presidents and former vice presidents always seem to look. Perhaps he wished for invisibility. Perhaps he had good reason to wish for invisibility.

She gazed around again. The voices of the crowd receded to an insect buzz in the background. Did anyone else wonder if a mannequin replaced President Henry's body? Was the First Lady conveying a double message with the open casket in the Rose Garden? If he wasn't really dead and Merrill Henry suspected this, the ploy made perfect sense. Henry had told Tess he preferred cremation, and though cremation had gained popularity with Earth's soaring population and lack of ground for burial, most people who chose it eschewed any rites except a memorial service. But the crowd seemed at ease; she saw no evidence anyone noticed anything strange. Even the press seemed oblivious, though many had eyes pasted to video and still cameras. She searched the rows of guests and their faces seemed suitably austere. A willowy woman in a row of chairs nearest the press, dressed in an elegant three-piece eggplant-colored ensemble with matching veiled hat, shoes and bag, dabbed at her eyes with a crushed blue tissue. She snapped the picture because the woman carried herself like the "lady in black."

Only a portion of the First Lady and the Henry twins' faces were visible to her in the front center row of mourners. They appeared genuinely stricken. The auto shutter on her camera whirred as she snapped a series of photos. The trio clasped hands, their heads held high. But their tense faces left the impression that they clung to one another for dear life. Was it fear rather than grief that etched their puffy faces?

She squeezed her eyes shut again. The stress of the past few days had jumbled her marbles. She doubted herself more than ever.

The hunky honor guard and other dignitaries nearest the casket took their seats. Reverend Arthur Blivens, the Henry family pastor, stepped up to the podium stationed near the President's casket and began the eulogy with a prayer. She flipped a switch on her handheld recorder to note anything worth remembering.

"Family and friends, we are gathered in this moment of national grief . . ." began the unremarkable eulogy. Reverend Blivens concentrated, as expected, on highlights of Harris Henry's life, enlivened a bit with his personal observations of Henry as a youth. He invited others to speak, making the planned speeches following the eulogy seem more spontaneous. President Allen came forward first to elaborate on the accomplishments of the Henry administration.

Secret Service agents in black suits scanned the crowd intently as sunlight broke through the heavy cloud cover. She scanned the crowd again. No one seemed interested in anything but the flow of speakers. She shook her head to clear it. It was difficult to keep her mind focused on the surreal proceedings as a spectator, let alone focus upon it as a reporter. She'd best come up with some prose that satisfied Lou and the Gazette's managing editor. She was ready to race to the airport, get home, ride Mulan with Mikka, and listen to her daughter's zany giggle pierce the desert air.

But here she stood like a big dog, as Mikka would say, ogling an American president's funeral service on the White House lawn. While she grieved for her people and pondered the future of her nation, her personal grief was beginning to dissipate. She'd loved Harris Henry but didn't want to love him anymore. Her only heart's desire now was her peace of mind and her daughter's safety.

Tess was beginning to feel more perplexed than sad. And though the situation seemed absurd, very, very frightened.

::: Chapter 9

Marshall and Savannah Updike

"Hey, Reverend . . ."

". . . Yes, Reverend?"

"Got a missive you'll wanna read. Almost tossed it out with the junk mail."

"Mmm, just leave it there . . ." Marshall Updike motioned to the heavy glass and iron scrollwork coffee table where he rested one foot. He lounged near the living room fireplace, holding a draft of Sunday's sermon on a legal pad against his belly. At first, he didn't hear his wife padding in stocking feet across the tiled floor near the hearth. When he noticed her approach, he shot a distracted smile over his transparent red plastic reading glasses. He returned to his sermon, bouncing a pencil on the pad. Suddenly, he grabbed his laptop computer and booted it up.

Savannah curled up on the sofa across the room and sorted through a week's collection of bills, catalogs, junk mail, and early holiday cards (why was it they came before Thanksgiving now?) not noticing at first the plain number ten envelope addressed in blocky capital letters, almost shuffling it into the "circular file" pile. Stamped with the new holographic American flag postage, there was no return address. She patted through the papers littering the cushions until she located her stainless steel letter opener underneath her business calendar and sliced the end of the envelope open. A quick scan of the letter, computer generated on unlined paper, jarred her Saturday morning mind awake.

Cradling the computer in his lap, Marshall looked up and patted the arm of his favorite chair, a plaid wingback facing a northern wall of tall ceiling-to-floor windows. Savannah rose and perched beside him. He reached up to smooth an unruly curl at his wife's temple with thick but nimble fingers. They both gazed for a moment together through a huge plate glass window at the spectacular Catalina Mountains.

"Must be a Very Important Letter to bring the pony express right to my side."

"Pretty darn interesting letter. Want me to read it?"

"Go for it."

"I'll begin at the beginning." Savannah spoke in a posh British accent, an inside joke she and Marsh had shared since college. "The date and heading, Sir Updike."

December 12, 2011

Reverends Marshall and Savannah Updike
Church of the New Millennium
Tucson, Arizona 85718

Dear Mr. and Mrs. Updike:

Your names were given to me by a friend, a minister you may be familiar with who also lives in Pima County and shares your interest in shadow government and conspiracy theory. It seems you're both unofficial experts on such matters.

Enclosed are some personal journal excerpts from various dates over the past three years, compiled into a narrative illustrating my dilemma. I'm afraid that communication with prominent experts would violate my privacy and worse, exacerbate my precarious situation. A neighbor spotted strange vehicles in my rural neighborhood recently, suggesting I may be under surveillance. I fear for my young daughter's safety.

I intuitively trust you. If you choose to disregard this letter, I would understand your silence. Although you have a great deal of knowledge, according to my friend, I realize you may not be able to recommend what actions, if any, I might take.

If you're able to offer some assistance, please drop a line at my P.O. box number. It seems safer than communication via phone or e-mail. If you send a postcard with only a Tucson address written on it—a restaurant or other public place—I'll know that you understand my predicament. I'll be in town visiting relatives on Christmas Eve and can meet you at mid-day if you're available.

It's imperative that you destroy this letter and the narrative after noting my return address below. I made a pledge to myself never to divulge details about this topic to anyone, and it's of life and death urgency that you respect my wishes.

Yours truly,

Teresa Vaughn
P.O. Box 2144
Valley Junction, AZ 86324

Savannah's eyes lingered on the woman's old-fashioned complimentary closing. She handed Marsh the Xerox copies of the dated entries scrawled in the same capitalized script as on the envelope. He scanned them quietly, grunting a time or two in response to choice passages.

"So what do you think, Marsh?"

He glanced at Savannah and then at the journal copies, his wide, chocolate face impassive at first. Then he pursed his full lips into a long, slow whistle and shook his left hand as if he'd touched fire.

"Mother of our man Henry's love child. Weird, huh? With the

controversy that's brewing over his death, she must be in a tight spot. I figured it was a joke at first. Considering Mr. Henry's rumored love life, it might be true. But there's this little tidbit of information . . ." He motioned at his laptop and tapped the touchscreen to magnify the text.

Marsh had found something new with his Bible Code software, information that corroborated his findings in October. Savannah devoured the pages unfolding in the video display on the screen. The names Harris Henry, the term Starchild, and words of warning melted from Hebrew into English. They crisscrossed each other in slow motion like the lines of a three-dimensional crossword puzzle.

"Oh, my God. What are we going to do with this?"

"Go with the flow, Sa'nnah. Meet this girl and take it a step at a time."

"You sure? Might be too big for us."

"If it's what I think it is, this is bigger than big." Marshall spread his arms wide. "Before the assassination, Henry was definitely swinging left—well, farther left than he presented himself before his election, and appeared to be bucking the system. Overhauled the health care system and manhandled the insurance industry. Prepared to goad the Senate and House to redraft his bill if they didn't pass his global warming resolutions before someone took him out of the game. We're sure he held secret briefings about UFOs and black ops technology early in his term. He may have had some sort of extraterrestrial experience soon after his election, according to insiders."

"Showtime?" Savannah arched her eyebrows.

"Showtime, Baby. Validation. A chance to shine a light into the dark corners. History with a capital H, dropped by divinity through the U.S. mail."

Marshall fixed a stare at Savannah, his soft, watery eyes glittering.

Savannah's reflection darted back at her from his nearly black irises. She held her gaze even with his, connecting a full minute before she spoke again. "If the gig's what we think it is, we're all in danger, anyway. Let's *do* it . . ."

"Exactly. My gut says this chiquita ain't lasting long without us. Most anyone she'd turn to for help is too high profile or part of the system. We have the gift of near-anonymity. For a while, anyway."

Savannah nodded. "Seems to be a good fit."

Marshall placed the fingers of both hands together in a little church steeple. "Yeah, Baby, a very good fit."

::: Chapter 10

Tess Vaughn

Restless and mad at her restlessness, Tess tossed from side-to-side well before dawn on December 23, kicking the pine footboard of her bed between bouts of staring at the ceiling. First she worried about going to Tucson, and then she worried about staying home. She wasn't due to meet the Updikes until Christmas Eve at noon; afterward, she and Mikka would celebrate the holiday with their Vaughn relatives.

She fussed some more, tormenting herself about her journal and the letter she'd drafted to the Updikes. They understood her plight, she thought, kind enough to destroy the original letter and return a festive postcard memento from a trip to México long ago, the Updike's confirmation of the suggested meeting date. But of course that didn't guarantee that no one else had handled her mail or checked ownership of her box number. What if the Updikes wanted publicity and copied everything to release to the media? They could make it big on *Entertainment Tonight* or *Inside Edition,* cause a stir in the *National Enquirer*. She had to be batshit crazy to give them her post office box number to begin with. Now she'd stumble on down to Tucson and let them see her face.

Anxiety won. She threw off the quilt and stumbled through the house to her desk. She retrieved a swatch of documents—a second copy of the letter and papers she'd sent to the Updikes, their reply on the Mexican beach scene postcard confirming their appointment, and airline ticket stubs from her trips to meet Harris. She stuffed them into a manila envelope, licked the seal, marched to the fireplace, stirred the coals, and dangled the envelope over the dying fire. She wanted to watch the physical proof of her dilemma shrivel into ash and finish any need or temptation to get involved with political intrigue and quash her desire to expose government corruption. That stuff was inevitable and would never stop. More than anything, she simply wanted a calm, normal life for Mikka.

She let the envelope slip from her fingers into the hot coals. Instantly she regretted the move. She snatched the envelope by a corner and beat it against the mantelpiece to dislodge the sparks smoldering along one edge. She sighed and pulled out a loose stone from the front of the fireplace, dislodged a wad of folded twenty-dollar bills and curved the envelope into the dark, cool hole.

If something happened to her or to Mikka, her family might need evidence of the truth. She might be an impractical airhead, but she wasn't stupid. She scurried back to her computer to back up data to a flash drive, the word-processed version of her journal and her letter files to the Updikes. Then she deleted the files on the hard drive and ran the computer's shredding program to clear any file traces.

To whom could she give the data? She didn't want anyone looking at the stuff unless she died or disappeared. Mom and Dad were definitely out. Brother Paul would peek. She trusted Uncle Mac implicitly. But anyone she gave it to might be at risk, so family was out. Jim would love to get his hands on this stuff and would publicize it to benefit people, if there was something beneficial in this mess, but she didn't want him hurt either. If someone was truly surveilling her the past few months, this stuff could literally be something to die for. That definitely left Darcy and other politically savvy friends out. She wouldn't want her worst enemy to flirt with the danger involved.

How about a lawyer? She almost snickered aloud, thinking of an old joke about worst enemies. She rummaged through the deepest drawer of her grandmother's old maple desk and pulled out the thick, dog-eared US Dex yellow pages for Phoenix. After she lit a stick of the sandalwood incense she always burned when she needed to think, and a votive candle in a sky-blue globe, she placed one hand on the phone book cover and asked for guidance. Then she turned to the attorney pages and fumbled through them. What type of attorney? Probably one not practicing in criminal law, ironically, or anything remotely related to her plight. She wanted utmost secrecy. She chose a page of attorneys engaged in environmental law and ran her finger down a column until it reached an expensive color ad for a practice specializing in the field. A large, busy practice in Phoenix. One too swamped to do anything but honor her request to stick the flash drive in a file and hold it until further notification. The primary attorney in the practice was an honorable man she'd heard about, a real friend to those he served.

She wrapped the flash drive inside her wad of new multi-colored twenties and sealed it with a bit of packing tape by the bluish light of the flat screen monitor and candle. With grim satisfaction she scribbled the attorney's name and address on the front of a small manila envelope, stuck a sheet of high-quality ivory paper she used to print CVs into the printer, and reopened Microsoft Word. Soon she had a letter printed and the package ready for posting. That left the dilemma of whom she'd ask to contact this attorney's office in the event of her death or disappearance.

She started chiding herself—what made her think she'd die or that anyone who shared her secrets might be in danger? She probably needed to get a grip. On the other hand, both her irrational and rational thoughts about the situation made sense. Her paranoia might be justified. Darcy and a neighbor up the lane, an elderly but outspoken widower, reported another black sedan cruising the lane the night before. The same one, both thought, that they'd seen weeks before. This time the car parked for more than an hour at the intersection of the neighborhood lane and a paved, moderately used road that connected to Highway 89. The previous summer on a late-night return from her nursing shift at YRMC, Darcy remembered noticing a plain white van bearing federal government plates parked in the same spot. Had someone kept watch for over a year?

Just ten days before, in mid-December, new reports related to the Henry assassination flashed from every news magazine, television program, website, and blog imaginable. A mortuary assistant noticed some irregularities in the identification and condition of Henry's body when the mortuary received it for cremation. Probably he'd been paid by a tabloid or a group to leak information. Political spin doctors in Washington soon doused the flames of controversy with a plausible explanation. That alone made the "assassination" suspect. The mortuary assistant's observations confirmed what Tess observed at Harris's funeral. Maybe the cremated body wasn't even Harris's. The assistant suffered a tragic accident during a weekend hike shortly after the story broke. Mainstream media was spinning info and disinfo like crazy. Her paranoia truly wasn't out of line.

Sleepy, Tess went upstairs, crawled back into bed, and then crawled out again. She returned downstairs to the desk phone and dialed her cell phone from the landline. The muffled ring issued from the bottom of her bag where she'd left it in the kitchen. When the call went to voice messaging, she left a message instructing the listener to contact the Phoenix attorney she'd chosen to hold her data. Surely someone in her family would think to listen to her messages if the phone was left behind after she died or disappeared. If it fell into the wrong hands, her best hope was that they couldn't produce the proper ID. Lots of big ifs. Of course, big intel could undo whatever she tried to do, but at least she'd done her best to inform her family of the situation.

The house breathed and settled in the rare windless silence. She checked Mikka by the glow of her favorite seashell nightlight and crawled back into bed again, eyelids drooping with the promise of sleep. But she couldn't calm her mind. Her eyes fluttered open for the gazillionth time as she lapsed into a semi-wakeful dream. She tried to transform the awful vision of a zombie Harris back into the man she loved, but the image stuck.

Spooked, she stomped out of bed in an irritable fury, flinging her star patchwork quilt to the floor. Between her crazy thoughts and bad dreams, she hadn't enjoyed a full night's rest for more than a month. She padded to the closet, fumbled for the light string, and pulled an overnight bag from the highest shelf. She packed basic essentials, tugging drawers open, flinging things toward the bag and piling some holiday gifts she'd hastily purchased on the internet into a cardboard box. She hated buying personal things online but felt more afraid each day to leave the house, or to put Mikka in daycare or with a sitter. She'd stayed close to home since returning from her foolish trip to Washington.

When she finished packing at 3:00 a.m., she tried to lie down again. Sleep didn't come—no surprise—and she gave up twenty minutes later. At 3:45, she left a message on Darcy's answering machine asking Ramon to start caring for the animals a day early. She gently opened Mikka's door and put her jacket on over her pajamas, then took the sleeping toddler outside, tucked her into the car seat, and fired up the truck.

Mikka awoke an hour before dawn on the outskirts of north Phoenix, unconcerned about not being at home. She instantly started chattering about the gifts Paul and Jay said they'd piled under their tree for her. Tess threaded her way through the relatively quiet streets and knocked at Paul's front door in the early morning twilight

Mikka nearly leapt into her beloved "Unca Pa's" arms when he opened the door. He held her fondly, brushing sleep out of his eyes, looking at Tess with suspicion. "Good thing I'm off work today."

She displayed her puppy dog eyes. "Could you give me some space until Christmas Eve dinner? Mikka would enjoy some quality time with you . . . would you mind taking her today and meeting me at Aunt Xénia's and Uncle Mac's tomorrow evening?"

Paul shot her a look, sensing something fishy. "Sure," he said, shrugging. "Jay's out finishing a shoot, so I don't mind some company. He kissed the flaming curls atop Mikka's head. "We're buds, huh, Meekeroo?"

Mikka started chattering about the gifts again, and he took her to the tree with a promise she could open just one before Christmas. She felt grateful for the diversion and that Paul played along with her.

She still didn't quite understand her dogged compulsion to keep her mouth shut, but figured she'd better roll with it. Usually she confided in Paul—a good guy, almost like the sister she'd always wanted. Would Mikka be any safer if Paul knew who her real father was and how crazy Tess felt? Not likely, and she didn't care to involve Jay, his significant other, who lavished cloying, fake sweetness on Mikka. She felt pleased he wasn't home and wouldn't join the family on Christmas Eve. Paul mentioned that at the family Thanksgiving gathering, which she'd missed, Jay had pronounced her mothering skills deficient—as if childless gay men were parenting experts!

The surface streets were relatively deserted after she left Paul's condo. She dawdled on her way back to the I-17 ramp at Thunderbird and 19th Avenue, where early birds were cruising to work or heading out for Christmas destinations. The holiday rush was cranking up on the freeway. Motorists and eighteen-wheelers slashed along the interstate in both directions, making long trails of red, white, and amber light. A couple dressed as Mr. and Mrs. Claus waved at her from an out-of-state rig as they flew past in the fast lane, the slant of the rising sun reddening their faces. A teddy bear with a tinsel and satin bow tie vibrated from its perch on the hood of their tractor cab.

She wished she could share the holiday joy. Her stomach chewed on itself with hunger and stress. She felt more like disappearing, driving south through Tucson to the Mexican border, and on into Central and South America until she found refuge with a tribe of penguins. Was it even possible to drive the entire length of the

Pacific coast to Antarctica?

As she neared Picacho Peak, the rugged plug of the old volcano rose like a wavering flame from the desert floor. She felt an odd tingle in the top of her head, pulling at her like some magnetic energy emanated from the single peak. What was this sudden attraction to the mountain? She'd passed it dozens, maybe hundreds of times without wanting to get closer to it. Did she need some nature? Not likely, since she lived in the country, but the Picacho trails became a favorite local hike when the saffron California poppies and purple penstemon bloomed after winter rains. The peak began to glow in the otherworldly sunrise, and she recalled a high school history lesson about the westernmost battle of the Civil War near the mountain.

She questioned the wisdom of stopping but her resistance weakened. She needed to stop somewhere; she was a day ahead of schedule. This seemed as good a spot as any. Her intuition told her to not rationalize about it. She yanked the steering wheel toward the freeway off-ramp at the last possible second and meandered into the Picacho Peak campground. She'd jog and hike, take in some scenery while she figured out exactly what to say to the Updikes when she met them.

The sunny morning, a bright holiday gift bestowed with the Sonora Desert's customary generosity, made it easy to forget that winter was beginning. The "snowbirds" loved it. Most folks at the Picacho Peak Campground buzzed around in their shirt sleeves and light jackets as the early chill subsided, some preparing to pull out for the next leg of their journey, while others basked in the sun at picnic tables outside their campers and trailers.

Her inner critic relaxed and went silent in the sunshine, but she had the good sense—and paranoia—to reconsider the stop. What in the heck was she doing? Hiding out, she guessed, though she intended to go back home right after Christmas despite her months-long feeling of being observed. Would anyone think to look for her in Picacho Peak campground? Probably not unless someone tailed her, and she hadn't noticed a tail. Wasn't hiding in plain sight supposed to be effective?

She found a niche to park in, close to a trailhead with a view of the exit. The tingling in her head progressed to a spacey, apprehensive feeling, so much she wanted to keep an eye on her escape route. She didn't want to circle around in a panic, not able to find her way out if push came to shove. She pushed away that dark fantasy and another of being kidnapped from the hiking trail.

After she'd dug out her black nylon duffel bag in the hastily tossed pile of stuff in the truck cab behind the seats, she pulled her running shoes from it and laced them up. She strode and jogged along the hiking trail, up the side of the mountain and back, until her groin ached. Her period? She counted back—her last was about thirty days ago. She'd been bleeding when she went to DC, so another was due. A heavy sensation, the onset of a hormonal headache, rooted itself in her head. No wonder she felt half out of her mind.

She hoped there wouldn't be a line in the restroom—there'd be a rush to toilets and showers this early and she really didn't need the exposure. She turned back to the truck and dug for her cosmetic bag in the duffel, then gave up and lifted the entire bag from the jumble of gifts. She locked the truck up and headed toward the squatty brown shower house.

When she pushed the rustic plank door open on the ladies' side, she noted the odd silence and the heavy, sodden air. Water hissed across the room in the showers, and steam poured from several stalls, yet the place felt empty. Every cell in her body jolted to attention. But her strong denial mechanism kicked in. Everybody's focused on getting ready for the holiday, she rationalized. A shiver edged up her spine and she looked behind her. People were milling around their campsites, but no one headed toward the showers.

She let the big door shut and passed a long mirror hung over a row of oval lavatories on her way to the toilet stalls. Her cosmetic bag fell at her feet and into a wet spot as she fumbled with it to search for a tampon. She picked it up and pushed through the half door of a toilet stall, her feet making sucking noises on the rubbery safety mat blanketing the floor. She didn't find the expected red stain in her panties even though PMS thrummed like a kettle drum through her head.

She washed her hands under a motion-activated faucet and dried them under an electric dryer. A toilet flushed and a bulky blue-haired matron emerged from a toilet stall. She held broad hands with short, shell-pink nails under a bubbly stream of water for a few seconds and rubbed them under the hand dryer just long enough to shed excess water. Then she dusted off the seat of her baggy black capris and headed for the door, nodding at Tess in a sweet, grandmotherly way, her plastic Christmas ornament earrings swaying garishly. Tess nodded back, wondering if she'd also succumb to bad taste in jewelry in twenty-five years. Her attention returned to the mirror, and she stalled for a moment, brushing her hair and checking it for split ends. Suddenly, it struck her that no one had emerged from the showers even though steam billowed in clouds that filled the room and beaded in droplets on the mirror.

She shrugged and glanced in the mirror again. She needed more sun. Picking up her duffel, she walked past the row of showers toward the exit, noting someone's feet and ankles visible through the gap between a short shower curtain and the floor.

The woman's feet seemed oddly pale and still.

"Hello?"

Her inquiry echoed back. She tried again. "Hello-o."

No answer, and worse, no movement. She held one edge of the natural-colored canvas shower curtain between thumb and forefinger and shook it, rattling the metal rings. No response.

Tentatively she pulled it back a finger's width. Horror slammed her in the gut. With a rush of nausea, she snapped the curtain back, grunting involuntarily to bite back a scream. The middle-aged white woman hung by her neck from a soggy clothesline rope tied to the showerhead, water cascading in steamy jets over and around her.

Tess's heart challenged her legs to a race. She forced herself to inhale deeply and stand still. She stared at the rope, looped twice around the woman's neck, tightened until it left her face gray-blue. A weird place to commit suicide and an even weirder way to do it. She shuddered and looked away from the macabre, pop-eyed expression and thick, lolling tongue.

Another electric current of dread raced through her gut. The woman wasn't nude, as she'd expected. A drenched red calf-length skirt and ivory blouse clung to her curves, revealing the outline of bra and panties. A murder or a suicide? Her heart beat faster and she gasped for her next breath. She moved forward as if pulled by something outside herself. Reaching an arm out almost involuntarily, she pulled back the curtain of the next occupied shower and then a third. Metal shower curtain rings screeched on metal bars. All dead. All with identical ropes doubled around their necks.

My God. She tasted bile rising from her stomach. Her thoughts raced and fell like a line of dominos, tumbled by terror.

She'd call the cops. No, she'd call the cops and leave. She shouldn't stay. She'd end up in the news. What if this incident brought attention from Washington? What if the truth came out about Mikka? Her panic rose. She'd stayed at the campground long enough for people to notice her. But leaving might cause her worst fears to be realized.

She shuddered. Why not go? She was innocent. She'd slip out, force someone else to notify the authorities. The killer might be lurking around somewhere, watching her. Or worse.

Caught between fear and panic, she wanted to flee but hesitated, almost shuffling in her tracks. She prowled to the exit and gingerly opened the shower room door a few inches to peer through the crack. The coast was clear. No one headed toward her. A fortyish couple in matching khaki outfits and sunglasses stood at a pay phone fifty yards away. A young girl slipped into the campground convenience store a few yards beyond the phone booth, and in the far distance, the old lady in the baggy black capris led a young boy toward a camper.

Her heart seized for an instant with longing for Mikka. Then she launched into a full-tilt panic. Every muscle in her body urged her to run. She held the door open just enough to squeeze outside. First she took one nervous and jerky step forward, willing herself on. She started to jog up a lane of campsites toward her truck, then slowed to a stroll, trying to appear nonchalant. A slightly stooped, silver-headed man walking a black dachshund on a red leash nodded as she passed him.

"Great spot, huh? Where ya from?"

"Uh, great, yeah. Montana!" She forced a smile without breaking step, wondering if she should have mentioned a state east of the Mississippi.

It took three attempts to unlock her pickup door. She shook from head to toe as she threw her duffel bag into the passenger seat and slid into the driver's seat. She tried not to look around like an edgy prey animal as she eased the truck out of the campground and melted into freeway traffic. As her heart tried to pound its way out of her chest, she prayed under her breath to become another cog in the daily wheel.

Would anything ever be normal again? She cursed meeting Harris, dissing herself for her decisions. She tried to clear her mind again. With some effort she relaxed her breathing in a slow rhythm and started to assess the situation. Harris had impressed her with his ability to organize his thoughts and his daily life even under the extraordinary pressures of a president's life. She tried logically ticking off her concerns like he did: One, she hadn't yet registered at the campground. Two, therefore the campground personnel didn't know she existed. Three, though her state of mind currently bordered on insanity, it seemed possible that the elderly gentlemen who spoke to her wouldn't connect her with the chaos soon to ensue back there. But the older lady in the black pants clearly saw her in the shower room. And what did the lady do there? Used the restroom, logic told her.

She scanned radio stations for nerve-soothing music, settled for classical, and pulled out the remnant of a marijuana cigarette she'd found in the ashtray a few days earlier. A friend had borrowed her truck for a weekend run to the county landfill and apparently smoked a "j" while he worked. There wasn't a lighter installed on the dashboard, so she fumbled through the glove box for the matches she'd used to light incense when she'd heard about Harris just the month before. Had it been such a short time ago?

She hadn't toked any cannabis for years, but it sure tasted good and she didn't even care that she sped through heavy holiday traffic on an interstate highway. She took another deep hit and snorted a little smoke from the lit end for good measure. Though the old, familiar cannabis warmth smoothed her rough edges, she'd never forget what she saw, the misery of violent death. She tried to imagine a beautiful place in the desert, tried to push those ugly thoughts back, flooring the accelerator as though to propel herself into that better world. What would she do the rest of the day?

At eighty miles an hour, the pickup suddenly swerved from the slow lane and onto the shoulder. She gripped the wheel as it careened back into the slow lane, the left rear tire sputtering and thudding on asphalt. A blowout. The pickup bucked to the left again, nearly putting her into the path of a big rig steaming along the fast lane. She pulled hard to the right until the vehicle responded. Her heart danced in her chest again and she broke into a sweat. Remembering to brake evenly, she pulled onto the shoulder, the flat thwacking on the pavement, and then steered into the wide dirt track bordering the highway. She cursed herself at the smell of marijuana in the cab and rolled down both the driver's and passenger side windows.

When she eased out the driver's door, a tow truck pulled up behind her like a big clunky white angel from heaven. She thanked the universe—she hated fumbling with a jack, especially on a busy thoroughfare.

"Merry Christmas." The driver touched the brim of his purple Arizona Diamondbacks baseball cap. "Let me give you a hand with the flat—no charge today, ma'am."

"I can't tell you how much that means to me." She muttered to herself about being old enough to be called ma'am and fetched the jack from its holder behind the driver's seat. The tow truck guy soon had the pickup jacked up, the spare tire off its rack, the lug nuts loosened, and the tire off its rim.

"Ma'am, anyone you know ticked off enough to cut your tire on Christmas Eve?"

"What?" She couldn't get the bluish face of the dead woman out of her mind.

"Yeah. Um, looky here. This tire's cut to blow." He traced a dirty finger around a roughly triangular hole on the back side of the tire. "Someone made shallow cuts back here. With enough speed and distance, that triangle blew out."

"Sheesh," she whispered. She buttoned her denim jacket against the sudden chill and dug in her purse for some money. What if the tire blew out on the edge of a canyon rather than here in the desert flats?

"Guess it's a good thing I got out of town, huh?"

The mechanic appeared puzzled by her lame joke.

She cleared her throat. "I can't thank you enough. Accept a tip?" She held out a ten-dollar bill toward the mechanic, who grunted with the exertion of tightening the lug nuts.

"Just pay it forward. My good deed for the day. You have a nice Christmas." The mechanic hitched up his droopy black denim jeans with a wink and hopped into his truck.

She smiled and waved at him while he merged into heavy traffic with a dull roar. Before she stepped back into the truck, she examined the other tires. Did someone hop her rancheria fence to cut the tire, or did this happen at the campground? Was someone following her?

She kept casting uneasy glances in the rearview and side mirrors as she blended into freeway traffic but couldn't detect anyone tailing her. She took an exit a few minutes later at a strip of cheap motels, paid for a room, secured the door lock, bolt, and security chain, and collapsed onto the bed fully clothed.

Tess pulled the scratchy, starched sheet up over her head and spent the rest of the day and night pondering her questions.

:::Chapter 11

Marshall and Savannah Updike

Savannah Updike watched the gypsy-like woman angle across the plaza toward her and Marshall. Teresa Vaughn's easy gait seemed to mirror her sincerity. But when she drew closer, Savannah noticed the woman seemed dazed despite her graceful movements, a study in contrasts. When she looked past the regal posture, her slender body seemed slack, an empty sack in crumpled clothes that appeared slept in. Her long hair hung lank and was frizzy, as if she'd washed it but left it uncombed to dry, and her oval face seemed blurred, by what? Difficult decisions and lost sleep, she supposed.

Tess, as Teresa liked to be called, gazed into her eyes as she approached, reminding Savannah of an iron filing inexorably drawn toward a magnet. They'd never met nor described themselves to one another but had identified each other immediately anyway.

"Hello. You must be the Updikes." Tess eyed the Pima County Courthouse, the mission-like walls and pillars rosy in the high-noon sun, and the blue-green dome a bright eye turned skyward. "What a beautiful day," she added.

Marshall found it appealing that Tess appreciated beauty in her state of mind. "Another beautiful day plucked from Tucson's magic bag of days—we're definitely not having a white Christmas," he replied.

She gave Tess a quick hug and Marshall offered his hand. "Tess, this is my husband, Marshall. Most everyone calls us Marsh and Savannah. It's a lot easier than Reverend Updike and Reverend Updike."

Tess nodded and smiled tentatively. She shook Marshall's hand as though grappling for bashful words before she spoke.

"Thanks. It's good to meet you both." Tess glanced around again. "This place is a good choice for a meeting. I worked downtown at the Old Pueblo Weekly awhile. I used to eat lunch at that bench often . . . could we sit over there in the sun?"

"Of course," he said. "It's a bit chilly in the shade, anyway."

Dried olives on the brick paving made a muffled pop underfoot as they moved to the only empty concrete bench facing west, dappled with shadows cast by the small, windblown olive trees. The courthouse plaza started coming to life, bustling with a lunchtime crowd in spite of the pending holiday.

Tess gazed uneasily at Marshall and lowered her voice. "I feel silly. This might be laughable under other circumstances, but as it is—Harris—uh, President Henry was rattled when we parted. Things were really hammering him. I'm still having bad dreams about it. I don't dream like that without a reason." She turned her head upward to study the sky again, tears pooling in her doe-like eyes.

Marshall and Savannah looked at one another. "Do you mind sharing what President Henry said? Your experiences may give us some clues about what you're up against," Marshall said.

"He seemed bedeviled by more than the usual political stress," Tess explained. "He mentioned weird things about extraterrestrial 'watchers' and 'reviewers.' About cloning technology being more advanced than people realized, about people around Washington being 'replaced.' He said he was searching for proof that extraterrestrials were involved in U.S. government. Only once, but the desperation in his eyes scared me . . . I thought he'd gone off the deep end. He also talked about his friend, Drew Forrest. Most investigative reporters 'never got deep into the dirt of the issue, except Drew,' he said."

Marshall and Savannah exchanged another glance and Savannah scanned the wide terraces around the courthouse as though checking for intruders. "Tess, Drew Forrest was looking into more than environmental issues," she said. "Our research suggests he discovered some strange things about UFO disclosure and what you're telling us seems to corroborate this."

"President Henry talked about how much he feared NIHSA, 'The Agency,' he called it." Tess encased the phrase in quotation marks with hand gestures. "He always said his biggest goal was to make a difference in the world, to see people everywhere living in peace and prosperity. He claimed there was a conspiracy to keep us at war and in poverty."

"These extraterrestrial rumors must seem genuinely off-the-wall," she said. "It's startling enough to connect social ills to greedy elites and corporations or political maneuvering rather than the usual practice of blaming the victims."

"What do I do about any of this?" Tess pleaded. "After the assassination, I thought I might not have to worry any more."

Savannah offered her a tissue and squeezed her hand.

Tess struggled to steady her voice. "I thought he was trying to have me and Mikka killed. I thought maybe he couldn't handle the love child connection. Many people think he had Drew Forrest killed. Why not me?"

"I don't see our man Henry as a guy who'd have his love child or his offspring's mother snuffed out," Marshall told her. "Or even his best friend. You're probably being harassed by the same source."

"I pissed off some local business people with my environmental articles ten years ago, but that's blown over. I don't have anything anyone would want . . ."

She noted that Tess's eyes shifted downward as if she hadn't told the straight-up truth. Someone knew about the child, Savannah figured, or wanted something Tess had, or both. According to what she'd witnessed, Henry had clearly turned on NIHSA and maybe NIHSA had dug deep to discredit him. On the other hand, Tess bore his child, true, but she'd never used that to her advantage, so Henry was unlikely to harass her.

Marshall answered Tess obliquely. "There are many rumors about Harris Henry's goals for his administration. Obviously, he was invested in moving beyond petroleum technology, willing to drag Americans who don't believe that global warming exists kicking and screaming into the future. But he had a deeper agenda too. Insiders say he was fascinated by the UFO/extraterrestrial question and wanted full public disclosure about data that U.S. government intel has collected over the past sixty or seventy years."

Savannah chimed in. "That topic alone is enough to get anyone into hot water, especially if his advisors dug deep enough. Put the two topics together, and it's a surefire way to annoy people who don't want their boats rocked."

"But both topics are heavily researched—there are hundreds of books, websites, and blogs published each year about them."

"True," Savannah said. "But much of it is repetitive, speculative material. Any time anyone digs too deep and puts something with teeth forward, those in the know ridicule the researcher or someone gets hurt."

Tess raised an eyebrow, wondering what kind of X-File story she'd gotten herself into. "But who?"

"Whoever stands most to profit. Follow the money trail. Elite bankers, corporations, the intel operations that support them," Savannah said.

"Fuck," Tess whined, thinking of Mikka, her eyes tearing up. "Is there anything in this goddamn country not tainted by power and money?"

"Tess, I'm sorry. We're making you cry." She spoke gently, taking Tess's hand in hers again. It felt small and cool, the skin tight and rough across the knuckles as though she worked with her hands.

Tess began to sob. "You won't believe what happened on the way down here, Savannah. You won't believe what I saw." She wiped away her tears in a clumsy motion, her voice tinged with desperation as she described murder victims at Picacho Peak and the tire blowout. "I'm so scared. Something else happened yesterday."

Savannah gazed around cautiously. She put an arm around Tess, who felt small, her bones prominent under soft skin. Tess sniffed and wiped her eyes while she spilled a longer narrative about the events.

"This surprises me. We didn't know this had anything to do with you. Do we have some synchronicity here?" Marsh pulled the morning edition of the Arizona Daily Star from his valise and offered it to Tess.

Tess held the paper gingerly and read the article heading and subheading aloud.

"*Campground slaying baffles authorities. Pinal County Sheriff's Office seeks mystery woman.*" Damn it, that man walking his dog remembered me! I should have turned on the radio or TV, or gone online."

She read the rest of the article silently. "My God, this says there was only one victim. I saw three! It says they couldn't pick up a fingerprint in the entire shower room, as though the entire place had been wiped down. I can tell you this—the scene was weirder than your ET stuff." She shuddered and wrapped her arms around herself. "Why did they find only one victim?"

Marshall raised an eyebrow. "You really saw more than one?"

"Yes," Tess murmured.

"If someone monitored you at home and jimmied your truck tire, is it not possible that someone set the scene up at Picacho? Were you more upset than you realized? Sometimes our sense of reality becomes skewed under stress. There are also ways to alter consciousness from a distance electronically. Perhaps someone used holograms, maybe other types of projections. It's a long shot, but possible. Maybe you're even the unlucky recipient of a tracking implant."

Tess suppressed her desire to roll her eyes at the Updikes. "I don't recall any woo-woo ET implant experience. Holograms at Picacho Peak campground? How? Why?"

"This situation may be more complicated than you think. Keep your mind open, Tess," Savannah urged. "You flirted around at top levels of government, so to speak. Maybe an agent lured you to Picacho, set you up to intimidate you . . . On the other hand, stress can cause your mind to embellish reality. And we know enough about so-called 'reality' to fill a teaspoon."

Tess cupped one hand to her forehead. "Okay. Go on."

"Simple explanations often point to the greatest truth," Savannah said. "Anxiety likely caused you to see things that weren't there. On the other hand, implants have many uses, including the alteration of visual and auditory perceptions."

"We have a doctor friend who's found and removed implants from ET abductees. He could check you if you're interested," Marshall added.

Tess closed her eyes uneasily for a moment, thinking about the weird triangular mark on her arm the summer she was pregnant with Mikka. But she didn't have "missing time" and didn't recall any possible contact. "I don't know. I've read about ET abductees receiving implants. I'm pretty sure nothing like that has happened to me." She shuddered and changed the subject. "That poor woman—I nearly reached out and touched her. She was *there.* By the time I looked into the other showers, I truly freaked. Maybe my mind did manufacture—"

"The human mind is mysterious," Savannah said in a soothing voice.

"Moreover," Marsh added, "if you have an ET contact, you might never recall it. Studies of documented cases indicate ETs take many precautions to ensure victims won't recollect contact. Plus, it's my understanding there are several ET and terrestrial groups with different agendas who abduct people. Historically, military and intel agencies have also experimented with implants, often using drugs and hypnosis to persuade you that nothing ever happened. People sometimes have false recall of getting abducted by ETs, a story the government likes to ridicule or ignore to keep their cover."

Savannah shot Marshall a glance to indicate he was talking too much, maybe even being insensitive.

Tess fidgeted for a moment but kept her eyes glued to Savannah's. "Harris told me he was investigating UFOs, that he had a plan for public disclosure. Indicated there *is* a deliberate cover-up, but not for the reasons some people think. I didn't ask him about it—I really didn't want to know anything. He sounded like he was losing it. He wanted to give me a nano chip thingy, some data, but I wouldn't take it."

Marshall tightened his lips again. "Then the Henry administration—actually, whoever's opposing it—is the source of your problem. Rumors have circulated since Henry's election that he's held regular UFO briefings in the White House. Knowing he mentioned disclosure to you points toward a possible relationship to your Picacho event. You'd be prudent to distance yourself from it. You didn't commit a crime even though you might be a prime suspect. You weren't described well by someone who saw you near the scene. Authorities are looking for a generic, long-haired woman in her late thirties or early forties driving a white pickup truck or SUV."

Tess grimaced and drummed her fingers on her notebook. "Which I drive. It doesn't sound good to me. They might have enough info to find me. What if they think I had something to do with it? That seems to be the set-up, isn't it? Doesn't someone want me charged with murder?"

"Yes, possibly, or to silence you through intimidation. But half the population of Arizona drives white pickups or SUVs," Marsh countered. "Unless PCSO has more details than they want to reveal, the chances of you getting tagged seem slim, Tess. Plus, they claim you're wanted for questioning, not wanted on suspicion."

Tess groaned. "It looks bad if I don't go in."

"Not necessarily," Marsh said. "PCSO doesn't know if you've seen anything. They're trying to unravel a mystery. They don't even know if they have a good description of you. Eyewitnesses are notorious for providing poor ID. Besides, the agency, and I use that term loosely, the agency bothering you might infiltrate PCSO or impersonate officers to get closer to you. This is a cat and mouse game you should avoid."

With a wave of her hand, Savannah signaled her articulate and sometimes overwhelming husband to slow down.

"Would you care to talk more over lunch? That old Mexican place across the street has a new owner and a healthy new menu." Savannah rolled her head toward a café and patted one hip.

"I'm game." Tess's voice suddenly held new or pretended confidence as she stood and followed the Updikes across the plaza and a broad avenue to a row of shops and restaurants.

::: Chapter 12

Marshall and Savannah Updike

The Updikes guided Tess into *Los Abrigos.* Handsome in a velvet Navajo blouse and blue jeans, she turned heads in spite of her disheveled appearance. Her heavy silver and turquoise Indian jewelry and soft deerskin moccasins drew attention away from her rumpled clothing. The deep blue blouse complemented her chestnut hair, large brown eyes, and the creamy olive skin that revealed her multicultural heritage. Her face was likely even more striking with make-up. Twenty years prior, her look was common with Arizona city girls but Savannah saw it now only in ranch or rez country. Tess made the old fashion fresh again, a strong woman who embraced her natural style.

Savannah chose a corner table in the busiest central section of the café, opting for privacy in the midst of holiday hustle and bustle. After the stately senior hostess seated them and the vivacious young waitress served cervezas, limes, salsa, and unglazed clay bowls of warm chips, the trio engaged in light chitchat.

As the conversation trailed off, Savannah shifted her weight to the edge of her mesquite wood and cowhide dining chair and assumed a relaxed meditation posture. She placed her hands palms up on the glass-covered cowhide tabletop, her favorite stance when channeling healing energy. Tess scooted her chair back a few inches and glanced nervously around the room, wincing at the sudden noise of a drinking glass shattering on the tiled floor. She rocked herself almost imperceptibly for a moment, self-soothing like a small child.

Marshall reached across the table and patted her hand. "You've heard about our research, or you wouldn't be asking for our help. To begin with, we'll give you a crash course in the history of humanity, a somewhat different viewpoint than the conventionally accepted version. We'll kick some theories and facts around, and then I'll show you my recent Bible Code discoveries."

Tess gave him her full attention. Or nearly full attention—the young waitress returned with their meals, balancing the heavy tray on one hand at shoulder height. Tess immediately attacked her steaming chicken and green chili enchiladas with gusto, taking big bites and washing it down with half a frosty mug of Corona.

Marshall savaged his carne seca chimichanga for a minute, then continued talking with fork poised in midair. "There are remnants of an old and advanced civilization scattered around the world. Maybe you're familiar with some sites. Archaeologists ignore or misinterpret many features of ancient sites because they don't fit the current archaeological paradigm." He paused to see if Tess followed his train of thought.

"Gotcha," Tess affirmed. She swallowed hard and dug her fork into her rice and beans. "I'm familiar with scientific paradigm. Science, even social science, tends to view society through a particular frame of reference. I majored in anthropology for a semester before I switched to journalism."

"Then you understand that the scientific community, for the most part, postulates that mankind began growing crops in the Middle East some 10,000 years ago. Prior to that time, it's believed that humans lived in tribal hunting and gathering societies deemed somewhat irrelevant to the rise of civilization, as were the foraging societies who didn't adopt agriculture. And the rise of civilization is considered a linear process, of course, advancing with each significant technological discovery." He stopped to gnaw on a lime section meant to be rubbed on the beer mugs' rim.

"I've heard about hard to explain artifacts . . ." Tess replied. "I mean, in terms of the strata they were unearthed in. And legends that point to the existence of ancient technology that equals or surpasses our current technology."

The girl did her homework. "Precisely," he said.

"But what does that have to do with me, my little girl, or Harris Henry?" Tess named the President without hesitation this time.

Marshall traced the circles of moisture left by the mugs on the tabletop with an index finger. "There are many layers in the story we'll construct. First, we'll discuss history, and then we'll relate it to your situation. We'll present intelligent conjecture based on legend and some little-publicized facts as well. The trick is to visualize the components as a coherent whole despite the gaps in knowledge and the leaps of faith."

Savannah raised one eyebrow. "It's a challenge to accept at first."

"An advanced culture existed on Earth before the rise of organized agriculture in our current historical era," Marshall said. "Since the 1970s, an international group of scientists has quietly mapped a huge subterranean city underneath the area of the Sphinx and Giza pyramid. The culture is at least 15,000 years old. We believe that *Zep Tepi*, the First Times, as ancient Egyptians called it, is the *actual* beginning of our current historical era. Scientists are still cataloging and studying artifacts and extensive records from this culture, and as a result, some well-known sites and antiquities in Egypt are now believed to be thousands of years older than previously thought." He stopped to sip his beer and have a bite to eat, nodding at Savannah to continue.

Savannah unfolded her legs, put her feet on the floor, and neatly picked up where her husband left off. "Early era monuments like the Great Pyramid dazzle us with their ingenuity. But they may only be surface markers for bigger underground structures. Important surface markers, because many follow the geometry of the human body *and* are maps of constellations as viewed in 10,500 BC. These reflect a sophisticated knowledge of astronomy and possible links to a culture or cultures outside our solar system."

"I thought I heard something on NPR about the Egyptian government not letting anybody dig for the past decade or more," Tess said.

"Egypt allowed a select group to excavate in the late 1990s and early 2000s using radar and laser technology—as have some other nations with monumental architecture," Marshall explained. "Every continent is represented except Australia. Extensive underground chambers and tunnels were discovered around many monuments. At Tikal in Guatemala, tunnels range across the country for more than 1,200 miles. There's a big, deep silence from the U.S. government about what's going on underneath us. Rumors circulate about miles of existent artificial tunnels and constructed caverns that our military has incorporated into their underground installations."

The corners of Tess's mouth turned down in disapproval. "Why is the research such a big secret? Almost everyone's fascinated by the old monumental sites."

"That's the point. These facts aren't exactly secret, yet they're not well-publicized either. Tabloid publicity makes the topic seem outlandish." Marshall glanced at Savannah, and she picked up his narrative impeccably.

"There's talk about little explored sites in other nations," Savannah said. "Rumor has it that the Chinese have discovered major sites in Tibet and have witnessed spectacular UFO sightings on the Tibetan plateau, but they're keeping a tight lid on the subject. Some think they invaded Tibet not only for land and resources, but also because of alleged entrances into underground sites. And perhaps because they want to make extraterrestrial contact."

Tess raised her eyebrows.

"Well, anyway," Savannah continued, "none of this fits within the paradigm promoted by anthropologists and other scientists as the accepted history of civilization."

"Does that truly matter?" Tess asked. "Why not adjust the darn paradigm and move on?"

Marshall answered her question. "This will happen eventually, but it's not a quick process even though whomever masters the secrets of this advanced culture may well possess unparalleled power, for good or ill. Hopefully for good. It seems this ancient civilization possessed advanced spiritual knowledge with their advanced technology."

Tess brightened. "Ohhh. I get it. A spiritual science?"

"Seems so. A philosophy linked spiritually and genetically to other galaxies."

"Hitch your wagon to a star . . ."

"Understanding our galactic origins is our intended birthright. There are allusions in the Bible connecting Enoch, the father of Methuselah and great-grandfather of Noah, to extraterrestrial civilization. Five thousand years ago, either extraterrestrial visitors or survivors of a previous advanced culture roamed Earth. Or both."

Tess was silent for a moment. "Wasn't Enoch known as Hermes to the Greeks?"

"Yeah," Savannah affirmed. "And Thoth to the Egyptians. He's the god Mercury in Roman mythology and Merlin in the Celtic tradition. He attained immortality, so the story goes, and promised to return at the end of time to teach mortal men to live as gods."

Tess tapped the tabletop lightly with a forefinger and glanced at Marshall. "Literally?"

"Of course," Marshall assured her, "his promise may be metaphorical, and he used terms understandable to people at the time. We feel it leans toward the literal—humanity has come full circle since the First Times. We now have a rare window of opportunity to quicken our spiritual nature."

"The Age of Aquarius."

"It's called that," Savannah said. "Sixties hippies and now twenty-first century New Agers take some ribbing for it. Serious astrologers point to many correlations between the new millennium and the Medieval Renaissance. Some say we've entered the Age, and others feel we've got a foot on the threshold and enter the doorway in a year, a decade, a century, or even longer."

They fell silent, each taking stock of his or her personal utopia.

Marshall finished his beer and cleared his throat. "This projected new renaissance will be more than an artistic and intellectual rebirth. Earth civilization will take its rightful place in the circle of galactic brotherhood. The crucial point to remember is that we're unquestionably not alone."

"Who's in this 'galactic circle?'"

Savannah stirred from her meditation posture. "Pleiadians, Sirians, Lyrans, Andromedans, and Arcturians, among others. They visit Earth frequently and some walk among us. Some, like Arcturians, move as energy fields among us, working to elevate government, science, education, and the arts. They are fifth-dimensional, non-physical beings."

Tess wasn't convinced. "Why now? Why not a hundred years ago?"

"Both positive and not so positive extraterrestrials have taken an interest in Earth throughout recorded history for a variety of agendas. But timing is crucial to a spiritual and intellectual renaissance—humanity is ready for the next step, and why our current systems are failing. Hindus, Buddhists, and some Native American groups count the early twenty-first century as the end of an age," she added.

"Oh, that's true, actually." Tess moved her eyes upward in recollection. "The Diné and Hopi speak about the end of the fourth world, 'the glittering world.' Doesn't the Mayan calendar also end soon?"

"Yes, and the Egyptian calendar too," Savannah recalled. "The Mayan calendar ends, or curiously emphasizes December 21, 2012. That's when some astrologers predict a shift—or the beginning of a shift in human consciousness. Others feel we've been immersed in the change for several years, and that the process will be complete then."

"Do you guys believe any of this?" Tess probed. "I mean, these are intriguing ideas and some people even bank on them, but do you think any of this stuff matters? There was supposed to be some earth-shattering, incredible event on 11-11-11, but . . ." She winced, thinking of Henry's assassination or disappearance on that date.

Savannah and Marshall shot a look at one another, knowing how simple events can rock the world. And how complicated the word "belief" is.

"The assassination is likely part of this unfolding drama," Marshall conceded. "Tess, we're not sure anything we're talking about here is subject to belief or disbelief. When we started studying the cultural and spiritual development of mankind, we were mainstream Christians, interested in but skeptical about anything outside of conventional Biblical philosophy. As we followed these stories layer by layer, our inescapable conclusion is that we are children of God, creators in our own right. We are Gods."

"Or God-des-ses," Savannah enunciated with a mock-serious look.

Marshall grinned. "That we possess capabilities beyond our imagination is a key element of this belief. Religious scriptures allude to our inherent divinity or our ability to develop a higher consciousness. Buddhists clearly demonstrate that even laypeople are capable of achieving the Buddha mind. The Bible and the Quran tell us we may become greater than angels—Jesus said men could do even greater things than he. Egyptian, Tibetan, Incan, and Mayan societies recorded legends of Wanderers or Star Walkers such as Enoch, Padmasambhava, Viracocha, and Quetzalcoatl. These teachers, fabled prophets or "gods," brought knowledge to ordinary people and sometimes left time capsules containing knowledge to be discovered later. And they promised to return at some unspecified time. We believe that all religious traditions originate from a single, ancient source."

"Hmm . . . I've heard these legends about gods among men." Tess's face began to glow. "A Hopi legend says a White Brother will return from the East. Do you think they mean from Asia? Some think it means the Tibetan lineages that are setting up retreat centers around the world. Does it mean a genetically superior being? Was Jesus a Wanderer from space?"

Marshall encouraged Tess's unbridled enthusiasm with another smile. "It's possible that all these stories have a common origin. We feel that groups of 'gods'—extraterrestrial humanoids—brought the rudiments of their civilization to earth during human prehistory and our early historic periods, and have been around ever since. It seems that both positive and negative cultures visited Earth. There is some speculation that that human stock was genetically altered 10,000 or more years ago in Sumeria, an incident reflected in the Biblical Adam and Eve creation story. Scientists who search for a missing link between apes and humans are looking in the wrong direction, but not because religion says God created Earth. There's more than a seed of truth in the old Genesis story."

"Weren't the Sumerian stories about their gods?"

Savannah nodded. "The Old Testament mentions "watchers" or angels created by Yahweh who rebelled and impregnated the females of our planet, creating the half-ones. In Sumeria, the Annunaki were the elder gods who taught farming and other skills to mankind. We feel the Annunaki were extraterrestrial beings who seemed godlike to earth dwellers."

Tess wrinkled her brow. "So, you're saying that we have extraterrestrial genes?"

"Yes, in more than one sense," Marshall said, "since we inherited genes from the Reptilians and the Sirians employed or enslaved by the Reptilians to create a slave race using simian hominids and Neanderthal man. The Sirians secretly gave the genetically altered slaves some humanoid attributes that allowed them to rebel against their masters."

"You're familiar with the brainstem." Savannah spread her palms in the air, golden-pink butterfly wings. "It's the oldest and smallest region in the human brain that evolved hundreds of millions of years ago, and is more like the brain of present-day reptiles. Our brainstem may literally be a heritage from the reptilian race."

"Too much data," Tess complained. "I'm confused."

"These are legends and myths from deep mists of history. Again, there are many layers in this story, and many mysteries," Marshall explained. "But at the root, there is unmistakable evidence that all earthly cultures, all languages, and all religions can be traced to one highly evolved civilization. Archaeological data suggests that the Fourth Root Culture was more spiritually and technologically advanced than any modern culture."

"Are we also genetically related to them?" Tess finished her last bit of food and reached for a tumbler of ice water, sweating on a cork-lined plastic tray that the thoughtful waitress swooped by to deliver.

Marshall thanked the waitress and turned back to Tess. "Quite possibly. Fourth Root culture cracked the genetic code and had a firm understanding of higher physics. Humankind *could* progress greatly by studying this culture, our heritage, if only that history were publicly available."

"But perhaps we'll have a chance to learn directly from the direct descendants of the original culture," Savannah added. "According to many Earth cultural legends, advanced beings return at the beginning and end of each time cycle, the 13,000-year half-point of our solar system's 26,000-year zodiacal orbit around the center of our galaxy. These intervals seem to be separated by cataclysmic upheaval. And we're definitely seeing some of that upheaval, both in terms of climate change and in human behavior."

"That's not hard to see," Tess agreed.

"Let me tell you a little more about Fourth Root culture," Marshall said. "Many scientists and investigators—Hurtak, Hancock, Bauval, and Sitchin, to name a few—made astounding discoveries in Egypt. There's irrefutable proof that the Great Pyramid is a sophisticated harmonic record of exact positions of heavenly bodies and of chakra systems of the human body. The empty sarcophagus in the center of the pyramid isn't an empty tomb, but a harmonic device tuned to the frequency of the human heart. Experiments around the world indicate that many of these structures are voice and sound-activated computers."

"Amazing," Tess conceded.

Savannah took over for Marshall as he concentrated on the last remnants of his meal. "Yes, Space Age without the hardware. A team of scientists produced waves of light from these structures by creating sounds from the most ancient form of Hebrew, Hiburu, a harmonic language said to transform DNA. Again, this culture was not only active in Egypt. Around 10,500 BC and beyond, there was a worldwide pyramid temple system whose ruins we preserve today. These sites are located on key energy meridians and were used like a musical system to stabilize Earth's tectonic plates, a system we badly need now with more frequent quakes . . . Mankind's link with the stars has existed for centuries at Giza and other points around the world, right under our noses!"

Marshall hand-signaled time-out and raised his mug. "A toast to evolving humanity!"

Savannah noticed movement from the corner of her eye and turned to look. An older woman sat staring at Tess from a small table in the corner across the room. Very ordinary, wearing a simple pair of gray slacks and a pastel blue blouse a little too tight on her large frame, gray hair, little or no makeup. Her eyes looked enormous through the thick lenses of her goldtone glasses. An average grandma type. Savannah lowered her voice to a whisper. "Don't look now, but we're getting some attention."

Savannah glanced at the woman again. A waitress was serving her a hefty combination plate big enough to feed two people. "Check her out now, she's eating."

Tess twisted in her chair to look and then leaned toward Savannah. "Oh my God, she seems familiar."

Savannah tried to jumpstart Tess's memory. "Anyone you've seen lately? Was she outside on the plaza?"

"I can't place her, but something about her gives me the creeps," Tess answered.

"She looks so normal," Marshall said. "Except for the appetite. Older women don't generally wolf down their food. They take half the meal home."

Tess squeezed her eyes shut. "I know her. Who is she, who is she?"

The woman rose from her seat with the little plastic tray holding mints and her tab, and slipped a big navy vinyl pocketbook, the type favored by seniors on a budget, over her shoulder. She glanced toward them again, her eyes resting on Tess just a little too long.

"She seems to know you." Savannah cast a sharp glance at Tess.

Marshall jumped up from his chair, then plopped down again, thinking better of following the woman. He was an internet sleuth, not a gumshoe.

Tess and the Updikes watched as she paid the cashier and eased through the café's fancifully carved double doors.

Tess continued to stare toward the entrance. "I should be able to place her. This feels like not recognizing your next-door neighbor or your schoolteacher at the grocery store—"

"She's leaving, at any rate. Let's act normal." Marshall raised his mug again and patted Tess on the hand. "A toast to transmuting this situation into one that will benefit humanity!"

Savannah extended her mug. "To life!"

In the spirit, Tess put the woman at the back of her mind and joined the fun. "To love!"

::: CHAPTER 13

HARRIS HENRY

The last thing Harris Cantrell Henry recalled was clambering up a rocky hillside under the starriest sky he'd ever seen. He'd awakened with a start from a dream about shape-shifting into a lizard ET and found himself curled up under a pale morning sky, teeth chattering blue with the cold and perched smack dab on the edge of a wide cliff face like some lonely beast, his throbbing head resting on his battered shoes.

Every cell in his body felt as sore as a whore's behind, his mouth so dry he could almost spit dust. When he rubbed the sleep from his eyes, he felt whisker stubble grazing his hand. A scraggly beard more than twenty-four hours old! Much older, in fact. The question hit him like a lightning bolt. How long *had* he been gone, anyway?

He ran his hand over his head. The every-hair-in-place 'do felt punked out, with curly and matted tufts bristling wildly in all directions. He looked down at his clothing and sniffed. A whiff of something dead welled up, his suit didn't seem much more disheveled than one would expect after a sleeping on a cliff in business clothes for a night or two. He gazed at his shoes again. Scuffed to hell, but they'd get that way climbing up the cliff.

How did he get way up here, anyway? He recalled scrambling through the dark for what seemed like hours, terrified he'd get captured or shot.

Then it hit him. More missing time? He only remembered sleeping away from the White House for this one night. But the overgrowth on his head and mug meant weeks had passed since something grabbed him from the West Wing. He reckoned that by now, Gap Allen was president if the same thing hadn't happened to him.

Sour panic surged from his gut and lodged like a leech in his throat. He'd hit the proverbial wall each time he tried to retrieve any memory between waking up in a bland room with walking stick doctors and standing in line underground with other abductees.

What could he do about it? First off, he'd dump the downward emotional tack and scope out his environment. The rocky, red landscape must be in Arizona, New Mexico, Utah, or maybe Colorado, he thought. Desolate Nevada maybe, though that would be a bigger problem. Under the circumstances, was it lucky to be lost in the USA? Was he lost somewhere distant: Mexico, Australia, even Asia or Africa?

Simple assumptions usually proved to be correct. KISS—keep it simple, stupid, he reminded himself. After all, he recalled a recent examination by extraterrestrials in some weird, colorless room, probably in a craft. Then another "bad dream" surfaced, one in which he'd escaped a raging battle that must have occurred at one of those underground bases that DoD people make veiled references to. Rumors circulated about above-top secret underground installations constructed in vast natural caverns and tunnels that honeycomb the United States. The whole planet, actually. Those stories weren't just the stuff of tabloids and the internet. Parts of the underground NORAD facilities in Colorado were installed into already existing cavern and tunnel systems, he recalled.

That's right, Jack, already existing. The infamous Area 51 at

Groom Lake in Nevada seemed to be testing ground for recovered ET craft and the test copies engineered with ET assistance, though the Air Force publicly denied this. Henry heard reports about another installation in northern New Mexico, run jointly by U.S. military and extraterrestrial forces. And another in northern Arizona, possibly in the beautiful and desolate Four Corners area; some said Native Americans had cleared the Four Corners of this intrusion, but that another base appeared further to the southwest, hidden under some little boom towns that sprang up in the mid-twentieth century in Yavapai County.

He'd reached a damn dead end each time he tried getting a chain-of-command briefing with the Air Force on extraterrestrial contact with secret U.S. military installations. Those arrogant flyboy shits always zipped their lying lips when probed for details. Most of his info came from disaffected military retirees or civilian employees of the military who had grown tired of the deception.

He eased himself into a sitting position and rotated his neck and shoulders, stiff from hunkering down on cold rock. As the sun edged above the stone spires towering along the horizon, rays of colored light shone between them. It took his breath away to see everything bathed in solar fire. The sun seemed to melt the stone formations from grays and lavenders and purples into mauve and amber, saffron and crimson. Most men didn't know specific color names, and he felt inspired to spout some aloud.

He sat with his fatigue and cottonmouth, poised like a rajah over the side of a magnificent canyon, enjoying the play of light on stone. When the sun rose fully over the horizon, his eyes nibbled at the contrast between the reddish shades of rock and the clearest of azure blue skies. *Azure—listen to me!* He'd mostly forgotten to look up at the sky in DC. Except for his occasional runs and workouts, he hadn't taken much time to smell the roses.

His stomach reminded him with a grumble that the feast for the soul wouldn't feed body or brain. He crawled to the edge of his ledge and looked down, shaky with dehydration and brain fuzz. And down, and down some more. Maybe it was just his aching head, but the bottom seemed a mile away. This was a grand canyon, if not *the* Grand Canyon. But what did he know? Many scenic overlooks in the western states probably looked grand after three years of negotiating the concrete-covered swamps of DC.

A narrow ribbon of light sand rippled at the bottom of the gigantic cavity. Might water be down there somewhere, a hidden spring, or a pool left over from a recent rain? Maybe if he dug deep enough in the sand he'd find moisture enough to keep him going, if he had enough energy to climb off the cliff.

He stood and pissed a spoonful into a concave spot on the ledge. Making a face at his unnatural thought, he lay down beside the little yellow pool. Stretched out on his belly, he stuck his tongue out. The sour smell made bile rise in his gullet. He gagged, closed his eyes, and stared at his piss again. Thirst ruled. Desperation more than courage helped him lap it up. At a mental level he wanted to vomit, but his body seemed to appreciate the water and minerals.

Hey, I haven't risked my hide in a war, but I sure can survive with the big boys!

Or was drinking piss bad, like drinking saltwater? Why get so happy about sipping piss anyway? Good Lord. He needed to get back to reality. It was imperative to put some distance between himself and the underground base. He couldn't have traveled far by foot—in fact, he was probably standing nearly on top of it.

What were the obstacles? Exposure, for one, his biggest problem. He hated cold. Winters all over the country had grown unseasonably warm during the day, but nighttime temperatures became extreme too, plagued by record lows. If a storm front came in, he'd be toast, frozen toast. Not much better than being shish kebab for the Agency's extraterrestrial keepers, but at least he'd go down a free man in the wilderness.

In spite of the pressing need to move for warmth and water, or maybe because of it, he sat awhile longer, rebelling against the instinct for survival. After some minutes of discomfort, he felt warmer anyway, and more relaxed, happy just to sit. The natural beauty turned his mind from the agonies that brought him there, and the profound silence felt proportionate to the size of the canyon, awe-inspiring, holy.

His worldly ambitions melted away like butter in the sun. He could get used to this. What was it like to spend one's life in pursuit of spiritual goals? He felt compelled to list things to be grateful for: his mother's tenderness, his exhilarating hero worship of John Kennedy and Martin Luther King, his courtship with Merrill and the birth of their twins, Delaney and Leigh. And Tess—so like the spirit of this place. He closed his eyes and wished her the peace and beauty of the sunrise.

A sudden realization snapped him back from contemplation. Denial had always been his greatest weakness and his greatest strength. What was he in denial about now?

His headache compelled him to get off his bum. Dehydration and exposure were taking more of a toll than he cared to admit. Cracking a half-grin in a face that felt like a fossilized prune trying to unwrinkle, he imagined his freeze-dried carcass displayed in the Smithsonian, a latter-day mummy.

So, how to get down? He gazed around the almost insurmountable cliff, feeling like one of those TV commercial cars dropped by helicopter into an inaccessible setting. Then he noticed a few faint scuffmarks where he'd climbed up, whitish scratches on golden-red sandstone. He'd follow these down, figure out where to head next. He guessed his captors would have pursued him if it hadn't been for the battle. If he got lucky, maybe they wouldn't regroup to find his trail, even if he was close to the crack he escaped through. It was a big fucking place out here.

"Away!" he trilled. He spread his arms out and almost giggled until he almost lost his balance and fell over the edge.

"Damn it, Harris," he said, counseling himself. *Keep it together. Get going. Find water. Elude capture.*

He took one last look into the wide, windswept bowl below him.

Directly opposite the sun lay a hill covered with reddish-black, bubbly pumice rocks, a lava formation that marked a geological change from the area he stood in. Worn rows of stacked rock stretched across the middle of the hill, the ruin of an old wall, maybe, tucked into a hollow on the hillside. It looked as good a place to head as any. There were lots of cactus around it, the type with flat, oval pads. Prickly whatever they called it. Juicy and edible. Wasn't any other food or water on that rock, unless you counted some old weedy-looking grass that might bear seeds.

He began to scramble painfully over crunchy ground toward his breakfast. After a short rest, he made several finger-stabbing attempts at picking and dethorning the cactus pads, finding that thin, flat stones made good scrapers. He removed most of the cactus spines except the tiny hair-like ones lodged in his fingertips. Biting through a pad's bitter skin into the bland juicy flesh, he ravished it, then dethorned and chewed at another, and another, nearly growling with pleasure like a starving beast. When finally sated, he stuck a few on a stick and shoved the end of the stick into his back pocket like some desert hobo. He rubbed at the teeny spines that seemed to spread from thumbs and forefingers to his palms with a burning itch. Some lodged in his tongue, too, and he rubbed it against his top front teeth. Just another prickle in the face of a bigger predicament, he conceded.

When the moisture and nutrients entered his bloodstream, a slight warmth oozed almost palpably through his body, clearing his head. He stretched, did a few windmills and jumping jacks, and jogged in place for what seemed like an eternity, but probably only a minute or two in his weakened condition.

When he checked his watch, the immobilized hour and minute hands were permanently stopped at 3:02. Now what?

::: CHAPTER 14

MARSHALL AND SAVANNAH UPDIKE

Marshall, Savannah, and Tess extended their mugs in a glassy tap, affirming Marshall's toast. He dug back into last few bites on his plate, savoring the picante sauce on his oversized chimichanga.

Tess wrinkled her brow. "So, Marsh. This ancient language from the Fourth Root culture. They've actually discovered how it sounds?"

"That's what's reported. Hiburu is thought to be a natural tongue formed by phosphene flare patterns of the brain. A natural construct of our nervous system. A language of light, if you will," he explained.

"I've heard that chanting in some languages, like Hebrew and Sanskrit and Tibetan, can be powerful. I've experienced Native American chanting that nearly blew my head open, if you know what I mean," Tess said.

Savannah nodded, her eyes glowing. "I'm no physicist or linguistics expert, but they say Hiburu mimics the waveform properties of light. If all modern languages are descended from this harmonic language, then some must contain original sounds even today."

Tess's face brightened again. "Wow. In the beginning was the word . . ."

"You got it!" Marshall said. "The word of God. Om, the primordial sound of consciousness contains the sound of everything in the universe. Join this perception of sacred sound with the latest discoveries about living matter . . . Scientists are realizing that DNA isn't just a fixed recording—its qualities are similar to light."

"So, another layer of this story is the ancient Egyptian fixation on the afterlife. What scientists thought was a clumsy stab at immortality may have been an experimental attempt to create a higher form of human. Perhaps they understood better than modern scientists that DNA comes from light, from the stars." Savannah folded her arms and smiled, satisfied with her proclamation.

"Then these new revelations not only rock the paradigm, they shatter it . . . And civilization as we know it is . . . well, there's much more to it." Tess rolled her neck rhythmically. "Our so-called advanced culture is all about material consumption. In other words, it is shallow and it sucks."

Savannah smiled at Tess's soul sister routine. "Many of us ask ourselves what our lives are really about."

"A test, a spiritual journey," Tess countered.

"Yes," Savannah agreed. "A search for truth. We hope our ignorance and suffering are not endured in vain. Some religious dogma and the scientific paradigm surrounding mankind's so-called linear evolution from hunter-gatherer to city dweller conditions us to accept not only our personal suffering, but the pillage of the Earth, tribal genocide, and the virtual enslavement of willing and unwilling participants, human and otherwise. We have much to learn from our nearly extinct tribal societies that existed for millennia without doing our planet serious harm. Now we're offered solid proof that a highly evolved civilization existed on Earth long before our destructive attempt at superior living. Both options show we don't have to destroy the world or live apart from nature in order to live comfortably."

"Of course, truth is pissing a few people off," Tess put it simply.

"I imagine some megabuck organizations that thrive on consumption aren't too happy about truth or change."

"True," Marshall agreed, "but bless the visionaries who embrace the new paradigm. It's not a snap to change from Petroleum Man to Galactic Human. But look how fast the internet and digital technology fueled free exchange among the masses, creating new industry and new ways of sharing information. There's great stuff down the road. But you're right—there will be forces to reckon with until the tide of rising consciousness transforms everything. These forces care little for individuals or democratic principles and are geared for survival at any cost. Power manifests with dark aspects and these dark aspects are what you're contending with." He chopped at the air with his hands, emphasizing his thoughts.

They ordered another round of beer and polished off the chips. The crowd thinned and the hustle and bustle receded into a trickle of late lunchers. Long afternoon shadows began to fill the corners of the café.

Tess looked Marshall in the eye. "You better describe this dark force. Obviously it's not rising consciousness that's troubling me."

He took a deep breath. This would take some explaining. "Well, you've heard the '90s stories about the Illuminati, the Trilateral Commission, the Council on Foreign Relations, and the Bilderbergers . . . imagine the influence of the world's wealthiest and most powerful individuals and corporations rolled into super-intel organizations like NIHSA. Power has been quietly assimilated into massive corporate and government intelligence liaisons spawned by 9-11 and the subsequent war on terror. While NIHSA and other superpower intelligence agencies are not quite as shadowy and conspiratorial as the political far right and far left think they are, they do have agendas and a huge influence on world economy. They control who is elected to high public office—"

A lanky, pimpled teen-aged busboy arrived to gather dishes, a hank of glossy, dark hair covering one eye. The vivacious waitress returned and recited a list of desserts in a charming accent. Marshall asked for more chips and salsa instead. The waitress and busboy disappeared through the swinging doors of the kitchen, busy with post-lunch duties. The hostess, an elegant Hispanic matron with salt and pepper hair swept up in a dignified French roll, remained sitting at a front counter, partially hidden by a carved wooden partition hung with Mexican Indian masks. Jaguars and fierce gods leered back at Marshall when he glanced at the woman, apparently also an owner or manager because she tallied out the cash register and entered figures into an account book.

He turned to Tess. "Unfortunately, these groups are loosely united—let's call them the Council—no, the Agency, what you said Henry calls NIHSA, for lack of a better term. The Agency controls major elections affecting the world's balance of power. They give the word that starts wars and they decide when to end them. They determine monetary issues, such as inflation of currency and rates of exchange. Shortages and surpluses of necessities such as food and fuel are manipulated to their financial benefit. They control world media to a great degree, the spin of reports on national television and radio and our mainstream newspapers. You might say they determine critical policy issues and shape the choices gullible voters think that *they* determine."

Tess tilted her mug back and took a hearty swig of beer, wrinkling her nose. "I can vouch for that. Major newspapers often bury important news in little articles on back pages. The AP and UPI wire services rewrite versions of their stories from day to day. Some are legitimate changes in the development of a story. Other changes are manipulation, calculated to spin stories for public consumption."

"So you follow Marsh's drift," Savannah said. "Back when you went to college, there were fifty corporations controlling mass media. Just ten years ago, there were fewer than ten, and we're down to five or six now in this era of corporate mega-mergers. The same is true with the book publishing industry."

Tess nodded. "Good point. Most Americans don't realize this when they watch TV news or read newspapers, magazines, and books. Because of the wealth of choices in television programming, print media, and the internet, Americans think their news is not controlled, even after the backlash about news suppression during the second Bush administration. Even though there are many complaints about the whitewash of mainstream media now. The Henry administration is no stranger to suppression."

"Yes," Marshall said. "Even our leaders, President Henry included, are members of the Council on Foreign Relations, now under the NIHSA umbrella. So are prominent figures in our national media venues. Major banks, corporations, the Federal Reserve, and top military leaders all play a role in the distribution of power."

"In a sense, NIHSA shelters a secret government within the legitimate government," Savannah added.

"From what Harris said, he wanted to see major improvements in our system and was questioning everything." Tess opened her palms upward and shrugged. "We're all suspicious of the system, and sometimes feel like our strings are pulled to its advantage. When I began investigative reporting, I learned about corporate government, but when I left the field, I stopped thinking about it. The manipulation is obvious to many people. But nobody likes to think the control is so—so pervasive. We Americans believe in our freedom."

"The manipulation isn't easy to see, so people simply carry on," Savannah agreed. "It's glossed over in day-to-day survival."

"What's harder to swallow," Marshall grasped for words, "are some of the hidden agendas and actions of the groups absorbed or controlled by NIHSA. Many were never what their names implied. The Council on Foreign Relations is an American branch of a British secret society founded by Cecil Rhodes of the Rhodes Scholarships. Their mission statement extols the preservation and expansion of the British Empire."

"So what you're saying is that foreign powers are screwing around in American politics. Nothing new. The Saudis and Chinese have lots of dough invested here now."

Savannah shook her head in the affirmative, her curly hair bobbing around her face. "Foreign powers with a history of centuries of despotic royal rule and agencies with dark agendas work here alongside honest people trying to do what's right. Corporate and government interests have become indistinguishable—a hallmark of fascism. It's somewhat natural for a corporate world to shift in that direction, but we're also dealing with some literal, old-school fascist influences too. Many historians feel the Nazis weren't shattered at the end of World War II. Some Reich members fled to South America and resurfaced in corporate empires in North America. Maybe even in another galaxy."

Tess laughed with a little series of snorts. "Get outta here. Galactic Nazis. Sounds like a bogeyman under every bed. How 'bout galactic Chinese ruling the universe?"

Marshall grinned. "It's not such a stretch. You may have heard how Hitler's scientists designed spacecraft during World War II. There are credible stories from extraterrestrial abductees after the war witnessing blond, blue-eyed humanoids aboard craft with the small gray ETs depicted in our TV shows and films. Some abductees have said that the Grays indicate they serve our old friends, the Reptilians, who seem to conveniently appear when humanity is poised to take an evolutionary leap."

Savannah's face lit up as she clarified Marshall's statements. "According to some ET researchers, the Reptilians love disorder, and they love war. Both Grays and Reptilians collect human body parts in war zones because both feed upon human glandular secretions and use human DNA in their cloning and reproductive projects. There's evidence that the more morbid Nazi experiments on humans were instigated by these extraterrestrials. The Nazis feared the Reptilians, and somehow disassociated themselves from their alliance by linking them with Jews and others they discriminated against. Confused by these creatures, they also confused Jewish proclivities in financial affairs with the acquisitive, abusive commerce of the reptilian society. Well, I don't buy that, but that's one theory."

Tess shook her head. "Doesn't do it for me, either," she complained. "There's no smoking gun, no definite proof of extraterrestrial contact except words on paper—at least not accessible proof. Even if there are ETs cruising around, we surely can't blame them for Nazi atrocities. Humans are the biggest monsters." She cast a bemused look at Savannah. "Do you really want to be an apologist for Nazi anti-Semitism?"

"Of course not. These are simply theories," Savannah replied. "Theories based on real but little-known data. Anyway, we all complain that our governments and our corporations are becoming more heartless. That's the nature of corporate activity. Simple human greed is the motivation. NIHSA is alleged to have illegal money streams tied to organized crime, the drug trade, and human slavery, as well as conventional government support in fighting the same. Why not ties to extraterrestrial races? Marsh and I postulate that NIHSA is truly controlled by the Annunaki—not the Sumerian gods, of course, but a convenient catch-all name for the extraterrestrial descendants of those who influenced human culture in ancient eras . . . Before NIHSA was formed, the Annunaki already had business with the NSA, CIA, M16, and MOSSAD. If you follow the pattern of evidence, there's reason to be paranoid."

Marshall picked up where Savannah left off. "Not only has a great battle between forces of light and darkness raged for millennia, there's been a struggle within the world's intelligence communities for decades. We're not so much engaged in a war to bring democracy to the entire world, as we are at war to defend Earth from an extraterrestrial threat that's spanned millennia. There are photos available of football-sized fields in remote areas of the United States and Russia filled with crashed ET craft. If that isn't an invasion, what is?"

"But we take comfort in the adage that when dark and light forces clash, light prevails," Savannah added.

"I should hope so." Tess tapped the fingers of her right hand on the table. "What about us? How do Mikka and I fit into this, this invasion?"

Marshall cleared his throat and looked down at the table for a moment, then gazed into Tess's eyes. "This is my opinion . . . how can I say this? Guard Mikka carefully. You say you have nothing anyone wants, but someone powerful is shadowing you. Clearly this dark power wants to use or to destroy your child. At the very least, she has political value as the president's illegitimate daughter . . . Our man in Washington, though supported by Illuminati powers, came from humble roots and wanted to overthrow—"

Tess clutched her head in her hands, and then sat up straight with an indignant stare. "You're not telling me to go to his people. No. I refuse."

Savannah held her hands out to Tess. "I'm sorry. Marsh isn't suggesting that. Quite the contrary. Under the circumstances, you should continue to keep a low profile."

Marshall hesitated a moment. ". . . We've covered a lot of ground, Tess, but we digressed from a topic I mentioned at the outset of our conversation. I want to give you some background . . ."

Tess quizzed him with her eyes. "What are you trying to say, Marshall?"

"We talked about Star Walkers. Human time capsules who disseminate vital spiritual information . . ."

Tess closed her eyes for a moment. "Yeah. I've read about such things in Tibetan Buddhist lore. Sometimes information is embedded in the minds of teachers born at particular times and is shared when the time is right."

Savannah spoke up again, her timing impeccable. "Have you ever heard of the Bible Code?"

"Yeah, I have. I remember reading magazine articles about it when those popular Code books were published a decade or so ago. Interesting stuff. But can't you prove almost anything with scripture?"

"Don't confuse the Code with scriptural dogma," Savannah said.

"I thought Bible Code was old news. There's more to it?"

Savannah and Marshall nodded together.

"Listen," Marshall said, "this is big. The code is visible in the

Torah, the Hebrew Old Testament. Apparently it's always been there and scholars speculated about it, but for centuries, no one could access it. Sir Isaac Newton of gravity fame spent half his life trying to find it. His biographer John Maynard Keyes was shocked to find Newton's unpublished papers about his quest for the code. Newton applied every known mathematical model to the Bible until his death. It wasn't until the twentieth century that a physics graduate student, Doron Witztum, a mathematician, Eliyahu Rips, along with an Israeli computer whiz, Yoav Rosenberg, were successful in publishing proof of the Code's existence because they possessed a tool not available to previous generations of scientists—the computer."

Tess sat up straight. "That makes sense! . . . One article in *Newsweek* discussed how the Code contained dates of historical events."

"Oh, yes. Accuracy with mathematical probabilities that are staggering. Many have tried to disprove Rips's work and ended up conceding that it's nearly flawless. The Code seems to contain the span of human history. Names, events, dates, " Savannah added.

"Amazing. An akashic record."

"Yes, but in the physical plane rather than the ethereal."

"So it makes accurate predictions, too?"

"Most scholars believe that the Code contains probability, not prediction," Marshall explained. "Probable events. In fact, multiple probable events are listed for certain dates."

"But there are warnings every century about a possible Apocalypse," Tess argued. "The Christian right loves that stuff—they want Jesus to physically return . . ."

"Exactly," Marshall agreed. "And much of the research has covered contemporary Middle Eastern events because of the Israeli/Arab conflict and Islamic fundamentalist terror activity around the world." But every culture, every phase of human history is found in the Code. Jewish tradition says everything and everyone who exists or will ever exist is recorded in the text of the first five books of the Bible. That's why Rabbis always reminded Torah copyists that miscopying or losing even one letter could bring about the end of the world."

"And we're pretty sure that the Biblical and Mayan predictions about 2012 and the end of the world aren't about earthly wars or terrorists," Savannah added. "They're about awareness of the ancient battle between spiritual and galactic forces."

"I'd rather think about the beginning of the world," Tess said. "Does the Code solve any mysteries there?"

Savannah's eyes softened with compassion, her smile bright with love. "You recall where Marsh interrupted our musings on the Word? Light? DNA from the stars? A spiritual science?"

Tess looked blank for a split second.

"The Genesis and Jehovah stories in the Bible," Marshall reminded her.

She shut her eyes and thought for a moment. Then her eyes snapped open. "Bingo. The Garden of Eden. The chariot of fire in Ezekiel."

"Yes," Savannah said.

"You mean . . ."

Marshall nodded. "Yes."

". . . the Bible Code substantiates that human DNA does come from the stars? And the stuff about the Reptilians creating half-breeds?"

"The coded information in Genesis states "DNA brought in a vehicle. And in Ezekiel, the words "human alien, steel vehicle, and alien codes, " Marshall said.

Tess clicked her tongue. "Humans were given both types of DNA, then. And the Code and even the Bible might be influenced or created by extraterrestrials."

"Advanced philosophy and technology seem like magic. God-like magic."

Tess shook her head. "The implications must stagger organized religion. So what about modern people in the Bible Code? Who's in it?" She looked at Savannah, then at Marshall. "I'm sorry for jumping ahead—my brain is buzzing."

"Oh, it's incredible." Savannah held her palms up. "The Wright

Brothers. Edison. The Kennedys, of course, the assassinations of Jack and Robert, and Martin Luther King . . . Bill Gates, 9-11, the 7/7 London bombings, the assassination of Benazir Bhutto and the Peruvian president, the resolution of statehood for Palestine, the wars in Iraq, Libya, and Syria, and possible conflict with Iran . . ." Savannah hesitated. "Even Henry . . ."

Tess made a visible effort to appear composed, but her eyes teared up. "I don't get it. I've never heard of Harris mentioned in the Code. How do people keep finding new things in the Bible? Isn't that flaky?"

"No, not at all," Marshall countered. "All the possible skip sequences of the letters of the Old Testament will take years to decipher, even with computers. Many researchers, including myself, look for new sequences."

"You really found something on Harris?"

"Yes, I did. So did some big-name researchers. It's rather cryptic, though. Open-ended, I guess you'd say, because even the immediate future is never fixed."

"I'm all ears . . ." Tess leaned forward like she might grab his collar across the table.

Savannah tried to look Tess in the eye, but Tess's eyes remained on Marshall. "Now that we know more about you and Mikka, we're pretty sure you're both involved, too."

"What? Tell me," she demanded, finally gazing at Savannah.

Marshall reached into his shirt pocket, unfolded a sheet of copy paper and placed it in front of Tess. "Here's a page of Old Testament text analysis by Bible Code software. See Henry's name in this sequence? It's crossed by the Hebrew date of his assassination—or disappearance—and by the words "Death–Mystery." Nearby are words surrounding this configuration in a rough circle. 'Empire C, Flying Serpents, Desert Sojourn, Starwalker, Starchild, and . . ." he hesitated for a moment," . . . Annihilation–Evolution."

The blood drained from Tess's face. "Starchild," she whispered. "And there *is* something fishy about Harris's death . . . when did you find this out?"

"Does the look on your face mean we've come to similar conclusions? We overnighted a letter to Henry a few weeks before his death. Many Code researchers relay information to world leaders and policy makers if their names are connected with future probabilities."

Tess's mouth dropped open. "Why didn't it help?"

Marshall shrugged. "Maybe he didn't see it. With the latest terrorist threats and weather chaos, plus the controversy surrounding the global warming bill, maybe the letter didn't make it to his desk. Most outside mail is opened and screened by aides. It could be sitting in a to-do pile somewhere. Obviously, he had problems with NIHSA as well."

Tess closed her eyes and shook her head.

"Be careful, Tess," Savannah urged, her voice low. "You're right that there's something fishy about the assassination. A coup. And your daughter may appeal as a lab rat. Or worse."

"In addition to this galactic war raging for centuries, we believe Earth has engaged its old Reptilian enemy, or soon will," Marshall said.

Savannah reached out and squeezed one of Tess's hands in hers.

Tess pulled her hand back and covered her face with both hands. Then she held her head between her palms as if holding it together.

Savannah fixed a cool stare at her. "That race uses humans as both food and slaves. Their motivations may be even darker than any we've discussed."

"Starchild," Tess murmured. She sank back in her chair, her face weary. "So you're saying what?" She put her head in her hands. "I'm sorry . . . I'm so tired—"

"Keep a low profile. Stay on the move. Don't park your truck or sleep in the same place twice. Perhaps change vehicles as soon as possible." Marsh patted her hand. "Can you do that?"

Tess nodded and stared at the table. "I don't know about another vehicle, but I can move around. For a couple of months, anyway," she mumbled into her hands.

"You might want to cut your hair, wear glasses, dress differently," Savannah added. "A new look wouldn't hurt."

"God, I don't know." Tess wound and unwound a strand of hair around her forefinger. "I'm afraid I'll blow this. Maybe I should turn myself in." Obviously she was skewered on the horns of a dilemma.

"It's up to you, of course," Marshall said. "But I feel apprehensive. Better to roll with your first instinct to steer clear of the law."

"Wish I knew for sure who I'm running from and exactly why. I'm not exactly hiding, either. I'm meeting my brother and daughter this afternoon at my great uncle and aunt's over in Picture Rocks for a Christmas Eve dinner."

Marsh's voice became huskier with urgency. "Go ahead with your holiday plans for the time being—you're 250 miles away from home. Don't stay long, and guard yourself and your little one. Your primary concern is your daughter's safety."

Tess nodded wistfully.

Savannah softened her voice. "I can't help asking about your little girl. Is she particularly bright?"

The question unsettled Tess. She shifted in her seat and stared at the horizon again. "Yeah, Mikka's quite a character. Talkative. Spoke in full sentences before she turned eighteen months old. Quite an artist, too, so good it's scary. She acts older, like an 'old soul' as the expression goes."

"Strong and healthy?"

Tess's eyes filled with apprehension but she answered the question. "Yes. A nine-pound baby and now she's a full head taller than most kids her age. Why?"

Savannah chose her words carefully. "Indigo kids, brilliant kids, are being born with greater frequency now. Many have special abilities. It's rumored but not proven that a few transcend time and space, somehow physically rearrange their molecules. They seem to operate in fourth dimensional frequencies, disappear and reappear at will. We've heard from a reliable source that the U.S. military is interested . . ."

Tess froze and gazed at the sky as though she longed to fly away. When she regained her composure, she spoke in a smooth, sure voice.

"That must be quite a talent. Can you imagine?"

Marshall and Savannah exchanged another look. Was this the trait Tess didn't want to reveal about Mikka?

Tess's face blanched again. *The older woman*. "Oh my God, Savannah. Now I remember who that woman was, the one watching us from across the room. It should have been obvious. She was in the shower room at Picacho Peak! Maybe it's a coincidence—maybe she's visiting Tucson too . . ."

Savannah's eyes widened with Tess's realization. "Or she's following you. You *must* take precautions to throw these people off your trail."

Tess's face blanched. "I remember seeing her lead a young boy to a campsite. A grandchild, I thought."

Marshall's soft eyes glowed with a fierce light. "Take care, Tess," he said. "*Your* thread is woven into this design."

::: Chapter 15

Tess Vaughn

As Tess returned to her truck with the Updikes looking on, her mind spun faster than it could form words, tossing the loose debris of plots, subplots, and addendums to subplots around in a mental hurricane.

But one term stuck in her craw. *Starchild.*

What did it all mean? She gazed around the street and waved goodbye to the Updikes while unlocking her pick-up. The downtown street was quiet with the lunch hour long past and some workers leaving early or already off work on Christmas Eve, although a few tourists still straggled here and there, enjoying the desert sun. She didn't see the older woman or anyone else following her, and apparently the Updikes didn't notice anything or they would've called her.

She unlocked and started the truck, thinking of Mikka. Since she'd moved to northern Arizona, she'd spent hours and hours gazing at stars. No, she assured herself, that couldn't have happened when she was pregnant with Mikka . . . could it? She recalled with vivid clarity the strange light surrounding her that summer night during a meteor shower, right before the odd mark appeared on her arm. That night progressed like a déjà vu experience—everything felt so familiar that she'd brushed it off as normal rather than surreal. She'd been more worried about how to conceal Mikka's identity after she was born than anything else. Now her gut churned. The Updikes briefly mentioned extraterrestrial abduction and tracking implants, and truthfully, might her experience have featured both?

Tess understood what those marks might mean now. It made sense, fit what Harris had tried to tell her. Were she and Mikka being tracked by extraterrestrials? Savannah mentioned highly evolved Indigo kids . . . Was Mikka some experimental ET hybrid? What did it mean to be a Starchild?

Tess heard of women having hybrid babies, another supermarket tabloid spoof, she'd assumed. And women who had embryos placed in their uteruses, finding themselves inexplicably pregnant and then suddenly and inexplicably not pregnant after the embryos were harvested. Miscarriages with no fetuses.

A chill ran up her spine. Her friend and neighbor, Darcy, suddenly lost twins in her first trimester two years before, when Mikka was a baby, but all she'd delivered was a mushy placenta with two cords. Her doctor said the babies must have been rapidly absorbed after they died. It didn't make sense, but what woman would question this in the midst of her grief?

Tess shivered and tried to stop thinking about this mind-boggler. She hurried through one of the old barrios near downtown Tucson, looking ahead for cops to avoid a traffic citation. She didn't need any more attention.

She gazed wistfully through her dusty windshield, wishing she could stop and stroll around this neighborhood as she had when she'd worked downtown. The crumbling adobe cottages seemed both aged and ageless, the same after the passage of years. Many were spruced up into states of elegant, maintained decay by the artisans who moved there for the affordable housing and cultural ambiance. She'd almost bought a house in the neighborhood before

Harris Henry, before Mikka.

At Speedway Boulevard, she swung the truck west toward Picture Rocks and mashed the accelerator to the floor until she cruised five MPH over the speed limit, anxious to meet Paul and Mikka at Uncle Mac's and Aunt Xénia's. Her mind inevitably glommed back onto her conversations with the Updikes, and wrapped itself around yesterday's horror.

Her guts began to churn again. The sky darkened suddenly but the obscuring clouds melted away and the sudden wink of sunlight blinded her for an instant. She pulled the sun visor down and fumbled in her bag for her sunglasses. She spied a chunky dark-haired man in an empty lot ahead selling chimineas and cheap Mexican statuary. Tucson street vendors still sold their wares along the boulevards, and the city had a hometown feel despite massive urban sprawl invading the surrounding foothills.

She sped by the vendors, checking her rearview mirror. An Indian or Mexican woman sat near the statuary guy, silver jewelry spread out in front of her on a plywood sheet table supported by carpenters' horses. At the opposite end sat a selection of CDs and DVDs in their bright plastic holders, and a dozen pairs of sunglasses. Remembering Savannah's advice, she made a quick U-turn. A new pair of sunglasses in a style she normally shunned might come in handy. Paying cash made the transaction untraceable.

The vendor yawned, barely acknowledging Tess when she handed her a ten for a pair of retro grannies with nearly opaque, square black lenses. Some good-looking pieces of jewelry winked in the sunlight, tempting her to browse, but she was back on the road in less than a minute, leaving the vendors in a puff of dust.

When she pulled into the dirt lane leading to Mac and Xénia's house, the sun was still an hour or two away from sliding behind the nubs and teats of the Tucson Mountains. She ran her fingers through her tangled hair. She figured if she must change it, she may as well do it now. She pulled the truck on a narrow shoulder where the lane curved around a volcanic rock formation, and pulled out her cosmetic bag from the duffel. First, she chopped her hair ear length with the blade of her Swiss Army knife, then struggled with the tiny scissors, bending to watch herself cut tiny locks of hair in the truck's driver side mirror. Twenty minutes later, her fingers ached from squeezing the tiny scissors hundreds of times. She scrabbled through lipstick and eye shadow to find a slightly larger pair of fingernail scissors. Not much better, but by the time the sky turned a blazing pink, she'd created a fashionable textured inch-long hairdo. The new cap of hair looked much darker than the old, sun-streaked length. Trading her tortoiseshell sunglasses for the grannies, she peered in the truck window at her reflection and smiled. She looked like a punk pixie waif from the pages of Vogue. The 'do would do.

She stuffed the clippings into a grocery store produce bag she'd packed around her running shoes. She'd have to remember to burn it—Mac and Xénia's fireplace probably had a Yule log burning already.

Her heart did a double flip when she pulled in front of Uncle Mac's big neo-Spanish house. White twinkle lights and luminarias bathed every nook and cranny in a misty glow. Paul's car wasn't there. She pawed through her handbag for her cell phone, but it needed charging. Paul's late for everything, she reasoned. Christmas traffic is heavy on the interstate. Then she ignored her logic and obsessed on other real and imaginary dangers, her stomach contracting in another slow burn.

"Get a grip, Tess," she muttered through clenched teeth.

Aunt Xénia responded to the doorbell as she always did, full of cheer, the scent of holiday seasonings and spices billowing around her. "Oh, honey! You're here!" she said in a subtle Mexican accent. "So good you of you to come this year!"

"Aunt Xénia, hello!" Tess placed the carton of gifts and Santa Claus stocking stuffers at her feet and extended her arms.

Xénia air-kissed Tess on both cheeks and she reciprocated, trying to look suitably festive as her great aunt enveloped her in one of her famous bear hugs and nonstop monologues.

"Your hair! Fashionable!" Xénia leaned back to admire the hairdo.

Tess flinched. Xénia's plastic smile indicated that maybe she needed a hairdresser fix.

"Oh, honey, Paul called. He's outside Marana. He'll be here any time now."

Tess fought to hold back tears and rubbed her hand over her shorn head. "Changes are good. Do you really like my hair? I was thinking of a bleach job with dark roots."

"Oh, no, no, you have that lovely chestnut luster, don't do that." Xénia plucked at Tess's hair with agile fingers, then smoothed a stray lock of her own dyed raven hair, coiffed in an elegant twist. "Your natural color *is* lovely."

Tess smiled and Xénia launched her quicksilver mind in a new direction. "Oh, I do wish that Rich and Lizette were here. It's a shame they're missing little Mikka at Christmas time."

Tess's heart ached again. Mom and Dad moved to Santa Fe after Dad retired from his teaching position at the university two years ago. Several of their old school chums from the Midwest moved there and pestered Mom and Dad to join them. "I'm sure we would have gone to New Mexico if Mom and Dad had stayed home. Once they planned their winter trip to Wales, they decided it would be fun to stay for holidays. They'd wanted to go eleven years ago for the millennium celebration but with all the terrorist warnings . . . I'm glad they *finally* went. They won't be around forever." She flinched. She sounded too defensive and shrill.

Xénia didn't seem to notice. She called Uncle Mac from the Arizona room, where he lounged half-asleep in a black leather recliner, a big coffee table book from his huge World War II collection open in his lap.

"Mac, for goodness sake, Tess just came in from up north . . ."

Mac Vaughn embraced her with a twinkle, his perennial grin and Welsh accent a balm for her heart. "Hiya Tessie, luv, how ya be?"

"Oh, my troubles are many, but I'm safe with my Uncle Mac now," she teased.

"That ya are, that ya are." He threw a few fake punches around her and growled, sounding a lot like the Wizard of Oz's cowardly lion.

"I'll take those bags, luv. Do take Xénia and her lip to the kitchen. She's been cooking and yakking for days. There's brandy, new world-class wines from Wilcox and Sedona, do ya believe it, and my world-famous eggnog, of course."

The simultaneous jangle of doorbell and phone interrupted. Relieved to see Paul and Mikka at the door, Tess rushed to hug Mikka. She looked at her mother's haircut and smiled, always accepting of whatever she found in the moment. Tess hid her emotions in the flurry of activity.

She was rubbing noses with Mikka when Xénia handed her a mobile landline phone. "It's a fellow for you, didn't say who." Xénia kissed Mikka and ruffled her curls, then turned to fuss over Paul. He eyed his sister's new haircut with raised eyebrows.

Tess pretended to expect the call. "Merry Christmas," she chirped, turning away from her family and trotting with Mikka on her hip down six carpeted steps into the sunken dining area.

Tess," said a smoky, unfamiliar male voice.

Mikka tensed in her arms. She thought to disconnect but compulsively replied. "Yes?"

"Did you like the ride?"

She wanted to throw the phone across the room. Exaggerated breaths wafted from the receiver, followed by a soft click and the dial tone. She froze. Obviously someone had discovered her location and procured the phone number. Did someone follow her as well? She hadn't noticed anything amiss. Perhaps she did have some sort of implant, or a bug in her phone or belongings. She glared at the mobile phone, knowing if she dialed *69 that the dialing number would be blocked. Mikka looked up at Tess, a question mark in her face. Tess tried to smile. Should she leave or would it be safer to stay? Getting through this night would take some acting. She couldn't possibly share her fears with a three-year-old or her family on Christmas Eve.

She wanted to run outside and merge with the night to sit alone and obsess under the stars until she made sense of the situation. But she'd have to shift into automatic and get through the evening without ruining it for anyone. She wanted to find comfort in the bosom of her family, no matter what it took.

Mikka brought her back to the present moment by responding to her dismay with a reassuring smile. "Mama, Santa has presents. Some for you too."

"Oh yes, Sweetie, Santa has presents for you. Mama and Uncle Paul and Aunt Xénia and Uncle Big Mac have presents for you!"

She tickled Mikka and the sound of her pure liquid laughter bubbled out to Paul, Mac, and Xénia, drawing them into the room. Tess's older cousins Trey and Trevor soon joined the crowd, both home from a jewelry buying trip in Asia, accompanied by their pretty Korean and Vietnamese wives and a crew of athletic, multicultural kids.

Good food, good company, and good cheer soon pulled her to the surface of her mind's deep waters. Mac slipped out after the dinner of Welsh lamb and Mexican delights. Santa arrived a few minutes later with an enormous red velvet bag of gifts and Christmas stockings stuffed with goodies for the little ones. They clamored around the tree and near the fireplace with their new toys, sucking on old-fashioned ribbons of hard candy. Adult gifts were opened, admired and tucked away, after-dinner wine imbibed, prayers and carols and family Christmas stories recited.

Finally, at midnight, after many hugs and goodnight wishes, Tess found sanctuary in a guest wing bedroom. She considered explaining herself to Paul, who disappeared into an adjoining room, but she was too tired. Tomorrow would be another day. She undressed and molded a dozing Mikka into fuzzy pink pajamas, tucking her into the queen-sized sleigh bed. She pushed aside the richly embroidered maroon and gold coverlet and lay down on the bottom sheet in her clothes. Mikka sighed beside her. A scarlet candle nested inside a golden ceramic star flickered from a glass-topped side table, softening the room's deepest shadows.

Tess thrashed around on her side of the bed in spite of her fatigue, dreading an anxiety-ridden, restless night. But the shimmering flame and scent of spice soon carried her into the other world.

Reclining on a narrow couch, scores of oil lamps gutter in a soft breeze that swirls pungent smoke across their nude bodies. Harris caresses her cheek, sucks tenderly at her lips, her neck, her nipples. He cups her vulva, a swelling flower in his warm palm. He smells of soap and new leather, freshly washed. She melts in the fire of his passion.

Hieroglyphics etch the walls and ceiling. The faces and symbols of kings and queens, their achievements spun in a tangle of passion, wheel over the lovers. The room spirals in a blaze, revealing a night sky spattered with a million stars. A trio of stone monuments shine in the moonlight, golden yet austere. They pant now, his shadow rising and falling in the luminous room, her tongue searching the sweetness of his lower lip.

In the distance, a child cries out, a sound that seems to emerge from a cave or tunnel. The lovers loosen their embrace suddenly as though ice water dashes over them. The child's cries become louder, more insistent.

"I'm scared, Tess." Harris buries his face at her breast.

She holds him again, whispering comforting words in his ear, but he starts to melt away. She grasps frantically at his arm as he morphs into an amorous, human-sized lizard. She screams and pull away, but when she looks again, Harris opens huge wings and a breeze snatches him like a giant kite.

A big black car races away in the distance, its engine roaring. A gleaming handgun emerges from a rear window, extended by a gloved hand.

Everything whirls away in a spiral of muted colors. All that remains is a man's shoe in a pool of moonlight. Tess jump ups, adjusts her sheer, cape-like gown around her, and runs in the direction Harris vanishes. But she seems to be running toward the child, for its cries grow louder and louder.

"Where are you?" she howls.

The more the child cries, the more frantic she is to find Harris. A small figure crawls from a crevice opening at her feet. It holds out its hand. Tess reaches out, but the hand is not human when she grasps it. She recoils with shock at the pearly white face and huge moist eyes like great golden-green almonds.

She turns and runs toward the setting moon, wailing with fear and longing. She should be safe on the desert horizon, away from those strange temples, but the moon turns on its axis and shoots toward her. It wobbles slightly, hovers over her, a transparent, illuminated jellyfish.

She falls to her knees. The moon is a circular craft, an extraterrestrial ship. A blue beam shoots from it to the ground, and then another. She can't move her limbs. The child cries incessantly, interrupted for a moment by a husky voice she seems to recall from a telephone conversation.

"Did you like the ride?"

She recoils. A brilliant light fills her up. She becomes empty space, lifted up for a moment, then condenses, streaking like a meteor across the sky, a strangely cool ball of fire. She tumbles inexplicably until she becomes an icy cinder hovering in darkness.

Tess awoke in a cold sweat, thinking again of the incident under the stars during her pregnancy, and the Christmas Eve phone call. The digital clock on the nightstand read 3:33 a.m. The candle still burned across the room. Beside her, Mikka was sleeping peacefully, though she'd turned herself nearly crosswise and lay on top of the lush duvet.

She forced herself from the bed, drawn to the large casement window facing it. As she passed the candle she blew it out, and pulled the lush draperies aside to peer through an immaculate window pane. She drank in the view of Tucson lights sparkling in the distance like a pile of gemstones. So calm, so bright.

But she couldn't shake the paranoia and panic of the dream. Tucking the drapes back firmly against the window and wall, she felt someone watching her and knew she must leave. She showered and put on her running shoes and sweats, clothing appropriate for her situation. Then she tiptoed to the kitchen, filled a stainless-steel teapot with distilled water from a dispenser. Herbal or regular tea? She'd cover all her bases and dropped a bag of each in an extra-large mug.

Paul shuffled in, hair tousled, denim robe falling off one shoulder, feet bare. "You couldn't sleep either?"

"I did, and quite well, too, but had a hell of a dream. Woke me up. Peppermint or green tea?"

"Peppermint. You sharing?"

Tess took a deep breath and exhaled just as deeply. "Yeah. I need to share. I'll start with the dream."

Paul listened patiently and shrugged when she finished. "That doesn't seem like anything to keep you from a good night's rest. Kind of a kick. Funny choice of lovers, though, if you ask me."

She turned to the window over the kitchen sink and pried two coppery miniblind slats apart, momentarily forgetting her paranoia with big brother at her side. She loved looking at the city from these hills on winter nights, at peace in the mountains' dark arms, splashed with Christmas colors. She gazed for a long time and then let the blinds snap back in place, wrapping her arms around herself, tears welling in her eyes.

"Tess?" Paul sensed her discomfort even though she'd turned her back to him.

She took a deep breath and related the entire story through her tears—the truth about Mikka's father, her suspicions about his death, the dark sedans lurking near her house, the incident at Picacho followed by the cut tire, her meeting with the Updikes, and the Christmas Eve phone call. Paul was one of few people who would believe her. When she finished, she felt worlds lighter, if only for a moment.

"And now that I've dumped all this in your lap, I think I'd better leave. At least Santa came last night, so I won't deprive Mikka of Christmas . . ."

"I'm going with you."

"There are enough people in this family in danger already."

"You've got a kid, Tess. You'll need more eyes and ears. Let me help you get situated wherever you're going."

"What will Jay say?"

"He just got back from a shoot, is busy in the darkroom. I think he'll understand once the urgency hits him. He'll deal with it."

"During the holidays? I doubt it." Tess wouldn't forget Jay's rude remarks about her at Thanksgiving, nor his ridiculous jealousy of any relative close to Paul.

"He's not as selfish as you think."

She disagreed, but let the statement ride, grateful for Paul's company. "I'll put my stuff in the truck and warm it up. Just before we take off, I'll write a note to Xénia and Mac and tell them we've decided to spend the day with friends down in Patagonia before we head home."

"So where are we *really* going?"

She shrugged, pretending to be relaxed. "I'm not sure. Out of Tucson?" She paused and brightened a little. "No. Let's go see the Updikes. I'm sure they'll have some suggestions. They said to call any time. I want them to know about this."

Paul saluted her. "Check."

They padded together down the hall to the guest wing, Paul in bare feet, Tess in her Adidas, both lost in their own thoughts.

::: Chapter 16

Paul Vaughn

Paul stripped the sofa bed in the den of its sheets and blanket, folded them, and gathered his things. Sighing, he wondered what the day would bring. It wasn't that he minded helping Tess out, but truly, he *was* due home early that afternoon and Jay *did* have plans.

Born just twenty months apart, he and Tess had been both inseparable and competitive growing up. They felt puzzled by the frustrating emotional distance their parents maintained from them throughout their childhood and were glad to have each other. Before puberty, the siblings were so close they'd practically been able to read one another's minds. And they shared many unusual interests. He recalled the long twilight talks about psychic phenomena, ghosts, flying saucers, and other paranormal stuff.

Their similarities diminished in his mind when he came out of the closet in his late teens. Tess accepted him like nothing had changed. But he began to find her perplexing, even dense at times, like a tire slightly out of round. There was just something about Tess he wanted to fix or change. She said he was projecting. Maybe. Anyhow, he wasn't sure what to make of her Christmas morning confession to him. It wasn't that he disbelieved her, but that her occupation as a writer was suspect. All too easy for her to embellish reality. Plus, she was prone to high drama.

Thinking back, he recalled the day Tess claimed to have met President Henry. She came to Phoenix that weekend to visit him, no special reason. They'd dinked around the house, did some swimming, went out for drinks, dinner and a movie on Saturday night. His ex-boyfriend was away. Good thing, because he was envious of Tess. At least he treated her with more respect than Jay, whose jealousy was pointed, to put it mildly. He couldn't have her around unless Jay was on a shoot. Jay couldn't handle *any* female attention toward him—not a relative, not a child, not even the sweet octogenarian down the block who shared doggy stories.

Tess was up early that Sunday, way before him. When he stumbled out of his room, she was eyeing herself in the living room mirror, decked out in a colorful long skirt and tunic, festive with her copper jewelry and shiny copper lamé sandals set with turquoise stones.

"What's the fuss?" He yawned and rubbed sleep out of his eyes.

"I met someone out running on the mountain. He invited me to brunch. Good thing I brought something to wear besides shorts." Tess frowned at herself in the mirror and adjusted her dangly copper and turquoise earrings.

"Oh. Where you going?"

"Somewhere near here, I think. He gave me a midtown address. I pulled the newspaper out of the sprinkler. It's out on the patio on your chair."

Tess changed the subject so fast he barely noticed at the time. He grunted. "If I'm asleep when you get back, wake me. I've gotta run over to Home Depot and pick up stuff for the patio."

"Hmm." Tess ignored him, caught up in her primping. She made a final pass at her head with a hairbrush, picked up her bag, and fluttered her fingers at him on her way out.

When she came back a couple hours later, he was conked out on a patio lounger near a bubbling fountain with the Sunday paper over his face. When he opened his eyes to her tickling jab in the belly, Tess twirled around, her skirt poufing out in an upside-down flower. She looked starry-eyed and somewhat jumpy, but didn't say much, implying that her date and the food were exceptional. This guy must have dazzled her, he figured, because she played her cards close to her chest that afternoon. Tess generally offered more information than asked for, a regular storyteller. He was so preoccupied with his Sunday afternoon to-do stuff that he hadn't paid much attention. If she'd told him that day what really happened, he'd have thought she was pulling his leg.

He set his suitcase down near the kitchen door. Tess breezed in from the hallway, handed him a sleepy Mikka, setting her car seat at his feet, and picked up her and Mikka's gear from the pile near his suitcase.

"I'll take these things out. I'll be right back."

"Why don't I follow you? I'll bring the car seat."

"Let me get this stuff situated first. I'll be back in a minute." Tess hustled out the kitchen door toward Mac and Xénia's driveway with her and Mikka's duffel bags, a colorful Guatemalan fabric bag over one shoulder, and a box of gifts cradled in her arms.

⁂

Tess's breath formed misty puffs in the nippy air. The little four-cylinder Toyota pickup, its windows shimmering with a light frost, sat at one side of the circular drive, several car lengths behind the other vehicles, as though she'd intentionally planned to leave first. She wouldn't have to wake anyone to move their vehicle, and was glad for the circumstance.

She fit the key into the door lock, remembering how her hands shook at Picacho Peak. If she hadn't confided in the Updikes and Paul, she'd be in the same shape today. But she felt stronger and more proactive now. She pushed the driver seat back and deposited the cardboard box in the jump seat area, then unlocked the camper shell and put her and Mikka's duffel bags in the bed of the truck.

Remembering that Mikka left one of her new toys in the living room, she hurried to retrieve it, then thought to start and warm the truck up first.

She went back to the driver's door and fit the key into the ignition by reaching around the steering column, her fingers stiffening in the cold air. She tried to turn the key, but it wouldn't move past the locked position unless she sat squarely in front of it in the driver's seat. As she perched lightly on the edge of the seat with both legs outside the truck, a tiny momentary whir, a whisper of some mechanism sounded underneath her. Or was it a sound in her head? Something felt odd, and she imagined one of Mikka's silly arcade game toys stuck under the seat. But she'd cleaned out the truck a few days before, vacuuming in each nook and cranny of the interior. There was no toy.

Suddenly instinct propelled her when one of her favorite action-adventure car-bomb movie scenes flashed through her mind. She took a few running steps and dove away from the truck as a mighty force sent the truck door sailing into her right hip, tumbling her head over heels and across the brick driveway. She landed in a pocket cactus garden while a deafening boom lifted the truck in slow motion from the ground into a searing ball of flame.

Any doubt in Paul's mind about his sister's Christmas morning confession diminished as the house convulsed, rising a millimeter from its foundation, absorbing the explosion with its double adobe walls and thick wooden doors. In half a second, the house settled back into an eerie silence.

Brilliant winter stars burned over the rising smoke like needle tips in a blue-black sky. He strained to see Tess, a gray lump curled up in the blue-black shadows between a barrel cactus and a stand of cholla. Just a few bone-shattering yards, he thought, from the wreckage of Tess's little pickup, which shuddered in petals of flame and pungent smoke.

Lights went on all over the inside and outside of the house. Aunt

Xénia and Uncle Mac, second cousins Trey and Trev and their wives and kids stood in the kitchen entryway, faces reddened and somber in the firelight.

"Holy shit, are you okay?" he yelled, frozen in his tracks. Had Tess moved her head and groaned? He exhaled hard, relieved. He'd thought she was dead.

Mikka scrambled out of Paul's grasp and ran toward her mother, responding like any frightened kid. "Mama, Mama!" she cried.

Tess tried to sit up, oblivious to her brother and to Mikka, her eyes hollow with shock and confusion. She held one arm away from her body, the other frantically slapping and brushing at her side. Cactus thorns and sandy debris covered one side of her body, the other steamed with fragments that burned little holes in her polyester jacket and sweatpants.

His doubts about Tess's relationship with Harris Henry evaporated, mist on the desert wind. He dashed past Mikka, brushing clumsily at Tess. "What in the hell?" He tugged at her, not thinking of burns or internal injuries or broken bones.

Mikka whimpered again and reached for her mom. Tess eased herself back to the ground with a breathy moan and Mikka plopped down beside her, patting Tess all over, simultaneously craving and giving assurance. Tess seemed physically sound for the moment, so he didn't wait for an answer. He tore up the driveway to the garage and tried to yank the door up to look for a fire extinguisher, but the electric door refused to budge. It suddenly opened and he realized Trey or Trev had probably used an electronic opener when it rose to the glare of motion sensitive flood lights aimed at the driveway. He found a small fire extinguisher mounted near the door and he dashed from the garage to the truck, wrestling with the extinguisher's catch. The truck might blow again, who knows.

Trey and Trev ran past him and ducked inside the garage, grabbing shovels from a wall lined with tools.

"Trev, Trey, got another extinguisher?" He succeeded in dampening the fire around the truck's bed, but the cab and engine compartment still crackled in smoky flames.

Uncle Mac shouted. "There might be another extinguisher in the old dune buggy."

Trey disappeared around the back of the garage to a high, open ramada where his folks' RV and boat were parked. Paul counted the seconds, half-expecting another explosion.

Trevor foamed the fire until only stubborn little flames danced here and there in wiring and burning plastic. Putrid smoke lingered in the air. Aunt Xénia rustled around Tess in a ruffly silk bathrobe like a showy bird and Tess stood on one side of the driveway gaping at the remains of her pickup. She wouldn't let go of Mikka and wouldn't go inside. Trey and Trevor's wives, torn between gawking and behaving like polite adults, herded their kids back inside.

"My God, my God. Honey, it's cold and dark out here. Bring Mikka in. You have a burn on your cheek. Let the men handle this."

Tess shook her head as if to clear it and eased herself to her feet. "I'm okay, Aunt Xénia. I'll be all right."

Xénia insisted. "Come inside. Let Mac have a look at you. Get cleaned up. I'll make some tea."

Tess picked up Mikka in a bone-breaking embrace, her voice almost a monotone. She spoke as if she'd heard nothing that Xénia had said. "Sorry to leave you with this mess, Aunt Xénia . . . we've got to go."

Xénia's voice became shriller. "Go? It's too early . . . you can't go. You're in shock. Why, we've got to call the police!" Xénia pulled at Tess's arm.

"Xénia, half the neighborhood and the authorities will be here soon whether we call them or not," Mac warned. "I think Tess needs some help." He held his chest higher and motioned to his sons, still circling the burned-out truck. "Lads, the sand pile. Get the wee John Deere cranked up. We'll try to hide the mess. Quickly now." Paul could see in Mac the young Welsh shepherd who'd enlisted when he was underage and served with honor in a British RAF intelligence unit during World War II. He seemed to understand without being told of Tess's desire to avoid the authorities.

Paul bit his tongue and walked in circles, not knowing where to help. "Holy shit, if her pickup was parked anywhere else it might have taken out several vehicles," he said to no one in particular.

And no one answered him. While Trey and Trev started the mowing tractor that sported a grading blade used to level the dirt lane, Paul watched Mac examine with a flashlight the singed mesquite tree and huge saguaro stippled with shrapnel at one end of the semicircular drive where Tess landed in the cactus garden. "It's a puzzle, isn't it?" he said.

The pickup had exploded more upward than outward—glass and stray parts collapsed around the pickup's shattered, twisted remains in a shallow crater, a perimeter about twelve yards wide that arced beyond the paving bricks of the driveway. Some stray shrapnel had landed on Paul's car, making a few spotty scratches and burns. Looked like he was in for a new paint job, he thought.

Trey and Trev scraped debris toward the truck, eyeing Tess and Mikka curiously. Then Trev started the mini-tractor and pushed sand toward the wreckage from a humongous pile that Mac had dumped at one side of the driveway for his perennial outdoor projects—he was forever adding brick walks, garden beds, and repairing the adobe walls that coiled around the house. Trevor hefted shovelfuls of sand with an old metal snow shovel onto the wreckage. Paul shook his head to focus and began to throw sand with a garden spade he found leaning against a wall.

Mac joined Xénia at the union of a brick walkway and the driveway. Paul shot him a pleading look. Mac put his arm around Xénia and pulled her aside, talking to her in his forceful but soothing Welsh accent. Paul coaxed Mikka from Tess, who stumbled toward Mac and Xénia, spewing some almost unintelligible words in a soft, flat tone. Xénia looked incredulous, like she might bolt. Mac nodded and pressed his lips together while absorbing Tess's story. He pulled Tess to him and hugged her so tight she grunted. "I believe your story. God be with you, luv. Go now, call if you can. I'll be thinking of ways to help."

"Tess." Xénia motioned with an outstretched hand, looking for the right words. Her mouth moved like a swimmer fighting for air.

Young faces peeked around the draperies at the front windows of the house, eyes big as saucers. Who could blame them? This wasn't your typical Christmas morning.

Paul's heart still pounded as he shoveled hard and fast to stop his hands from trembling. The adrenaline began to wane with his vigorous shoveling, but his underlying anxiety still blossomed in his tight chest. Tess wasn't the only one who wanted to run.

He pierced the sand covering partially covering her truck's remains with the shovel and left it standing. He pulled at the sleeve of Tess's warm-up jacket, motioning toward his car. "We'd better get going. The law's going to show up any second."

She turned and followed without hesitation. Uncle Mac followed and shut the car door after her with an air of finality.

"My God, Paul. What if I'd taken Mikka to the truck with me?" Tess burst into tears.

After he turned the key in the ignition, he reached over and patted her arm. Still petrified, he forced himself to speak softly, no small feat for him. "Lucky girl. Hey, we've got the car seat, how handy is that?" He motioned to Mikka, sleepily chewing on a quarter of blueberry bagel in the back seat.

"Great ride, Unca Pa." Mikka's little voice cut through the tension like a bell. Tess giggled in a short hysterical burst.

He flipped on the headlights. "Where to, Madame Trouble?"

Tess tried to smile. "Thanks for the rescue. I love you, facetious brother."

He gunned the accelerator and eased down the driveway in reverse. Tess stifled a sob with her fist, reached to the floor for her shoulder bag, one that no longer existed, and sobbed harder. Paul's heart clenched at her deep pain. He handed her a tissue and she wiped hard at her eyes and nose.

"What's the Updikes' address?"

Tess stared at him. He repeated the question.

“Oh. Across town . . . Campbell and Sunrise,” she replied, her voice weary. “99144 Via Encanto, something like that. I just added the address to my phone yesterday.”

Tess fell asleep barely two miles from Picture Rocks. Her head angled back on the tan leather headrest, a tiny trickle of saliva trailing over her puffy lower lip. Over the purr of his engine, he noticed the mechanical sputter of a helicopter approaching. He cocked his neck, straining to see it through reflections on the windshield. Police. He pressed the accelerator harder, presuming the chopper headed toward Mac and Xénia’s, searching for the site of the explosion. His was one of few cars tooling around the Tucson Mountains early on Christmas morning. He hoped the helicopter wouldn’t follow them.

Paul’s respect for Tess soared along with his anxiety.

::: CHAPTER 17

TESS VAUGHN

Tess woke up with a start as Paul shut his engine off in the wide driveway of a Santa Fe-style house. Not the nicest house in the neighborhood, or the largest, but it carried the polish of a well-loved home. Tucked into a niche of the Santa Catalina foothills, its vine-shaded entry faced east. A pair of gleaming, turquoise-glazed pots sat at either side of the front door, and the matching turquoise door and window trim seemed a bit too bright for the mud-colored walls in the rising sun's unforgiving light.

It took Tess a moment to remember why she was there. One achy hip felt badly bruised and bits of metal, glass, and cactus spines adhered to her warm-up togs and exposed skin, where little blisters and burns were beginning to sting. Her eyes felt watery and raw, and her hearing was off, like her head was underwater. Adding insult to injury, her mind felt peeled raw by the foreboding dream that awakened her in the wee hours.

Mikka chortled in a singsong voice, counting the vigas supporting the house roof. Then she counted backwards, adding to Tess's apprehension that another explosion might find them when she reached zero. She hushed Mikka gently and released her from her car seat, helping her outside to the ground.

Savannah appeared at the Updikes' front door in a velvet robe of the same turquoise shade of the decorative pots and window trim. Her hair fell in little spirals around her face; even without makeup, her skin shone clear and smooth as a scoop of mocha ice cream. Tess envied those exotic high cheekbones and upturned eyes.

"Merry Christmas, what a surprise! Come in, come in. So this is your little angel." Savannah knelt to Mikka's level and extended the long, graceful fingers of one hand. Mikka extended her small hand and wrapped her fingers around Savannah's ring and pinky fingers, shaking them gravely. As their hands parted, they grinned and twinkled at each other.

"Marsh is in the kitchen fixing his famous apple-cinnamon pancakes and fresh blueberry syrup. You're right on time." When Savannah rose to her feet, she zeroed in on Tess's dishevelment.

"Tess, my God. Let's get you inside. Are you all right?"

She clenched her jaw, willing back a surge of panic. She could barely hear Savannah. Her hands began to shake and her voice wavered. "Savannah, this is my brother, Paul. I'm so sorry to bother you on Christmas morning . . ."

Paul squeezed Tess's shoulder, offering Savannah his free hand.

Savannah looked at Tess without guile, her eyes soft with compassion. "Hush." She held Paul's hand for a moment, twisting on her manicured toes to call Marshall to the door.

"Let's get you into the bathroom and out of those clothes. No more apologies."

She burst into tears, babbling like a basket case about nearly being blown to bits.

Savannah led her through heavy carved double doors, one arm draped protectively around her shoulder. "Girl, never in a million years did I expect this. What happened to you the day before yesterday was crazy enough. I should have known better than to let you go anywhere."

She whimpered and Savannah clucked with empathy through the foyer and formal living room, a cabinet of curiosities decorated in a montage of earth tones punctuated with bright splashes of modern Indian art and artifacts. Rows of katsinas, Hopi nature spirits, danced archetypically on massive bookshelves, and jewel-toned rugs and feathered ornaments flew across rough plastered walls and a mantel over a stone fireplace. She wanted to linger among the collections, to savor the textures of feather, wood, and mud, and trace her eyes along the angular geometric designs. The people who crafted these treasures were rooted to Earth, propelled and sustained by the mystical nature of their desert environment. She longed for the same stability.

Mikka headed toward the scent of pancakes with Paul close behind. Marshall was already dressed, looking almost businesslike in his plaid shirt and jeans pressed with sharp creases. Tess strained to hear his commanding but gentle voice extol the virtues of his cooking to Paul and Mikka amid the clatter of plates and kitchen utensils. Savannah led her down a long hallway into a sunny bathroom worthy of an empress. Savannah pulled a plastic first aid kit from a row of cabinets underneath a gleaming marble counter. First she daubed at Tess's cheeks with a cotton sponge soaked in peroxide, then dabbed blistered spots with a bit of aloe vera spear she plucked from a pot perched at the rim of a turquoise, cobalt, and gold-tiled jacuzzi. After that, she set to work plucking splinters of glass and metal from Tess's right side, clucking like a mother hen. Savannah dug through the first aid kit and found a cooling patch for the huge dark red and purple splotch forming along the back of Tess's right hip.

"Are you sure you feel well, Tess? Being so near an explosion might be an emergency room situation."

"I'm tired more than anything," she mumbled. "I'm worried about my hearing. My ears aren't right. My hip hurts, but I don't feel any extra pain when I walk. I'm probably good to go. Will you give me some ibuprofen or aspirin just in case? It'll keep the inflammation down."

Savannah went to rummage around the spacious master bedroom.

She came back with a small bottle of ibuprofen and a pair of jeans and a T-shirt Tess's size. "Just five more pounds to go and I'll be back in my old jeans," she joked.

If Savannah carried any extra weight, it certainly didn't show. She forced a wan smile.

Too hungry to shower, she settled for a quick sponge bath laced with more peroxide, and downed a therapeutic dose of three ibuprofen, the same she'd taken when she'd had a bad toothache once. When she and Savannah returned to the kitchen, Marshall held out steaming plates of mouth-watering pancakes dressed with dabs of yogurt, walnuts, and blueberry syrup.

"Merry Christmas, Vaughn family."

Marshall and Paul were hitting it off, judging by Paul's reasonably relaxed demeanor. He could appear inscrutably serene even when wound up like an eight-day clock.

"Yum, Marsh, I'll take some seconds on these pancakes," Paul mumbled through a full mouth. "You're the cook, man!"

Marshall passed a covered serving plate toward Paul. He locked eyes with Tess, acknowledging her pain, and gave her a thumbs-up. She felt encouraged, yet even more ragged and tired under his kind but unrelenting gaze.

Marshall's deep tropical voice pealed through the room. "Plan A—let's satisfy our nutritional requirements, then talk about plan B." He turned to Mikka. "Do you know *Deck the Halls?*"

To her surprise, Mikka nodded yes. Never much of a Christmas carol fan, she hadn't often left Mikka in daycare near the holidays when she might have learned Christmas songs. Not that she had anything against Christmas; she and Mikka spent a lot of time at home around the winter holidays. Mikka must have remembered the song from the night before, Christmas Eve.

Marsh and Mikka launched into the carol, her tiny soprano melody floating above his rolling bass harmony like a breeze over a rumbling ocean. Savannah chimed in, then Paul, and finally Tess, her voice wavering. At the last chorus of tra-la-la-la-la, Savannah held her orange juice aloft. Everyone, including Mikka, held their glass up too, toasting the glad tidings of the day.

For an instant, Tess blocked out the events that brought her there. But her apprehension crept back like an unfaithful mate. Paul gradually became quieter, too, as they finished the festive meal. She felt his distance wedge between them. He always said she was overly sensitive, projecting his own defensive nature. Her stomach gnawed at her. Worry had darkened his face and he must have second thoughts about this entanglement in a situation that might destroy his life. He'd just opened up a year ago to Jay, an award-wining gay photographer. Surely he didn't want to jeopardize the relationship—he was happier the last few months than she'd ever seen him. She reached out across the table and touched his hand. He looked at her in that soft way of his, but didn't say anything. It'll pass, she tried telling him with her eyes.

When the last delicious morsel on the table vanished, Savannah interested Mikka in a pair of ferrets the Updikes kept in their Arizona room. She had to admit the weasel-like critters were engaging, bouncing and prancing like little clowns in a huge cage crisscrossed with colorful plastic "habitrails" and sleeping hammocks.

The adults reconvened around the massive round oak table in the kitchen. Marshall opened a book of Arizona county and city maps. The name COCHISE sprawled across a rectangle of light green ink that Marshall drew his finger down. From behind that page, he pulled a sheet of typing paper with a hand-drawn map scrawled in the center. Some initials—CH—and a stylized feather stood out at the bottom right-hand corner.

She swung from her tongue-tied state to jittery and manic. Once she started to talk, it became hard to stop chattering. Her voice sounded distant and hollow in her own ears. She interrupted Marshall to describe a quick rendition of the explosive events in the wee hours.

"I'm surprised by the tire slashing . . . shocked by the violent aggression." Marshall glanced toward Mikka, still playing with the ferrets in the Arizona room, and lowered his voice. "But this attempt to kill you and Mikka—you're a hell of a lucky lady, Tess. Spirit stayed with you. I originally considered kidnapping only. I figured they wanted to snatch Mikka and wondered why they didn't just grab her from your house. Seems someone wants you both out of the picture. Did someone listen to our conversation yesterday? You might be bugged or implanted. I hope they're not catching this conversation."

"Why would they watch me, murder a woman, let me find her, try to kill me in a way that would look like an accident, harass me with a juvenile phone call, and then make a serious murder attempt that could have killed half my family? If they wanted Mikka, why not snatch her? And if they wanted me dead, wouldn't it be easier for a sniper or a drone to pick me off somewhere and be done with it? Wouldn't that be more professional?"

"It's bizarre," Marshall admitted, "but if NIHSA is involved, particularly some inner faction, well, they've done some extremely strange things. They're big on psy-ops and studying how people respond to terror. Sometimes they make deaths look like accidents or inject people with substances that give them a heart attack or cancer. I'm wondering if they're not running some sort of experiment, maybe zapping you with microwaves and running a variety of scenarios on you to provoke a particular response. Maybe they want to provoke you to do something violent."

She knew for sure why NIHSA or whoever was hassling her might be interested in Mikka, but she still didn't want to share the most special, terrifying thing about her daughter. NIHSA might also think she knew more than she did about the odd things Harris mentioned. Was NIHSA scared of her or Mikka?

Savannah looked Tess in the eye. "Tess, yesterday you asked what more 'these people' could possibly want . . . we never discussed specifics. Money, power, advantage over everyone else. I think you see now how dirty this can get . . ."

Savannah paused, either for dramatic effect or to collect her thoughts. ". . . Back in the thirties, a psychologist advocated the use of hypnosis programming for spies. His ideas led to the MKULTRA program."

She felt puzzled for a moment by her rapid change of subject. "I think I've heard of that program, but I don't remember what it did."

"You remember the novel *Manchurian Candidate*—or did you see either the old or new version of the movie?"

She smiled. "Who'd miss Denzel in anything? 'Bout a spy or soldier who didn't remember his assignments. His actions were triggered somehow."

Paul twisted his lips and looked at the ceiling, but she noticed the uneasiness underneath his disdain.

"Exactly." Marsh put his fingertips together and closed his eyes, gearing up for a long explanation. "Here's a real-life story. Some Nazis didn't get killed, captured, or disappear into South America. A few of the best and brightest Third Reich scientists ended up in the States under the wing of Operation Paper Clip. Some scientists working in the program weren't connected with the Reich, but some of the Reich's bizarre work continued, this time in experiments with hypnosis, drugs and head injuries. Eventually the CIA was born from the OSS, and experiments continued under the MKULTRA name. Their programs were connected to a variety of government agencies, hospitals, and universities."

"Isn't it normal for governments to look at some odd things in relation to defense?"

"Yes and no. These programs were particularly brutal. Some strange American characters began to get involved with the Nazi scientists. Some had ties to the Church of Satan."

"You're kidding!"

Savannah eyes turned fierce. "No. True. Documented."

"They started messing around, trying to create the perfect spy. Spies who behaved with perfect precision in the field, who would not divulge secrets if captured. Cold-blooded killers with no conscience," Marshall emphasized.

"Psychopaths?"

"Not exactly. The operatives were disoriented with drugs, with extensive physical, psychological, and sexual torture to break down their egos and cause divisions in their personalities. Then their psyches were rebuilt with new personalities. The program created "super" soldiers and spies triggered by code words. One hand didn't know what the other was doing."

"Split personalities?"

Savannah nodded. "More or less. They took healthy people and made them crazy. Turned them into mental servants whose disassociated personalities had no choice but to obey."

"Sounds like slavery, Marshall."

"The worst kind," Savannah and Marshall said together.

She glanced from Savannah to Marshall and back. "So they abducted people to do this? Who'd wanna be a lab rat like that?"

The couple shared their story in alternating narratives as they had in the restaurant the day before. "The amazing thing is, many subjects signed releases," Marshall said. "Some families were military people. The military told them they were special patriots. Survivors who went to court later revealed there was no clear disclosure about what they were in for."

"Good grief. When the experiments became abusive, why didn't they pull out?"

"Unfortunately, most subjects were children, Tess . . ." Savannah's eyes teared up as her voice trailed off.

"My God. What kind of parent would subject their child to that?"

"Again," Marshall said, "No real disclosure. Sometimes military families heard about these studies or were approached by researchers. In some cases, they were flattered by compliments about their children's intelligence and were led to believe they'd be enriched by the program. In other cases, some hard-nosed parents had a vague idea about what their kids might endure, but accepted this as service to their country. They signed releases. Sometimes the program recruited runaways; other times children were kidnapped . . ."

"How sick can you get? They'd have to keep kids for years to accomplish those objectives. They must have had more training than breaking down their minds."

"They did," Savannah said, her voice rising in anger. "Once researchers were able to control their subjects' minds, they were given the training that any CIA agent or high-caliber soldier receives. The programs were often run on weekends and school holidays, flying subjects to various bases around the country. Weapons training, flight training. The reprogrammed alter egos who performed tasks that their normal personalities wouldn't consider. Some of the best pilots were subjects scared of flying in their daily lives. Ordinary-looking girls were trained as femme fatale Mata Hari spies who drugged their victims and killed them in their beds."

"That's disgusting."

"Worse than disgusting. Some remember being molested by their trainers and passed off to other pedophiles. The abuse happened to the split personality. In those sickos' minds," Marshall added, "the beauty of the situation was that the operatives would never remember what had happened to them, theoretically. They could honestly say they knew nothing about incidents because these were either forgotten or perceived as dreams."

"Dreams are rarely honored or observed in our society . . . there's always a catch in reality, isn't there?" she said.

"The catch is that we're all psychologically geared toward survival and equilibrium," Savannah said. "Sometimes subjects rebelled years into their programs. These were deemed failures and left alone. Some were used for a time, especially the Mata Hari girls, and then abandoned as the international political climate changed. The need for a new type of soldier emerged, one good at infiltrating terrorist organizations rather than diplomatic scenes. The programs began to create subjects who could be provoked into acts of aggression. Like bombings attributed to terrorists. Perhaps school shootings . . . stuff that manipulates public fears and opinions. Considering the documented abuses of MKULTRA, our undocumented suspicions about some incidents both here and abroad aren't unbelievable . . ."

She plucked a lime peel from her teacup and worried it between her thumb and forefinger. "So, if these operatives weren't constantly reinforced by trainers, wouldn't they begin to remember?"

Marshall nodded enthusiastically. "*Exactamente.* Repressed memories sometimes return spontaneously, although some operatives received electronic implants that kept them in line temporarily."

"How long did this go on?"

"The MKULTRA program ran pretty much unimpeded from about 1953 up until 1980."

She shook her head. "That long! Amazing."

"That's not all," Savannah said. "When some CIA officials' distaste for the program spawned a memo requesting the program's termination in 1972, every MKULTRA document that could be found was destroyed with Director Richard Helm's approval in 1973. Over the next two years, Congress and a Presidential commission, the Rockefeller Commission, raked the CIA over the coals. The furor didn't die down until the late seventies. Then in 1980, five Canadians came forward and sued the United States and Canadian governments for their part in funding Dr. Ewen Cameron's work under a CIA grant at Montreal's McGill University. He took about fifty subjects and put them to sleep for several months. Then he gave them LSD and electroshock to eliminate normal behavior, put them back in sleep rooms, and attempted to reprogram them with recorded messages . . ."

"Sheesh . . ." Her eyes moistened. "How do we know if this really stopped?"

"That's the point, girlfriend." Savannah's voice softened. "Excuse me, I don't mean to be rude . . . It did and it didn't. There's always someone willing to take chances with radical research. Some programs end for good. Others resurface with different names and different players. Some high, hush-hush echelon of NIHSA is rumored to be playing around with all sorts of mind-control techniques. There are rumors they've cloned some sort of genetically-enhanced super-soldier and brought it to full maturity in a year's time."

"War slave?"

"Yes, and likely faster, stronger, and smarter than any normal human." Savannah went silent for a moment. "Anyhow, back to the past. In 1964, a gathering of the world's most powerful nations signed an agreement to restrict research experiments on children, pregnant women, fetuses, and prisoners. Our government held out until 1991."

"Savannah, that's not so long ago!"

"Revealing, isn't it? What's to stop rogue intel factions from doing anything they want in this post-9/11 world?"

"To make the proverbial long story short," Marshall said, "stuff keeps surfacing. Soldiers involved in the CIA's remote viewing programs—Sunstreak and Stargate—came out of the woodwork in the mid-1990s and wrote books and articles about their experiences. They want remote viewing and other psychic phenomena to be used for the greater good, not for warfare. New programs using improved technology keep popping up. Because of the real and the exaggerated threats of terrorism, NIHSA channels anything imaginable into espionage and warfare research. Sa'nnah and I are convinced that they're probably more interested in controlling the masses than dealing with external threats. Climate change is affecting agriculture, the economy is unstable, and more and more people are unable to make ends meet or prepare their daily bread. Unrest is stirring around the globe."

"Perhaps even more restless, understandably, as the wealthy take advantage of the situation to keep their nests lined," she said.

Savannah nodded. "We've noted there's always an especially shadowy side to an already dark agenda—if not some sort of high-level drug dealing with profits in the billions, then organized pedophilia and prostitution tied to high levels of government . . . national and international child pornography rings that service the wealthy and powerful, cater to perverted homosexual and heterosexual abusers."

Her guts turned to water. "Harris?"

Paul hadn't uttered a word during the entire conversation but glanced from Marshall to Savannah to Tess and back with discomfort written all over him.

"You'll be happy to know there's no evidence President Henry has been involved in human trafficking, but the Collins family, now that's another matter. There may be links."

"Mm-mm-mm," Savannah clucked, reached over the table and patted Paul's hand, while focusing her keen-eyed gaze at Tess. "Lord have mercy. Your baby is clearly special and they think you have information from Henry. Your life has been threatened more than once, Tess. Marsh and I think it's time you go see a good friend of ours."

"Um. I dunno. Who's that?"

Marshall cleared his throat. "Carson Hodges. His friends call him Crazy Horse. He's a Native healer."

She groaned. "I respect that, but—

"This is beginning to sound like some bad movie," Paul said, holding a level gaze at Marshall.

She glared at Paul despite her reluctance. "Don't offend our hosts. Maybe you have a better idea?"

Paul frowned at her. Marshall's face tensed with a trace of surprise. "No, no, Carson's not what you're thinking. Not a New Age fake, yet he's not entirely traditional, either. Quite a character. Mixture of Navajo and Hawaiian, if I remember correctly. After college, he roamed around with Hare Krishna folks for a bit, and then did some long Tibetan Buddhist retreats."

Tess didn't say anything. Paul raised his eyebrows and shrugged. "Sounds better than Mr. Prez," he teased. "At least when he walks all over you, he'll do it in moccasins or Birkenstocks."

"This is hardly personal," she huffed. "And I didn't exactly get stepped on in my last relationship."

Savannah put on her brightest face. "I understand your apprehension and Paul's concerns. Carson's an incredibly gentle man, Tess. He's well-respected as a seer and healer. Some of his mother's Hawaiian kin were Kahuna, and his Navajo father's great-grandmother was a much-loved traditional medicine woman. He'll help you find direction."

She groaned again. "Direction. I wanna go home."

"I thought you liked adventures," Paul said in a singsong lilt, a note of sarcasm in his voice. "Hanging out with a medicine man sounds like more fun than getting blown up."

She forgave Paul his mood swing—he had to be tired and confused too. "God, I'm exhausted. Please let me go home," she complained again.

"Well." Marshall flipped a pencil between the middle and forefinger of his right hand, tapping the table with the eraser end. "We're trying to get you home in one piece. Carson will have some good ideas about maintaining your mental and physical stability. If I were you . . ."

"Okay, okay. I'm at the mercy of the situation. Shall we call him now, or wait until tomorrow?"

Marshall and Savannah looked at each other. "You should go now," they said together. They turned to one another, smiling brightly at the coincidence.

She witnessed this complementary harmony every time she spoke with the couple and was still amazed by it. "On Christmas? I'm wrecking everyone's day . . . what about your plans?"

Savannah tried to reassure Tess with a smile. "Oh, don't worry about us . . . we spent the holidays with our families last year. We're glad you reached out. We're concerned about you and your family."

"What about your friend? I don't want to impose . . ."

"He doesn't have a phone, but he welcomes spontaneous visits. He might even be expecting us . . . you and Mikka, anyhow."

Tess wondered why Carson would expect a visit from someone he didn't know. Guess that's why they called him a seer.

Savannah gathered the map and two six-packs of bottled water from across the kitchen. "Let's put Paul's car in the garage and take ours. Marsh, would you warm the car up while I throw some clothes on?"

The Updikes and the Vaughns soon left the Catalina foothills, headed west to Interstate 10, and then south along Interstate 19. Mikka sat in the back seat between Paul and her mother, playing with a new toy. Tess leaned against Mikka's car seat, wishing she could take her baby back into the safety of her womb. Marshall started another round of Christmas carols. Mikka and Savannah were soon revved up in the holiday spirit again. Tess chimed in for a few lines and faded out. She alternately embraced and fought sleep, drifting in and out of consciousness. Paul sat in silence, staring straight ahead. He definitely had something on his mind, but she was too blitzed to question him. If he wanted to share, he'd say something.

She drifted off and suddenly came to as Marshall swung through a long, curving interstate exit. Mikka held a little hand atop hers, watching her face with grave concern. "It's okay, Mama. You like a picture?"

"Oh, Sweetie, you know I love your pictures." She reached for her bag, then realized the second time that day she didn't have one anymore. She sniffled, nearly bursting into tears.

Savannah pulled a little spiral notebook and a pen from the glove box and handed it to Mikka. "Here you are, honey. I'm anxious to see your drawings."

Mikka uncapped the pen carefully, holding her pinky aloft. Her first stroke on the paper took shape, a flattened oval. An eye emerged, or more than an eye, for the picture looked multidimensional.

"What'cha got there, Meekers?" Paul reached out and touched the pad. He shook his head and smiled. A spacecraft angled across the page, its movement traced by lines that became a face, an Indian male with hair loosened to the wind on a background of stars. The craft itself was like an open eye with a penetrating gaze that reached beyond the sheet of paper.

"You like it, Mama?"

Tess didn't answer, pulled by the sketch into a reverie.

Savannah leaned over the seat to look. Her eyes widened. "Mikka, how do you do that?"

Savannah held the sketch up for Marshall. His look of surprise caught Tess's in the rearview mirror. She looked away.

Mikka pursed her lips. "I see pictures. I put them on paper," she said, trying to translate adult concepts into words. "The paper talks to my fingers."

"Oh. I hope you'll always make your pictures," Savannah said. "Make them no matter what anyone says. They're wonderful, Mikka."

"Savannah's right, you know," Paul added. "Always follow your heart."

Marshall chimed in with a lyrical "amen." Tess wanted to add 'you were born to it,' but held her tongue. Mikka beamed. She squeezed Mikka's hand and kissed her forehead, squinting against the bright sunlight that pierced the car windows.

When she opened her eyes again, she noticed Marshall and Savannah's mental wheels turning, their faces tenser, the air thick with unasked questions. She wrapped her arms around herself and settled deeper into the cozy leather seat, drawing an imaginary physical and mental boundary of protection around herself. She fought sleep, tried to rest but stay conscious, afraid of what might happen next.

The voices of her daughter, brother, and companions gradually became soft interwoven tones at the edge of her perception. Over the next half-hour, she periodically surfaced and forced her eyes open, fatigue pulling them out of focus and closed again. Each time she seemed to drift in two worlds simultaneously. Steep jagged mountains superimposed themselves over the flat, dusty fields along State Route 191, formerly Route 666, she recalled, uncomfortable with the symbolism. The path of her vision mirrored the highway but was narrower, splayed through solid rock towering thousands of feet high on either side. She seemed to hover sans vehicle a few feet above the path. Dusk fell in that world, the shadows turning maroon then charcoal in the waning light. She'd seen such places in National Geographic—in photos of Kashmir, Bhutan, Nepal, and Tibet.

She blamed the strange episode on fatigue. It didn't make any more sense than anything else at the moment. The Updikes had talked about Egypt and her weird dream the night before seemed to be set there. Why, then, would she visualize Himalayan countryside superimposed over Arizona high desert grassland?

An unseen presence seemed to beckon her along some visionary trail. Where? And to what?

::: CHAPTER 18

CARSON HODGES

A vision of a woman fleeing something drifted into Carson Hodges's daily contemplation. The woman crept and paused like an animal pursued by a predator, cycling through postures of caution and panic. At times, the serrated blades of sun and shade spiraled through her like a pinwheel, but he noticed no other clue to her stalker's identity but the geometric patterns of light and shadow.

Instinctively, he called upon the powers of the four directions. He burned cones of temple incense and bundles of sage and sweetgrass to cleanse his own and her perception, praying also to his spirit helpers and the Buddhas and bodhisattvas to grace her with clarity.

This is what he did, always, for the people who appeared in his life.

While reflecting further upon the woman's identity and the nature of her dilemma after his prayers, he received a few more vague clues—a sense of brutal authority squatting in his heart like a cold fog, followed by a powerful feminine energy both raw and compelling.

The woman's great suffering had moved him toward this vision, no doubt. Still, it appeared only in brief wisps with little context.

Sometimes the universe gave him much more to work with. The future was never fixed, so clear outcomes were sometimes elusive, even with vivid visions. Though unclear in this case, a fluid situation seemed assured. The woman's journey seemed more important for her than the outcome, an angle suggesting great trials, much learning, and the probability of spiritual transformation.

In essence, responding in compassion was his only concern. He thought little of the visions outside his hours of contemplation and had no clue how this woman might enter his life. But he wasn't surprised when his friends Marshall and Savannah Updike pulled up his driveway on the morning of the Christ-teacher's birthday.

Carson heard the car shudder over the cattle guard first as he bent over a hay bale near the tack room at one end of the stable. Dust Devil, one of his Appaloosas, nickered gently and bobbed his head hello when Marshall's brown Jaguar sedan edged into sight.

He straightened up to observe the car. Marshall Updike sure liked his toy—the restored auto's finish glowed in the sun like a polished agate. Marsh's lovely wife Savannah sat beside him, sparkling as always. And behind Marsh, the woman of his visions. She had cut the flowing hair in the vision close to the scalp. A man resembling this woman, and a child, a bright spot of a girl, sat with her in the back seat. She was clearly special. He fixed his eyes in a quick vajra gaze to see why. The girl was surrounded by a broad oval of clear, white light edged with a rainbow, a sign someone is free of most negative karma and obstacles.

Beneath the brother's smile, Carson sensed a veil of uncertainty. His energy waffled around like Jell-O. His basic goodness shone through, but was he trustworthy? Fear caused people to stand in their own way.

This woman would call on him for help and he'd do whatever he could to assist her. Responsibility equals the ability to respond, though he didn't know in what form his response would manifest. He continually strove to understand, to "stand under" situations, opening himself to wisdom offered by Spirit, by the clarity of his natural mind.

Savannah emerged from the car first and rushed at Carson with a big bear hug. He smiled, inhaling her lemony scent as he pressed his forehead briefly to hers in the Tibetan custom. Marsh emerged from the car next, followed by the vision woman and her family.

"Hey, Marsh, maybe you'd show me how to make my horses shiny like yours," he teased. "When I go to the bank for a business loan, the man might fork over some nickels."

"Hey, you old warrior. So, you ready to open that healing center?" Marsh always urged him past his self-imposed obstacles, encouraging his abilities and the use of his land to serve people.

The two old buddies embraced. "Seems like the way to go," Carson agreed. "There's plenty of space and good energy out here. Hot spring's the icing on the cake. Still treasure my solitude, but I'm almost ready for the change."

"I met a possible investor in Tucson. Doctor interested in starting a multidisciplinary clinic. He might want to work with you."

"Awesome! Maybe it's time to roll." Carson grinned at the synchronicity.

"I'll mail his business card when we get back." Savannah hugged him again, enthusiastic about his endeavor. "If you think you'll have others hold workshops, please let us know. We'd love to come down and teach."

He glowed, thankful for the Updikes' support. "You bet!"

Marshall introduced the woman and her family. Tess and her brother Paul were solemn, not entirely at ease. The little girl bubbled without inhibition, her ginger curls bobbing in the wind with a life of their own. They walked back to the cabin for the refried beans he'd left simmering on the woodburner. Carson's sister had delivered a platter of her homemade tortillas and tamales that morning, wrapped in bright red cloth. The meal looked happy and nourishing as he laid it out on the pine plank table. He lit sage in the circle of friends and gave thanks for the meal and the holy day.

After the afternoon meal, they trailed outside to enjoy the sun and stretch their legs. Carson noticed little Mikka was a magnet for all life on the land. Her gentle, bright aura drew animals to her, the horses whinnying and stamping their hooves at the corral's edge. His Australian shepherds cavorted at her feet. Off-season butterflies and lizards appeared like magic, reveling in the unseasonably mild weather spurred by global warming, but they probably came for Mikka too. He reluctantly returned his attention to the grownups' speculation about the wisdom of bathing in the hot spring and making a bonfire afterward, a little ceremony to mark the day.

"Maybe you and Tess better figure stuff out," Marsh countered, always the cautious one. "We'd best be off, under the circumstances. Probably safer for Tess and Mikka to be alone with you."

"A good point," Savannah agreed. "Celebration may not be a good idea today."

Paul laughed, opening up for the first time. "You're contending with the Vaughn women—may the force be with you! Seriously, Carson, take good care of these girls. They're in extreme danger."

Paul's lips tightened and his face became somber. He fixed his eyes on Carson and then looked away. He picked up Mikka, hugged her, promised to visit her soon, and kissed his sister on the cheek, wishing her courage. He held his cell phone out to her. She shook her head, spoke softly and returned his hug like she might never see him again. She let go only when he pulled away. Marsh lay a hand on the Paul's shoulder.

Nearly a male twin to his sister, he had lighter eyes and hair, Carson noticed. Only his chin was different, more rounded and weaker, as if it wanted to recede from his face.

Then they stood without speaking for several moments, gazing across the land. The hills around Carson's cabin flattened into wide plains crossed with roads and fields and wrinkled back up again into purplish foothills and low mountains in the far distance. Carson eventually turned toward the cabin and everyone followed him down a different path than the one they ascended, a faint animal trail littered with rocks that cut down the slope and merged with the driveway. Paul couldn't seem to get back to the car fast enough, his long legs planted in hard, sure steps. He took his place in the back seat while Tess and the Updikes exchanged more hugs and promises to stay safe. Then Paul studied him through a back window.

The car's engine purred under Marsh's hand. Carson, Tess, and Mikka stood in the center of the drive and watched the gleaming car pull away. Tess held one arm up in a wave and the other across her chest, guarding her heart, blinking back tears. Mikka bobbed up and down between him and her mother. As the Updike's sedan quivered over the cattle guard in the last curve of the lane, Paul turned his head, green eyes fading into dark question marks while he searched Carson's face in one long, last look.

::: Chapter 19

Harris Henry

Henry hadn't walked long after leaving his cliffside perch, an hour and a half, maybe two hours. He headed first for a streambed that joined others in a web snaking down to the canyon floor. Then he followed instinct and left the sand, stumbling over rock and thistle to make his tracks harder to follow. He avoided thoughts about becoming a buzzard snack by visualizing the soul food dinner he'd celebrate with if he came out of this shit alive. Baby back ribs dripping in spicy barbecue, dense, crumbly old-fashioned corn bread dripping in butter, roasted corn on the cob, collard greens garnished with onions sautéed in butter, molasses baked beans, and mashed red potatoes with the skins still on . . .

He didn't think of beer, but of water instead: bubbling from springs, splashing from cool, deep wells, fat streams gushing from faucets, fancy bottles of spring water stacked to the sky. He could almost taste the simple purity.

He stumbled onto a road, a teeny, two-track road, but a road nonetheless. His mind buzzed in paranoid circles, wondering if it was coincidence or a direction that the Agency intended for him to take.

Maybe there was a script to this drama. Were the lizard masters of the universe still up his ass?

Henry sat on a rock at the edge of the road, trying to figure out what to do, knotting himself up in a spasm of guilt. He wasn't proud of himself. He'd done some good in the world, but he'd caved in to Agency dictates to save his own ass and protect his family more often than he wanted to admit. Whenever something big goes down in a country, a war, a financial downturn, even a natural disaster, just ask who profits, he'd always thought, but he was never allowed to state this to the public. Profit is the bottom line, he mused, and power flows down from those who stand to gain the most.

He'd sucked up to that power. Stopped illegal immigrants from signing up for health assistance because that phase of welfare reform became a popular issue, driven mostly by corporate need to cover corporate greed. Henry put more cops on the streets because the dubious, government-created war on drugs continued with a vengeance despite many states legalizing marijuana, for medicinal use or recreational use or both. Profits from the drug trade and prison construction were bigger than a pig's belly, especially in states where the real estate bubble had burst, leaving thousands of workers without jobs.

The Agency had indicated in no uncertain terms which bills to sign and which bills not to sign. He was forced to satisfy a rabidly Moral Right Congress and conservative corporate interests. They showed him how to wipe his ass or they'd surely have wiped it for him. Between the Agency's control and the Moral Right media campaign riding him about everything from politics to his personal life, he was jammed between rock and hard place.

He began to hum the opening bars of "Billy Boy" using his own lyrics. *Oh, where have you been, Henry boy, Henry boy, oh where are you now, charming Henry?*

So which way to go, literally and figuratively? Judging from the sun, fading now under a gauzy puff of clouds, the road rolled east and west. East for the rising sun. West for . . . the Western White

House . . . which resided in him at this moment, he hoped. West for heroes riding into the sunset.

He chose west. The road must be a four-wheeler by the looks of it, too narrow and too eroded for conventional vehicles. He walked alongside it on rocks and packed soil, leaving as few tracks as possible. The landscape began to vary, the dramatic spread of reddish flats bristling with tufts of dry grass and cream-colored cliffs that gave way to a voluptuous plain rich in piles of boulders and evergreen trees. Junipers or cedars, he guessed, and little pines about his height, coated with dust and craving water just like him.

Henry walked another mile or so, the road smoothing out into tire tracks from the deep ruts and holes that cut it until then. A glimpse of flashing metal startled him when he rounded a bend in the road. He edged forward. A big water tank. About fifteen feet in diameter, flanked by an unmoving windmill. Even more astounding was the pickup, a late fifties Chevy, dappled with a different color paint for each decade, chewing dust in front of a dilapidated shack.

His ticket to safety: water, shelter, and transportation. He walked toward the truck. The nicker of a horse and a soothing voice rounded the shack and startled Henry again. He scuttled sideways and ducked below the far side of the truck bed, his blistered feet begging him to stop mashing them. He caught a whiff of old dry rubber, rusty metal and fresh petroleum mingling with his rancid body odor.

The rider and his horse soon appeared in his line of vision, a lean, middle-aged man with wire-rimmed sunglasses and a generous waxed mustache not stylish since the turn of the twentieth century, except in the Middle East or in cowboy country. He rolled with the horse's easy amble as if born in the saddle, his well-worn brown felt hat riding low and easy too. The horse carried a pair of tooled leather saddle bags in front of a pair of plastic five-gallon water cans roped to the rear of the saddle.

This guy either planned to travel awhile, or was hauling a small amount of water to a specific location to camp. Henry wondered if he should ask him for help. In a split second, his gut said no. He was trying to figure out the man's intention when a pair of mules moseyed out behind the horse carrying identical water cans lashed together with yellow nylon ropes tied to their halters. They carried no other supplies.

Henry held his breath and hoped the horse and mules wouldn't notice him. He smelled like rotten garbage and horses were tattletales with keen protective instincts. He'd heard stories as a boy in Iowa about horses smart as bloodhounds. Folks didn't need a watchdog if they had a good horse.

The seconds passed like schoolboy hours. Easy Rider whistled a low tune and turned his gaze east, down the road. The noon sun arched along the southern sector of sky, bright as a smile but without its summer strength. Henry shivered at the same time the chestnut horse laid its ears back and flicked its tail in what looked like annoyance. The mules paused a bit in response to the horse, falling back to the full length of their leads. Henry exhaled lightly and held his breath again, resisting the urge to gulp air as he watched the hindquarters of the horse and mules sway away from him.

Henry crouched behind the truck until Easy Rider disappeared around a bend in the road, the rust-colored dust his convoy stirred up drifting into ghostly forms. A little dust devil spun out of one form, scouring the ground with a mind of its own until it disappeared, either losing power or feeling satisfied at what it found. Henry heard Native Americans thought these dust devils to be spirits, and he hoped the spirits weren't spying on him too.

As he stood cautiously from his crouch, his bones protesting, Henry noted the obvious—the truck had license plates. Not the standard cactus and mountain design he'd noticed in his state-by-state travels, but the copper-colored plates with red trim designating an antique vehicle.

Arizona. His wanderings now had a sense of place. He realized he hadn't been in *the* Grand Canyon, or he'd have seen a place contained by massive sheer cliffs of sandstone, even beyond the main canyon of the national park fame. Was he near Page, Arizona and the alleged underground base? Or in southwest Arizona, at the big air base with heavily guarded military secrets? If so, he knew little or nothing about either place, except that neither was heavily populated and that he could easily get lost.

As if you aren't already lost, Henry Boy.

He shuffled furtively around the shack, a one or two-room ranch outpost abandoned to the elements. The big ribbed water tank that flashed in the sun stood on a little rise behind the shack, more interesting to a thirsty man than the truck or the building. Sheltered by an old tin roof, a *ramada*, he thought they called it, which seemed to serve the dual purpose of providing shade and gathering rainwater. The rainwater must roll down the slight incline of the roof, through the eaves and into the waterspout aimed at the tank. Obviously the windmill pumped water into it too, if it worked.

When Henry reached the tank, he tapped it with his fist along the side vertically, listening to the tones it produced. The water line started about halfway down. He circled around it, looking for a foothold. The top of the tank stood about even with the bridge of his nose. He tried pulling himself up to look into it, but his strength wavered. He found a water release valve frozen with rust when he tried turning it. But a step-sized rock leaned against a ramada support post inches away. Henry stood on the rock and hung from his armpits, confronted by his reflection when he peered down into the water.

He didn't know how in the devil Easy Rider got his water from this tub. He was stuck in hell with a short spoon. But necessity is the mother of invention. He found another stone, stacked it on the first, giving his arms more leverage. Then he stepped up and slid over the edge, hanging from the tops of his thighs. He scooped up water in handfuls, avoiding the dead leaves and insects floating on top, until he couldn't stomach another drink. He hoped he wouldn't get sick from drinking too much, or from imbibing bacteria. Then, so shaky he thought he'd plunge in, he washed his face and tried to slick back his unruly hair. The icy cold water shocked some life back into him. He took a breather and leaned against the post, angling himself toward the sun.

Now for the shack. He needed to shove some food down his neck and he hoped to find something to eat inside. The dilapidated dwelling was weathered to gray wood, the back door flexing as if it might disintegrate into slivers under his hand when he pushed at it. He lifted the door by the knob and pushed it aside because it had sagged and stopped swinging long ago.

The interior of the shack was in no better shape than the exterior. The futile-looking place matched the dark mood rising from his gut. He mentally ticked off his observations to soothe his nerves. The wood frame windows, minus their glass, had been lined inside and out with plastic nailed to the frames that now fluttered aimlessly in a slight breeze. Shards of old window glass lay under the windows on tattered linoleum decayed to the tar paper base. The kitchen boasted only a short row of empty, sagging cupboards with a wide, undivided sink in the center. A hand pump mounted above the sink served as indoor plumbing. There was nothing in the open shelving cupboards but dust and rodent shit.

Henry jerked the pump handle aimlessly for a few seconds even though he'd satisfied his thirst. It spit out a papery spider carcass. He wandered into a short hallway and peeked into a doorless cubby. The room looked like an afterthought added to the kitchen; a bathroom, by the looks of it. Plumbing sized holes stared from walls and floor and a dirty cord descended forlornly from a broken light socket. The room had space for only a standing shower; the scarred walls and missing plumbing suggested it had been ripped out. Henry pictured one of those enameled metal stalls that only the most prosperous folks in the Mississippi Valley owned when he was growing up.

He found the house consisted of two main rooms, a kitchen and living area of almost equal size, both with two windows and a door. He stepped gingerly around the groaning and perforated plank floors of the living room. Light welled up from the holes, revealing the ground underneath. The place reminded him of an old farmstead near Leafy Mound, his childhood home. Scenes from his childhood began to bloom behind his eyes. Ghosts murmured in his head, the soft twang and dropped consonants he'd internalized as a baby. He followed this homely melody right back to his childhood.

Young Harris Henry rode in the tattered front seat of an old car so rusted even the floors were eaten away, watching the ground speed by like a brown river through the holes. He dangled and bounced his little feet below the bench seat, shod in worn black high-top shoes. He wanted to get down and press his face to the holes to see better, but a hand pulled him up by his thin and faded overalls and a warm voice laughed heartily at his curiosity. Daddy. They rode for a long time, it seemed, twisting and turning out of the wooded hills along the Mississippi onto a flat dusty road bordered by fields of corn and soybeans. Next, he remembered a big brass bed in a lopsided, decaying room, its massive tarnished posts and dowels gleaming dully in the late morning sunlight. To his young eyes, the bed was fit for a king. Its colorful but ragged patchwork quilt and sagging mattress dominated the small room. Someone rustled in the next room, a kitchen, he thought, which made him feel hungry and thirsty.

"Go out and play now, boy." Startled, Harris looked up at his father, who'd come from the next room, his white summer t-shirt glowing against his tanned chest.

"But Daddy—"

"You heard me." His father motioned with an open palm toward the door. "There's a tin of scratch for the chickens. You can feed them."

Dejected, he walked into in the yard of the tumble-down country shack, his stomach growling. He didn't understand being banished to the yard. A few scraggly hens wandered around, clucking softly in their throats, bobbing and pecking among patches of weeds and tall grass to find the last bits of feed he scattered about. He soon grew tired of the novelty of chasing the chickens and spied a little knothole in a plank at the side of the house. He stood on the old Crisco can filled with chicken scratch to level his eye to the hole.

He peered into the room, dimly lit by sunlight filtering through closed curtains made from old flour and feed bags. A big glass bottle, empty except for a thin band of golden liquid, sat on the floor beside a massive brass bedpost. There seemed to be a scuffle atop that big bed. A tangle of limbs and bodies, smooth brown and hairy tan, stirred against geometric patterns of faded red and yellow patchwork. A small brown breast, brown like him, flashed against a white sheet. Grunts and groans leaked through the uninsulated wall. Was Daddy okay? Harris wanted to rush to the door and help him, but thought of the butt scuffing he'd get if he didn't do as he was told stopped him.

The day got hotter, making the yard smell of vegetation and warm earth. A trickle of sweat ran down the front of his neck into his overalls. He squinched one eye shut and looked closer. His daddy's face was fused to the brown lady's face, his tongue rimming her full, rosy lips. She didn't look anything like his mama, his step-mama really. Daddy seemed overcome this lady's sleek brown body with his larger, pale one. Was he angry? What did those motions mean?

Harris's immature mind couldn't follow one topic for long. He turned away, kicked the shortening can at a wandering hen, and went to get a drink at the rusty outdoor pump. Then he noticed a garden patch rimmed with chicken wire. Maybe he could nab something to eat. Lots of people grew tomatoes and rhubarb in their kitchen gardens. He loved the prickly, tart feeling of green tomatoes and crunchy rhubarb on his tongue and hurried to find some.

Harris eventually realized the woman under Daddy was probably his real mother. His father once told him his mother died when she birthed him and then refused to talk about her when Harris was older and pried with more questions. But that day the woman watched from the window when his father backed the pick-up away. When he got home, Harris stared in the bathroom mirror at himself and the same angular lines of cheekbones and lips as the brown woman stared back. His eyes teared, thinking of this now, even though his stepmother loved him the same as his white half-brothers and half-sisters. The memory of the tangy rhubarb he'd picked that day almost moved him to tears too, a sharp reminder of his mother. He never could eat rhubarb again.

:::

But there wasn't anything tasty here. The empty shack probably sheltered hikers at times. Perhaps Easy Rider spent the night curled up inside—maybe he even owned the place. Beyond the water cans he carried, Henry had no clue what the guy might be doing. Or what he'd do himself when he found civilization. At any rate, he had no reason to stay here.

The wind picked up when he went back outside, the air slicing through a thick, audible silence. It spurred an odd thought—that he would enjoy dying like this, in open country. He imagined his spirit comforting his bereaved wife and children, telling them, "He escaped his captors and lived for a few days, nourished by rainwater and cactus, and died with the sound of the wind in his ears."

Henry scanned the yard around the shack but found nothing to carry water in, so he went to tank for one more long drink, leaning into it. He eased back down and stripped off his silk socks and scuffed wingtips. Cold water braced him, numbed his burning blisters. The haze in his mind cleared. He remembered the pickup—how could he forget? He stuffed his feet back into his filthy socks and shoes and made a beeline for the truck.

He skirted 'round the shack and stopped dead in his tracks to appraise the pickup with new eyes. In his thirsty delirium, he'd only cowered behind it. The chalky rubber tires looked iffy and the rear glass trembled in the shreds of old rubber seals. He nearly jumped for joy when he leaned through the open driver's side window. A single key on a short chain sat in the ignition switch next to a starter button. He almost rubbed his eyes in disbelief. The driver's door groaned mightily when he opened it and he couldn't scramble into the sun-rotted bench seat fast enough. It took a minute to orient himself to the clutch and gearshift—three-speed on the column—and to the weird sensation of being in the driver's seat. Senators and presidents don't get behind the wheel much.

Here it goes. He turned the key and pressed the starter button, expecting a dead battery or, from the looks of it, no battery at all. To his surprise, the engine wheezed and turned. He depressed the accelerator pedal once, like his father taught him in high school, and tried again. More wheezing. Encouraged, he jabbed the starter button once more; the engine turned again, catching this time, and it farted in little backfires until the engine smoothed out to a fairly respectable hum. Jubilation—he had wheels!

He turned the pickup around, grinding the unfamiliar gears, and congratulated himself on his lucky strike. As he settled into the drive, he grinned and parade waved to an imaginary audience lining the road—President Harris Cantrell Henry does Podunk, Arizona. He bounced along the flats for a couple of miles, until the deep ruts in the road got shallower and his cruising speed fast enough create excitement. He relished the wind in his hair. Whatever Arizona county he was in must be maintaining the road at this point, perhaps the Forest Service, for he suddenly passed a Smokey the Bear sign at the next bend.

He must be getting closer to civilization. What if he encountered a rancher or a ranger? His mind raced ahead, trying to focus upon what to do next. The road began to rise, and he slowed to take a few turns, twisting the old truck through a rocky incline dotted with twisted, red-limbed shrubs and scrubby, weather-beaten evergreen trees. But the truck's front end suddenly sank and a dull thwacking sound echoed back at him from a cliff face nearby. Startled, he pulled as far to the right as possible and hoped no other vehicle would come flying around the curve.

Shit, shit, shit. He peeled himself out of the truck. Not one flat tire but two. He'd creep along on the rims; they'd hold up in the dirt for a little while. He got behind the wheel again. The truck purred to life this time with one try. But a dry metallic sound suddenly pattered a rhythm from under the hood, increasing in intensity like a mechanical heart attack. The truck shuddered and died. Damn it, he hadn't checked the oil. Hadn't brought any water, though he couldn't fault himself for that. There wasn't anything to carry water in. The damn engine was probably hot and thrown a rod or blown a head gasket. Frantic, he tried the starter again even though he knew better. The engine wheezed once and froze.

"Goddamn it." He sputtered aloud, feeling a tizzy coming on, as Grandma Opal used to say. He wondered what his capable grandmother would do in his shoes. He pounded the steering column and blew the horn until his fist hurt, then wrenched the driver's door open, almost springing the hinges backward. The truck seemed to sag into the ground, the earth gradually sucking the vehicle into its belly. He sagged too, collapsing to his knees, arching his body to the sky, howling in frustration.

His voice filled up his head for a brief moment and then dissolved into the desert. He picked himself up and trudged down the narrow ribbon of dust, still headed west.

::: Chapter 20

Paul Vaughn

Stress sank its jagged teeth into Paul Vaughn. If something bad happened to Tess, then what would happen to him? He wanted to ask Marshall his opinion, but didn't want him thinking "what a ninny."

He might be anxious about some situations, but he certainly wasn't weak. Who wouldn't be nervous if their sister just announced that her kid's father was President of the United States, assassinated a month ago by a fruitcake, and then her truck blew up thirty minutes after her confession?

He loved his sister, truly, but she was downright weird sometimes. He was practical, more grounded than Tess. If he were her, he'd lay low, maybe leave the country. She wasn't running far enough from home, he figured. And there was nothing a good infusion of money wouldn't fix. It was only a matter of finding funds. Maybe their folks could shell out some moolah. Or maybe Tess should go to the authorities, get into a victim protection program. The Indian hocus-pocus seemed like a waste of time, though Carson did seem to exude a certain charisma and compassion. Guess it was harmless for her to hang out with Carson if it made everyone feel better. It seemed to give Tess hope.

Paul rubbed at his crotch, willing his cock to stay down. He felt attracted to the man, excited by the thought of touching him with lust or tenderness. Attractive dude, magnetic even. Blunt and angular face, soft and fierce like a wild cat. At the same time, something unfamiliar repelled him. Indian guys, blacks, Arabic types. It wasn't that he figured only white is right; his own mother was Mexican, for chrissakes. He just felt safe with the familiar. He'd dated and lived only with Anglo guys or mixed guys like himself who looked and identified as white. Hard enough to deal with his sexual orientation, let alone cross a cultural divide. But he had friends of color. Lady friends, mostly.

Hell, he didn't know why he bothered with any of this. Probably guilt over his attraction to Carson and not getting back to Jay on time.

He continued to mentally meander on the uneventful return trip to Tucson. The Updikes remained quiet too. Savannah drove and Marshall snoozed in the passenger seat after they stopped for gas and fruit drinks at a convenience store at the intersection of Highway 191 and Interstate 10. Marshall's occasional snore punctuated the soft music Savannah played from an MP3 player connected to the Jaguar's stereo system. Glad for the instrumental music and the relative silence, Paul spaced out on how many miles they'd traveled until he glanced over and the TEP power plant south of Tucson whizzed past. Traffic was light, almost nonexistent. Most people were off the streets, still celebrating Christmas.

The day seemed condensed into minutes and he wondered how time vanished like that. Soon Savannah pulled the car into the Updikes' driveway, flicked the ignition off, and turned to face him in the back seat.

"Well, here we are."

"Wow, short day," he said.

"Coming in for coffee? I'll make some sandwiches too." Savannah said in a voice soft with concern.

Paul declined her invitation, anxious to get back to Phoenix. He considered going back to Mac's to see what happened there and because Mac might have some tricks up his sleeve, but the thought of all Xénia's questions and projections exhausted him. And law enforcement might be surveilling the area. Surely Mac and Xénia would understand if he called tomorrow.

"I'd better be getting home. My partner's waiting, and I have gifts to deliver." He hoped he sounded apologetic but felt more tired and cranky than anything.

Savannah shook Marshall lightly on the shoulder. He woke to his wife's touch, rubbing his eyes and grinning a little.

"Hey honey," he yawned. Then he remembered his passenger. "Oh. Sorry, Paul. Needed that nap." He noted Paul's posture, his hand poised on the door handle. "You're going? You're welcome to spend the night. Stay long as you'd like. Need to call your family? I imagine they're plenty worried about you and Tess."

"Thanks, I've got my phone. I'll call along the way. Or let it wait until morning."

"Understandable. You have a safe trip. How about letting Sa'nnah pack some cookies for the drive?"

Paul started to put up his hand to decline, but what guy in his right mind walked away from homemade cookies? While the Updikes went inside, he fired up his BMW's engine, eased the car out of the double garage, circled the cobblestone drive to the driveway entrance, and walked back to the front door to chat with Marsh. They made small talk, watching Christmas lights in lower Tucson begin to glow and shimmer, a holiday mirage.

Savannah returned with a gallon-sized Zip-lock bag decorated with snowflakes and filled to the brim with colorful Christmas cookies. "Be safe, then, and stay in touch. Keep us posted about Tess and Mikka. We're deeply concerned."

Paul swallowed hard. "I'm glad she has someone to look after her. Hope the rest of your holiday's good."

After a quick round of hugs and handshakes, Paul beat a hasty retreat to his car before the Updikes could walk him to it. He tried to look casual as he climbed inside, gave the engine a quick rev, and pulled into the street. These were good people, but he couldn't get out of Dodge fast enough anyway. He'd had enough stress and family commitment. High time to think about other things. He put on the loudest, hardest rocking Motorhead CD in his collection and settled in for the two-hour drive home.

Soon he approached Picacho Peak, the darkest shadow in the post-dusk shadows along the highway. He noticed a helicopter cruising not far ahead, following the interstate. Then the obligatory patrol car in his rearview mirror, lights strobing, winding its way through traffic until it pulled behind its target—his BMW. He hit the steering wheel with his fist. Tess had her Picacho experience, guess he would get his.

Paul performed the obligatory pullover, slid his driver's license from his wallet, retrieved the auto registration from the center console, and rolled his window down before the officer walked to his vehicle. He watched the officer's partner in the rearview mirror, standing with one hand spread on the hood of the patrol car. When the first officer arrived at his window and looked down at him, Paul could barely see his face because of his height. Paul glanced at his wide, black belt and polished Wellington dress boots, and then the light from the patrol vehicle bouncing off his shiny identification tag: Deputy Brad Merritt, #1744.

Paul held his ID through the window. Deputy Merritt bent at the waist to address him. "Thank you, sir." He fingered Paul's license and registration thoughtfully. "Mr. Vaughn, do you know why I stopped you?"

Paul shrugged and mustered a wry little smile. "Sorry, Officer. Wasn't watching the speedometer . . . my Beemer's pretty peppy."

"In this case, we weren't monitoring your speed. We have some questions to ask you."

No shit, he thought. Obviously, they were using those damn GPS chips in newer cars to track him. Or that helicopter racing toward the Tucson Mountains had scanned his car. He wasn't so much fazed that

Deputy Merritt wanted to chat, but the emphasis on "we" didn't settle well.

The helicopter that spotted his car for ground support personnel still sputtered over the area, swinging in a lazy arc. Who else galloped around on this expedition?

"Sure. What's up?" Paul raised one eyebrow and furrowed his forehead, making an effort to look bewildered.

"Are you related to a Teresa or Tess Vaughn?"

"My sister."

Merritt nodded, his eyes glued to Paul's. "We've tried contacting her at home in Yavapai County but were unable to reach her. Would you know how to contact her?"

Paul let his jaw sag a fraction of an inch. "Is there something wrong?" His feigned ignorance and alarm didn't make much of an impression on the deputy, who patted one hand against the car roof and probably knew the answers to the questions he asked.

"We'd just like to ask her some questions."

"Questions. You seem to have lots of questions," Paul said awkwardly, tapping the gearshift knob with his right forefinger in counter rhythm to the deputy's drumming.

"Mr. Vaughn, if you'd provide us with the means to contact your sister, we'd greatly appreciate it." Deputy Merritt inclined his head toward Paul, his gaze unwavering. He patted the roof hard one time. "Follow me to the station, please." He put emphasis on the please, both softening and accentuating his command, and the expression in his eyes changed subtly from firm to firmer. "I'm working from the Arizona City substation today, but we'll head to the main—"

"Hey, wait a minute. To the station?" Paul interrupted. He tried to keep his tone calm. "Am I under arrest?"

"No, of course not, but we need a statement. We prefer doing that at the station. Of course it's your right to have an attorney present, and we can schedule this in the next few days, if you prefer."

What the hell would PCSO do if he declined right now?

As though Merritt read his mind, he reached out and touched a small mottled spot on the hood of the Beemer where the explosion had scarred it.

Paul took a deep breath and sighed. "I'd rather get this over with. I don't need a lawyer."

"Follow me, then." Merritt took a step back from his window.

Paul's cell phone emitted the first two bars of Beethoven's Ninth Symphony, his folks' ringtone. Lousy time for chitchat. He reached to the passenger seat and retrieved it from his fanny pack, eyes still glued to Deputy Merritt.

"All right. I'll follow. Mind if I answer this call?"

"It's your call. Just do it safely." Smug or not, Deputy Merritt didn't miss a cue. He turned toward his vehicle and gave his partner a thumbs-up.

Paul sighed, pressed the phone call button on the last note of the ring, and grinned, hoping to make his mood sound light. "Hello, Paul here." He dreaded their small talk, especially Dad's bumbling attempts at connecting with him. "Hey, how's the Welsh holiday?" His fake good cheer echoed into the phone's hollow electronic world. He and Dad batted pleasantries back and forth for a few seconds. He sounded oblivious, as usual, and soon passed the phone off to Mom. Why is it that mothers, even mothers of grown children, have eagle eyes and keen ears? The strain must have surfaced in his voice as he eyed the road ahead, pressing the accelerator firmly to keep up with the blue and white patrol car.

"What's the matter?" Mom whined. "Why are you going back to Phoenix on Christmas? Where's Tess and Mikka?"

They spent most Christmases with Mac and Xénia, or at either set of grandparents when they were still alive; or Mom and Dad hosted the extended family back when they still lived in Tucson. First the family had lived in the university area in the little pink adobe house where he and Tess grew up while their dad studied electronics and engineering, and later, over on the far east side, with the Rincon Mountains practically in the back yard of their sprawling ranch-style house after their dad earned a PhD and started teaching at the U of A and consulting for Raytheon. Paul wanted to get lost in the memories but couldn't deny his mother the answers to her questions. She'd given him almost anything he wanted if he'd be her confidante. Money for school, plane tickets for vacations; she was generous to a fault, but the price was telling all. Paul braced himself to give her the goods. In thirty seconds, he ran through the bare bones version of what happened early that morning, giving himself a mental pat on the shoulder for not telling her about the bombing.

"I don't understand your sister, why on earth . . ."

Relief and nausea rolled around Paul's gut. It should be Tess's story to tell, but she'd probably let it play out before she'd confide in their folks. If she ever did. They could help her, in his opinion, but Tess always played her cards close to her chest. Independent, private. She was content to let second-hand information circulate, even when it was a crock. Blithely ignored it or bitterly bitched about it, which always drove him crazy.

"I don't want you and Dad to worry . . . but I thought you'd want to know," he said weakly. "Tess has some help, but she needs more help, in my opinion."

The phone crackled while Mom said something about Mac and Xénia. "I'd better go before we lose the connection. Call me at home after you get some sleep," he shouted, easing into the freeway's right-hand lane.

He turned his music back up to high volume, trying to force his thoughts out of his head. He lagged as far behind Deputy Merritt as he dared, picturing their two-vehicle convoy edging through the desert in slow motion. They left I-10 at the Eloy exit ramp and cut due north on Highway 87 through Coolidge, then east to Florence, picking up speed on the nearly deserted highway. Every Arizonan knew Florence as the home of Arizona State Prison, a fact that gave him a brief chill. His imagination raced with thoughts of himself in an orange jumpsuit, shuffling down dreary hallways with chains around his waist and ankles.

Get a grip, Paulo. But he started to fret about getting home. He should call Jay. He picked up the phone from the passenger seat, then thought better of it. While he felt compelled to spill his guts to Mom, he hated explaining anything to Jay. Jay had the infuriating talent of twisting his insecurities into humiliation.

Too soon, the patrol car pulled into a lot behind a sturdy two-story brick building edged in white wood, maybe stone or concrete, with an elongated cupola on top. A typical small-town courthouse like many around the state. Light posts illuminated the flat, grassy lawn and a few palm trees served as the sole winter landscape motif. The two deputies exited their car, speaking to one another for a moment. The shorter, stockier man headed into the building first, and Deputy Merritt disappeared into the same entrance.

A few moments later, Merritt returned to his vehicle, and waved at him to follow. The pair jockeyed through a few more blocks of deserted streets, the pulled into the driveway of a squat and modern brick building labeled Pinal County Sheriff's Office. They parked, Merritt in a reserved employee space, and he in a row of visitor spaces opposite. He motioned Paul toward the building with a clipboard in hand. He exited his car and fell in line wordlessly behind Merritt, imitating his manly gait. They passed through sets of double doors, the first held open by Merritt for him, the second buzzing open electronically, controlled by personnel inside. At the end of a cramped waiting area, a wall of brushed stainless steel and bulletproof glass separated the public from the female receptionist, a thirtyish Hispanic woman in civilian clothes, and other employees in brown and khaki uniforms.

"Marisol, if Sheriff Little has arrived, please let him know I've returned with Mr. Vaughn."

Paul held his breath for an instant, wondering at the mention of the sheriff. The reception area door clicked, startling him, drawing his attention back to the deputy. The deputy held the door for him and led him through the group office area into an adjoining room, furnished with only a rectangular table and six chairs, two at each long side and one at each end. Fuzzy instrumental Christmas music tinkled from small black speakers mounted in two corners near the ceiling. Looming over the table on both sides were room-length windows covered in closed miniblinds, though one side was a wall between rooms and the other, an outside wall. He imagined detectives viewing his questioning from behind one-way glass, eyes narrowed in disbelief, the fingers of both hands placed together in tents of superiority.

Merritt pulled a chair out for Paul at the far end of the table, and chose a chair for himself near the outside window, glancing at the empty chair flanking him as if an invisible cohort joined him. Marisol tottered in on red suede platform shoes, dressed for the holidays, and placed a hanging file jacket on the table in front of a chair opposite Merritt. She smiled at the deputy but made no eye contact with him.

A rangy man in a civilian suit and an immaculate gray Stetson strolled in as if he owned the place. Under the hat, his shock of sandy hair was threaded with wiry gray hairs that looped out from the rest. He offered Merritt a perfunctory nod and Paul a tight smile. Paul reached out to shake his hand but the sheriff didn't offer his.

"Good evening, Mr. Vaughn, Sheriff Little. In the interest of getting back to our families this Christmas night, we'll take your statement as quick as possible. Do you mind if we record this session?"

He wanted to ask if he had a choice, but thought better of it. He wanted to get out of there fast too. Jay would be livid by now.

Marisol returned with a small voice-activated recorder and some cheap pens. Paul tapped his fingers lightly on the tabletop and studied the atomic digital clock on the wall opposite him. 6:28 p.m.

The sheriff pulled a manila folder from the brown jacket, then some forms from the folder and passed them to Merritt. Merritt asked his permission to record the session again, scribbled something on a form, and placed the recorder on the table in front of him.

Sheriff Little cleared his throat. "Mr. Vaughn, you are the brother of Teresa Renee Vaughn, a resident of Yavapai County, are you not?"

He nodded. Little reminded him to voice his answers. "Yes."

"And when was the last time you had contact with your sister?"

He hesitated for a split-second. “This morning. We spent Christmas Eve at our relatives’ home in Tucson.”

“You traveled there together?”

“Separately.”

“So you left Tucson separately, then.”

“Correct.” He resisted the urge to rearrange himself in the chair.

Deputy Merritt continued the Sheriff’s line of thought. “And your sister, she remained in Tucson or . . .”

Good they asked. If Mac and his cousins dumped enough sand over the blasted truck, maybe the authorities never figured out the exact location of the explosion. They probably wouldn’t be chasing him around if they’d found it. Any smoke from the explosion would have been hard to see in the dark and probably cleared before daylight. He bit the inside of his lip to keep from exhibiting a deceiver’s grin.

“I’m not sure. I left early Christmas morning and went to visit other friends ‘round town.” His cheeks warmed up and he hoped he wasn’t blushing.

Sheriff Little and Deputy Merritt cast a look at each other.

“So, the two of you didn’t share your holiday plans with each other? She didn’t tell you what she’d been doing lately or what her schedule was for the rest of the week?”

“Not really. She mentioned she’d been busy this week and was glad to get away for Christmas.”

Little rotated a pen thoughtfully between his forefinger and thumb. “Mr. Vaughn, we’d all like to be at home right now,” he reiterated like Paul were wasting his time. “You don’t know if your sister stayed in Tucson, headed home, or planned spending some time elsewhere this week?”

He groped for a plausible answer. “We were pretty focused on enjoying our relatives. You know how Christmas is with kids around—lots of Jingle Bells and eating cookies, lots of eggnog and wine with dinner, not as much connection among adults as at other times.”

“I see,” the sheriff said in a mechanical tone.

"I think she might have mentioned visiting friends outside of Tucson. I'm not sure."

"And where might that be?" Little's tone was neutral, but his eyes scanned Paul's.

"Umm, let me think. Patagonia . . . Tess has some friends on a ranch down there, and some around Ajo, if they haven't moved yet. I think that couple was going up north soon to teach at Hopiland." He hoped he'd get the cops off track with minimal lying. He always stretched the truth rather than subverted it—fewer problems later.

"Santa Cruz, Pima, and Coconino counties." Sheriff Little addressed Marisol, scribbling now in shorthand on a steno notebook, and Merritt, confidently penning on the department forms in all caps. "May as well add Apache County, too."

"Mr. Vaughn, I notice you haven't asked why we're questioning you." Little punctuated his remark with a tap of his pen on the table.

Oops. He reminded himself not to let his guard down. "I'm following your lead. Wanna get this done fast. I just saw Tess this morning," he backpedaled. He drew one hand across the tips of his gel-stiffened hair. "She was fine. And I asked Deputy Merritt why he asked so many questions when he pulled me over."

"So you're curious why we'd ask you these questions, huh?"

"Of course." Paul narrowed his eyes, adding the compulsory bewildered tone to his voice. "What *is* this about, anyway?"

Little appraised Paul with steely gray eyes. "Your sister may have witnessed a crime. Or a crime scene. We'd like to ask her some questions about it."

"You don't think she had anything to do with a crime, do you?" His incredulous tone was sincere. Tess's biggest crime was standing in her own way.

"At this point, we only want to talk to her."

"You have her phone number and address."

"We need current contact information."

"I'd tell you if I could." Not exactly a lie since Tess's phone blew up with her truck. He didn't have Marsh and Savannah's number memorized, and he didn't know how anyone reached Carson Hodges. Fucking smoke signals, for all he knew.

Sheriff Little flicked his tongue across his lower lip. "Her friends. Do you know any surnames, precise addresses?"

He forced a little chuckle. "Sheriff, my sister and I haven't shared any friends since we were kids. It's been awhile."

Little glanced at Merritt, his face cool with disbelief. Deputy Merritt handed him a business card. "You can reach us any time. Have your sister call us if she contacts you. Merry Christmas. Marisol will see you out."

"Merry Christmas," he replied in kind, glancing at the clock. Shit, nearly half past seven. Jay's *chones* were in a bunch by now.

A dark car pulled out of the PCSO parking lot as Paul unlocked his car, probably someone finished with a shift. He couldn't get out of Florence fast enough, breaking every speed limit along the way, knowing his chances of getting stopped again were astronomical so late on a holiday. Soon he sped along I-10 toward Phoenix, watching the glow on the horizon growing while he neared the southern suburbs.

Crap. Hope he'd done the right thing. The *best* thing. He didn't need a perjury charge. The law might help Tess, but he'd steered PCSO away from her. His conscience was clear, temporarily, anyway.

And he hadn't seriously spilled the beans to Mom, either, just ran down basics, he rationalized. Mom might keep the story to herself, worrying it to a frazzle the way she did with stuff she didn't want anyone to know. Tess would get angry, livid even, when she found out he'd spoken to Mom. She should know he considered her best interests. Even when she didn't seem to care about herself, he tried to protect her, a good older brother. The cloak and dagger stuff wouldn't help anyone in the long run.

::: Chapter 21

Tess Vaughn

Mikka and Tess strolled hand-in-hand behind Carson across the yard of his cabin, curious about his intentions.

"I'll sit outside and do my practice," he said. "You and the little one may want a shower. A nap, maybe? You'll find clean towels in the bathroom closet. My bed has fresh sheets. We'll do some spiritual work at sunset."

The man sure didn't waste any words. She understood the Native way, but did he also consider her a nuisance, not worth his energy? She searched his face for clues. He radiated a comforting aura. She simply thanked him and went inside. Gratitude was her middle name at the moment. She'd come unhinged if it weren't for the strength and kindness of her family and newfound friends.

Energized by the hot shower, she wrapped Mikka in a big blue bath towel and herself in a plaid flannel robe she found hanging behind the bathroom door. It smelled faintly of cedar and sandalwood. Apparently she and Mikka had the same nosy thought and started browsing the bedroom together, brushing the Mexican blanket curtains aside from the multi-paned window. Carson sat outside on a flagstone terrace bordering the front porch, legs folded in a half-lotus position. His dark shoulder-length braid glowed with reddish highlights and his bandana headband, blue jeans, and multicolored flannel shirt played a bright counterpoint to the traditional black meditation cushion and mat beneath him. Dappled patterns of sun and shade under a small cottonwood tree still bearing leaves fell across him like a web of dancing hearts.

Mikka pursed her lips and looked up at Tess. "We're safe a little bit," she said with rising inflection that sounded more like a question than a statement.

"Yes, sweetie. We're safe a little bit," she said, repeating the childlike statement. She let the curtains fall back into place and squatted to hold her daughter, Mikka's wet curls tickling her cheek. "Carson's working on that."

Mikka placed her forehead to her mother's and peered into her eyes. "He knows how to look, Mama."

The statement surprised her. But life was full of surprises lately. She responded with a hug and drifted toward some framed certificates hanging over a battered roll-top desk, still holding Mikka in the fluffy towel. First in line was a faded high school diploma from a high school on the Navajo reservation in New Mexico, and more impressive, a Bachelor of Arts degree in Psychology from UC Berkeley. Two certificates of completion—a healing program at a Sikh ashram on the East Coast and a three-year Buddhist monastery retreat and ngakpa ordination in India, whatever that was—hung side-by-side next to a MS degree in Counseling from the University of Arizona, tucked into shiny brass frames.

This guy did his homework and then some. She reminded herself she'd better do hers. She dressed again in Savannah's old jeans, topping them with her damaged warm-ups, and helped Mikka back into her outfit, still clean except for a trace of buttered bagel on one sleeve. Tess hoped they'd get a chance soon to pick up something else to wear and wash what they had on. She nosed around the kitchen, but didn't see a washing machine, then located the leftovers

Carson mentioned, plus some fresh homemade salsa and a gallon of organic apple juice in a 1950s style refrigerator that covered its contents in droplets of moisture. The leftover tortillas, tamales, and beans were easy to reheat on the apartment-sized range.

Carson waited for them at the weathered plank picnic table like he knew they'd arrive. He spoke to her in his spare way again, his smile kind and receptive. "After we eat, we'll start a fire and we'll look into this business, Tess."

"Thank you. And thank you for shelter, Carson. I feel good here." She kept her eyes on his, projecting sincerity. She missed her own little homestead, but the open land brought out the best in her here, as it did at home. She glanced at Mikka, twirling now in a pool of sunlight, singing songs she said she made up for the trees and sky.

"And all our relations," Carson added, referring in the Indian way to four-leggeds, the winged ones, and those that swim.

"Of course," Mikka said.

Tess smiled in spite of her effort at keeping a straight face. Carson nodded soberly at Mikka as though small children always dispensed wisdom.

Carson picked up his cushion and mat and led her and Mikka to blankets and cushions arranged at the edge of the terrace by a fire ring facing west. At one side of his mat and cushion, on a hand-woven placemat, lay sage bundled with red yarn, a braid of sweetgrass, a feather fan, a turtle shell rattle, a glossy card with some Tibetan characters on it, and some stones and crystals. A large silver coin or medallion with some vague engraving on it sat at the top of the placemat. After eyeing the objects with some curiosity, she felt embarrassed, as if she invaded Carson's privacy, and averted her eyes.

"Please sit." He motioned her toward the blankets and pillows.

She imitated his cross-legged half-lotus position. Mikka leaned against her and she ran her fingers through her baby's curls, comforting herself with their silky warmth.

"You're familiar with meditation?" Carson asked.

"Yes. I have some guided meditation tapes at home. I learned to do TM for relaxation a long time ago."

"Good." Carson paused. He stood and faced the east, prostrated three times in Buddhist fashion, then turned clockwise and bowed to the four directions, Native style. "I want you to begin by simply relaxing in clarity."

"Clarity?"

"Timeless awareness. The sky-like nature of mind. It's compared to a clear blue sky—it's a practice of lifetimes, but we all catch glimpses of it now and then. Tibetan Buddhists call it rigpa. You're familiar with the concept?"

"No, not with that term, but I understand observing the mind, allowing it to settle."

"Good. Then you know where I'm coming from." Carson lowered his eyes, relaxed his jaw, and straightened his back, placing his hands in a meditation mudra.

Mikka sat up and folded her little legs in half-lotus, imitating Carson and her mother. Her breathing was as soft and even as an experienced meditator.

Carson led Tess through some cleansing breathing exercises and the recitation of a protective mantra. "Now rest as best you can in timeless awareness."

The gaunt December sun slithered toward a line of low mountains on the horizon. She gloried in the last golden light of the afternoon and a gathering silence broken only by nature's whispers—the piercing cry of a hawk, some branches rustling in the intermittent breeze. From this, she understood the nonjudgmental peace beneath her frantic reality, what Carson described as the "true nature of mind."

Carson began chanting forcefully in a low tone. A Tibetan style, she thought, what her friend Jim used to call "chanting frogs" when she played CDs of sacred music in her cubby at the weekly paper. But Carson's words sounded Native American. He accompanied himself on a one-sided skin drum, beating it with a simple padded stick that still had bark attached. After several repetitions, he motioned for her to join him. After what seemed like limitless repetitions, she felt like the top of her head was bulging open.

"Open your eyes, Tess. Gaze beyond the tip of your nose. Watch your thoughts but don't follow them. Let them dissolve like waves in the ocean. When you see your mind's clarity and luminosity, try to rest in that state." Carson's voice resonated as though it originated inside her head.

She resisted the urge to glance at him. Mikka settled into a new position, and Tess felt her child's movement without labeling the process. Carson stopped chanting for a minute or two, and then began again, gently this time. The phrase didn't feel repetitive, even after dozens of rounds. She felt her consciousness drawn into this lengthy mantra recitation, and noted a funny movement at the crown of her head, like a budding flower unfurling its petals.

Her eyes focused on a gray stone that soon became illumined from within. A drop of sweat rolled from her temple down the side of her cheek. Her body seemed to slowly dissolve even though she could clearly see her lap and beside her, the flagstone against earth. Everything became even more radiant in the day's last golden light. There seemed to be two voices now, two Carsons, harmonically interwoven, one chanting, one directing her to take his hand, whispering at Mikka to hold the other. The same blooming sensation that she felt at the crown of her head began at her forehead, her throat, her chest and just above her navel. A mild euphoria seeped through her body. She'd experienced sensations at these chakras during meditation before, but never like this. It took every ounce of detachment she could muster not to think about it. Damn hard to remain in this radiant perfection.

"Stay with the true nature," Carson whispered.

She could hardly believe it, sitting as she was, yet lifted by a soaring sensation. There were no words to describe the bliss, the freedom, the immensity she felt in that moment. She felt no ego, no sense of "I." Tess became a label, as did Mikka and Carson. The three identities flowed and merged into a vast ocean of consciousness, the true reality.

The light became brighter and brighter and her surroundings dissolved into it until she thought, "my God, a cosmic experience." She fell back laughing and Mikka giggled too. A little white butterfly, unusual even in southern Arizona's relatively mild winters, fluttered over Mikka's head.

"Aaaah." Mikka stood and twirled in circles, her face to the sky, exuding joy.

Carson regarded the butterfly and the mirth with detachment. A hint of pleasure danced in his eyes. He took a long glance at Mikka.

"We'll have tea and watch the sunset, and then practice again."

She thought to tell him about Mikka's talents, but decided against it. Her connection to Henry was enough shared for now. She was full of questions about what she might do, but Carson had little to say except that they searched for a safe haven or an understanding of her enemy.

"Enemy." The back of her neck prickled at the term. Clearly, she was under siege, yet never in her wildest dreams had she ever imagined having enemies. It seemed negative, unspiritual even, to think of it. She told Carson so.

"You're right. In essence, there are no enemies, only misguided perceptions. Your enemy may have been your beloved friend in former lives. Our so-called enemies are also our teachers," he instructed.

"And you are my teacher, too. I'm grateful and . . ."

Carson interrupted. He leaned toward her and lay his hands lightly on her shoulders. His coffee brown eyes penetrated hers deeply. "And you are *my* teacher. I am most grateful."

Arizona delivered yet another picture postcard sunset. They watched in silence as the sky blazed with rainbow colors, fading by slow degrees to gray. Carson fetched their jackets and extra blankets from the cabin, rearranged his blanket and spiritual paraphernalia, and prepared for a campfire and tea.

At the appearance of the first star in the indigo sky, Mikka sat in her lap and recited the rhyme that Tess had so earnestly repeated in childhood. "Starlight, star bright, first star I see tonight, I wish I may, I wish I might, have the wish I wish tonight." Mikka solemnly closed her eyes.

"What are you wishing, sweetie?"

"Mama, wishes are secret," Mikka chastised.

"I know, I know, I'm just curious." She kissed the curls at the crown of Mikka's head, feeling guilt at her prying.

"I can say this, Mama. My prayer is for you."

"For me? Oh, Baby . . ." A lump formed in her throat. Mikka had never used the word prayer before.

She and Mikka were coaxed by Carson to relax with their big stoneware mugs of sweet tea and milk, watching stars "turn on," as Mikka said. When they finished tea and the sky was sprinkled with a swirl of stars, Carson squatted in front of her and Mikka, smudging them again with his sweetgrass and sage. She pretended that the smoke caused the tears in her eyes. He motioned her to the blankets to sit. Mikka curled up on her cushion and closed her eyes, wrapped tight in a coarsely woven Mexican blanket. Within seconds, her breathing quieted to a shallow whisper.

Carson leaned over and touched her arm. "We'll sit in clarity again. This time I'll ask my spirit helpers to reveal what we need to know. They may gift us with a vision or take us on a journey."

"A journey?" That sounded scary. She'd had enough journeys. "You mean a state of mind?"

"Yes. No." Carson grinned as if he anticipated something funny. "It's somewhat like astral travel in one's sleep in New Age terminology, but we'll be awake. Our bodies will be sitting here, meditating."

"But . . ."

"Clear your head of negative thoughts." His tone was imperative. "Do you have a mantra?"

"A personal mantra, no. I've chanted a few in my day. *Baba nam kevalam* is one we chanted in the first yoga class I took."

"That's a good one." Carson looked thoughtful, gazing at the sky for a moment. "We'll use *Om mani padme hung hri*. It's potent with compassion and many eons of use."

They chanted in an unhurried cadence at first, gradually gaining speed until her tongue couldn't keep up. She fell silent, and Carson switched into one of his prayers, part Tibetan, part Sanskrit, and part in the Native American tongue he used earlier. Regaining clarity seemed easy under the stars. Her mind rose on his words like wind drifting to the heavens. She'd always loved sitting under the stars in the desert and felt at peace doing so.

She found it easier to meditate at night with eyes open. Gazing past the tip of her nose, her eyes relaxed in the darkness. Her body and mind seemed lighter, readily dissolving into the clarity she'd experienced before sunset.

"Stay clear. Have courage. Follow me."

Carson's imperative touched her senses like velvet. But she found it difficult to concentrate afterward without adding to her mind's chatter. No wonder Asians called everyday consciousness the monkey mind. She kept hers busy with Carson's mantra and eventually the wild thoughts stopped. Then she felt a sensation that she imagined as floating through a long corridor or tunnel in a deep twilight, though the floor, ceiling, and sides of the place were in deep shadows. It reminded her of cruising inside a living organism, pushed forward with peristaltic waves that she could vaguely see as spiraling stripes arcing around her. Not an unpleasant feeling. She relaxed further, oblivious to possible change.

Without warning, the pulsations stopped. Carson instructed her to be aware or beware, she wasn't sure which. She started silently reciting the mantra again, hoping it ran interference with the unnecessary thoughts threatening to pull her from clarity.

Although still in meditation, she began to have the perception that she and Carson stood in an open field. Without warning, a huge brilliant form raced at them like a freight train. She resisted the urge to latch onto Carson.

"Tess, concentrate on clarity." Carson sounded stressed, his voice lowered as if talking surreptitiously. "Peace be still."

She closed her eyes, hoping the change would relax her. Suddenly the mother of all light shows began under her eyelids. A multi-limbed rose from the shimmering rainbow light like sea foam rises upon ocean waves. It uttered a powerful, gut-wrenching bass roar that vibrated in her bones.

She shuddered and watched it only for seconds before she squeezed her eyes shut tighter. She resisted the urge to rub her eyes. Somehow the scene materialized as though she were watching a film or experiencing a dream. The creature's face looked stony yet malleable, like a sculpture of tough leather. Each well-built arm tapered into long-fingered hands, talons actually. One hand held an enormous rippling snake, and something bright and round in the other, a chalice or small drum. The creature's hair gyrated wildly, standing on end and flaring up into a circle of flames surrounding its massive head. An apron of animal skins held by a waist cord circled the creature's loins, the excess cord drawn across its barrel chest and slung over one shoulder. Muscles flexed around the exposed breast, its large dark aureole punctuated by an inverted nipple and a few hairs. The gigantic being stood with one leg extended and the other forced upon a struggling animal scaled like a lizard, its double mammalian heads and four stocky legs planted upon what looked like a damp and bloody human skin.

"Carson! What the hell!" She opened her eyes and looked around. The sky arched above them like a bowl of dark crystal, the Milky Way a spattering of diamond-like points of light inside. Mikka still lay peacefully beside her. "Where . . . what's so damn funny?"

Carson burst into laughter after one look at her sputtering red face. "You look scarier than her, a Dharma protector, a good sign."

"Dharma protector? You mean one of those Asian deities? It's on our side? Holy shit, you'd think they'd be pretty but mean. She's ugly!"

Carson slapped his knee and another spurt of liquid laughter spewed from him, the most emotion he displayed thus far.

"Maybe she wouldn't dispel demons and obstacles if she was pretty."

She rolled her eyes and flung herself flat on her back. "Whew. Then everything's going to be okay?"

"In a cosmic sense. We might have experienced more. You'll have protection from higher realms."

"*In a sense.* Higher realms. Oh great, no guarantees, huh?" She knew this, but held a hand to her forehead, feigning drama, alone again.

Mikka woke with a start and flew into her arms. "Mama, buildings fell down. Cars went up in the air. People ran away."

"Hush, sweetie, it's okay."

"No, mama, big trouble. Things in the sky." Mikka's little golden face screwed up in a tearful grimace.

"Sweetie, you had a bad dream. Look, we're with Carson." She scowled at him. "My God, now she's having nightmares. This baby *doesn't* deserve it!"

He returned the most loving look she'd ever experienced. "You must listen to her. What she dreams may be more than dreams. Her involvement may be crucial."

"More than dreams?" Protective of Mikka's privacy, she pretended not to understand what he meant, someone with perceptions like his. That the world might need Mikka.

"As in psychic premonitions. You both are involved in a future that affects many."

"Carson, aren't we all . . ." She dug for words, exasperated, not wanting her little girl to suffer, to lose her childhood because of her brilliance. "We all have the capacity . . . it seems anyone who's alive right now . . ."

Carson suddenly leaned forward and tore Mikka from her arms and grabbed her by the hand. Mikka looked at her mother with wide, teary eyes. Confused and slow to react, Tess observed nothing out of the ordinary.

"Run," he urged in a tone at once calm and commanding. Mikka's arms and legs tightened, clutching at his clothing.

Her heart jumped into her throat. She wanted to ask why but she ran.

They scrambled west, away from the house, toward a dark clot of shrubs and brush that surrounded the hot springs. Just a few rocky yards from the terrace, a half-dozen figures erupted from the shadows. She gulped and held her breath. Carson eased Mikka into her arms and leapt forward, lobbing a well-aimed rock toward the aggressors. One figure, shorter than the rest, responded with a feminine yelp. Carson winced, repelled by causing pain to another human, but as the group rushed toward him, he displayed a martial arts stance. The next intruder confidently raised a handgun. Carson froze. She made a conscious effort to hold her bladder and Mikka stiffened in her arms. The other intruders raised a variety of weapons, their eyes glaring from dark ski masks. Few sounds were audible in the ensuing scuffle except the scrape of boots on the sandy path. A volley of spinning arms threw Carson to the ground, tore Mikka from her, and twisted her arms behind her back. She spit in the face of the one who bound her arms, screaming at him to stay away from Mikka. He responded by gagging her and tying her wrists together, knotting the rope in hard tugs until it burned her skin.

"Alpha One, target secured." A tall wiry man spoke into a thin smartphone-like device that glowed blue around the edges. Light skin showed through the holes of his and most of the figures' ski masks. Except for the beefiest figure, whose broad shoulders and bulging biceps pushed against the fabric of his coveralls. His skin blended into the shadow of his mask. He seemed to take an unusual interest in Tess, his eyes narrowing and boring into her as if she might vanish. Unblinking, she stared back.

"Getting an eyeful, sister?"

Her stomach turned at the sound of his smoky voice. The voice on the phone at Mac and Xénia's? His words—*did you like the ride?*—rang in her head. She struggled to breathe, her chest constricted with new fear.

"You creeps tried to kill us yesterday," she said with venom in her voice. "Why the hell are you kidnapping us now?"

He responded by yanking a rough canvas bag over her head. She presumed he did the same to Carson and Mikka. She shook with frustration that she couldn't protect her child from these thugs.

She felt something near her head, perhaps the beefy kidnapper's head. A big rough hand trailed from the ends of the bag at her shoulders down her upper arm and over one breast. She squirmed and grunted with disgust.

"Bet you'd like what I've got."

She balled her fists up, wishing she could spit in his eye.

Within moments the captives were hustled aboard a helicopter that swiftly descended and then ascended, blades cutting the dark sky with deafening malice.

Pushed and pulled by many hands, Carson and Tess boarded the craft. Tess kicked furiously at someone who shoved her by the buttocks, a move that got her ankles tied together so firmly that the bony inner knobs ground together. But she surely deserved the pain. She'd barely made any protective gestures to save Mikka, who'd taken the capture like a trooper. Mikka cried out once, kicking and lashing out at the goon who grabbed her, and now sat wedged between her and Carson like a bag of potatoes. Mikka's little body trembled as Tess leaned against her protectively, and then she relaxed in what Tess hoped was a deep and forgetful sleep. Her breath came in rapid, uneven bursts.

The chopper cut its way through the night like a hungry mechanical beast eating up the miles. Maybe a few hundred miles—they'd been in the air for what seemed like three or four hours. She nodded off several times in exhausted sleep only to wake with a start minutes later.

As she yearned to embrace sleep and yet fought it, her eyelids began to twitch. Her thoughts about their predicament careened through a spectrum of helplessness, panic, resentment, and remorse. Despite knowing how suddenly they'd been assaulted and kidnapped, she wondered why Carson hadn't guided them to the cabin to lock themselves in and call for help. Then she felt remorse for laying blame where there was none.

But one thing ate at her. Someone she loved had snitched on her. Who had tattled? And who exactly carried them through the sky?

::: Chapter 22

Paul Vaughn

Paul could see that Jay's *chones* were in a bunch when he pulled up at their condo. His spurned lover leaned against the frame of their maroon French doors, sucking furiously on a cigarette under a porch light, his body language oozing ugliness. Jay always smoked privately on the back patio with the sliding doors closed, never like this at the open front doors. They both hated the lingering scent of stale tobacco on carpets or upholstery, but the grayish haze of smoke over his head was drifting into their living room.

Paul pasted a stupid grin on his face and eased out of his car. Jay tossed his burning cigarette down on the brick entryway and mashed it underfoot, another new gesture. Finicky and meticulous, he always took butts to the kitchen sink, ran water on them, and stashed them in a baggy before tossing them in the trash. And Jay insisted they wash ashtrays with hot soapy water every day.

He launched into an apology, throwing an arm around Jay's shoulders and leaning his forehead on Jay's. But Jay's arms remained crossed against his firm abs.

"Merry Christmas, my love—"

Jay abruptly interrupted him in a tone so poisonous, Paul imagined the arrangement of poinsettias at their feet wilting in response to his anger. "Jay, Tess—"

"Oh, *Tess*, of course." Jay motioned dramatically, backing into the condo as if he'd been shoved. "Listen . . ."

He followed, swallowing hard to push down the knot rising from his gut. "*You* listen. Drop the drama queen shit."

"Drama queen?" Jay mocked. "The big T holds the copyright on drama. When the hell is she getting out of our lives?"

"Jay, I don't live in a vacuum She's my sister . . . no threat to you. She likes you. My family likes you."

"Oh, they *like* me. They like me so much I spent Christmas Day in my darkroom, trying to forget you said you'd be home early."

"Jay." He held a palm up as if to negotiate. "Tess had a major problem. I had to help out."

Jay's face flushed with anger. "Oh, she's got major problems, all right. What woman doesn't?"

Paul stared at him, trying to delay the conflict for a moment, enjoying the contrast of Jay's prematurely silver hair and his rosy cheeks. "What, like women aren't people? Get off that trip, man. You hate women because you love men? Tess is my family. And Mikka. What about her? I'm worried about her."

"I'd take that baby in a heartbeat." Jay's anger subsided for an instant. He had a thing for Mikka. "In fact, you ought to. Does she still find Mikka outside when she 'disappears?' *Freakin'* God!"

Paul resisted rolling his eyes. There were times when Tess seemed like a flaky mom, but he wasn't in the mood for dumping on her.

"Look, I've got gifts upstairs for Mel and Manny. They'll be in party mode until the cows come home. Let's change . . ."

Jay insisted upon continuing his negative spiel. "Oh, you *dance* home like nothing matters, expecting I'll put up with your shit!"

"What shit?" Paul's voice rose a couple of notches. "*You're* the one dishing out shit!"

Jay picked up a Cardin sweater from an ivory leather loveseat and tossed it at Paul's feet.

"You're *hinting* I should put this away?" He snatched the sweater from the terrazzo floor and turned to the spiral staircase. He took the steps two at a time, muttering to himself. "Why do I have to work so hard to make you happy?"

He shouldn't have voiced that thought. Jay had what he and Tess called "cat breath" ears. It seemed he could hear anything and everything within a half-mile radius.

"Ho. You *work hard* to make *me* happy?" Jay broke into the fake laughter of a B-actor, his feet pounding a staccato rhythm up the steps behind Paul.

This exchange would lead nowhere. Paul kicked a pair of boots aside from the walk-in closet doorway. The closet smelled of cedar and the stash of good weed tucked away in a mahogany box on a top shelf. He shook off his anger and tried to level his thoughts as he added the cashmere to a stack of neatly folded sweaters in a cedar cubby.

"Jay, we both work hard to make each other happy . . ."

"Let me tell *you* who works hard to make you happy! *Who's* on the street with a camera day in and day out? *Who* hangs out alone in a darkroom breathing chemicals to create just the right shots? *Who* busts their ass to get into the glossies?"

"We're not talking about *that* work." Jay's ego was wrapped up in his art. His photos won awards and some predicted the next Pulitzer for photojournalism would be his. *If* he put the reins on dabbling in the bizarre photos he shot for underground galleries from time to time. Jay alienated some of his biggest supporters of mainstream work with the shocking violence of his artsy stuff. Some of the staged photos sickened Paul. But he admired Jay's dedication to working with old-fashioned 35-millimeter film and developing his own photos.

"How we approach our passions is as much a part of a relationship as the emotional stuff." Jay's silver-blue eyes dared Paul to disagree.

"It's not supposed to be this hard."

"*Hard! You* come dancing home hours late on a holiday like nothing matters and tell me *your* life is hard?"

"*Dancing?* Who the hell is dancing? And I didn't say my life is hard. I meant we're engaged in a struggle that's not necessary."

"Oh, not necessary?" Jay mocked him in a singsong voice, backing him into a wall of shelves covered with shoes, his face lined with eerie shadows in the soft light. "You don't owe me *any* explanations?"

"I didn't say that. I'm *trying* to explain. Let's get out of the fucking closet."

Jay stepped aside, waving his arm in an exaggerated bow as Paul headed toward their king-sized bed, ornamented with the metallic-threaded brocade hangings of a medieval emperor. He tried defusing his anger by looking around the room, one so large they'd put a Christmas tree there as well as downstairs, both decorated in shimmering gold and crystal ornaments. The ornaments reflected as stars of light in the huge floor to ceiling window that looked out over the garden fountain. Jay's lavish and oversized interior decorating style was in distinct contrast with his starkly evocative black and white photos. Four shots of cross-dressing revelers in a gay club, clipped between huge sheets of wavy glass, hung on the custom-painted wall across from the bed. Paul sank down on the lush duvet cover, heavy with exhaustion. He watched Jay's reflection swirl across the photos as he approached.

Jay spread his long, elegant fingers across his hips, his eyes icing Paul. "So fill me in."

"*Anything* I say about Tess ticks you off. Let's open gifts. Or call Mel."

"No, tell me what happened. What's the *big* excuse, Paulie?"

Paul hated it when Jay called him that. "It's *not* an excuse. Someone is shadowing Tess. A not very nice someone. They blew her truck up down at Uncle Mac's."

"Oh, *good God.*" Jay tossed an arm up in disbelief. "You can't come up with something more *real* than that? I know you've got *plenty* of friends in Tucson."

"Let's cut to the chase. You're worried about Ronald. Is that it? That's a dead issue." Just saying his ex-boyfriend's name made Jay livid. He'd been totally in love and the relationship was tight until Ronald dumped him suddenly after five years for someone who looked like a weasel and pranced around in full make-up all the time.

"Ronald and the others. That *entire* plebeian crowd."

"I didn't see *any*damnbody except my family. It was Christmas Eve, for chrissakes." He hoped he didn't sound whiny.

"I suppose you'll have *Teresa* vouch for you."

"I don't need *anyone* to vouch for me. Either you believe me or you don't. The truth is the truth."

"I don't believe that's the truth." Jay's chin jutted forward, his sensuous lips twisted in a sour sneer.

"How can you *be* this jealous? Someone as good-looking as you? You're the damn *celebrity*—you've got young guys crawling all over you—*I* should be the jealous one . . ."

"So, what precipitated this *imaginary* car bombing? I watched the six o'clock news. Full of dancing sugar plums, *no* Tucson explosions."

"That's chilling." He thought of telling Jay about Tess's experience at Picacho. Too bizarre a tale, though not so bizarre that Jay wouldn't want to create a macabre photo depiction of it. "She says Mikka's father is Harris Henry."

He felt sorry the instant he blurted it out. This fact shouldn't be repeated. Not here, not anywhere.

Jay's face darkened. He picked up a heavy ornate brass lighter shaped like an Arabian lamp and juggled it from hand to hand. Paul hoped he wasn't in a throwing mood.

"Gimme a break. Anyway, who *cares* what story the bitch concocted. *You* said you'd be home on Christmas Day. *We had plans.*"

Paul bristled at Jay's harsh language, but noticed he didn't maintain his ferocious glare. "I'm *sorry*," he snapped back. "I *wanted* to be here. I had an *extreme* family emergency. I couldn't get home until now. I spent a couple of hours at a sheriff's substation in Pinal County . . ."

"Oho, the plot *thickens*." Jay's voice rose, grating on Paul's ears. Jay sneered again, but somehow his expression looked artificial. He slammed the lighter on the end table with a dull thump. At least the lighter had a felt liner underneath, or he'd snivel about dents in his cherry wood furniture tomorrow, blaming Paul for the outburst.

Paul tried another tack. Jay wanted a commitment, so he said, one he'd obviously made. Paul thought he needed visuals, so he picked up a little package—matching rings—from under the tree.

"Merry Christmas, honey." He stood to embrace Jay, but Jay snatched the gift, flung it at the tree, and stormed out of the room. A few moments later, his darkroom door slammed with a thud that rattled the photos and a six-foot square oil painting over a long occasional table at the bedroom's far end.

Paul wanted nothing more than to climb in bed and pull the covers over his head. Pooped out, his day had started way too early. But Jay wanted him to follow, so he did. Jay would lock the darkroom door and he'd end up whining outside. Jay loved domestic soap opera scenes and staged them weekly. He felt ashamed to participate.

Paul pushed the darkroom door open a few inches, expecting things to fly out at him. Nothing. He opened it a little farther and tried another route.

"Let me make it up to you, Jay. I'll be home for New Year's. Come outta there and have a glass of wine with me."

He pushed the door wide open. Jay studied a row of photos clipped on a stainless steel cord over a short countertop. His face softened, but he grasped the edge of the counter with one hand as though he had a hard time letting his snit go.

"You *think* you can make today up to me. I suppose you *might*, if you approach me the right way." Jay's eyes took on a crafty gleam.

"What the *hell* is that supposed to mean?" *Goddamn imperious shit*, he thought. Exasperation strangled what little patience he had left.

Jay slammed his fist on the counter. Paul stepped toward him, wanting only to hold Jay in his arms, to feel the stubble of Jay's day-old beard against his cheek, taste the salt of his lips. When he edged closer, lips poised to meet Jay's, he inhaled the tangy scent of photo developer and Versace cologne. But Jay mistook his affection for an act of aggression and gave him a shove that sent him flying into a file cabinet. A stack of files left on the open topmost drawer scattered to the floor.

Paul literally bit his tongue trying to restrain his bodily response. His lower lip quivered like a scared kid's. Jay had always been emotionally abusive but this was the first time he'd gone physical except to throw inanimate objects around.

Paul rubbed the back of his head and sucked his tongue, bending to pick up negative strips spilled from a file folder. "Damn, Jay. Why the hell did you do that? What's wrong with you? I'm tryin' to kiss you . . ."

"Yeah, right." Jay kicked at him, grabbing at the negatives. Paul turned around, hunching over the negative strips, trying to get a better look. On the first, one of Jay's stupid, violent art poses, a woman hung from a showerhead by her neck . . . what was vaguely familiar about the scene?

Tess. Picacho. Paul's guts turned to water. *How in the hell?*

Jay swiped at the negatives, sending them spinning across the room like leaves. *It was him.* Jay was harassing Tess. Paul spun around to confront him. "What are you doing to my sister?"

Another flash of intuition hit him in the gut. "You snuffed that woman in the campground, you slimebucket! What the hell else is in this file cabinet?" He shoved his hand into the half-open drawer, grasped something hairy and pulled it out as Jay slammed the drawer against his wrist. Paul bit his lip and yanked his arm from the cabinet. A curly gray wig dangled from his already swelling fingers. He turned and shoved his hand into the drawer again. Jay hammered at his back and tried to yank him away from the cabinet. Paul dug deeper and pulled out a glossy multipage brochure, like a sales brochure, but lined with photos of young boys and girls, most with hands tied and mouths gagged. Jay ripped it from Paul's hands and shoved him sprawling to the floor.

"What the fuck was that, Jay? Children for sale?"

Jay looked at him as if he had answers that didn't involve words. In reply, Jay brought a folded tripod crashing down on his skull. Flesh and bone flexed under the blow, and stars whirled past his eyes as his lights dimmed out.

:::CHAPTER 23

MARSHALL UPDIKE

The Christmas sojourn was right up Marshall Updike's alley but his return home from Carson's place had diminished the sense of adventure. He and Savannah would miss the challenge of sorting out Tess and Mikka's dilemma. While they prayed for a speedy resolution, the drama would continue to unfold, and they hoped to be of service again.

After a spate of holiday calls, e-mails, and instant messages to family and friends, he and Sa'nnah settled down to a late supper in front of a roaring mesquite fire in their living room. He fetched the rum and limeades that were their drink of choice ever since they'd met at a jazz club during their university days. Savannah surprised him with his favorite Philly cheesesteak sandwiches, served in skintight, low-rise hip huggers and a clingy, cleavage-revealing top.

"Red-hot mama always takes care of her man," he said, chowing down. After they finished their meal, he unzipped Savannah's jeans, tickling her chubby little belly button. The hot pink velvet push-up bra and thong panties were the point of no return and he howled prodigiously under the Christmas moon.

When the last strains of their favorite John Coltrane album faded away on the new sound system, their holiday gift to one another, the couple watched the multicolored tree lights blink and twinkle in patterns on the ceiling. Savannah rested with one leg over his, something she did every night of their marriage. Of one mind, when he stirred to get up, she stood up too. They checked doors and the security system. All lights were out except a blue twenty-five watt bulb over the back and front doors, the glow of the banked fire, and some strategically placed nightlights in various rooms. They headed for the sack. He still had enough sauce left to chase his wife around the room. When he caught her, she squealed, a not-so-innocent schoolgirl sound. Marshall pinched her firm buttocks and tweaked an ebony nipple.

"Hey, big boy, you haven't had enough?" Savannah's deep, satiny laughter filled the room, echoing from the rough-hewn beams of the high ceiling down to the Navajo rugs.

"Super-hero and his sidekicks haven't seen much action lately."

"You jest." She hung her 34 C bra from his ear.

"Truly . . . truly I do jest." He stifled a yawn. "But I'd sure 'nough be happy to spoon ya, ma'am."

Savannah winked and arranged the duvet at the foot of the bed, angling back the southwestern print sheet and intricately woven cotton blanket. "Jes' set it down there, mistah."

Happy to comply, he pantomimed a diver and jumped in. Savannah nestled beside him, tugging the covers up from the bottom of the bed. She pulled them to their chins and once again, eased one deliciously long leg over his. Thirty seconds after his head hit the cool pillow, He was out for the count.

Just as suddenly, his eyes shot open again. The darkness sliced through his mind like a box cutter. Every cell in his body buzzed. Had he heard something? Everything felt wrong. He went for the MagLite flashlight under the edge of the bed and swung. An arm slithered around his neck in a choke hold. The heavy flashlight fell from his hand in a dull thud to the floor. He strained to see in the dark. Gasped for air. Yanked opened the bedside drawer. The 38. Unloaded. Childlock, how to remove it? Bullets, how to load them? A beefy limb gripped his neck tighter. A hand shoved at his head, jarring the back of his skull to his spine with an electric shock. Another hand slammed his hand in the drawer. Bone gave way, a curious crushing sensation. Savannah? His good hand reached out for her, patted the blanket, but only felt folds of fleece empty of all but her body heat. His head filled with the sizzle of bursting bubbles. An opening appeared, a tunnel yawning wide in the dark, a dim light miles away from him.

"Marsh. Marsh, Baby."

His heart swelled with relief. He sat up, rubbed his hands over his face and along the sides of his nappy head. He'd pulled the covers askew and decorative silk and plush pillows lay scattered on the floor.

Savannah rubbed the tips of her fingers lightly along her husband's vertebrae. "Must have been quite a dream. You rolled around like an eggbeater and left me nekked, boy."

"Whoo. Too real. Do I have some subconscious anxiety, or what? Is this what Tess feels like?"

Savannah brushed her cool lips across his cheek. She retrieved their thick cotton bathrobes from the master bath, pausing at a shrine table they decorated together when they'd moved into their home. She lit the pair of tapers held in polished crystal formations, and some Nag Champa incense, repositioning a Celtic cross in a collection of ethnic crosses that covered nearly half the table.

He reached to a tier of glass shelves at his bedside and flicked on an MP3 player attached to a stereo. Soft strains of chanting nuns wafted through the room. He wrapped himself in his robe and took his place beside her on prayer cushions in front of the table.

"Heavenly Father, Mother, Protector," he prayed, "Let your grace descend upon us as our loving arms ascend to reach yours. Cradle us, Universal Spirit, with your heart of compassion. Guide us on the path of knowing your light and your love."

He turned to Savannah. A glowing, golden angel, her face turned upward, dark eyebrows like butterfly wings. Incense smoke drifted in lazy tendrils in the candlelight.

Savannah's voice was husky with sleep. "Help us, Cosmic Creator, that we may in turn help others. Remember our friends Carson, Tess, and Mikka. Walk with them; grant them Your illumination throughout their difficult journey. Please guide and protect them and all beings with Your love and compassion. Bring those who live in darkness into the light."

The couple joined their voices together. "In the name of our Elder Brother Jesus, the Christ Consciousness, Amen."

Their prayer finished, they closed their eyes in meditation, quieting themselves so that their minds might join the greater mind of God.

The muffled chime of the grandfather clock striking two from the living room broke the silence. They put on their nightwear this time and yawned their way back into the sack. It wasn't long before drowsiness overtook him again. "I love you, wife," he whispered against Savannah's shoulder. The last thing he remembered was her breath coming in soft ragged bursts, the slight movement of her body toward him, the sweet East Indian incense still lingering in the air.

What seemed like minutes later, he gained consciousness in what seemed to be another dream world. *Oh no*, he thought. Though the dream bedroom seemed peaceful and Savannah lay quietly beside him, he had a sense of impending disaster. "Recurring dreams may be a sign of deep frustration," he recited from memory, a line from one of his workshops.

This time the dream proceeded civilly. Two tall gentlemen in navy blue prodded him gently from his pillow, handling him with restraint. He barely felt the needle inserted into his thigh. He studied the surgical gloves they wore, thinking illogically that stealth required tight black leather. They wore their stocking caps tastefully, pulled skull-tight, but still reminded Marshall of the gangbangers who roamed South Tucson's parks and avenues.

He felt panic, then relief that Savannah was with him, sitting up like a goofy rag doll against their Mission-style headboard. Her angel face wore a crooked, pasted-on smile. He couldn't bear to look for long, her face further distorted by his fear and his vision, hazy and kaleidoscopic. A nightgown strap slid from her shoulder, causing her gown to ride sideways. One breast spilled from the bodice, and the soft shin-length folds of skirt gathered around her upper thighs. He wanted to touch her long, lean knees. He commanded his brain to command his arm to reach out, to no avail.

He felt pulled through time on the softest of deceptions, a fleecy, feathery euphoria. Words surged around him. Questions. Statements. Evaluations. Computations. Levitations. Precise locations. Ruminations. His friends helped him remember. Philosophy, chronology. His skull split open, its contents spilling from his cranium, eyes, ears, nose, and mouth. Savannah laughed at him gaily, one hand plucking at the paisley pattern of her nightgown. The microcosm of their bedroom inhaled and exhaled in trails of colored light. He glanced at the stealth men. They blended into the deep winter gloom of the unlit room and weren't much fun to watch.

"Ahhh," Savannah exclaimed, her eyes wide and glassy. She tossed her head back in another throaty laugh. A still graceful hand ran up and down her arm as though she tried to find herself.

The words continued. Their voices bubbled under cloudy water, sentences rising to the surface of a deep, deep pool. The stealth men's voices baritone, patronizing, beseeching, soothing. His went an octave higher, defensive, patient, explaining everything. He could help, he could make things easier.

The dream faded into oblivion. His chest rose and fell. Inhalation, exhalation, heartbeat. He sighed and rolled onto his side. Savannah lay across the foot of the bed with a pillow over her head, one bare leg dangling over the edge.

Then two hot wires pierced his eyeballs. He rubbed at a strangely cramped-up thigh. A slice of light pushed wickedly through a tiny gap between the draperies across the room. In a driveway just across the rocky wash separating their property from those down the street, an engine gunned, making his head throb. He flicked his tongue across sandpaper lips. He only had a double shot of rum in a tumbler full of limeade the night before.

Then what? Confused, he kept flashing on the words *Delta Force* and the narrow, black-rimmed eyes of a lizard.

:::Chapter 24

Tess Vaughn

The chopper coughed, staggered and dropped like a rock. Tess Vaughn's numb, exhausted heart fell with it. She regretted getting Carson mixed up in this drama and shouldered a momentary crushing devastation over her daughter's brief life. But their impending deaths might be for the best. Her tainted sense of relief grew as they plummeted to the ground—her dilemma was over.

The faint odor of burnt wiring wafted into the cargo area. Somehow, through the clatter of the struggling rotors, loud curses spewed from the cockpit. The crew's muffled attempt to stabilize the plummeting bird seeped through its noisy descent. Someone pounded on a window, a lonely, desperate, hollow sound she felt in her chest. By the thrashing sound that followed, she imagined the pounder trying to bail out, scrambling like an animal that clawed its way to safety.

Bound, gagged, and tossed around like cargo, she and Carson could do nothing except surrender to the process. Mikka scrambled in the air toward her. Carson positioned himself as a cushion between the craft and Mikka.

When Tess came to, dazed, poignancy clung to her like a wet membrane. She thought she must be dead, ripped from the physical plane to the after-death world, even though she seemed to be consciously thinking. She couldn't see anything with her head covered, but she "saw" Carson's as well as her own body in a hazy, dream-like light below her, simultaneously feeling herself floating around and slumped against a hard surface. But where was Mikka?

When Tess stirred, the pain shooting through her rib cage and into her right hip brought her back. She sagged back to the hard surface, gagging to force vomit back down her throat because the canvas bag over her head would channel it down her chin and into her lap. She gagged a second time and heard Carson talking to her as though he shouted through a wall.

"Tess! Tess, can you hear me?" Carson stood over her and removed the bag from her head, sawing at the bindings with a military knife, a medium-length blade with a stainless steel grip. An ominous dark streak stained the sharp edge. He eased her into an upright position, mopped her face with a mechanic's rag, and propped something behind her back.

She squinted at Carson, trying to bring his features into focus. She looked around for Mikka. Her heart slammed against her breast bone. Where was she? "Oh, God," she moaned, her voice rising an octave.

Carson stared back with sad eyes and reached for her with outstretched arms.

"My God, no!" She struggled to stand, but Carson held her down. She balled her hands into fists and pummeled his back, her face contorting in a wet fury. She'd done everything a mother could to protect her child. Almost. Better than most. *Where is she?*

"Mama?" Mikka suddenly sat at their feet, holding the canvas bag that had covered her head. Tear tracks lined her soiled cheeks. She lunged for Mikka, clucking in distress, examining every inch of her little body like a first-time mother with a newborn baby.

Carson looked toward the sound of Mikka's voice, then at her, his dark eyes wide with surprise.

Tess exhaled hard, swallowing back bile. “Mikka disappears. Rearranges her molecules somehow . . .” She thought of something that made her brighten. Mikka had disappeared the same way she had at home, but this time the act may have saved her life. Maybe even Carson’s and hers too.

Carson gazed hard at Mikka, nearly looking through her. Perhaps he perceived some energy around her, an aura. Satisfied with something she couldn’t see, he grunted softly. Then he took another long look at her child.

“Whew—I thought the worst. Mikka’s not a child of the Earth. She’s a child of the stars . . . I’ve heard some old tales, but this is my first encounter.”

Wild grief rose in her chest again. She hugged Mikka harder, intrigued by Carson’s remark, yet not wanting to know more, not now. “Please. Don’t tell anyone.”

Carson gazed at Mikka again and shook his head. Tess knew he understood.

Mikka examined Tess in return, noticing her mother wince at her weight against her thighs. “Mama, are you broken? Here’s a fix-it kiss,” she crooned, using her mother’s expression of comfort. The toddler kissed her cheek as Carson held the medical kit cold pack to the back of Mikka’s head.

“She has a pretty good egg on her head despite her transformation,” Carson reported matter-of-factly.

“Egg? Oh, bump . . . is your head okay, Sweetie . . . how did you untie yourself, Carson?”

“With a prayer and some concentration. I used a piece of debris, then found the knife on one of the men . . . do you want a weapon? There’s plenty of ‘em. We could use one . . . but I’m thinking bad karma. Firearms may draw more violence.”

Carson’s calm voice was a salve to her spirit. She squeezed Mikka’s hand gingerly and raised the other to Carson in a weak high-five. “I’m so glad you said that. Maybe it’s crazy—I can’t stand the sight of guns.”

"You sure? I'd hate to get into a position where we need one. Maybe I'm too much a pacifist."

She groaned again, rubbing at her hip. "If we live by them, we'll die by them, pure and simple."

"Then let's rely on our good merit to see us through."

She tried to smile, but even her face felt sore and lopsided. "This is good merit? How come we're so lucky?"

"Friendly trees." Mikka shook the juniper branch that poked through a hole in the fuselage.

Tess looked toward the hole with crossed eyes in the hopes of hearing Mikka's pure, melodic laughter.

"Mikka's so right. By the grace of our protectors and the Standing Ones." Carson's expression was deadly serious, but his eyes radiated kindness and serenity like he sat in a temple rather than a helicopter wreck. He picked up one of the big Zip-lock bags strewn around like so many dirty pillows. "And a little help from our friends."

"What's that?" she murmured, too shaken to hazard a guess.

Carson slit the tape wrapped around one of the bags and tugged it open. "Looks like marketable cargo. If I'm not mistaken, some mighty pure rock."

"Cocaine?

"Yeah. Piled up under the tarp in the tail. We were leaning against a pile of bags."

"Geez. Traffickers?"

"Loaded to the gills. I don't have a good feeling about this. Somebody will home in on this stuff."

"Can we get out of here?"

"We can. Let's make sure you're okay first. I'm worried about internal injuries. Whiplash, concussions—we're all banged up."

They sat staring at one another for a few more moments, the shock and enormity of the situation washing over them. They'd sprawled out, not on the floor of the chopper, but the wall of one side, with the tail tipped above them. The smashed cockpit area sat below, jagged shards of metal and glass pushed menacingly into the front seats. The cockpit had come to rest in a group of jagged boulders. She glimpsed a bloody hand dangling from a torn sleeve where the pilot sat. Another form lay behind the seats, covered by a tarp Carson presumably placed. Two canteens, field glasses, rappelling rope, and a small pack lay piled near the body. She guessed Carson had already harvested stuff worth taking. A hole next to the hatch above their heads in the copter's roof reminded her of a tin can ripped open. The hatch door extended like a broken wing. Beyond it, the sky brightened to light gray, the stars vanishing one by one.

"What happened to the others?" she asked.

"Dead, outside." Carson spoke softly to prevent Mikka from hearing. "Funny, two of them look like twins. Blond as blond can be. Tall handsome rascals. I think maybe some of our captors may have stayed on the ground at my place when they put us aboard."

"I think the one you accidentally bopped with a rock was a woman." She thought again of the big beefy guy, the dark one with the familiar voice. Her relief at being alive warmed into anger. She hoped he was dead, burning in hell.

"Ready?"

"Ready as I'll ever be." She winced with pain. "Let's get out of this thing."

Carson pulled her up gently, his arm around her waist. "How does it feel? Anything out of place?"

A surge of pain flooded her already aching hip. She wasn't sure why she felt like hiding it from Carson. Mikka imitated Carson from her other side, uttering little grunts in an effort to support her mama. They stood for a few moments until certain Tess would stay vertical. Carson squatted on one knee, and gave her an old-fashioned boost. She stepped on his thigh, rattled by feeling like a hollow wooden puppet with limbs in segments, pulled this way and that by strings.

"Okay, now what?"

"I checked the way out. Watch where you put your hands and feet—don't cut yourself. There's only one way to step down. Get out on the skid, and then I'll give Mikka to you."

"Careful, Mama. I'll be right out," Mikka reassured her.

"Okay. I'm okay. I'm okay," she repeated like a mantra while she squeezed through the hole in the craft. Carson's statement about internal injuries worried her. "Are you sure we're okay? Do we have internal injuries?"

Carson raised his voice so she could hear him. "Intuition tells me we'd know by now. I'm not a conventional medical person, but I'm sure we'd feel weak or even collapse."

"Okay. I'm okay." She found a secure handhold by grasping the cable of the door, catching her breath as she brushed past the cable and stretched her good leg down to a brace that secured the helicopter's landing skid to its bottom. But her injured hip ached with a new stabbing pain, her weight caused the craft to shift slightly, and she responded to the grating sound with a panicked screech.

"Steady, Tess, steady." Carson pulled himself up through the hole and looked down at her with concern. "I think we're lodged in pretty well. Our friends up front came to rest on a pile of boulders. The junipers are holding the fuselage up."

She looked down. The distance to the ground was no more than her height. She held her hand to her heart and exhaled forcefully, puffing her cheeks out. "Sorry, I'm okay." She paused and repeated herself. "Okay. Help Mikka up, I'm ready for her."

Tess brushed her hand across the dull black finish of the helicopter's exterior. There were no markings, no identification numbers. Her eyes darted around the scene. The chopper's rotor sported only ragged stubs of blades. Shards of glass and small bits of metal littered the ground. A trail of blood streamed onto the ground where the cockpit met the rocks. She looked away.

"Carson."

"Yes."

"Who *are* these people? Government?"

"Definitely looks it. The chopper's a Blackhawk. Military, I suspect. Druggies wouldn't mess with you unless you're involved with them. Who else would grab you?"

"Question of the year," she said in a flat tone.

"I looked for ID and didn't find even a toothbrush," he explained. "These guys were traveling light. Looks like they planned on crashing at the Marriott tonight."

She appreciated the pun. "Then besides messing with me, they're doing some Oliver North thing?"

Carson grunted thoughtfully, studying the side of the chopper. "I hadn't thought about that in years. The Iran-Contra affair. Yeah. Guess that was probably the tip of the proverbial iceberg. I've heard there's billions of dollars still being laundered into the U.S. economy. NIHSA and the Collins family allegedly run drugs . . . That family got richer faster than any mortal humans should. Hardly anyone understood all the convoluted connections until the Forrest book came out. Maybe this is proof . . ."

Tess didn't reply. She admired Drew Forrest, but even though she had her own career as an investigative journalist, she'd avoided reading his book. His topics scared her and it seemed just a matter of when, not if, he was silenced. His death came as no surprise, a hazy counterpoint to the larger drama of Henry's disappearance.

Carson gazed around. "If this is a government operation, you'd think they'd use civilian craft as a cover. Mighty bold, using a military bird."

"A group of rogue agents?" She remembered Harris talking about the Collins family. He felt they were out to get him. Their eyes locked, the gravity of their situation hitting home. "Carson?"

"Yes?"

"This sounds stupid right now—thank you for being a good friend."

"My pleasure. And thank *you*." He disappeared back into the hole.

She raised her voice. "For what? I've wrecked your holiday."

"Upsy daisy." Carson grunted as he picked Mikka up and eased her outside the torn doorway. "You haven't wrecked anything. I was a little bored yesterday, to tell you the truth. This is a lot more fun." An appreciative chuckle bubbled up from deep in his chest.

Tess didn't respond to Carson's humor as Mikka wrapped her legs around her waist. She steadied herself with one arm, gingerly stepping from one skid to the other. "Honey, Mama's going to put you on the rock. Stretch your legs down. There you go, Mik."

Mikka's little sneakers scuffed the boulder lightly, her curls glistening and quivering in the sun and wind. She turned her face up toward Tess, and then gazed back across the valley. A wide canyon rimmed on three sides with buff and vermillion cliffs like steep crowns. Pretty, but scenery was the last thing Tess cared about. What she wanted more than anything was to propel her butt to bed.

"Like home." Mikka spoke matter-of-factly. "Big snow mountains."

Tess and Carson glanced at one another.

What was Mikka talking about? Then she remembered her vision on the way to Carson's. Were these mountains where Mikka went when she disappeared?

"Meeks, do you go to the 'snow mountains?' When you . . . go away," she said, stunned she'd never thought to ask before.

Carson cocked his head, ready for her answer.

Mikka took her mother's hand with a serene smile. "Yes," she simply said.

Tess wanted to ask another question, but was distracted by the familiar country. Were they really back home in Yavapai County? She stood and sniffed the air, trying to get her bearings, her jaw involuntarily stiffening in response to the pain in her hip. "Looks like home. You know as well as I do that there's a hundred and one places like this in the Southwest. Northern Arizona, southern Arizona." She hobbled through a 360-degree turn, scanning the landscape and her memory. A name popped into her head, one she associated with a pleasant day hike and stories from a friend who often camped there. "Manzanita Canyon? I don't believe it."

"You know it, then?" Carson's eyes brightened. Mikka beamed.

"I hiked there just once, the area around it. Not inside the canyon itself."

"So, it was like this? Carson pulled at his chin with thumb and forefinger.

"Country sure looks the same. I hiked the road connected to the canyon's trailhead. Got rough toward the end and I didn't have time to walk the seven or eight miles into the canyon and back to my truck. There's water—a creek in the canyon."

"Then if we head northwest, we're aiming for your place? We could backtrack and get water in the canyon, but we'd still be without supplies."

Tess almost choked with the exertion of speaking. Words seemed to bunch up behind her teeth as if she couldn't share them fast enough. "There's a cabin out there, just before the road gets bad. My little truck isn't four-wheel drive, so I parked it near the cabin. The road intersects with the trailhead a couple of miles from the cabin. I hiked those with Mikka on my back. There's a sign-in sheet at the trailhead gate. You know, a form they keep in a wooden box, so the Forest Service knows when people are out there."

Carson quizzed her with his eyes. "You're mighty talkative for someone who just fell from the sky."

"Nerves. Guess I'm a little hyper." She rubbed at her hip again, Mikka's affirmation about visiting "snow mountains" temporarily forgotten.

"How far from your place?"

"Oh, a good ways. About fifty miles, a little more. Maybe forty as the crow flies."

"We might head toward your house and hope we find water on the way. It's not safe, but neither is wandering around out here."

We're beyond safety, she thought. It would take a miracle to avoid being tracked from the air. "Let's get out of here."

"My feeling too, Tess. We can try to find something to eat, regroup, and decide what to do next. It may be a few hours before the wreck is located."

"If our buddies in blue already know about it, they'll presume us dead . . ." Hope perked her up.

Carson looked hopeful, too. "By the time they arrive to secure the crash site, we're long gone."

Mikka suddenly lost her smile. "I'm hungry." Her little voice cut through the conversation, more like a bell than a whine.

Tess felt helpless and angry knowing there was little she could give her daughter.

"These guys had water, but this roll of mints is *it* as far as food goes." Carson offered Mikka a wintergreen lifesaver with one hand and a sports bottle with the other. "Suck it slowly, Mik. And have a little drink of water."

She nodded, accepting the meager offering.

"I'll see if I can catch a rabbit, little one. I was good at it when I was a kid. First we have to get away from here."

Mikka wrinkled her nose but didn't reply.

They gathered the gear, their backs to the watercolor sunrise display—the sky tinted violet, then pink. They headed into the wilderness of barren, grassy basins and rocky mounds. If it were summer, Tess thought, they would have encountered scorpions, rattlesnakes, cougars and coyotes, but the creatures had withdrawn into the ground or the shelter of caves and canyons for the winter. They'd probably see only an occasional rabbit like Carson mentioned, a raven or hawk, maybe pronghorns if they roamed this area.

Tess found if she leaned most of her weight upon her left leg, it minimized the pain in her hip. They walked at a slow pace for two or three miles, then her body protested. "Exhausted. Need to rest, Carson. I'm sorry."

"Don't be. Let's go up around those boulders." He faced south and motioned toward a cluster of hills covered with big boulders at their base, just a few hundred yards away. He squatted down, positioned Mikka on his back, and ambled toward the boulders. Shuffling through the light brush behind him, Tess kicked up some fine dust that made them all sneeze. More misery.

"You okay?" Carson asked.

She shrugged and apologized with her eyes. "Just the dust."

"We'll rest here," Carson assured her. "I'll look for game. We'll feel better after we eat."

"We're so close to the helicopter, though."

"But not right on top of it. We won't stay long. We can chance it."

"Don't worry, be happy, huh?" She managed a thin smile. "Funny thing, after that hike I told you about, I dreamed bin Rashid rode up in a jeep and asked me for directions."

Carson grunted. "Reality is dreamlike and dreams mirror reality. Have courage, Tess."

:::Chapter 25

Carson Hodges

Tess held Mikka so close they looked like neither could breathe. Carson studied Tess's face, considering the panic her heart must hold. Even under these conditions—and with the pain she thought she hid from him—her magnetic sensuality shone through. She stripped off her gray sweat pants and wrapped them around her shoulders over her matching hoody sweatshirt. Her torn blue jeans fit like a second skin, revealing a slender waist and gently rounded hips that tapered into long, firm thighs.

Tess winced with pain and his heart opened in compassion. It must be difficult for her to avoid attachment and aversion in her condition. Who wouldn't feel panic in her shoes? He didn't share her panic, though. A sense of urgency, yes, but no personal panic. He was committed to putting one foot in front of the other, living in the moment. A good practice at any time, but in the midst of a crisis like this one, essential.

Tess and Mikka curled up on the tarp he'd salvaged, soon falling into a deep sleep. They insisted upon lying with their faces turned upward against his advice to protect themselves from sunburn. Tess and Mikka craved light. After a few minutes, their fair cheeks were warmed red in the high desert altitude. They'd soon have serious burns. He propped his jacket on a frame of sticks supported by fist-sized rocks to shade their faces.

He felt torn for a moment between doing a meditation practice and finding food. He wanted to maintain his balance but their need for nourishment was critical. He settled on a compromise. A short practice, then walkabout.

He was fortunate in the hunt. Doubly fortunate because he had only the hunting knife and stones for weapons. Soon after his brief prayers, a little cottontail appeared from the brush to give itself up. Within minutes, he'd skinned the rabbit and built a little fire against his better judgment—raw meat wouldn't be palatable for the ladies. He passed the cottontail to the four directions, wishing it a better rebirth, grateful it had surrendered its life.

He ate a portion of the stringiest muscle meat and saved the tender parts for Tess and Mikka. He debated about waking them, but the cooking smells brought Tess back. She sat up, rolled her eyes skyward and arched her back, her fingers stretched high above her head.

"It's good you stretch when you wake up. It realigns the body," he said.

"Feels good. Must know it instinctively. My vertebrae always pop." Tess yawned. "Wow, what smells so good?"

"Rabbit."

"I'd love to see you hunting, Carson—Indian brave prowling the desert scrub . . ."

He put a bent finger over his crown to indicate a feather and mimed a stalking hunter. "When we were kids, my brothers and I used to catch rabbits for fun."

"By hand?" Tess wolfed down the meat he cut for her. "That's amazing."

"We were young and limber. It doesn't take too long to wear a rabbit out if you keep them running in the open."

"I didn't know that. Boy stuff, I mean. Mmm, this is good. Super good," she said, mumbling with her mouth full.

"Food's always better when you're camping."

Tess flashed a megawatt smile and winked at him.

"What?"

"You joked, Carson. The first time I've heard you crack a joke."

He blushed. He didn't mean to attract that much attention. "The second time," he teased. "You ignored my crashing at the Marriott joke."

"I loved that one, too! Guess I was too preoccupied to tell you. Two jokes in one day—how cool is that?"

Tess obviously enjoyed his funny bone and he blushed again.

Something skittered through the underbrush. They startled and Mikka woke up, crying out for her mother. Probably another rabbit or woodrat, maybe a lizard. Simultaneously, the sun disappeared for a moment under the only cloud in the sky. It was nothing, or was it? He took even small signs seriously.

He watched Tess rocking Mikka in her lap, offering her meat and studying her face when she thought he wasn't looking. Clearly she trusted his judgment and looked to him for decisions. He asked Spirit for the strength to respond to her trust.

"I think it may be best to move. I'm not sure." He didn't care for his own uncertainty. "I hope you're up to it."

"I'm bushed . . . but we'd better take advantage of the daylight. Might get hellish wandering around at night. The wind's getting colder." Tess sounded more at ease, but her face looked somber again and she gathered Mikka into her arms as if she wanted to draw the girl into her bones.

They extinguished the fire, covering it with dirt, then brushed away their tracks and resumed the journey. Mikka's energy increased after her nap and meal. She zoomed ahead of the adults, marching and swinging her arms, reciting a preschool song in a high, sweet voice. "Stop pickin' up field mice and bopping 'em on the head," she scolded imaginary rabbits.

A brushy, skittering noise ahead interrupted her joy. She altered her course abruptly, turning around, her little legs pumping like pistons.

Tess panicked at Mikka's panic, stampeding after her. "Mikka, what happened? What are you doing?"

"Cows!"

Carson grinned from ear to ear. "Cows," he chortled, looking around. He didn't see any.

"She thinks cows will charge at her," Tess explained. "She always runs when she sees cows opposite our fence on state land."

A second skittering sound sent Mikka flying in another direction. He turned toward the sound to see a ragged piece of cardboard box scooting along the ground.

"Was it more cows, Mama?" Mikka frowned from Tess's arms into the twilight.

"The worst." He arched his arms over his head, making giant horns. "Ghost cows!"

Mikka regarded him with eyes narrowed, her face screwed up tight. He meant to make her laugh and scolded himself for his insensitivity. She brightened suddenly with a huge grin that spread from ear to ear. Her arms shot over her head.

"Moo-ooo," Mikka lowed at him. She wriggled out of Tess's arms, pawing at the ground and mooing to the sky in imitation of a fearsome bull.

"Good mooove, Carson," Tess punned.

Mikka giggled with delight, and pawed the ground again. He pawed back. Tess watched their cow antics, laughing aloud only the second time since they'd met. Then she joined him and Mikka, shifting her weight to one leg and pretending to chew her cud.

For a moment, they left gravity behind, happy in a bovine rumpus.

:::CHAPTER 26

HARRIS HENRY

Harris Henry's brain ricocheted from the plan to his fears, his heart heaving with terror for Merrill, Delaney, and Leigh. How could he keep his family close to his heart, contain his fear, and still function under duress?

Impossible. He'd have to forget about them for now. He couldn't afford to worry about his family or feel their pain while he fought for survival or he'd go stark raving mad.

Shit. He squatted and tied his shoe, yanking up a baggy, annoying sock. Hiking in dress shoes and thin dress socks had caused painful blisters on his heels. The crackly skin of one calf itched and he rubbed an equally dry hand across it. How did people live in these infernal deserts?

He kicked a rock down the road like a frustrated kid. *Whoa, Mama.* It tumbled in a high spinning arc that made him feel better. He swung his arms harder, matching the rhythm of his breathing to his walking pace. Inhale, one, two, three, four, exhale eight, seven, six, five, four, three, two, one.

He fought his mental urge to dally in the politics that brought him here without success. That the Agency would pull this . . . this coup, was no surprise. Their protocol . . . he snorted out loud. Stick it up the Agency's protocol. He'd find some way to pay 'em back and expose their sordid little secrets. They'd clipped him to screw up environmental renewal and prevent UFO disclosure. They'd keep the world in chaos, exterminate poor people, their own countrymen, in profitable wars and quietly cull the population further through biological and weather warfare. And fund it by using unsuspecting taxpayers to cover the overhead.

He snorted and kicked another rock sky high. It seemed like the natural evolution of a powerful nation-state to engage in imperial conquest when resources become scarce. Earth was caught in the web of a carefully planned operation spanning not only years, but generations, an extraterrestrial conspiracy.

Good Lord. For the nation's sake, the entire world, he had to figure out his next move. He needed a goddamn plan of action—food, water and shelter. Worry and conjecture wouldn't take him anywhere. He couldn't waste any more time on nonsurvival issues, but his mind compulsively nibbled at his political frustrations. Ever since his experience on Air Force One, he'd smelled shape-shifting fascist lizards in every dark corner of his predicament.

Space Nazis were the subject of his administration's strangest briefing. Lody Ramirez, his Chief of Staff, brought in this kooky, world-renowned medium, a mysterious Eastern European with a Dracula accent. The guy went into a trance like some actor in a B movie, churning out odd nonhuman sounds, strange electronic whines and whirs. Then he began to speak in an accent no one had heard before, part Transylvanian and part something else.

"You may call me Sumari the Sumi," the "channeled" character murmured. "My people, ve populate a vorld that orbits the star Aldebaran, in the constellation Taurus."

Lody shot Henry a look. He raised an eyebrow in return. Next, Sumari explained that Sumis were a humanoid race who briefly colonized Earth 500 million years ago. "The ruins of ancient Larsa, Shurrupak, and Nippur in Iraq were built by these Aryan race ancestors," he intoned in a deep and sorrowful voice, "and they survived the large flood of Ut-napishtim."

Henry noted Sumari's fascist language. Sumari suddenly grabbed a document from Henry's hand and began scribbling marks on it. Damned if these didn't turn out to be Sumerian, the tongue of the ancient Babylonian culture. Of course, the man could easily practice for the briefing by copying hieroglyphics from a book. But it turned out, Lody said afterward, that some Nazi sympathizer had a similar contact with the Sumi through a medium in the 1920s. He'd carried the story into the Reich, who had incorporated it into their occult and UFO technology research.

When the Transylvanian medium emerged from his "trance" he related a captivating history, claiming that the Reich had indeed succeeded in creating space-worthy vehicles that reached the Moon and Mars. When the Reich disintegrated, they took their technology to Antarctica, he claimed. By the time their base was discovered by an Allied Task Force in 1946, the Reich had already tested the *Andromeda*, a large cylindrical spacecraft. They decided to launch it before the ATF secured it. The medium claimed that an untested device aboard the spaceship was believed to be capable of putting the ship into a "wormhole," enabling it to achieve interstellar flight. Veterans of Himmler's Waffen-SS volunteered for the flight.

The *Andromeda* was thought capable of traveling only up to three thousand miles from Earth without the untested device, the medium indicated, but the Nazis supposedly pointed the *Andromeda* at the star Aldebaran and made the interstellar jump. Three years later, the *Andromeda*, or other ships like it, began being spotted around the globe. A ship, or some ships, were seen releasing dozens of discs—flying saucers—that flew off in all directions. U.S. fighters captured gun camera footage of these cylindrical, cigar-like ships in the 1950s.

The Transylvanian claimed that a German psychic heard from the mysterious Sumi again in 1967. "Oh, Herr Hunt says the

Andromeda traveled far beyond the three-thousand mile limit to Aldebaran. They sent a big armada, two-hundred eighty battle cruisers that hold hundreds of saucers. The Armada is coming to Earth soon, to start again the World War II."

Henry wondered why they didn't make an interstellar jump like the *Andromeda*, but didn't ask. He and Lody bit their tongues to keep from laughing while Dottie escorted the medium from the Oval Office. Then they had a thigh-slapping hoot until tears streamed down their faces. Ancient Sumerians claimed to have made contact with an extraterrestrial culture, and their language relates to no other on Earth, but their Transylvanian had melded history and some imaginative fiction into an entertaining sideshow act.

Or so he'd thought. He'd relished the irony until Lody shared some old intel reports suggesting that the Nazis may truly have traveled to another galaxy. Perhaps those damn goosesteppers had not only infiltrated U.S. government and industry after World War II, they'd also penetrated the farthest reaches of space itself . . . The bizarre experiences aboard Air Force One and after his abduction from the White House pointed to the fact that life was truly stranger than fiction.

His guts clenched in a cold chill thinking about it. The beautiful American dream had become the biggest drug-dealing, oil-sucking, vile empire in the galaxy, totally in cahoots with an extraterrestrial civilization. Hadn't the Reviewers instructed him not to think about this? Was he insane, coming to this lunatic fringe conclusion pried from the darkest corners of the internet?

He still doubted himself in his darkest moments. But unlike some of the nutcases spouting this ET invasion stuff, he'd had reams of official briefings with credible researchers, enough to grasp the probabilities.

He picked up his stride, stomping little clouds of dust up to his knees, mentally reliving another briefing on UFO phenomena.

"The Grays are mercenaries, Mr. President." Dr. Pride, an eminent UFO researcher, shook his crinkly mane of salt and pepper hair as he spoke. "Mercenaries with a hive mentality. They serve a Reptilian race, a cruel race of losers, as teenagers today would say. Renegades who consider Earth to be one of their colonies and the human life upon it their stock, their prey. They've dominated Earth's prehistoric past, hence so many stories about ferocious dragons and flying lizards. Adam and Eve stories from different cultures refer to genetic modifications made by the Reptilian race on early hominids to create a servant race. This extraterrestrial culture is one driving force behind our current global economic system, a system embracing the acquisition of wealth by an elite class."

"Where do you get this stuff from?" Henry asked, annoyed by Dr. Pride's cloying certainty.

"These are details given to some abductees by Grays. We thought these details either delusion or fantasy, but researchers documented an overwhelming number of stories. There are also eyewitness reports of interactions between groups of blue-eyed Caucasians and Grays on craft harboring abductees used for harvesting genetic material."

Dr. P's briefing left him speechless at the scope of the UFO cover-up. One theory he shared extrapolated that more spiritually evolved human relatives from other galaxies took pity on Earth's modified hominids and genetically enhanced them after they had been forced to accept the Reptilians' modifications. The slaves were given the capacity for higher thought, allowing them to free themselves from servitude.

"This may be the reference to Adam and Eve being cast out of the garden," Pride explained. "Modern humanity teeters on the brink of unprecedented evolution or annihilation. Our enlightened relatives have a hands-off policy and wait for Earth humans to evolve enough to join their Galactic Confederation. Some of the UFO activity on earth is friendly investigation or harmless research by galactic bioscientists. Our world has more biological diversity than most and this fascinates extraterrestrials. Other visitors, like the Reptilians and their representatives, pose a threat to humanity."

Again, he felt annoyed at Pride tossing plausible theories around as certainties, but he had documentation of human experiences with humanoid extraterrestrials and a variety of nonhuman species.

"Abductions by Grays," Pride informed him, "may be as high as one in twenty humans on earth, an event so common it *cannot* be ignored. Eyewitness testimony points to a secret military operation in the 1970s. A large group of Grays were attacked and perished in an underground base in New Mexico, yet the U.S. government continues to deny the allegations, despite participant testimony. Thousands of abductees have offered jigsaw puzzle pieces of information both under hypnosis and from memory since the Betty and Barney Hill abduction case took the world by surprise in 1961."

"Now *that* was an interesting story," he affirmed.

"Yes. And after more than four decades, the scattered pieces have been assembled into an unbelievable but recognizable picture."

Henry continued to listen to reams of UFO stories and theories from the mouths of competent and credentialed researchers. The scientists took the off-the-record briefings seriously and backed their own work with credible evidence. Still, they'd been the laughingstock of conventional science for quite some time. Debunkers loved to hound them because there's nothing like ridicule to put a big chill on the truth.

But hell, he had to stop daydreaming. He reminded himself that it was only a matter of time before someone or something caught up to him again. He shivered and picked up his pace, casting a glance over his shoulder now and then. But his mind soon wandered, picturing the face of another researcher, Dr. Sterling. What a honey. The hot, redheaded ET abduction expert briefed him not long after the meeting with Dr. Pride, soon after his experience on Air Force One.

"I'll be damned, Doctor, I've read about this stuff, but you've worked hands-on with these folks, helped put their lives back together," he said.

"Yes, sir. Most abductees don't recall a thing at first. Sometimes memories bleed into consciousness months or years after the fact. Others suffer immediately from recurring dreams and panic attacks. After they realize what has happened to them, most subjects keep a low profile. Still others get psychiatric help and go public, write books and make TV appearances."

"Might they do this for the money?"

"Mr. President, I haven't seen many abductees get involved in revealing a false ET abduction for attention or money. The abductees I've examined and interviewed are the most sincere people I've ever met. They're truly puzzled by and traumatized by their abductions. They undergo extensive, rigorous batteries of questionnaires, background checks, lie detector tests, hypnosis. It's not a fun process. They're driven by compassion to publicize their suffering to help others. I've met only a handful who seemed to enjoy spinning a tall tale, and only one or two who seemed to be agents of disinformation."

He nodded. "Their stories are disturbing, but I have deeper concerns—like the reports of human harvesting. What about the *permanent* disappearances of children and adults? An astounding twenty-five hundred people go missing each day in the U.S. alone. You know that most cases are later resolved—runaway kids, estranged husbands and wives, people who want to escape unsatisfactory lives. But the permanent disappearances are generally explained away as unsolved crimes. Some abductions have human perps, of course. Like the recent case of the young model who vanished from a New York agency office recently . . . her body was found in some nutcase's freezer in a little town in Maine."

"Yes. Most cases do have "Earthly" circumstances. But as you may know, Mr. President, perhaps 1-2 percent of missing person reports, nearly as many as solved stranger abductions, are accompanied by UFO sightings reported by witnesses near the victim's temporary or permanent disappearance."

Henry stared at Dr. Sterling's tapered fingers and unvarnished oval fingernails as she placed some documents on his desk. He wouldn't mind if she laid him out like those docs, he thought. "Tell me more, please."

"People disappear from vehicles abandoned on the side of the road. Often the vehicles are found with their belongings intact, including keys and handbags or wallets. Kids disappear a block from home or from their beds, monitored just a few moments before by caring parents or watchful neighbors . . . most return suddenly, but some do not."

Henry picked up a photo, a child's drawing of big-eyed extraterrestrials taking him from his bed. "Stealing kids pisses me off. I don't care if it's non-custodial parents or pedophiles or goddamn extraterrestrials." He thought of his own kids, how vulnerable they were before adolescence. He restrained himself from slamming his fist on the desk, silently wondering if there were some goddamn satanic link between organized pedophilia and the ET abduction phenomena.

Dr. Sterling ignored his language lapse and continued her briefing. "Mr. President, dozens of humans including U.S. military personnel have been found in the past four decades with all the hallmarks of cattle mutilations. A neat circular patch of skin is removed around one eye along with the eyeball. Anus and sexual organs are removed, often the soft tissues of the head as well—nose, lips, tongue. Sometimes part of the jaw is sectioned away."

She laid out a handful of 5x7 photos of dead cows. "The bodies are drained of blood, yet the ground under and around the bodies is bloodless and the incisions are surgically precise. One of the first documented cases of human mutilation was a highly skilled officer participating in an exercise on a New Mexico military base."

"I'm aware of that case. Some of his squadron members witnessed weird lights in the area . . . Is it true that ranchers have observed extraterrestrial beings participating in mutilations through binoculars?"

"That's correct. Also, a variety of other domestic animals and wildlife have been found mutilated in the same fashion."

"How can this happen to humans with so little notice by the media?"

"Both animal and human mutilations are brushed off by local law enforcement agencies as the work of predatory animals or Satanic cults, though there's startling evidence to the contrary."

"Denial is simpler than facing reality, isn't it? I intend to seek more intelligence on this matter." He toyed with the cell phone vibrating in his pocket, his chief-of-staff alerting him to another appointment. "I'm sorry. I have another appointment. May I?" He reached for her file.

"Of course, Mr. President. This is your copy . . ."

"I truly appreciate your time, for coming across the country. Thank you, Dr. Sterling. You're a courageous woman."

"The pleasure is mine, Mr. President. This is an exciting turn of events. You're the first president in U.S. history to openly acknowledge the depth and complexity of the UFO enigma. I wish you luck in your endeavor."

When she smiled at him shyly, he noted her captivating hazel eyes were dusted with threads of copper. He could also see she wasn't used to rubbing shoulders in high places despite her professional bearing. He reached for her hand, tempted to bow and kiss it in the old-fashioned manner, but shook it instead. He admired her shapely legs and the easy sway of her hips as Dottie steered her from the Oval Office toward the family quarters, where Merrill waited with lunch.

A gaggle of aides and a Secret Service detail surrounded Henry as he exited the Oval Office. The aides fell into an easy banter, trading jokes while the Secret Service observed all, their expressions inscrutable. He smiled, pretending to take it all in. He still mulled over Dr. Sterling's briefing and why full disclosure was in the best interest of national security.

Henry took a few minutes to grunt *hup two three four* aloud again, hoping to distract himself from his thought tsunami. The trouble with all this fucking walking outdoors was having *too* damn much time to think. At least the hike kept him warm. He broke a sweat and mopped at his face with a dirty sleeve. Gradually he felt dizzy with the exertion and had to look for a good sitting rock. He plopped down, fighting the urge to close his eyes and pass out.

What was his plan, the priority he couldn't seem to manage? He often embraced action from the foundation of free thought. But the wild horses of his mind weren't taking him anywhere. Wallow on, oh Henry . . . he sighed and spat. His loogie plopped into the dust, almost hitting his foot. He sighed again and gripped his head between his hands.

Chief of Staff Lody Ramirez's voice echoed in his head. "The worst of the weaponry is capable of entering minds and bodies either close-range or from a distance and manipulating them to the will of the user . . ." Good old X-Files Lody. What a kicker, a real patriot. Had they both cracked under pressure? Where was Lody now?

Last year, Lody had the balls to pick up the phone and start poking around when Bax started getting scared and losing his groove. Lody's desire to push the envelope for more material thrilled Henry. Lody stirred up a ton of hornets by declassifying more information. He and Henry pulled thousands of pages into the sunshine, more documents than any administration in history. Most people didn't realize that Lody had provided the impetus for Henry's signing Executive Order 12958.2011 directing that all Federal records five years and older relating to unidentified flying objects be immediately reviewed and declassified. A Kennedy family member, the administration's first briefing advisor, interested both in UFOs and in solving the mystery of JFK's death, wrote Henry a congratulatory letter afterward.

Just before he found himself in a spaceship, he figured the great thing about Lody's hornets, his opposition, was that they aimed their venom at Lody, not him, and weren't that hard to outsmart. At that point, he still had a shot at full disclosure. His biggest disappointment now was losing contact with Lody, losing their bid at disclosure.

He shivered and drew inside himself, looking up to mark the descent of the sun, still hovering well above the horizon. Night would fall hard. A stiff breeze started to pick up and he didn't have enough clothing to weather serious cold. How the hell he managed to survive the previous night without catching p-neu-mon-i-a was a mystery.

Which was worse, his old fears about environment and disclosure, or the new ones about plain old survival?

Despite his worries, his mind jumped the corral again and trotted through the previous night's battle in the underground facility. It *must* have been a galactic war scenario. Dr. Sterling had mentioned an extraterrestrial group assisting rabid national security types against another political faction disseminating information among more spiritually-oriented types. Maybe galactic Nazis, Reptilians, and Grays were fighting over Earth, opposed by Earth's benevolent secret forces consisting of enlightened galactic relatives. Possible? Henry thought of the soldier who'd spoken to him, the one he thought might be part of a rescue team. Surely the man was an ally. Were there *two* factions of secret government battling for dominance? That would make sense . . . He began to feel giddy and wanted to throw his head back in wild laughter. December 21, 2012—gawd, what a story!

He swallowed hard, trying to push the knot from his aching throat. To keep his mind in check, he quick-reviewed his status: Kidnapped. A squishy gray creep mentioned the "Draco/Orion Federation." He observed ETs underground working with U.S. military troops, meaning the U.S. military and extraterrestrial groups interfaced. Extraterrestrial interests held considerable sway on Earth. Maybe they lived on Earth somewhere despite their ET origins. Still alive and kicking, but throat getting sore, a sign his immune system was weakening. Faculties intact, mostly, in spite of his careening thoughts.

The plan. So what in the hell *was* the plan? Since he was clearly alive, shouldn't there be public suspicion that he wasn't really dead? Surely Merrill and the kids knew it, felt it in their bones. Someone must be looking for him. Where were his loyal Secret Service agents, his supporters, the shadowy patriots who called themselves "The Library?"

His throat itched and he coughed again. His head hadn't stopped throbbing since the day he'd been abducted from the White House, and every time he shut his eyes it felt like his head tried to morph into another shape. He had to find help. When he got out of this fucking desert he'd best make just the right contacts. Or his goose would get cooked, for good this time.

::: Chapter 27

Tess Vaughn

Tess had read somewhere that scientists credited mothers with stronger survival instincts than other adults. But she'd resigned herself to failure in spite of how much she loved Mikka. Her resolve to save her precious daughter had nearly dissolved and she felt she may as well dissolve too.

Even in her best moments, a dull ache throbbed from knee to hip and up into her rib cage. Her worst moments featured red-hot piercing jabs that left her breathless and gritting her teeth, the sharpest pains she'd ever experienced short of childbirth. In spite of the dropping temperature, her skin was beginning to radiate a dry heat. Fever or dehydration?

Why did she still try to hide her injuries from Carson? Maybe because she disliked appearing weak. No sniveling, as Uncle Mac liked to say. Maybe she didn't want to admit to herself how serious the situation had become. Plus, she'd leaned on Carson too much and didn't want to lean any harder.

She limped on, following Carson and Mikka as a murky darkness began to nibble at the last bit of twilight. They skulked like animals in the shadows, warily treading along hillsides, edging behind large boulders or through whatever vegetation cover they encountered. She tried to pad as gracefully as Carson over the desert terrain. Agile as a mountain lion, he sometimes retreated behind her and Mikka to cover their trail wherever possible. Sometimes he led them up stony ridges where they would stretch from rock to rock to avoid leaving footprints.

When she gazed up at the sky again, night drew overhead like a curtain. Scores of stars appeared one by one, a lacy veil sewn with sparkling beads. She stopped for a moment to find the few winter stars and constellations she recognized. Pleiades and the yellow star Aldebaran crept over the horizon, and the constellation Gemini, her sun sign. She recalled that the ancient Mayans described Pleiades as a snake's rattle, a vision appropriate for this environment and the occasion.

She stumbled forward, trying to catch up to Carson, who held Mikka in his arms. A barbed wire fence running perpendicular to their path interrupted his stride. She noted as they stooped to climb between rows of wire that they were probably crossing from forest land into a ranch or vice versa.

Carson ended his long silence and spoke in a deliberately gentle tone while he unhooked her sweatshirt sleeve from a barbed wire spur. "Tess, I don't know how to tell you this . . ."

She chafed at his words. "Just tell me straight out. I'm a big girl."

"I'm not keeping anything from you." Carson shifted Mikka from one hip to the other, and she wearily turned her head on his shoulder. He shivered, either from something he sensed or from the rapid desert nightfall. "I'm feeling anxious . . . I don't know whether we should take shelter soon or if it's better to keep walking. I had a vision of sand spilling from an open palm."

The proverbial hourglass, she thought. Fatigue and gravity pulled at her relentlessly. "Maybe we should rest awhile first?"

"Yes." Carson motioned with a stick he'd fashioned earlier from a juniper branch toward yet another rock formation, a big hulking shape. Her sore hip sagged under Mikka's weight and another round of searing pain began. She stopped and tried to squat, a mistake with her hip's limited range of motion. Carson disappeared for a few seconds, and circled back to her.

"A good place," he announced. "On the other side there's a hollow between rocks big enough for the three of us. Almost a cave. It's mostly out of the wind and free of snakes. I'll put the tarp over the opening."

"Thank you, God, thank you, Universe. My feet are like ice." Gashed by rocks and pricked by all manner of thorns, her ankles and high arches throbbed. Her running shoes and Mikka's suede sneakers didn't provide much protection from the cold or rugged terrain. Other than that, they were dressed pretty well—for a short jaunt, not a fifty-mile high-desert excursion in late December. Her sweatshirt hoody barely kept her head warm. At least Mikka's quilted nylon jacket and thick hood were fleece-lined.

Carson took off his bandanna headband and unrolled it into a headscarf. He took her by the hand and eased her into the womb-like hollow between the boulders. She collapsed inside, curling around Mikka on the hard, gritty ground. Her daughter exuded warmth, a radiant secret center at her mother's solar plexus. She whispered soothing words into Mikka's ear, comforted by Carson's energy as he squatted inches away, grappling silently with the tarp. He secured it as a door by weighting it with stones. Air pressure caused it to pulse gently in and out. She imagined the tarp as a giant heart pulsing over them. Carson lay down and nestled his broad chest against her back. Even when prone he radiated a silent, meditative state.

Despite her pain and her growing fear, she felt momentarily safe in their rocky nest. She'd never felt this secure with a man before. Desired, yes, especially by Harris, but . . . she forced Harr's face out of her head and placed a hand on Carson's shoulder. To her surprise, he didn't pull away, uttering a soft sigh and relaxing against her.

What seemed liked moments later, Tess came to with a start. Her dreams and waking life converged in the same murky anxiety, running again from God knows who. Groggy, she squinted at the tarp "doorway." A dim light shone along the edges, giving it a reddish glow. The moon?

Carson leapt to his feet and dislodged one side of the tarp as he pushed his way outside. She strained to listen but heard nothing except the loosened tarp thwacking dully against the rocks. She tightened her arms around Mikka, and then let go of her to creep up on her hands and knees. "Carson, what is it?"

"Lights in the sky." He crouched in a boulders' shadow, motioning at her with a flick of one hand to put her head back inside. His dark skin and clothing were barely visible. All she could see were the white lines in the collar and cuffs of his plaid shirt and the winter fog that obscured their surroundings, casting the world in a polarity of misty light and deep shadow. The night, though crisp, seemed balmier than when they'd fallen asleep under a clear sky. Large, dense, low clouds like black dragons began drifting through the lighter overcast, appearing to eat up the moon and coiling to rest along a distant mountain range.

Mikka moaned in her sleep. Tess murmured back at her, still riveted by Carson and whatever he thought he saw. She resisted crawling outside but did it anyway, scraping her wrist and causing another surge of pain in her hip that forced her to stand up straight. She pressed her back against the rocks, grasping for mental and physical stability in the act of connecting spine to stone. She felt momentary comfort with her friend standing before her and the sentinel of stone behind.

Though Carson waved her back, he didn't protest when she joined him. She gaped at the sky. "What in the world?" Her hoarse theatrical whisper caused Mikka to cry out, but Tess remained rooted until she spotted Carson's "lights in the sky." Three small orbs throbbed overhead, far away. They soared toward the ground, growing larger. Their glow diminished for a moment, changing from white to a golden orange. Then they brightened permanently, suspended in midair at some hard to determine height. When the orbs moved again, they seemed to sway in tiny arcs and figure eights, somewhat like the lightning bugs Tess had encountered on her travels in the Midwest and South. She held her breath and listened, but the sky in its vast silence remained constant until a jet passed over with a tiny, distant roar, its white strobes and red running lights blinking through the mist, probably oblivious to the orbs below it.

She pulled at Carson's jacket. "Shouldn't we get back inside?"

"Sometimes what makes sense isn't the right thing to do." Though Carson turned as he spoke and looked directly into her eyes, he seemed distant. Was he at a loss for what to do, or was she the one lost in her pain and anxiety? A dense feeling of being observed surrounded them like cotton batting. Carson plunged like a hawk into the rocks, grabbed Mikka, the tarp, and her arm in what seemed like one fell swoop. He scrambled away from the boulders. She uttered a guttural groan as she forced her hip to stretch and match Carson's speed.

One orb suddenly appeared in plain view, a slightly flattened globe with dozens of long, thick spines jutting from its sides. It closed in on them like a drone, and they slowed to a walk to gaze up. Familiar somehow, yet completely alien, it rushed them, plunging downward and arcing sharply up again, jetting with great speed and force through the fog. Another one, and then the third sped past. The three six-foot craft spun in random patterns, clockwise, counterclockwise, forward and backward, whirling like great spiky bubbles in a mechanical storm. There were no windows, no vents, no visible signs of a propulsion system, nor any sign of what caused the pulsating glow. The orbs looked dull and opaque now, and the moonlight that glowed through the mist barely reflected from them. She had another brief impression, one of huge snowflakes falling wildly in dark woods, as though the craft tried to inject a false memory into her mind.

Carson moved forward and yanked her by the wrist. "Run. Keep going!" he urged in his choppy Indian cadence.

Mikka whined and her eyes shot open. She flailed her limbs,

fighting against Carson for a moment. Tess stumbled alongside them, patting Mikka in a feeble attempt at reassurance. Mikka curled up and buried her face in Carson's denim jacket. Tess stiffened her injured leg to make its movement less painful, and then forgot her body entirely in the next surge of adrenaline. The probes repositioned themselves, arcing back toward them as though maneuvering for an aerial dogfight. Tess tucked her chin to her chest, expecting to be fried by a laser beam or crushed in an inevitable crash.

"Down that ridge," Carson yelled. They hobbled forward, visually handicapped in the haze. He pounded steadily along in thick-soled hiking boots. Like a tugboat in a syrupy sea, he labored with a husky three-year-old and her, a gimpy, exhausted, middle-aged woman.

Carson stumbled suddenly, grabbing desperately at a scrawny juniper for balance. She tilted precariously with him, trying to pull him back and keep the group equilibrium. Mikka squeezed her eyes shut and contorted her face as though bracing for a fall. She and Carson half-slid, half-ran down the remainder of the bank into a ravine.

Carson hesitated a split-second and chose a direction. She sensed the craft hesitating as well; then it dove toward them. Carson shifted Mikka from his hip to tuck her against his chest and pulled Tess along a narrow streambed. The relatively straight ribbon of sand and rocks cut deeper into the land to form banks that gradually rose ahead of them.

She glanced behind them briefly, biting her tongue in the process. Adrenaline and doubt surged in her. "They're on us," she screamed. "They're on us."

"Keep going!" Carson's staccato-sharp order contrasted with his syncopated, slow-motion trot.

Her chest heaved with the effort of running on rocky sand. Salty and swollen, her dry tongue grew huge in her mouth. Brush whacked their faces as the ravine narrowed, forcing them into single file. Carson dropped her hand, and she never felt so alone in her life. She glanced back again. The three craft looked like one now, linked somehow into a strand. They skimmed along, no more than a few yards behind.

Carson grunted a command. Was it *duck, duck,* or *jump, jump*?

The streambed narrowed again, making them stumble through a narrow slit. The earth and rock walls loomed over seven feet high, casting deep shadows over their path. Carson stopped abruptly, fell to the ground, and arched protectively over Mikka. She sprawled unceremoniously on top of them, unable to stop her momentum.

An earsplitting screech of wrenching metal, flying sparks, dirt and stones stormed over them as they instinctively balled up for protection. The three craft had miscalculated, thrashing through twisted forms of boulders, trees, and brush at the ravine's upper edges. Tess expected an explosion, but in the aftermath, she heard only silence. She opened her eyes. A few tiny fires sputtered in the brush. Nature and chance had taken their side.

Their tangled limbs waved around and somehow three people emerged from the dogpile. Carson panted like an animal and shook his head in relief. Tess sat up, gasping for breath. A single tear surged down her cheek. She grabbed Mikka's hands and looked around her wrists for the dotted triangle mark she'd found inside her own elbow after the strange stargazing interlude she'd had while pregnant with Mikka. She almost pulled Mikka's jacket off, wondering if more had happened than they were aware of.

Mikka's little voice rang out in the crevice. "What in the holy hell was that?"

Carson and Tess hugged Mikka between them, rocking in a fit of nervous giggles as the fog swirled around them in big, ghostly forms.

::: CHAPTER 28

HARRIS HENRY

Harris Henry followed the road's graded curves around boulders that seemed fancifully flung into place by a giant hand. He still held hope that his mental wheels would spin an action plan for his return to society. Something sneaky, brilliant, dramatic. To finally rivet the attention of the American public on UFO disclosure in an era of so many crises, his plan would have to be fucking dramatic.

His stomach dropped and chills revved through his body at the sound of an approaching vehicle. He turned to see a light green Ford pick-up truck pull into view. Forest Service. His emotions surged from elation to dismay. Was he safer here in the desert or in a population center?

A young man in a khaki-colored shirt rolled down the window and leaned his head out, making his face look as though it floated over the brown U.S. Department of Agriculture logo on the driver's door.

"How's it going?" The ranger eyed Henry's rumpled suit, scuffed shoes, and his eyes lingered on his natty hair and whiskers. "Need some help?"

Tongue-tied for a moment, he weighed the drawbacks of seeking the ranger's help versus brushing him off. His political instinct soon took control. He'd simply have to manipulate the conversation one phrase at a time.

"Oh, just lookin' around. Beautiful country." He sucked his gut in and stuck out his chest, pretending *not* to be a sight for sore eyes.

"Better carry some water." The ranger leaned out the window and handed Henry a sealed 32-ounce water bottle with a pull-up top. "So you enjoy taking the back way between Chino and the Verde Valley?"

"Thanks," he replied, ignoring the ranger's question, trying to mask his extreme enthusiasm for the water. He decided to play on the ranger's assumption that he was a local. Overall, Henry took the ranger's remark as a sign to let the guy go—he seemed more interested in passing out water than anything else.

Surely the guy must recognize him. His mug must have been plastered all over the news ever since he was abducted from the White House. Then again, maybe a low-level government employee just wanted to get through the day and go home to his family.

Henry's political savvy moved up a notch. He'd best offer a slightly extended answer. "Yeah," he added in a disinterested tone. Best case scenario was the ranger would assume his vehicle was around here somewhere, if he hadn't already noticed the stalled truck. But if this was the young man's jurisdiction, he probably knew the truck belonged to Easy Rider, or whoever owned it. How would he get around that?

"I've got to get back to town myself. Sure you don't need a lift?"

"I'm sure. I'll be on my way soon." He feigned disinterest, glancing off in the distance. This guy was too much, he thought. Didn't he recognize the President of the United States yet? Or was he one of those people who thought Washington, D.C. is a state?

The young ranger touched the brim of his brown baseball cap and eased down the road, the rear of the truck with its federal government plate receding into the distance. Henry stood watching the truck with his mouth open. Holy shit. He wondered if anything would dawn on the guy, if he'd turn around after a few miles. He'd always heard Arizona spent less money per student on public education than most states. When he got back to business, he'd lobby the Arizona legislature to appropriate more funds for schools in Yavapai County, Arizona.

The wild stallions of his mind soon galloped into forbidden territory again. Was he nuts to evade two human beings, Easy Rider and the Forest Service ranger, who might have helped him out of this wilderness? He hated second-guessing things and reminded himself that his first instinct always paid off.

He needed to focus with a capital F. Not only did he need to get out of the desert; he had to get back into a position of power somehow and act on this ornery combination of ET visitation, government secrecy, and advanced technology fueled by huge military budgets. He couldn't think about one problem without considering the others. He'd failed to bring full disclosure to the American people and he desired, more than anything, to reverse the long legacy of secrecy regarding the UFO question. What would the Agency do to the people without him?

When President Eisenhower left office, he advised the American public to not underestimate the power of the military/industrial complex. Henry occasionally thought about his remark, wondering exactly what event had inspired it. Rumor said Eisenhower went to Kirkland Air Force Base to see the extraterrestrial bodies allegedly stored there. He'd confronted, like every president since then, the biggest, strangest, and most fabulous secret in human history. And apparently shied away from doing anything about it.

Congressional committees considered military situations from time to time. Or tried to. Many times legislators sought to rein in NIHSA and the armed forces, but Congressional control remained superficial, illusory at best. Senators and Congressmen often failed to find or understand the hidden secrets. The transfer of ET technology and suppression of UFO information was just a tip of the U.S. military black budget iceberg, a formation of gigantic proportions. Henry had begun to realize that technology originating during the U.S.//Soviet arms race combined with exotic technology probably gleaned from visiting ETs seemed to result in twenty-first century satellite and internet surveillance of everyone on the planet. Terrorism, domestic or foreign, was always the excuse to cultivate this technology. Bax had been discouraged from pursuing this topic at his post in the Attorney General's office. Later on, a good number of his cabinet members were also coerced to forget about it. Lody had been the only one who forged ahead while the Agency scammed the public, creating situations to make many folks in his administration look like conniving rascals.

He hiked on, struggling to remember specific data about secret technology, and found he could retrieve some info by recalling the high, reedy voice of the British scientist Dr. O., as he called himself. The flash of his steely eyes and the way he held his fingertips together in a little arch before his breastbone at briefings was unforgettable.

"By directing laser beams, such as neural-particle beams, electromagnetic radiation, sonar waves, radio frequency radiation (RFR), soliton waves, torsion fields . . ." Dr. O. had buzzed like a busy insect about what sounded like the weapons of evil villains in science fiction stories. Henry hated thinking of using these on anyone but a hostile ET civilization—God help Earth if this evolved into galactic war.

"One of the most disturbing uses of this technology, Mr. President, is a system using pulsed RFR to manipulate mental processes. The victim is located and "locked" on to, finding himself or herself unable to evade the menace by moving around. Beamed energy causes anything from pressure on internal organs to cardiac arrest and bleeding in the brain. Messages, words that are heard inside a person's head, can be transmitted, similar to the way a mentally ill person experiences hearing voices. The use of RFR technology has many negative effects on human physical and mental health. Good heavens, even Sony has developed video games using bioelectromagnetism to create visual, aural, olfactory, and somatosensory sensations in players. Imagine the havoc created with pulsed RFR and bioelectromagnetism."

His eyes narrowed. "So this can be done without implants?"

"Absolutely. RFR renders RDIF technology obsolete."

"Geez, what's WalMart up to now?" he joked.

Dr. O. glanced at the president with an uncomprehending look.

Henry shrugged. "So what locations is this done from?"

"The United States of America, for one. As you are already keenly aware," Dr. O. said, his clipped accent taking on a dark edge, "the HAARP facility in Alaska is an installation with the capacity to use RFR for local and global mind control."

The name HAARP wasn't new to Henry. He sighed. "I've had many concerns about HAARP."

The project began as a harmless university research project to study the ionosphere. Early in his term, Henry's aides reported that HAARP showed definite signs of morphing into a full-blown military operation. Both DoD and the CIA had the balls to withhold info about HAARP from every president since Jimmy Carter. None had retrieved as much info as Henry, despite the stonewalling by NIHSA.

"I'm sorry to agree that the terrorists using mind control and weather control tech in crimes against humanity may be the federal agencies Americans look to for protection," he said.

Dr. O. leaned back in his chair with satisfaction at Henry's response, clearly pissed at the United States government's hand in the situation.

He didn't remind Dr. O. that the British secret services had an international rep as the hardest-nosed and most manipulative intel organizations in the world.

"Dr. O., what's your take on weather control technology?" Henry was so intent on full disclosure that he'd left some aspects of HAARP technology unexplored.

"Mr. President, surely you don't think all the level 7, 8, and 9 earthquakes since the 2004 Indonesia tsunami were acts of God or nature? Or the huge hurricanes on your Gulf Coast? Continental drift and global warming play a role in both, to be sure, but these phenomena are clearly manipulated through technological means."

Henry had heard a bit about generated electromagnetic transmissions that produce an extra low frequency—ELF—scalar energy grid over a predetermined point on the earth's surface to disrupt the atmosphere. But how many people kept up on the topic? Those transmissions zapped Earth's upper atmosphere with three million watts of electromagnetic power—sheer cataclysmic potential. HAARP and other transmitters were undoubtedly the world's most powerful weapons.

Dr. O. didn't have to explain further. The truth socked him in the gut.

"I'll never forget the Indonesian crisis," he said. "I heard rumors about that first tsunami having a manmade source. Then Hurricane Katrina hit our East coast, and later Typhoon Nargis mauled Asia. After that, the big '08 earthquake in China, the early 2010 rocker in Haiti, Fukushima earlier this year. Superstorms and major quakes are far too commonplace, all blamed on natural causes, mostly. But Hurricane Tyrell—"

Dr. O. understood where his thoughts led. "Of course, your powerful Moral Right is intent on suppressing anything disagreeing with the Christian view of the apocalypse. These crises fit that viewpoint—God punishes the sinner and raptures the righteous."

Dr. O. began to spout more info than Henry needed or wanted to hear. "The effects of HAARP include nuclear-type explosions, geophysical manipulation, weather modification, air, ground and underwater electrical failures, mind control, disorientation, heart attacks, illness, and other invasive acts. It is suspected that HAARP has been used as a weapon against Afghanistan, Iraq, and Syria, and is pointed at Iran—any country that corporate/military powers desire to dominate. Not to mention that your NASA is testing 'killer satellites' despite their ban by international treaty. Space weaponry far surpasses public knowledge of military technology."

No shit, he thought to himself.

Dr. O. shook his head. "All this information is in the 'public domain,' meaning there's much information NOT in the public domain. Such as who's truly in charge of this 'weapon of mass destruction.'"

The Russians used it. So had other major world powers, all trying to influence the outcome of sensitive political and financial affairs. Even corporate criminals had been caught harassing other corporations for their trade secrets with RFR technology.

Henry nodded, realizing that sooner or later, someone would surely come after him if his course of thinking was correct. And he prayed that a new leader might emerge from a less conservative, less corporate-driven republic like Belgium or France, governments more open than the United States about investigating UFOs and military affairs. He was enthused about the Brits' recent intention to give full disclosure about UFO matters in the United Kingdom.

But it hadn't happened yet. Maybe what he called his "courageous plans" were simply castles in the air. Merrill called them his "outrageous" plans. They had many conversations about full disclosure, the secret, ultimate mission of his presidency. His wife never spared him her expert opinion, even tried to dissuade him from full disclosure in his final discussion with her.

"Harris, you've done other fine things that stand as your legacy. You ended the Social Security fiasco, for God's sake! You finally pushed national health care through and now people love it. You don't wanna end up like Kennedy over disclosure, do you? He had a lot of life left. So do you."

"Sugar, you're an attorney. A dyed-in-the-wool political activist. You cut your teeth at Legal Aid. You've been in public life long enough to know that full disclosure is the best legacy we could ever leave the world. Think of it! Perhaps *the* most kickass act ever. To expose the truth about Earth's position in the universe—"

"Oh my God, we've gone over this a million times. Of course, the benefits would be tremendous. Kennedy must have thought so, too.

It would work only if we can chase the power mongers out of town. They're hugely powerful, so how can we? If we act foolishly, the backlash . . . think about the twins . . . What if the Agency takes vengeance? What if this sets the stage for a galactic war?"

"There's something brewing in that direction anyway, I'm afraid. But we can take it a step at a time. If we have to fight, the tools are ready. Star Wars technology wasn't developed lightly. Someone in Reagan's admin, specifically someone *using* Reagan's administration knew exactly what they were doing. "

"But the black ops people control it," Merrill pointed out. "Even with full disclosure, they can manipulate it their way."

"If the Agency can manipulate us, we sure as hell can manipulate them," he assured her. "If it's a matter of backlash . . . hell, disclosure information is spreading all over our administration. And across the nation. Millions of folks are waking up. The UK obviously hasn't disclosed everything they know, but at least they've opened their incident reports. Merr, people around the world would rise to the occasion, Independence Day-style."

"I don't know, Harris—you're too optimistic. Plenty of people are comfortable with the status quo. And the Moral Right's riding shotgun with NIHSA . . ."

"The Right's always on our back, true, and some people lack imagination, for sure. But Sugar, it's not like we don't have more protection than the average Joe. Gap and Ashara back us one hundred percent. We've got loyal people in the Service. A good group of patriots at the Pentagon, even a few in NIHSA. Influential researchers are on our side. Concentrating on us is truly not in the Agency's advantage. Too many eyes are watching. People around the world. Bax said there's even some highly organized opposition. The Agency's got too many fingers plugging leaks in the dikes."

Merrill sighed in frustration. "Harr, you're living in the zone between desire and addiction." She looked pensive, a soft honey-colored forelock falling across her brow.

Henry pulled her to his chest, wrapped his arms around her. She didn't encourage him to forge ahead with his plans, but despite her final remark, she hadn't discouraged him, either. His tough gal had an eye for history. A twenty-first century history that might include the Henrys in the domain of Washington, Jefferson, and Lincoln . . . the Henrys would have a legacy beyond being the first mixed-race family in the White House.

Henry planned to reveal his UFO briefing data along with a massive FOI in his first State of the Union address, right about the time he found himself on an extraterrestrial exam table. Why did he think he could halt years of false posturing about UFOs? How could he have answered questions about extraterrestrial life whether the Bible thumpers liked it or not? With the backing of millions of outraged citizens in the US and the industrialized nations, he thought he'd stomp the brakes on ET control, black military operations, and other Agency shenanigans.

He wanted to pull it off so badly he really thought he could. That there was no way he would ever skunk the Agency from the White House should have been clear. How he'd do it from outside the White House when he was supposed to be dead drew a complete blank too.

Disappointment left a bad taste in Henry's mouth. His skin began to crawl with goose bumps—this shit always gave him the shivers and the falling temperature didn't help. He was ashamed he'd been spoiled by executive mansion living, a service for everything. Slowing his pace, he looked around for shelter. The water the Forest Service ranger gave him would keep him hydrated through the night. He vaguely recalled reading about how to dig a pit and line it with plastic sheeting to collect dew. Or to dig in a dry streambed until water surfaced. He didn't have any plastic, but he'd sure as hell look for a streambed.

He pulled the stick of dethorned cactus pads from his rear pocket with a sigh. He chewed at the last ones, trudging along, cursing the meager meal. At least cactus contained moisture. He should be grateful he hadn't found a box of saltine crackers instead.

As he limped around a lumpy hill, he stumbled into a three-way intersection of narrow dirt roads. Ta-da, he thought. He moved up and down each one, trying to make sense of them. Two had fresh-looking tire marks. But he hadn't seen any other vehicle but the Forest Service truck all day, except the passenger jets high in the sky, traveling east and west, mainly. There were no markers of any kind except a weathered plank dangling from a rock pile. The intersection stood in a low hollow that allowed only a partial view of the sky and little of the surroundings. He still felt isolated from the world even though the intersection might be a cowboy cloverleaf for all he knew.

The high cloud cover soared past like a time-lapse film, though the wind was much less brisk down in the earthen bowl. Henry scouted the terrain, poking around rocks and small evergreen trees until he found the remains of another old wall. The narrow rows of stacked rock that looked at first like a natural jumble met at right angles, telling him that in the past, someone had constructed a hut or somesuch. He imagined a half-starved, bewhiskered nineteenth-century prospector staking a claim, gold dust in his eyes. The jumble might be the remains of something the Forest Service constructed during the Great Depression work programs. Native stone was used to construct dams, bridges and other public works in rural areas around the country.

He pulled up handfuls of dead knee-high grass with curly tendrils at the top. Clods of dirt clung to the shallow roots and exploded into his face when he pulled too hard. He tore the roots away from the bundles and carted them to the rocks until he'd made a cushy pile. Then he closed up the corner with his own rows of stacked rock until he'd made a lair. By this time, the sun began to set in a Technicolor explosion.

He knelt at one wall of his shelter until the last light faded from the sky. Stars emerged like points of ice as the sky darkened and the cooling air nipped at his hands and face. He hobbled and limped into his lair, one leg numb and rubbery, and burrowed as best he could into it, sneezing at the dusty chaff he stirred up. He curled up into a dog-tired fetal position, his stomach rumbling like an engine out of gas. Morbidly, he wondered if he'd even survive the night, then reminded himself how he'd hankered for normal stuff like camping trips when playing president got too big for him.

Far in the distance, high-pitched howls—coyotes, he supposed—reminded him he'd come not only far from home, but a universe away from who he thought he was.

"This is only one obstacle," he offered in a raspy voice to whatever beings were around to hear him.

Listening to himself, he wondered again if Merrill wasn't right. He sounded like some character in a half-witted sci-fi movie. Not only had his obsession with full disclosure led to this dilemma, it may have led him off the permanent deep end.

How much power did he ever have anyway? Not much, it seemed. Elected officials were always bound to their base. Power was directed to appease those who held greater power. Even if elections were fair, the money and power influencing them had greater impact. The presidential office was more about prestige than serving the people. Everyone on Earth served at the altar of the petroleum-based economy.

Holy shit. As Grandma Opal used to say, he surely "lived under the cross" now.

:::CHAPTER 29

PAUL VAUGHN

Paul gingerly thrust his thick, dehydrated tongue over the salty scab of his split lip and squinted into the twilight. Or was it dawn? It didn't take a rocket scientist to notice the stiff, orange nylon ropes digging into his cramped body. The top of his head throbbed but he couldn't rub it. His mind skittered like a scrambling jackrabbit from concerns about what happened in the darkroom to fantasies about his probable, imminent death.

When he heard Jay's voice, deep pain seared his heart.

"Tough luck, Bud. Had to happen sooner or later." Jay leaned toward him, aiming a flashlight at his head.

He searched Jay's face for any trace of regret, a wistful twitch of an eyebrow or chin. Nothing but disdain registered. A chill spread through him. Was there anything colder than a lover's betrayal? He pushed back tears and clenched his teeth against the metallic taste of bile. Forcing his already cramped body into a tight knot, he squeezed all tender memories of Jay from himself like the last bit of toothpaste from an empty tube.

Jay leaned down and leered.

Paul fantasized he'd bite the nose off Jay's patrician face if he shoved it any closer. "Remington, you fucking bastard," he moaned. He racked his aching brain for the precise terms of this monstrous manipulation. Tess would've reeled off some choice phrases. What kind of person based a year-long relationship on deception and didn't bat an eye?

Jay smirked. "Is that all you can say? You were never a great articulator, Paulie." He tore a piece of duct tape from a new roll and slapped it across Paul's mouth, smoothing it tight in hard motions below each earlobe. "I don't suppose this will help. You're not likely to share much more, are you, sweetie?"

He pushed out a deep grunting roar from his gut that startled even himself. Jay jerked back involuntarily. In Paul's peripheral vision, a figure sitting in a high-backed driver's seat swiveled to look. He caught a glimpse of a beefy, wide-eyed, baldheaded, African American face. "You okay, Picard?"

Picard? Paul's insides nearly erupted from every orifice in his body. Was that Jay's real last name? How in the hell did a minor celebrity like Jay take a pseudonym? He picked up his head and dropped it, wanting to beat his own brains out. He realized then he was stuck in the rear of a boxy vehicle, a panel truck, maybe. No, a large van or RV with the cab partially open to the cargo area. It idled in gear, a low, growling diesel sound that drowned out the tone in his ringing ears. He looked around as best he could with one cheek pressed against a floor lined with gray canvas. His head pointed diagonally toward a slatted aluminum roll-up door. By straining his eyes far to one side, electronic equipment and a computer terminal spread along a thigh-high counter appeared in his peripheral vision. Coiled ropes, dark crates, and bags of stuff were stashed underneath. Spy gear?

Jay's foot shot out, shod in a Bruno Magli sport shoe Paul had bought at a discount outlet. He pictured his bloodiest fears, vaguely recalling the ruckus about O.J. Simpson's Bruno Magli shoes in the '90s after he allegedly slashed his wife's neck. He hoped O.J.'s Maglis would be the only pair connected to a murder mystery.

Bracing himself for a kick, he heaved a sigh of relief when Jay shoved his ribcage with a molded sole. Jay bent down, grabbed the ropes around his ankles and wrists, and pulled him around parallel to the back door. His view became limited to the blank walls of the vehicle. Jay yanked his head back and tied a soft, fragrant piece of fabric around his eyes. It smelled of Jay—his pheromones—and his complicated cologne. He mentally beat back his tears again.

"You always were a nosy shit." Jay stomped to the front of the vehicle and slid into a seat. "Let's get out of here," he growled in a dictatorial tone.

Snatches of conversation wafted from the cab area. A loud classic rock beat began to chop through the air, music Jay always disdained. The driver pumped the gas pedal and the truck rumbled to life.

Paul shivered. Now he'd worry about the point of departure and the destination. Where were they parked? Not likely at their condo—tucked deep in a cul-de-sac, their place had only enough parking outside the two-car garage for Jay's little Alfa and his BMW.

And he thought Tess would suck him into danger . . . A weird haze began to clog his head, no doubt the result of being clobbered and drugged. The van's engine overpowered most sound but, sometimes he heard the occasional swish of tires on what sounded like damp pavement. What else but damp cold would he expect late on Christmas night? At least he hoped it was still Christmas night. The vehicle's interior was periodically slashed by oncoming headlights, but soon lightened with the approaching dawn. He imagined the sky a dismal gray that matched his mood.

The van stopped and turned twice at what must have been traffic signals, then sped up on what must be a freeway entrance. He wondered if they were taking a northern or southern route. If the van took on some altitude, they were headed north. They would eventually gain some altitude on a southern route too, but his ears wouldn't pop as much.

Tess and Mikka must be safe for now, he figured. She, Mikka, and Carson might have slipped out of Cochise County into Mexico. If they were smart, they would have.

He strained to hear the goddamn traitor and his terminator buddy talk sporadically under the loud chatter of a rock and roll drum set. A transmitter sputtered, and someone turned the music volume down to a respectable level.

"I repeat, unexpected engagement. Eagle hunt Manzanita—" A static burst muffled the rest of the transmission.

The music went off. Jay's partner requested a repeat. Paul cocked his head to try to catch the reply. Another burst of static elicited a choice epithet from Jay. A pause and the voice returned. "Dragon Wagon sweep northeast Yavapai County, Manzanita, Sector A, forty-seven miles northeast of last estimated position. Talon down and out in Sector A. Indigo Girls and Geronimo missing from scene. Two hunts in one. Probability of containment in Sector B. Sensors tracking intermittently." Silence and another sputter. "Copy, Welcome Wagon?"

Goddamn radio. Paul could hardly hear himself think. The volume swelled again, higher than before. *Inagaddadavida, ba-by* screamed over the next transmission. Fucking oldies.

Indigo Girls? He'd never cared much for solving riddles or playing games. Was someone monitoring the Indigo Girls? Lesbo politics might offend some, but the country had a pot-smoking, guitar-playing Prez . . . this didn't make sense.

Think, think, Paulo. Damn it! He wanted to hurl on Jay. Anger and despair tainted what wits he had left. Then it dawned on him. Tess lived in northeastern Yavapai County. Wasn't there a Manzanita Forest, ridge, or canyon up near the Verde Valley? Indigo Girls—Tess and Mikka? Geronimo might be Carson. Had they gone up north? What the hell was eagle hunt?

Pinal County had made their move, interfacing with Yavapai County law enforcement to knock on Tess's door, he guessed. Or worse. At least Tess and Mikka weren't at home. Those jerkwad cops just figured that out. And who else? What was Jay's neo-spy thing?

Federal connections? His mind went into overdrive, echoing with Marshall's recent words about organized child pornography and prostitution. Some foggy memory in Jay's darkroom . . .

The van picked up speed. The black guy's angry voice cut through the blaring music and rumbling engine. Jay's angry voice cut back. Then a thump sounded at the front of the cargo area, some padded footsteps stopping short of his head. "Nighty night, Paulie."

The sharp jab of a needle stung his ass. He vowed to keep his eyes open until they crossed but he drifted away on the rambling of his own internal voice.

:::Chapter 30

Savannah Updike

Eight o'clock? How could that be? Savannah pulled her face from the bunched-up sheet, its bumps and ridges impressed in her puffy cheeks. How did she become sprawled crosswise at the end of the bed? Not her style. And she'd missed the dawn, her favorite time of day. Usually she rose before Marshall and started the coffeemaker before she went jogging. She always looked forward to the early morning sights around their foothills home, the watercolor sunrises and dawn forays of quail coveys and roadrunners.

She hated her confused disappointment as much as missing her run. Marsh had started his day before her, by the sound of it. An old blues tune he liked to whistle issued from under the bathroom door on a veil of steam. Like a mockingbird, he whistled any tune from classical to jazz and imitated any bird he ever heard. She sighed. He also loved long, hot showers and always turned their master bath into a sauna.

She listened closely. Marsh started repeating the last bar of the song over and over. Anxiety creased her brow. She'd never heard him repeat himself like that. Distracted by her bathrobe lying in a heap on the bedroom floor, she picked it up, wondering how it got there. When she'd taken it off after their middle-of-the-night prayers, she'd thrown it over the back of an overstuffed chair near the vanity, her usual routine.

She winced and wiggled her tongue around her mouth. Why was it so dry? It felt like a sandstorm had howled through it. Must be getting old if one drink dehydrated her. She downed a full glass of distilled water when she checked the kitchen before bed. She'd start her day with another glass of water, then a smoothie.

Marshall forgotten, she mentally cranked into her list of to-dos and headed for the kitchen. They'd open the church office and get caught up for the next service. A couple of loyal volunteers might pop in with Christmas leftovers. She'd have to dig around to find something for them to do, then catch up on church e-mail and correspondence. One of their cranky computers needed servicing and she planned to run the hard drive down to their tech guy near the University. During the afternoon they'd visit a dear member of the congregation who lay in a hospice making his last transition. Finally, they'd rush home for some personal business delayed by the holiday and their meetings with Tess.

She and Marshall hoped they'd hear from Carson and Tess soon. Recalling Mikka's delight with the ferrets, Once and Twice made her smile. She and Marshall opted out of reproducing and settled for pets instead—they had too many other dreams and wanted to channel their energy into "making a difference."

The ferrets, affectionately nicknamed "little weasels," became their substitute babies. They originally had a trio—Once, Twice and Forever—their private wordplay about their relationship. But Forever was a little wild, always working at her grand escape. They joked about her disappearance, calling it an omen of their impending doom, knowing it would never happen. They were a "death do us part" couple and as Marshall always said, "a true blue duo."

She stopped dead in her tracks at the hallway's end. A shockwave tore through her. Patches of unfaded paint marked the spots where the Native American paintings and artifacts decorating the walls had hung.

"Marshall. Marshall!" Her voice hit a shrill note. She sprinted toward the bedroom. The sound of running water still issued from the bathroom. She nearly dislocated her wrist rattling the bathroom door's ornate pistol handle. Marshall never locked that door; rarely even shut it when he showered. In her quest to keep the room drier, she insisted an open door supplement the ventilation fan during his long showers.

She pounded on the door. "Honey, open the door! Open up!"

She leaned her forehead against the door and nursed the ache in her fists and forearms, listening to the shower go off, the glass shower door open, Marshall's feet pad across the terrazzo floor, the lock open with a dull click, and the doorknob turn.

It seemed to take forever until Marshall appeared dripping wet in the open doorway, a green Egyptian cotton towel draped around his waist. Water streamed from his hair, slid from his eyelashes and his chest hair in little drops. She stared at his chest, appreciating the little curled hairs and his firm pecs. Her dad and brothers had smooth bodies, and Marshall was the only black man she'd known with a deliciously hairy chest. But why was she thinking this? Why did she have all these collateral thoughts in the midst of a crisis?

Marshall's face contracted in a puzzled expression. "Sa'nnah? What's the matter?"

She couldn't remember the urgent thought she wanted to convey. She stood on tiptoe and brushed her lips across his. Marshall bussed her back, holding her wrist firmly with one hand, pushing her back to gaze into her eyes.

"*Savannah* . . . Are you all right?"

She smoothed her hair back from her forehead in a nervous movement. "You were whistling the same thing over and over."

Marsh moved his fingers from her wrist and intertwined them with her fingers. "I was?" He frowned. "That's odd, but why do you look so weird?"

"I can't remember. What's happening to my memory?" She stared again at her husband's chest. "Oh, Lord have mercy."

"What is it?"

"Lord have mercy," she repeated.

Marshall gazed across the bedroom and a perplexed expression shadowed his already dark face. She pulled him by the hand through the bedroom, noting the disheveled bed again.

Marshall gaped disbelieving at the barren walls of the wide hallway as they hurried to look at the rest of the house. "Holy shit. Who broke through the security system?"

In shock, she didn't reply, continuing to tug him by the arm toward the main rooms of the house. They entered the arched doorway of the living room almost joined at the hip. Marshall's mouth dropped open. "I'll be goddamned . . ."

"Stripped. Completely stripped . . ." Her voice echoed from the beams and walls of the empty room.

Marsh centered himself in the room and spun clockwise in a 360-degree turn. "Unreal," he muttered.

There wasn't a scrap left in the room except for the drapes, not a nail in the walls, not a dust bunny in the corners. Not even a pine needle on the tiled window seat over the missing antique Navajo rug they displayed their Christmas tree on. It looked as though they'd moved and cleaned the room.

Marshall marched into the kitchen with Savannah on his heels. His towel nearly fell from his waist and he rearranged it, tucking the end at one hip, his lips narrowed in a grimace. "How?"

The kitchen gleamed with emptiness. She ran into the Arizona room, dust motes dancing in the rays of morning sunlight that issued through the wooden slats of white shutters mounted on the huge windows. Potted plants, the rattan furniture, and the ferrets' multistoried cage, all gone.

"Oh, Marsh, our babies!" Her distressed squeal turned into a sob.

She turned and ran past her husband, who still stared, dumbfounded, into the empty pantry. She dashed through the living room and into the hallway, stopping at the door of their library, a large room arranged at one corner of the house. Taking a deep breath, she gingerly turned the doorknob with her fingertips as though not to disturb what she'd find inside. Then she held her breath as she peered into the solemn gloom. Like the Arizona room, the shutters were on the windows, still securely closed. The floor to ceiling shelves had teemed with books, videos, papers and memorabilia and now gaped at her like mouths missing their teeth. She touched the recessed light switch and track lighting bordering the walls came to life. Their desks, computers, the flatscreen TV, and wing back chairs were gone.

She ran to the next door, a guest room, and flung it open with a bang into the wall-mounted doorstop. A ruffled, girly room, she'd painstakingly collected and decorated it with country antiques and the beaded regalia of Plains Indian women. She sank to her knees where a floral oriental rug should have lain beside a canopy bed and stared out a window where a roman shade was half-drawn.

Marshall's familiar hand came to rest on her shoulder. "Sa'nnah?"

She snuffled through her tears like a little girl. Marshall tried to comfort her, but his voice held the same insecurity she felt. "Our babies. Our home. It's like everything vanished into the next dimension."

"Once and Twice . . ." Marshall cursed their loss. "We can replace things, but . . ." He kneeled and pulled Savannah into his arms. ". . . Can't believe the little weasels are gone . . ." The catch in her husband's voice caused a flood of new tears from her. "Except for our room, everything . . ."

Marsh quieted for a moment. "This reminds me of something." He cleared his throat. ". . . I heard a story once."

"A story?" She wiped her face with sweaty palms. Her mind seemed to sashay wherever it wanted to go. Why would Marsh tell her a story now, of all times?

He held her tighter. "I mean a true story. One that might explain this. You remember Heinz?"

"The German guy you used to write to . . . the one that invented all sorts of crazy things?"

"That's him. The one time I met him in the flesh, he told me a story over several beers. A curious story. Did I ever tell it to you?"

"No. I don't think so . . ."

"Back in the late sixties, before the new environmental movement peaked, Heinz worked on some devices based on the work of Nikola Tesla. He was determined to reintroduce wireless electricity on a practical, mass scale." Marsh spoke at a breathless rapid-fire pace. "Hardly anyone in the industrial world considered living off the grid back then. Just a few hippies and some remote ranchers and farmers who either equipped themselves with wind or gas generators or lived without power. Anyway, Heinz was snubbed by his colleagues and told by engineers that his was an impossible dream, to get off his cloud. Couldn't get anyone interested even though he was close to patenting his inventions. One day he came home from some university seminar, and found his flat in Munich was stripped bare."

"Like this?"

"Exactly. He said it was cleaner than he'd left it. Even his housecat vanished. He wondered at first if jealousy spurred the incident, then he took it as a warning. He abandoned his lease and never went back. Said he never had the heart to start over. Moved on to less controversial things. He married, had a couple of kids, and figured if he ever tried to resurrect the old work, it might mean his life or the lives of his family. He felt lucky losing just his belongings and research."

"The government did this to him?"

Marsh looked Savannah in the eye as though he wondered why she was incredulous. Then she remembered *their* research and felt stunned at his statement.

"Which government, is what I wondered," Marshall said. "German? I thought they were too busy regrouping from the war even two or three decades later to be bothered with the issue. Some international coalition of government and corporate interest, more likely. Same group we're up against now in the form of NIHSA, no doubt. Anyway, Heinz said it was possible to make things vanish. You remember the Philadelphia Experiment."

They stared into each other's eyes for a long time.

She wiped her eyes and took the initiative to ask the big question again. "What happened last night?"

Marshall shook his head hard, as much to clear his mind as to show he didn't know. He pressed his lips together, raised his eyebrows, and gestured with open palms.

"I woke up blank as an empty slate. Except for one weird image. Reptile eyes staring at me. I had more than one bad dream, Sa'nnah. The first time we got up and prayed . . ."

"We prayed; I remember feeling quite peaceful and protected when we went back to sleep. Then I woke up on the end of the bed, hardly remembering who I am or where I was . . ."

"That's not like you. You're a morning person."

"Marsh, you locked the bathroom door, you never do that. You whistled the same bar of a song in the shower over and over . . ."

"And you came screaming like a banshee down the hall . . ."

"A banshee, huh?" She gave him her best black chick head roll.

"Well, you know, you were shouting and pounding on the door."

"Neither of us remember anything after the prayers and meditation, right?"

"Right . . . but I had another dream."

"What?" She shook Marsh's hand impatiently. He had to remember something, anything.

"The second dream was like the first, the one that woke us up. Only darker. More real." He closed his eyes and took a deep breath.

"I dreamed of getting hurt the first time around. The second time, no one got hurt. There were men dressed in dark clothing. Asking questions. I felt scared but didn't seem to care, if that makes sense." He opened his eyes wide, surprised at this scrap of dream recall. "I remember you, Sa'nnah. You watched us from the head of the bed, laughing."

She gave him another soul sister neck roll. “Me? When have I ever laughed at you, Marsh? That *must* have been a dream.”

“No.” He shook his head vehemently. “No, I distinctly saw you laugh.” He suddenly pulled her bathrobe up and peered at her thighs.

“Sa’nnah.” Marshall’s voice went husky and he traced a finger around a faint bruise on her upper thigh. “Look at this.”

In the center of the uneven bruise was a mark. A puncture mark.

He stood up, yanked his towel off and turned to catch light from a bedroom window. While no bruise showed on his dark thigh, another puncture like a hairless pore scored it.

“You know what this means.” He dourly adjusted his towel.

“Yes.” A sour lump rose from the pit of her stomach. “That was no dream, Baby.”

:::Chapter 31

Carson Hodges

When the sky lightened, Carson figured the space probe incident had ended about four hours before. They'd lost some precious time before they set out walking because they stopped to pick out goatsheads, cactus thorns, and other prickly debris embedded in their shoes, socks, and jeans legs.

"These pokies are too much." Mikka shattered the silence, picking at her ankles again. He and Tess chuckled their anxiety away once more. They began walking again, forcing themselves forward on what they hoped would be the last leg of their journey.

The cold became colder and the dark darker in the last hours before dawn. Their anxiety and fear thickened like a crust around them. The hike became tedious, a plodding inertia through a murky bad dream. He suggested another rest, but Tess said her familiarity with the landscape made her want to press on.

Using hand signs, he insisted stopping for a brief meal, a cactus appetizer. There wasn't much edible plant life in the high desert in winter, just some rain-deprived prickly pear, thin pads curling in the cold, dry air. He dethorned some pads with the knife, peeling them down to the meager flesh. They sucked and chomped at the pads voraciously. Mikka was too drowsy to join them, so Carson packed some into the military issue backpack. Despite the meager pickings, he counted them lucky to be trudging through the desert in December—they'd never have made it this far in hot weather.

"How are you holding up, Tess?" he asked after the silent meal.

"I'm ready for a long, hot shower." She complained about feeling dirty rather than describing the pain she obviously tried to hide.

"When water was scarce, my ancestors "bathed" in the smoke of the creosote bush," he replied. "They believed creosote was the first plant created, and they believed its smoke was both medicinal and purifying."

"It's too bad creosote doesn't grow at this elevation. Maybe we'll find some more sage."

"Rare in the winter, but we could." He encouraged Mikka to climb on his back. While they prepared to trundle off again, the hazy predawn sky shattered piece by piece into brush strokes reminiscent of an Asian script. Brilliant golden cloud characters glowed against sky blue, inked by the hand of the Great Mystery. He and Tess drank in the sky until Mikka groaned from his shoulder. He pulled her around into his arms, patted her back, and glanced at Tess. She'd moved like an elder the past hour, hobbling a good ways behind him. He could see that she didn't want him to mention her pain. But her eyes said, "press on."

A short time later, when he glanced back, Tess looked "green around the gills," as his Hawaiian granny would say. Her slack cheeks framed eyes puffy with fatigue. She seemed dazed, as if too many thoughts whirled around her mind. In contrast, the sunlight grazing the rocky eastern horizon behind them backlit the reddish-brown peaks of Tess's patchy haircut, giving her the appearance of a benevolent but suffering pixie.

Responding to his look of encouragement, Tess limped harder to catch up. He slowed, pretending not to notice her uneven gait. She reached out and cuffed him playfully on his arm. He let her pass him.

Limping ahead, she walked no more than a few hundred yards, then stopped and pretended to admire the clouds and the sky's changing colors again. But she soon fell behind again.

A flock of sparrows appeared out of nowhere. They scattered in a gust of damp wind, struggling to stay together. The frantic fluttering of tiny brown wings looked fragile against the gathering clouds. He broke their long silence. "We're close to civilization."

"You're right. I've never seen sparrows in open country." Tess stroked Mikka's hair for an instant and balled her hands into her hoody's shallow pockets.

Leaning forward on the balls of his feet to balance Mikka's weight, he shivered, the layers of T-shirt, flannel shirt, and lined denim jacket not enough to repel the damp cold. His head ached and the back of his throat was beginning to feel raw. Now he wished for the medicinal powers of creosote *and* sage.

"Storm's coming." He offered Tess his arm. She smiled and her sweet nature shone through her dancing eyes. He took her radiance as a compliment and smiled back, careful to generate as much healing compassion as he could muster. Mikka stirred and stretched, her little body arching in his arms.

"I'm thirsty again, Mama." Her eyebrows rose and she looked at Tess with a trace of accusation in her eyes. "We going home? I'm so cold."

He stopped and gave Mikka the last bit of water from the canteen. "I've never seen you this finicky, Miss Mikka."

"Well, I've had it." She screwed her little face into a frown.

Tess shot him a look. He expected amusement, but she appeared motherly, emotional, and bereaved. He coughed to suppress his grin and coaxed Mikka to taste a bit of prickly pear pad, expecting her to snub the offer. She ate it, though, eager as a kid with a candy bar.

Mikka reached for Tess, who lifted her from his arms. Mikka wrapped her legs around her mom's waist.

"Mikka, Mama's so sorry, sweetie. You shouldn't be here." Tess sighed, her voice watery with tears, her face darkening as though a shadow passed over it. It was the first time he heard her speak directly to Mikka about the situation. Until now, Tess was motherly and kind, but divulged no extra information to Mikka. Trying, he supposed, to keep their lives in equilibrium. Whether Tess realized it or not, she'd done a great job shielding Mikka from adult worries. Mikka seemed unusually composed for a kid her age.

Tess turned to him, wiping a teary cheek with a wind-roughened, dirty hand. "I've thanked you but I never thought to ask why you're helping us, total strangers."

"I—"

"No, I'm sorry. Of course people help other people. It's a shallow thought. I'll zip my lip."

"There's nothing to be sorry about . . ." He leaned toward Tess, curving a rough brown hand around hers.

Tess smiled through her tears. "Your touch is as sweet as your handsome face, Carson."

He ignored her remark. "I think you need to hear this. I've come this far with you because you came to me needing my help."

"I intuit that it doesn't matter to you whether you're successful or not."

"Don't get me wrong." He smiled. "This sounds like I don't care about you personally. I do. But keeping you from harm is my most important intention. Yet karma is . . ." he started to say *immutable..*

The karma word fell like a dark curtain on a lighted stage. Tess's eyes softened and her happiness melted into poignancy, as if she felt something deep inside her heart that made her smile disappear.

"The word karma always unsettles me. So what happens is a result of my previous actions?"

"Yes. All our actions combined. No more and no less. It's always that way."

"Then why would you participate in my karma if it might hurt you?"

"That you showed up on my doorstep with my dear friends makes our karma intertwined."

"Group karma?"

"You could call it that."

"Then you think we've known each other before?"

"No doubt. Beings are said to be reborn for eons of lifetimes before reaching enlightenment. As Tibetans say, 'we've all been each other's mothers.'"

"So having a connection in another lifetime might not be as meaningful as we think?"

"Well, it can be important but it's definitely not uncommon. Our enemies return as friends, and friends return as enemies, they say."

"Like changing costumes on stage."

"Very much so. Right now you're the damsel in distress and I'm the tall . . . well . . . medium, dark, and uh . . . sorta good-looking wild savage." He felt another rush of blood to his face. He started to babble about Buddhist philosophy. "Wise human beings who 'see things as they are' transform the energy of desire into awareness and understanding—"

"Hero," Tess said. "You forgot hero, Carson. Don't let me forget to thank you again." She leaned over and planted a firm kiss on his cheek. She smelled of sweat, smoke and something sweet like vanilla.

Tess suddenly staggered back as though her legs were giving out. Her face tensed with pain she didn't try to hide this time. She handed Mikka back to him. Drowsy again, Mikka lay her little head on his shoulder. Tess placed her forehead against his, her eyes shining feverishly. A wave of serenity passed between them. They rubbed noses, felt the old magnetic pull of romance. Carson tingled at the thought of kissing her, pressing his lips to hers. Instead, he lay his cheek on top of her head and stroked her face. She rubbed her nose against his again. He put his eyes to her cheek and teased a laugh from her with a butterfly kiss. Tess needed laughs, not romance.

"You're funny," she giggled, laying her own butterfly kiss on him.

He jumped aside, tickling her in the ribcage. Tess tickled back.

"You're funnier." He sputtered, choking back a belly laugh.

Then they did a giggle dance, wanting to extricate themselves from the tickles and still remain in each other's grasp.

Tess laughed so hard she started crying. Dismayed, he wondered what he'd done. Maybe it wasn't a good time to play. Or maybe she needed him to kiss her. As he leaned toward her, she took one step back.

Mikka stirred, picking her head up from his shoulder. "Mama, don't cry." Her voice was thick with sleep. She leaned over and patted Tess on the head with a dusty little hand. "Daddy will find us. Just like Carson."

A look of astonishment crossed Tess's face. Mikka's unexpected remark caused her to utter a strangled sound from deep in her chest.

"Mikka," Tess finally said. She turned to him. "Carson. He's alive."

"Mikka's dad?"

"Yes! I haven't discussed our relationship . . . The Updikes must have filled you in on the story."

"They did. But I don't get it . . . alive, I mean. I heard about the controversy, about his cremation. The speculation it wasn't his body. Then the brush-off. Congressional briefings begin the day after New Year's."

"Headed by Chaz Collins? Tess made a little hissing sound. "The son of Harris's political opponent? What a joke!"

She explained what she'd dreamed in Washington—a mysterious double, Henry moving in an open casket. And then described the real funeral, a possible mannequin or double in the casket.

"I didn't tell Marshall and Savannah about it because I felt so overwrought the day I met them. I didn't want to play kiss and tell at the time. I've spent three solid years guarding my privacy and worrying about Mikka . . ."

"That's understandable."

Tess swiped at her runny nose with her hand. "Carson, if Harris wasn't assassinated and there was a mannequin or double in the casket, there had to be a coup."

"A power struggle. Interesting. Then where's Henry? In this context, your problems make sense."

"Why I'm on the run . . ."

"I'd trust Mikka to know his status. She definitely has Starchild medicine."

"Mikka . . ." Tess whispered, a look of genuine despair on her face. "I have to protect her at all costs. Please, please don't tell anyone."

"You have my word, Tess. More than my word." He took the risk of speaking in female language this time, leaned toward her gently, and kissed her on the cheek.

Tess glowed and Mikka's face glowed in response. Tess kissed the tips of her first and middle fingers on her free hand and brushed them across his lips. "You're one of the most generous souls I've ever met. You've kept me putting one foot in front of the other . . ." She grimaced suddenly as though warding off pain or unwanted thoughts. "Knowing Harris is alive gives me hope that he can make all this stop somehow."

His eyes met Tess's. "Hope is a good thing. Makes the impossible possible. I'll be around to help you until this situation is resolved."

Tess squeezed his hand and stared at him. Her large dark eyes brightened again in a feverish way. She began to walk with a little more spring in her step. Mikka toddled beside her mother, head held high.

He gestured across miles of open high desert. "After you, ladies. Our destiny awaits."

Tess took the cue and curtseyed. Mikka imitated her. They moved on in silence as the wind picked up, fanning the already chilled air that swirled around them like some damp, malevolent spirit. The sun suddenly broke through the thick clouds in a Biblical fashion. Snow clouds, it looked like. His Navajo granny owned a big, leather-bound Bible given to her by a missionary who failed to convert her from her Blessingway faith. It had a similar picture in the book of Genesis. Carson always imagined that picture to be the Christian God—the long, streaming light rays piercing through dark clouds of human anguish in a sunrise of mythical proportions. Like the picture, the momentary display of light above them softened the dreariness that threatened to swallow them. It eased the physical chill too, if only for an instant.

Tess seemed to fully understand how the human mind jumps from one extreme to another. With his support, her resignation suddenly shifted into resolve. She seemed newly determined to not let her pain slow her down or to let her suffering fester into bitterness. She had to survive this trial, if only to find sanctuary for Mikka.

He prayed for this positive outcome as fervently as Tess.

:::Chapter 32

Marshall Updike

"Marsh, I keep thinking of Tess. We need to contact her relatives," Savannah declared. "I mean her uncle and aunt."

His wife's hunches were always right on. Marshall grabbed for the phone book and snatched air, forgetting that the communication cubby in the kitchen wall was empty of directory and phone.

Savannah saved the day with the cell phone she'd tucked into her bathrobe pocket on Christmas night. "Tess said her uncle lived in Picture Rocks," she reminded him as she pressed the phone into his hand.

"We don't know what their address is. Picture Rocks Road, maybe? It's a long shot. If we can't get a number, we'll call Paul." He keyed in Directory Assistance. "Tucson. Vaughn. Picture Rocks Road," he said in a loud voice to the computerized service. The phone responded with a pleasant, generic photo of a female representative, reciting the name and number in a digital female voice.

"Yes!" He pumped his fist in the air. "It's gotta be the one." Jazzed, he pressed the numbers as fast as his big fingers could move on the touchscreen keypad. He prayed the Vaughns hadn't gone somewhere for the remainder of the holiday. His heart fell when he reached an answering machine and soared a second later when another pleasant female voice, a real one this time, said he'd reached Mac and Xénia Vaughn. Jackpot. He just had to mention Tess and the Vaughns would call him back.

After leaving a message, he called Paul's number on a whim, but his voice messaging indicated a full mailbox. "Can't get Paul and can't leave a message," he complained. "Must be busy."

Still wearing her "I'm getting a funny feeling" look, Savannah watched him press the phone's "end call" option.

"I'm . . ." they said together, ". . . getting a funny feeling about this."

They also jumped simultaneously when Savannah's new ringtone for Mac Vaughn—some rousing bars of "Bat City" by Avenged Sevenfold—blared from the phone.

"Updike's," Marshall answered.

Mac Vaughn's voice boomed loud and clear in his distinctive west Wales accent. Marshall explained how he and Savannah came to know Tess and Mikka, that they'd deposited them at Carson's remote rancheria in Cochise County for safekeeping. Mac shared his misgivings after dithering about speaking to a stranger.

"Marr-shall, I have some peculiar feelings about this, too. I'm relieved that Tess is away from Tucson. But we've not been able to ring Paul. Under the circumstances, I think he'd make himself available."

"My feeling too, Mac." His intuition told him Mac had a plan. "How shall we proceed?"

Savannah shot him a grin and shook her head, mouthing the word 'men.'

"Lad, I've already made some contacts. I could use more young blood . . ."

Mac must have suddenly covered his phone with his hand. Straining to hear, he made out a muffled female voice scolding Mac. ". . . you're almost ninety, you old codger. You've no business tramping around the countryside. Send Trey or Trevor."

Mac's irritation showed. "Xénia, I'll be handling this."

Mac's phone bumped something with a dull clack and Mac cleared his throat, resuming their conversation. "Head for Phoenix, then I-17 North. I'll keep you posted from the air. My sons will also be on the ground. They're warming up the Ram now."

Apparently, the old gent had a military background. Marshall wanted more detail, but Mac seemed satisfied he had the situation in hand. Savannah quizzed Marshall with wide eyes as he continued the conversation.

"Check. Let's coordinate our watches—oh nine hundred hours sharp."

"Roger that," Mac purred, his pleasure obvious. "Detail exchange every quarter hour. My contacts report two parties roaming Yavapai County forest land and a unit leaving Phoenix. Military transmissions and GPS satellite sweeps and no known military installation in the northern region."

Marshall marveled at Mac's quick mind. "Something's up." He nodded at Savannah. "Then you think . . ."

"Aye, Marshall. A bird is waiting. Marana Air Park. Check you in fifteen."

He replied in Mac's style: "Aye, aye. We're on our way."

"Well?" Savannah returned to the room, dressed in odds and ends she might wear to work in the yard, some old U of A basketball hoodies draped over one arm.

He explained Mac's conversation. "There's a "unit," a vehicle leaving Phoenix. Mac also mentioned two parties wandering Yavapai County forest land. Maybe Tess and Mikka are in one of those those parties . . . at least Mac thinks so." He did a little jig. "We're off to see the wizard . . ."

"How? Dressed in what?" Bemused, Savannah had found the walk-in closet stripped to the bone earlier. "I can't believe all the clothes we have left are in that storage bin under the bed," she said, motioning at her mismatched outfit. "At least they left us in our bed and left the bin underneath it. You had some halfway decent stuff in it." She pulled a pouty face and tossed his hoody toward him. "But me . . . never mind that. I bet the garage is empty, too."

"Blast!" He flung open the door between their kitchen and garage. "You're so right. Clean as a whistle." He glanced at his watch. "Thirteen minutes and counting."

Savannah shot him another look.

"We're exchanging location info with Mac every fifteen minutes."

She nodded, her eyes sparkling. Savannah loved adventure as much as he. "Wait! Maybe they missed old Guzzi . . ."

They tore through the kitchen to the Arizona room and outside across the back patio. The garden gate clacked open when Marshall pulled the string latch and they dashed to a canvas car shade tied at either end with waterproof tarps. He pumped his fist in the air again. "Good sign, Baby!"

He wrangled around behind the trailer constructed from an old Chevy pickup bed. The 1970 Moto Guzzi and sidecar gleamed through a layer of dust in the morning sunlight. He rubbed away a big cobweb that stretched from the exhaust pipe to the roomy sidecar. "Guzzi girl, go, go, go," he chanted. "Sa'nnah, get the . . ."

He realized again that there was nothing in the garage to get. He ran back to the patio and peered over the wall separating their property from the neighbor's house a half-acre away. Savannah kept him from falling back as he climbed the wall, steadying himself with one knee. Then he leapt down to bare, sandy ground on the other side. He hustled toward the riding mower and a five-gallon can of gas resting in the shade of a large shed in the neighbor's back yard. As he grabbed the can, a pair of freckled black and white pit bulls surged toward him, barking their asses off. He must have been a sight thump-bumping across the yard with the heavy can. He hoisted it atop the wall, flew up and over it himself, one hand scraping against an old granddaddy saguaro for balance, glad for his old Nike high-tops with air soles. As he hit ground, he pulled the can down while the dogs yapped furiously at the spot where he'd disappeared.

"Thank you, neighbor," he yelled over his shoulder.

Savannah unsnapped the sidecar cover and pulled out their old helmets, the same midnight blue as the bike. They gleamed in the sunlight.

"Hey, no dust," she said, holding the helmets up as he unscrewed the chrome gas cap, spilling fuel from the unwieldy five- gallon can. It had lost its funnel, but the better part of three gallons made it into the tank.

"Damn it! The key's missing." Their spare keys had hung from a brass plate in the kitchen.

"Hot wire in the old town tonight!" Savannah read his mind and brandished a screwdriver she'd dug out of a kit tucked in the sidecar boot. "Darlin', gimme that old time religion." She sashayed to where Marshall knelt near the engine.

"Just like old times." When they'd met in college, both the Guzzi and his old red Fiat had electrical peculiarities. He'd hot-wired them often to get them started, avoiding long, boring weekends on campus.

He selected wires from the battery, pulled the ends loose, twisted the throttle a few times, and motioned to Savannah to bridge the gap between the wires with her screwdriver.

Mounting the Guzzi, he stroked her tank like a horse's neck, toed the gearshift into neutral, twisted the throttle, and kicked the starter. "Battery's probably gone," he grunted. He used to be in the habit of servicing the old Italian bike every few weeks, then taking it out for a brief neighborhood spin. Lately he'd spent a lot of time on the internet or with the Bible code software, hunting for answers about government conspiracies and the Earth's future.

"Ten minutes, Baby. Chargin', bargin', Guzzi girl," Savannah chanted.

"Boogaloo, boogaloo, boogaloo!" They tossed their heads back and cheered the process like they had so many years ago. His blood warmed with excitement.

Savannah repositioned the screwdriver and wires. He nailed the kickstarter and gunned the throttle once more. The Guzzi coughed, sputtered, sparked, backfired, and coughed again.

"I don't know," he muttered. He kicked the starter and twisted the throttle once more, melding his body energy with the machine. She sputtered and then hummed in her characteristic Italian.

"Arrivaderci!" Their shout rose over the purring machine. They high-fived and pulled on the helmets over their sweatshirt hoods. Savannah swiped at the dusty cycle and sidecar windshields with a faded green mechanic's rag. He wished a moment for the black leather jackets, pants, and boots they'd stored in the cedar-lined walk-in closet.

Savannah slid into the sidecar, clipped her cell phone to her hoody pocket, positioned a wireless earpiece on her right ear, and settled in for the ride. Marshall revved the engine, blasted through the easement and into the narrow alley, hoping no one would notice the expired plates. One minute and counting.

Mac or one of his sons called them every quarter hour on the nose as he promised. Trey and Trevor continued north from Marana in Mac's Dodge Ram, "Big Blackie," they called it. Mac rode in the catbird seat aboard his pilot friend's red and white medevac helicopter.

Despite Mac's instructions that helped them wend their way around freeway construction snarls, they got snagged in slowdowns twice—a widening project just miles above their north Tucson home and another near Chandler, the burgeoning south Phoenix suburb. Worse than idling in creeping traffic was trying to breathe in the thick smog of a Phoenix winter temperature inversion.

Marshall gunned the cycle out of the right lane and around an RV with Polk County, Iowa tags, laden with lawn chairs and bicycles. A white-haired grandpa pointed at them and small faces appeared at the side windows as they passed.

They flew by green freeway signs and the corresponding exits. Camelback Rd., Bethany Home Rd., Glendale Ave., Northern Ave., Dunlap Ave., Peoria Ave., Cactus Rd, Thunderbird Rd., Greenway

Rd. Traffic picked up, lots of folks back to work the day after Christmas, starting another leg of a holiday adventure, or simply rushing to clearance sales at the malls.

Savannah slapped at his leg and pointed at the cell phone as the thrill of the ride began to wear off. "Mac's up on I-17 near Union Hills turnoff," she shouted. "Can't hear or see him very well. Think he's circling over the freeway ahead of us. Sounds like there's been an accident. Big Blackie's either in it or stuck behind it. But he was happy—'Unbelievable blessings this day brings,' he said and winked at me on Skype . . . he was aiming his phone at the scene when the signal failed."

That was odd. He nodded, trying to focus on Savannah's voice and traffic at the same time.

She pulled the earpiece from her ear, examined it, put it back, and pushed a redial option on the phone. "Shit, I lost the signal again!" she shouted. Her eyes snapped with annoyance behind her lightly tinted face shield.

He wished they had techno helmets with intercom radio so they didn't have to shout at each other. Or better yet, helmets with intercom and wireless hookup, so they could both talk to Mac and even see him at the same time.

"If you can't get Mac, he'll try you again." He tried to exaggerate his lip movements while he shouted to make sure Savannah knew what he was saying.

Cars and trucks ground to a halt in a sea of brake lights up ahead. He swerved the bike into the wide gap between the carpool and fast lanes, praying no one would open a door. Motorists shook their heads as the Guzzi whizzed past. An ulcer-making mile later, the source of the traffic jam appeared. A large van, a Class B RV, he thought they called it, plain white with Florida plates, sat with its right front wheel over the line of the Union Hills off-ramp. Its rear end was crumpled and fused to it was the front of Mac's big black pickup.

A red and white medevac chopper circled overhead, and a single motorcycle cop in tall black boots stood with two well-built gentlemen in sleek, uniform-like dark sweaters and pants—a large, burly black man wearing one gold hoop earring and a handsome, silver-haired white man wearing an unusually large gay pride ring, a rainbow of stones set in sterling silver or white gold or platinum wrapped around a large section of one middle finger. They both gestured with their arms, their faces ranging from expressions of annoyed impatience to anger. Marshall couldn't hear what they said, but ropy veins stood out on the white guy's neck while he spat out his words and showed the cop a wallet-like object, identification, probably. He gestured with his left hand, his ring glinting in the sun. Then the black guy reached into his jacket, displayed his identification and patted a bulge under the side of his jacket. Plainclothes detectives or agents of some sort.

Marshall took a deep breath and eased into a space a few vehicles behind the accident. Had Mac's twins Trey and Trevor accidentally or purposely rear-ended those men? The Phoenix motorcycle cop wasn't letting anyone pass around the scene yet. Though the left lanes were free, he'd parked his Kawasaki KZ 1000 so it partially blocked both and he busily lit flares and lay them down in a third lane. Trey and Trevor sat placidly in Mac's "Big Blackie," a Department of Public Safety cruiser parked behind them. A female DPS officer stood at the driver's window talking to Trey.

Savannah unclipped the phone from her pocket and flipped it open again. She sat up on her knees in the sidecar, lifted her face shield, and put her face close to his. "Mac's above us. Says they've intercepted some messages and triangulated a radio frequency to that white vehicle. He figures those two guys in dark clothes must be government agents looking for Tess. Mac wants us to make another diversion."

Mac had more gizmos than NIHSA. Marshall hesitated, confused for a moment, and then realized what Mac meant.

"Lean as close to me as you can, Sa'nnah." He took a deep breath, twisted the Guzzi throttle, revved the engine three times, then popped the clutch and spun forward.

Both cops' heads snapped in their direction. The cycle officer pulled at his chinstrap and took three big jogs toward his bike. The chopper dove lower, hovering over the officers. The DPS officer waved her arms at it, a stupefied expression on her face. The black guy and white guy looked at each other and dashed for their van.

He prayed for enough space to clear the parked Kawasaki, but when the sidecar's outside edge rammed its front tire, the officer's bike flipped and crashed. Marshall glanced down at Savannah. Her eyes were big but she circled a thumb and forefinger, signaling okay. He braked hard while opening the throttle, spinning the Guzzi around just in time to see the chopper knock the black guy on his ass with a runner. The blow should have killed him or left him unconscious. But he sprang up like some otherworldly thing from a thriller movie. Marshall wanted to rub his eyes in disbelief when the man's form flickered in the sunlight like a film image. Did he really see a bipedal lizard for an instant?

He took a quick look behind him at the cops, who regarded the black agent with narrowed eyes, their hands poised on their Glock service holsters. Both agents leapt at the driver's door of the van and tried to open it, but Trey and Trevor exploded from the black pickup, colliding with the DPS officer as the group surged toward the van. The DPS officer recoiled, trying to draw her gun with one hand while rubbing her nose with the other, one eye clenched shut. She bellowed at everyone to halt in a voice that could tumble walls, but Trey and Trevor still made for the agents. Trevor's long dark ponytail bounced and his face contorted with effort as he tackled the white man. Trey suddenly sailed through the air from a well-placed kick the black guy aimed at him. Then the black guy did something no earthly human could do—he ripped the van door from its hinges and swung it at Trey.

Trey rolled back on the pavement, wide-eyed with surprise. The DPS officer froze for an instant, another stupefied look crossing her face, then she decisively drew her Glock and motioned at Trey and Trevor just as the chopper swooped down again, so close it made her duck. The motorcycle cop drew his weapon, but didn't seem to know who to point it at either. Both officers glowered at the chopper, glowered at the agents, glowered at the twins, and then trained their Glocks on him. He made a split-second decision to rush them, revving the Guzzi engine to a high-pitched scream. The officers hesitated again, no doubt because it wasn't a safe location to fire shots. Suddenly, a volley of shots pinged around the Guzzi while it careened forward, but the shots came from the agents, not the cops. His heart jumped into his throat when Savannah doubled over.

The motorists idling directly behind the "accident" ducked or shrank in their seats, but those farthest away pointed and leaned forward. The southbound traffic in the other lane slowed down and sped up again as motorists rubbernecked and others instinctively forged ahead.

He glanced back. When the helicopter lunged at the agents again, the black guy soared upward in an old-fashioned "hoops" jump, grabbed a helicopter skid, and tried to fight his way onto it as the pilot shook the craft back and forth to dislodge him.

Another bullet whizzed over his head. He cocked the Guzzi clutch, shifted into high gear and kept going the wrong way, wedged between the outside lane and the tiny shoulder, the sidecar scraping with flying sparks against the freeway divider.

He looked back in the Guzzi's mirror. *What the hell.* A medium-sized figure in a patterned turtleneck sweater and a mussed-up, gelled haircut now stood beside the van with Trey and Trevor. Where did he know that sweater and that hair from? My God, was that Paul?

He knew the plan would be to extend a cable and basket from the chopper, but it still circled with the black agent hugging the top of the skid. The bikeless cop and the DPS officer hunkered down behind the DPS cruiser, Glocks in one hand, their heads leaned toward radios clipped to their shoulders.

He braked and turned the Guzzi next to a late model four-door Lincoln with two scared-looking senior couples inside. Savannah sat up, her face ashen. He almost grabbed her and touched her all over to reassure himself that she was okay. Holding hands, they gazed up at the chopper. It plummeted to within a few feet of the ground, and then soared in a looping arc worthy of a dragonfly, soaring nearly five hundred feet from the ground. The agent fell with a scream unlike any he'd ever heard, landing with a sickening thud on a shiny new Cadillac. But the man wasn't a man any longer—a blunt-nosed man-sized bipedal lizard lay crumpled atop the obliterated Cadillac hood. The agent's death must have caused him to assume his true form. Marshall thought of the crazy tabloid rumors about Senator C. Clelland Collins and figured the speculation must be true, that it must be the source of President Henry's and Tess's problems.

A chill iced his guts. Savannah reached up and gripped his arm. Motorists jumped out of their cars, cell phones aimed and flashing. Savannah grabbed her phone, her fingers shaking while she held it up to catch a quick shot. He wouldn't let his mind grapple with it—there wasn't time to think more about the creature.

The cops sprinted toward the lizard man as the chopper arced down again and hovered over the van, lowering the cable and basket. The white guy appeared from behind a bobtail delivery truck parked askew near the van, flattened himself on the pavement and fired shots upward as Mac appeared at the cargo door. The cops ran from the Cadillac when the first shot rang out, circled around the van, and tasered the agent. They looked back and forth between the helicopter, the Guzzi, and each other, wondering, no doubt, what to do next.

Mac hitched up his western jeans up on his ample belly and flat behind when the basket reached his boys and Paul. He crouched down to give Paul a hand into the chopper, and then Trey and Trev in turn. Grinning ear-to-ear, Mac stood and waved to him and Savannah with a thumbs up. They returned the signal.

Sirens began to wail in the distance. The chopper turned in an ear-splitting 180-degree half circle and hovered again over the subdued agent, making sure he was down for the count. Then it darted toward the cycle, lowering the cable again. Savannah cheered and fingered a victory sign and leapt up and grabbed the rim of the basket. He turned to look at the cops, who seemed transfixed, maybe too riveted by events or too safety-conscious to intervene without backup. Or maybe they just knew the good guys when they saw them.

Savannah raised her face shield and gazed down wistfully at the Guzzi and sidecar, stimulating his pangs of regret at leaving the old girl. He raised his face shield and their eyes locked for a moment. His wife's mouth curved into a smile and she winked at him. He laughed with joy. "We're finally seeing what we've suspected for years, Sa'nnah," he shouted.

When she was safely aboard the craft and the basket lowered again and swung toward him, he nailed the edge of it with all ten fingers like a cat hanging from a high tree branch, tension hardening every muscle in his body while he climbed inside.

As he sailed upward he tried not to look down, but he couldn't resist gazing at the lizard sprawled on the Cadillac's crushed roof. Ever since he'd fallen from the hayloft on the family farm at age eight, he hadn't climbed more than ten feet above the ground without feeling nauseated. That, and the fleeting thought that these lizard ETs truly existed made his stomach churn.

::: Chapter 33

Tess Vaughn

Tess felt a magnetic pull, a subtle tendril drawing her toward something . . . home . . . a resolution. If she was right about their location, they were hiking a beeline for the flagstone and gravel operation bordering forest land near her home.

She must keep her mind open and serene. She filled her head with the mantra Carson taught her, *Om mani padme hung*, one repetition after another, hoping these would continue to tame her wild negative thoughts. She almost laughed at the irony—Carson had taught her a new way to live. She'd never known anyone who laughed in the face of suffering before. Suddenly she lost the mantra and thought of the star quilt bunched up at the foot of her unmade bed, its warm colors and dazzling pattern clear in her mind. When they made it home, she'd gift Carson with it. Wasn't the star quilt an old Indian pattern?

She and Carson didn't talk about the early morning's strange happenings, letting go of one trauma to deal with the next as they plodded through more high desert prairie. She half-expected to see a pronghorn or jackrabbit, but the only thing that stirred after the flock of sparrows were wind-tossed clumps of gramma grass and swirls of dust.

When Mikka's words reverberated in her head, touching her with renewed surprise, she realized she'd reentered her thoughts and lost track of the mantra again.

Daddy will help us. Just like Carson, she promised.

As she mentally rehashed Mikka's words, her solar plexus tingled like it had when she felt attracted to Picacho Peak. She looked up. A tall, distinguished man stood in front of them, a lone figure in the middle of a narrow dirt road. She rubbed her eyes to brush away the crazy vision, then stood transfixed, gazing at the convergence of her past and future, her mouth wide open in surprise. She never dreamed she'd meet this man, not in the foothills of Phoenix and certainly not on this high desert plateau. Even from dozens of yards away, she knew him.

Her heart began to pound. Harris and Mikka had to meet. There was no avoiding it now. Could he help them or would his presence harm them?

Harris Henry tilted his head at a quizzical slant at the sky and then at them, sizing up the situation. Carson seemed confounded for a moment, almost as if he wanted to reach up and rub his eyes. Then he glanced at her and understood.

"Daddy!" Mikka tore herself from her arms and ran to Harris, dodging rocks and the spear-like tips of yucca leaves, her little arms outstretched.

"Yup, it's me, though I'm gettin' burnt black," Harris joked.

Harris turned toward her, one corner of his mouth twitching up in the lopsided curve that always revealed his surprise. She took a deep breath and raised her open hand to greet him, trying to center herself in the emotional tsunami that threatened to wash her away.

Ever kind and discreet, Carson murmured, "I'm going back up the hill and look around."

When Mikka reached Harris, he swung her up and into his arms as though he met her at his door every day after work. She had to hand it to him—he always could shift gears in an instant. By the time she reached him, he and Mikka were forehead-to-forehead, peering into one another's eyes and laughing.

Flabbergasted, she grappled for words. She'd try to play it cool too. "Care for an introduction?"

Mikka looked at her and then turned her relentless three-year old stare at Harris. "I'm Mikka Delaraye Vaughn. And this is my very important Daddy. He's smelly and needs a bath."

Harris lifted an eyebrow and grinned. She relaxed at this meant-to-be energy, as charmed and disarmed as when she'd fallen into his arms so long ago.

"Annnd," Mikka continued her announcement, "This is my mama Tess, who needs a bath, too. The gugos are after us and we want to go home."

"Ah, me, too," Harris assured Mikka. "I have a feeling I know what you mean by gugos."

"It's a monster word she learned from our Mexican neighbor's kids," she offered. "My mom's family is Hispanic, too."

"I'm runnin' from monsters myself." Harris offered his free arm to her and set Mikka on her feet. "Shall we?"

Taking his arm, she zoomed into another world, a sensation she'd often experienced around Harris. They ambled with some effort onto a narrow trail, a stock or wildlife trail perpendicular to the road. Harris shuffled like she did, his face slack with exhaustion. He complained of blisters and limped so much she didn't think he noticed her rolling gait. They were both haggard, hungry, and dehydrated.

"I owe you an explanation . . ." she bowed her head, looking for the right words.

"No. Miss Teresa, I owe you far more than that. And you, Miss Mikka D. My, your genes are popping out all over . . . you're quite a mix of your mom and dad."

Harris flashed his big ocean eyes and his lopsided grin again and she beamed back. He pulled each of them closer to him in a gentle, one-armed hug. "My girls."

A nervous shiver rattled through her, half-joyous, half-wary. Mikka gazed up in adoration at Harris, her eyes a mirror image of his.

"This is crazy . . . did you ever imagine we'd run into each other in the desert twice? It's been a long time, Harr."

"It has. I'm sorry. If I'd known . . ." Harris looked at her with uncharacteristic shyness, and then gazed at Mikka again. "I'm dazzled."

"Yes. I'm sorry, too." She didn't know how to apologize, still overwhelmed with fear and concern for Mikka. "It wasn't fair that I didn't tell you I was pregnant. It was all so complicated." She kicked herself mentally. There was no need to apologize.

His face turned grave. "And *that* is my fault. It wasn't fair to you or to my family to insert myself into your life. Or to expect you to go away . . ."

"Harris, I always accepted the limitations . . ."

"Tess, there never should have been any," he said with a hangdog expression, like a little boy caught with his hand in the cookie jar.

It must be hard for him to admit his error. She bit back her mental and physical pain while they strolled up a rise to get a clearer view of the area.

Scanning the horizon, anxiety knotted itself inside her gut. Was someone or something drawing closer, seizing an opportunity to pounce?

"I appreciate now why you sent me away. I appreciated it then even though I wouldn't listen to your tales. I was frightened. I still am." She told him about Mikka. He seemed stunned as she related her possible UFO experience and described Mikka's artistic talent. She underemphasized Mikka's forays into another dimension, still trying to protect her.

"I wish I'd known about Mikka. Perhaps I could have helped your situation, for awhile, at least. . . He looked down at his rumpled suit and laughed. "On the other hand, you did a fine job on your own. I'm so sorry, Tess. It's a difficult world, more so when you brush elbows with money and power . . . if it weren't for me and my plans . . . you look like you've seen some demons."

"You could call it that. Someone tried to kill us." She filled him in on the shortest version possible of their happy holidays. "I don't know if they want Mikka or want her dead. Maybe they just want me out of the way. I thought the villain might be you at first."

"No wonder you look so tired . . . Some element of NIHSA, the Agency, have done their damndest to block and discredit me. I've had many otherworldly experiences myself since we parted."

"I can only imagine."

Harris shook his head, his body tightening with anger. "Damn it. None of this was supposed to happen. Knowing about Mikka clarifies another piece of the puzzle. I understand now why the Agency's out to find Mikka and special children like her. They may use some and destroy others, depending on their objective to gain superiority with these kids' talents, to create a super-race, perhaps." He set his jaw. "I'm afraid my being here will only make things worse for you."

Mikka listened intently, staring with interest at her father's face. "Mr. Toad's wild ride," she quipped.

Harris threw his head back and a deep belly laugh bubbled from him. "I have a feeling you'll do just fine, Mikka D." He picked her up and tweaked her nose.

Mikka nestled against his chest. Tess marveled at her daughter's deep connection with her father. A spark of the old passion flickered in her heart, but their precarious situation nailed her feet to the ground. Life before Harris seemed nothing more than a static museum display, and yet she'd learned so much about life's deepest meaning from Carson in less than forty-eight hours. Her heart flickered for Carson too. How like her to want two guys while walking the razor's edge.

"We're all in it together now," she said, brushing her personal feelings away. She flashed on their strengths and how they might share them. "Three heads can come up with a better plan than two."

"Your Native friend, he oozes confidence. I take it he's on a quest with you."

Tess took Harr's remark as a question. "Carson is wonderful," she stated unequivocally. "I asked some friends of a friend for help and they introduced me to him on Christmas—the day before yesterday, if I'm counting correctly."

Harris shot her a stunned look. "Christmas, my gawd! Then I've been away over a month!"

She nodded. "We ended up here when a group of men kidnapped us at gunpoint from his ranch. Government agents, Carson says, based on the unmarked black helicopter."

"No surprise, since shadow government is what has me by the balls."

"The Phoenix Gazette hired me to report at your funeral." She told him about the funeral dream, the First Lady's insistence on a Rose Garden open-casket funeral.

Harris registered surprise again. "How strange they displayed a double or mannequin. Someone tried to create doubt about my assassination. Or it was just a clumsy cover-up. Might even be some sort of signal, or a warning."

"No doubt."

"Poor Merrill. She must be going out of her mind. My son, my daughter . . . And Gap must be under the thumb of the Agency." He confided some snatches of what he recalled after the abduction at the White House. "And how did you end up here?"

She finished her story about the chopper crash and finally related how Mikka disappeared and reappeared.

His face drained of color. "This makes perfect sense. You were smart to run, but I'm afraid the Agency can track us anywhere . . . shoo, they can read our watches from two miles in space. We're probably under surveillance right now."

"Probably. I couldn't figure out earlier if I was tailed, or implanted or both."

"I'm sure they have all their bases covered." Harris frowned. "I've been doing a lot of thinking . . ."

She smiled at his statement and Harris grunted in response at the unintended humor.

"I've got an idea or two," he said. "I think some people in the UFO community might be able to hook us up with good extraterrestrials . . ."

Her face must have given away her surprise, but she knew after her recent experiences that he wasn't loony.

Harris glanced at her as if wondering why she exhibited surprise. " . . . But we need food and water before we get into plan A or B."

"I can help with that one, Harr. I think we're less than a day's hike from my house."

Harris brightened. "My phone's dead." He pulled his Blackberry out of his suit coat's inner breast pocket. "Can I make some calls at your place?" He winked at her.

She winked back at him. "Of course, or from my neighbor's. Might be safer . . ."

"You know criminals often return to the crime scene, to their homes, or to meet a special person in their lives."

She shrugged, noting that Harris seemed thrilled to share his thoughts with someone who understood. "I know. I'm too weary to worry about it."

While Harris began to talk in an urgent tone about some library he said was really a group of patriots with documents, she thought she heard a faint mechanical chug in the distance. Her skin crawled in response to the sound and to the realization there was so much more to Harris's story than she ever thought possible.

She gripped his arm. "Listen, do you hear that?" She hoped it was the weird ringing in her ears again.

Harris turned his head toward her. His lips parted. He started to say more, but stopped and cocked his head.

A warrior's call from Carson cut the air. Her adrenaline surged and she felt a wave of exhaustion equally as intense. She trembled, the first ripple of a physical and emotional earthquake surging through her body.

Harris gripped her hand so hard it hurt and pulled her back down the trail. Mikka raised her head, a look of raw fear gripping her face.

Harris moved in slow motion, a man on his last reserve. He wasn't much faster than she was, her bruised hip throbbing with fire again.

The sound of a chopper suddenly echoed from the sky and in the distance, a low growl of land vehicles issued from clouds of dust flaring up from the ground. Another adrenaline rush flashed through her nervous system. They floundered for a moment on the hillside, lost the trail, and then righted themselves, the road appearing below them. Carson pounded up the hill like a piston. His mouth moved but the sound of his voice dissolved in the wind that swept ever-darkening clouds lower and lower among the hills.

The sound of helicopter rotors began to pound from the craft almost directly above them. Jeeps filled with figures in dark uniforms crawled toward them from all directions, clouds of dust rising, preceded by menacing red lines of laser light from their firearms. She fell sprawling into the dirt, her fingers unlacing from Harris's hand. One cheek scraped rock and her head bounced painfully in a slow motion impact. Shooting pain snarled through her hip again. Harris extended his hand toward her, attempting to reconnect. His face tense, he moved his mouth like a fish gasping for air. For a split-second, he took on an otherworldly cast, his skin turning into a dark, scaly mosaic, his eyes golden with vertical slits. She heard herself scream, but to her ears it came from outside, a shriek erupting from the windswept ground. Small drops of rain spattered in the dust, followed by sharp rays of sunlight that broke through the clouds and disappeared rapidly.

Time seemed to stop as another volley of shots rang out, then another, and then what seemed like endless pings and pops.

Carson leaped through the air, a martial arts wind spirit, braid flying behind him like a whip. Like Superman, he stretched out long, held up the sky, breath hissing from his lungs. Or was it the wind? His tumble met the ground, and he rolled to Mikka, his body arching in protection over the tiny bundle. He uttered syllables, another mantra, maybe, while she clawed at the ground, trying to get to her daughter. Harris crawled nearer, reaching for Mikka too, then flailed at thin air, red pouring from his shoulder. Red too close to his neck, red from Carson's back, from Mikka. Something red on Mikka! She couldn't stop screaming, her screams, her baby's screams, the screams from the earth.

Another flurry of shots like popcorn stuttered under engine growl. Then she heard another tremendous hissing growl, and she gazed up into the face of a giant lizard, a dark form with shining brown scales like some bizarre figure in a dream. Those scary sounds wouldn't stop, the growling and the deadly snap of helicopter rotors slashing like knives.

She strained to see Mikka's face, a miniature howling mask, every mother's nightmare. Horror exploded her mind into jagged fragments. An adrenaline-pumping shriek shattered her bones. If only Mikka would disappear now, Tess prayed. Oh, please let her do that crazy thing now. She opened her mouth to tell Mikka *go, disappear*, but all that came out was a howl of pain.

Tess tried to flee but managed only to pick up her throbbing head. Low clouds settled over them, a bank of fog spitting sleet that burned bare skin with its cold needles. Shots popped around her again. Someone returned fire, but whom? She dropped her head to the ground. Legs in camouflage fatigues and black boots pounded past her.

Her name echoed in a banshee scream atop a hill. She wanted to reply, but her dry tongue stayed glued to the roof of her mouth. Faces played in and out of focus. Paul, Uncle Mac. Were they really here? She heard her mom singing a lullaby, felt herself rocked in a scratchy old army blanket on her lap at a picnic long ago. Heard herself singing the same lullaby to Mikka under a sky so starry that it didn't seem real. She sobbed, a storm of saltwater turning dust to mud.

Help me, help me. Was she screaming? Harris came into focus. Harris looking like himself, cheeks panting and reddening with effort, plowing dusty ground on his hands and knees. She followed his lead. Pulled herself to her knees, crawled for what seemed like years. Screamed again, pushed at Carson, dug under him . . . nothing there.

Reddish gray dirt, stones, pebbles, sand, puffs of dust wafting away in a wind carrying delicate snowflakes.

Carson's eyes met hers, full of question marks. His lips made soft movements, caressing the vowels and consonants: *I'm sorry.* Did he also say she'd be fine? Would he be fine?

A thousand snowflakes gleamed in his dark hair and Tess could almost hear a swell of melancholy movie music as her heart ached for him. She gathered Carson into her arms, wanting to ask where Mikka went, where she could be inside or outside this dimension, but he grew pale and still.

Hands thrown skyward, she screamed again. Hands pulled at her then, attempted to comfort her, to arrange the scattered pieces of herself back into place. She cursed those hands, brushed them away, tried to get up, to run away, but her legs wouldn't work any longer. As though it came from outside her, she heard a high-pitched howl of despair, "Why, why, why?"

⁂

She groaned and pried her sticky eyes open to a blur of color. Tess expected pain but her body felt numb. The fuzzy euphoria of painkillers fogged her brain. Oh, no. Mikka. Where was she?

Then she remembered. Mikka always returned safely after she left this dimension. But had she reappeared in the desert, alone? Panic arose again and tore her heart in two. Grunting, she tried to pull herself upright without using the electric controls to raise the head of the bed. She couldn't move her lower body. Panicked, she blinked to clear her vision. Her legs encased in a stainless steel frame to weights and pulleys. She cried out in frustration, reaching for something to throw. Someone pulled the wheeled table over her bed out of her reach.

"I have to go," she said.

A face came into focus. "Tess? Welcome back . . ." Paul fingered the gauze taped around his head and shifted from foot to foot as though he didn't know what to say. An ugly, dark bruise partially covered by the bandage mottled his lower forehead, slashing across the bridge of his nose and around the inner orbit of one puffy eye.

"Your pelvis has a hairline fracture that worsened from activity. They're keeping you in traction to help heal it. You can't go anywhere for a month, maybe longer."

She moaned in response. She needed to find Mikka.

"The doctors can't believe you continued to hike for hours. Pelvic fractures can be deadly," Paul said. "We told them you got lost on a camping trip, fell from a ledge." He motioned with his good hand, the other held up above his waist, stiff in a blue fiberglass cast. "The nurses said you've been sleeping for nearly twenty hours."

"Not twenty days?" Tess moaned again. How would she ever find her baby? "What happened to you?" Her eyes met Paul's, registering the dozens of questions she wanted to ask.

Another familiar voice issued from a padded chair near the head of her hospital bed. "You had us deeply worried, luv. You went into shock . . . took us nearly five hours to find you and get you here."

"Uncle Mac? Her voice cracked. "Then you *were* there!" Two other bodies came into clearer focus. "Marshall. Savannah. How did you get here?"

"Girl, let's just say that we conspired to find you." Savannah grinned, then her face quickly softened with compassion.

"We really did," Marshall said. "Mac called some old military buddies. They follow police radios, military transmissions, and ham radio stuff. They heard about an air search for an individual and a group in Northern Arizona."

"My buddy's son is a medical helicopter pilot," Mac said. "We caught up to that wretched Jay and his scoundrel companion and found Paul with them. Those radio transmissions led us to you, luv. Those two rogues were one root of your problem. Another of my buddies heard rumors from a relative at the Phoenix PD that they found NIHSA documents and a memo from C. Clelland Collins in their van. Some odd security badges with microchips and Delta Force insignia, not your usual earthly ID. Some incriminating bits of kiddy porn, as well. Let's just say neither can bother anyone anymore."

Paul cringed. Tess's heart fell for him. But if he were as frightened as she was, his gratitude for his life must be greater than his grief about Jay. Now she understood Jay's weird attitude toward her. Her head began to spin with all her questions.

"You weren't hassled about my pickup exploding in your driveway, Uncle Mac?"

Mac grinned. "We managed to get the pickup and enough debris around it covered with sand to stall Pima County deputies."

Her weak smile conveyed her gratitude.

"Oh," he added. "I found your cell phone in the corner of the garden. Blew right out of the truck with you, luv. Scorched, but the voice mail worked. Took the liberty of playing your messages." He blushed. "Under the circumstances . . . I called the attorney who had your flash drive. Never thought he'd get the message on a holiday. Be darned if he didn't call me back early yesterday morning. He was puzzled by your request, but remembered some of your investigative reports from a decade past, so he figured you might be hardwired in some new crisis. He stashed the flash drive away, still sealed in the mailer. Did some mighty fancy talking to convince him to open it without your permission or presenting your death certificate. I convinced him you were involved in a matter of great urgency that might lead to your death. He read the information for me over the phone, but you have to sign this notarized form he faxed." Mac pulled a dog-eared, double-folded slip of paper from the breast pocket of his denim shirt.

She breathed a sigh of relief. "Thank the universe. The flash drive still needs to be copied and go somewhere safe."

"We'll see to that, luv."

"Of course none of this explains where nearly every material item in our household went," Marshall said.

She glanced at him, puzzled. Savannah outlined the ordeal she and Marshall experienced in Tucson while she, Mikka, and Carson trekked in the desert and Mac made his plans.

"Meanwhile, Mac and your cousins kept us posted . . . after the conflict on the interstate and in the desert, we brought you here to

Flagstaff from Yavapai County," Savannah explained. "We figured your pursuers would expect you to show up at the Yavapai Regional Medical Center, or at home, for what that's worth."

Her brother, great uncle, and friends formed a circle around her bed, taking her hands in theirs.

"You remember what happened in the desert?" Savannah's voice softened as she guided us toward the elephant in the room, the topic no one wanted to broach.

She nodded and stifled a sob that tried to rise from her heart. "Harris and Carson are gone, aren't they?"

No one replied, and in the uncomfortable silence, the door edged open. Carson gingerly walked to the bed, bent over Tess, and brushed his hand across her cheek.

The room went quiet as Tess and Carson held hands and shed silent tears of joy. She touched the bandage across his bare chest, the sling that held one swollen, wounded arm.

Paul cleared his throat, his voice husky. "I'm so sorry, Tess. We left President Henry in the hills under a stone cairn. We're trying to reach his family without being traced . . . we're not sure what to do about the county coroner." Paul seemed to relish his new involvement with her case. "We've gotta notify authorities some time . . . there's a dead extraterrestrial out there too . . ." He avoided speaking about the elephant in the room, Mikka.

"I guess the media would pass me off as just another druggy Indian, if that was my body out there," Carson said. "Can't imagine what kind of trouble will hit the fan about President Henry and the ET. We're not certain why the bodies were left behind. There seemed to be two types of soldiers out there. Both pulled out rather suddenly when Mikka . . . "

She gripped his hand harder but said nothing.

Marshall spoke up. "We figure the NIHSA unit, whoever pulled the coup, is invested in the assassination story. Maybe they didn't want to deal with Henry's body right off the bat. By now, they know what Mac and the Updikes pulled off. They'll want Henry's and the

ET's bodies to keep everything quiet, we would think. And the bodies of their agents who went down in the chopper crash, if they haven't already secured those." He gestured wildly. "Lord knows, maybe that ET is Senator Collins. There were people out there shooting at the people who were shooting at us."

Tess held back a storm of emotion. "Harris mentioned a similar firefight in an underground base where he was held, like good battled evil, or . . . I also have some weird memory of seeing him with the face of a lizard . . . my imagination? I don't know." She wasn't sure she cared what had happened. How could she lose her daughter and one of her best friends and still survive?

Mac shook his head. "It was confusing out there . . . here too. The medical center is swarming with suits. Coconino County deputies sniffed around, tried to question us, but the suits ran them off."

"I don't know why they're backing off," Savannah added. "Maybe they're afraid of more powerful suits, if we're lucky."

"We might have to go into hiding with you, girl, and soon," Marshall added, pocketing Savannah's cell phone and casting Tess one of his stern looks. "I just received a text from a friend. The media's beginning to report two drug arrests gone bad. They claim all parties, agents and smugglers, are dead in the desert, with that incident related to an attempted bust leaving one dead and one injured on I-17 in Phoenix. We're lucky they're tiptoeing around us for now."

"Maybe we can assume they're not concerned about me, just Mikka. But we shouldn't be too confident." Tess took a deep breath and related her story about the triangular mark she'd found on her arm after watching the meteor shower when she was pregnant with Mikka.

Marsh stroked his chin. "An ET intervention."

"I've heard of people finding marks on arms or legs after abduction experiences. Never heard of that particular one before," Savannah said.

"I'm sorry, Marsh and S'annah, I should have told you before. I didn't recall the connection until after our meeting. When we met at your house, I was too stressed . . ."

Savannah waved her apology away. "You were in trouble up to your neck and did what you had to do. Besides, this mess is complex."

Tess inhaled and exhaled hard, trying not to think of Mikka. "In the desert, Harris said his UFO disclosure plan caused the fake assassination. And that Drew Forrest died because he exposed Senator Collins. I think the Agency's trying to figure out their next move. Hopefully they're scared of what we can reveal. We definitely know too much now . . . by the way, did anyone else see the face of a lizard on a blonde man? Or a lizard in uniform, like Harris saw?"

Savannah affirmed her concerns again with tears in her eyes, describing the intervention on I-17. "What we suspected and what Harris found out is true, Tess. There truly is an extraterrestrial civilization involved in manipulating Earth affairs to suit their agenda."

She shook her head. "I would never have believed it before all this happened to us."

Marsh smiled. "Cell phone pictures of the dead ET have gone viral on the internet. Another reason, I'm sure, that the suits haven't yet bothered with us yet. If NIHSA wants to suppress disclosure, they certainly have some work cut out for them."

Mac reached out and patted her free hand. "We're behind you one hundred percent, Tess," he murmured, blushing at his own tenderness.

"Always," Marsh and Savannah said together.

Paul gave her a thumbs up. "I'll never doubt you again, Sis."

Carson sat on the edge of the bed and beamed at her. Then a flash of intuition hit—her vision of the mountainous region she'd seen superimposed over the highway on the way to Carson's place. And Mikka's remarks about snow mountains. Mikka must have gone there. Wherever it was, the high, rocky peaks were barren of everything but snow.

Carson glanced at her as if he read her thoughts, but no one else dared mention her daughter's name. Everyone looked at Tess again, their eyes watery with new grief and filled with a single question. Her chest became a sealed box and she struggled to take a breath.

"And . . . Mikka. She's gone . . . but I know she's alive. In my heart, I know she's fine, hidden in high mountains. The Himalayas, I'm guessing."

Carson squeezed her hand. Paul, Uncle Mac, and Savannah and Marshall looked at one another with raised eyebrows.

"You know Mikka has talents . . ." She swallowed her hurt and explained the disappearances that Paul partially witnessed and misunderstood, that Carson had witnessed after the helicopter crash. What she'd never fully described to anyone, except Harris, in their last few moments together.

". . . She could disappear from one spot and reappear in another. I think either she knew where to go or somehow Carson helped guide her. He prayed over her at the last." She gazed into Carson's eyes, so glad she'd met this incredible being. "Mikka went somewhere safe. I had a strange vision of high, snow-covered mountains on the way to Carson's on Christmas Day. Even Mikka mentioned snow mountains while we wandered in the desert. Why else would I have such a vision?"

Hot tears began to spill from her eyes.

"If you feel it in your heart, it must be so." Savannah squeezed her hand hard. "Let's pray." She and Marshall led the group through a poignant prayer, dedicated to Mikka's long life and return home, and for Harris Henry's journey to the light.

Tess nodded through her tears. Her spirit soared with the prayer's final amen, musical with the sound of their combined voices, Carson's hand warm around hers.

"Amen. So be it. My only heart's desire."

::: Epilogue

"May we not cling to this life, which is like a water bubble."

::: Khenchen Konchok Gyaltsen Rinpoche, *Supplication Prayer*

Ani Jangchub struggled to heave the shrine room's heavy rear door open. It slammed with an ominous thud behind her, its big hinges groaning more from the force of the howling wind than the muscle of the young Tibetan nun's diminutive arms.

The fabric of her monastic garb twisted and swirled in the thin air like a kite rising. Though the early afternoon sun shone bright in a sky of purest azure, the snowfall of the previous night rested in a shimmering layer upon the older, icier layers preceding it. Steam from the hot springs at the base of the ani gompa, the nunnery, and loose snow harvested from mountain slopes by the wind rose in fluffy white mares' tails that wafted above the highland. Strings of colorful prayer flags attached to eaves and posts of the high-roofed buildings rustled and snapped, their prayers to Mother Tara carried by wind to all beings in the ten directions.

Every afternoon after tea, she swept and straightened the shrine room, preparing it for evening puja. Ani Jangchub pulled an arm-length bundle of straw from inside her woolen outer robe, a fur-lined chuba. Her golden broom and heavy robe's maroon color added cheer to the monotonous white landscape of the Tibetan plateau, an unsurpassed but deadly beauty. She swept with youthful vigor at a patch of icy snow clinging to the stone steps, thinking that the other novices who swept before morning puja must have hurried through their duties. She reminded herself not to think poorly of her sisters, to be mindful of her thoughts, that her duties were important to others. A self-serving attitude would never bring happiness.

An odd patch of color on the tier of steps below caught her eye. Purple, a pastel shade from sunset's palette was not a color often used among the bright primary colors of her culture. She padded down the angled stairs to the landing marked by large boulders and audibly caught her breath.

"Ah."

Ani Jangchub's face brightened with concern and she felt her heart and mind radiate bodhicitta—loving kindness and compassion. A little person lay in a crumpled heap, the rounded, golden face peeking like a snow lion's from a hood rimmed with a white stripe. Coppery curls escaped the shiny lavender hood and played in the wind like tiny butterflies. Ani took a sudden step back. Blood trickled from a dark hole in the child's shoulder and the child's golden complexion seemed wan. The smear forming on the nylon jacket had already congealed into ice. She picked up the child's bare and dirty hand. The short nails were nearly white, caked with curiously red dirt. A thin thread of a pulse quivered in the cold wrist. She yanked off the length of maroon wool serving as her outer robe, tucking it as swiftly around the child, grunting with effort to gather the limp body into her arms. No good. She couldn't easily carry a child more than half as tall as herself in the stiff wind. In a determined motion, she tugged her maroon stocking cap over her ears, one bare arm protruding from her fur-lined chuba. No one walked the web of trails connecting the various buildings of gompa. She paused at a fork of two paths, one leading to the gompa keeper, the other to the nuns' quarters. With both speed and caution, she ran in the nuns' direction, then down the next tier of limestone stairs on a steep scree slope, toward a two-story building with a curved tile roof housing the senior nuns.

"Jetsunma! Jetsunma!" The nun called frantically as she approached the building. Her Dharma sisters would be reading texts or contemplating their studies now, perhaps hard at work on domestic tasks as she was.

"Jetsunma! Help me!"

A shaven head with a female Buddha's serene features emerged through the open shutters on an upper dormitory window.

"Ani Jangchub? Whatever is the matter? You'll raise the Maras with this racket."

She tried slowing her speech but words tumbled out of her like a mountain stream. "Jetsunma, oh Precious, come quickly, there is someone lying on the shrine room steps. A hurt child!"

"A child! Ani, one of our smallest novitiates?"

"No, hurry please, Jetsunma! A foreign child, bleeding, and too big for me to carry in the wind . . ."

"Oh, mm-mm-mm," Jetsunma "clucked" in the characteristic Tibetan expression of empathy. "Go back to the child. I'll be right down, Jangchub." The colorfully painted shutters closed with a mindful slap of wood against wood.

The little nun turned and rushed back up the path, chanting *Om Mani Padme Hung.* She felt sorry she'd forgotten to chant mantra when she fetched Jetsunma, and now she feared the little one would die. Death was but part of life and possibly this child's karma, but if the child left this world for the next, slipping into the bardos, she might never know the curious story behind the child's arrival at Terton Nunnery. She cringed with shame at her thought. Jetsunma always said her curiosity might be an obstacle to enlightenment, an obscuration.

The child lay as she left her, snugly wrapped in the maroon robe, signature of the four major lineages of Tibetan monastics and made famous around the world by Tenzin Gyatso, the fourteenth Dalai Lama. Only the child's loosely closed eyelids and forehead showed, reddened now from the extreme cold, showing that her life energy still flowed.

Jetsunma carefully picked her way up the last set of stairs toward the landing. Though not elderly, she walked like a person cognizant of her age and limitations. A fall on stone steps might cause a major nuisance. Her nuns needed her whole and healthy.

Jetsunma pursed her lips and made the clucking sounds again, her almond eyes misting over. She squatted and picked up the child as though lifting a bag of feathers.

"Ani Jangchub, run ahead to my quarters. There is hot water. Pour it over one of the big blessing pills from the bundle on my altar. Choose some of the clean red rags from the bundle as well, long and short. Pull back the quilts on my bed."

The coals from a tiny fire glowed in a little clay wood stove in an alcove in Jetsunma's private room. Ani Jangchub prostrated hastily under Jetsunma's kata laden photograph of the Dalai Lama, recovered from a hidden vault under the temple after the temporal and spiritual leader's triumphant return from India. Then she replaced the stoneware teapot on the stove and listened at the doorway for Jetsunma's footstep. A group of short-haired heads bristled from an open door down the hall. Ani Jangchub cast her eyes downward in deference to the older nuns. Jetsunma soon arrived with the child, whose sneakered feet bobbed with Jetsunma's exertion.

"Easy now."

Jetsunma lay the child in her bed and removed the robe. Her lips moved rapidly in silent prayer. She held a fore and middle finger against the girl's neck.

"Her pulse is weak and slow." Jetsunma pulled the jacket zipper down and eased the child's arms from it. Underneath the child wore a sleeveless vest the same color as the jacket lining, made of a fabric that looked like lamb's wool. Ani Jangchub reached out to touch it.

Jetsunma stripped off the vest, revealing a high-necked shirt printed with flowers. Both garments were dusty and soaked at the shoulder with blood.

"A girl, is my guess. A Western boy would not wear flowers."

Jetsunma brushed her pinkish-golden palm over the child's voluminous curls. "Hair of sunset," she said matter-of-factly, peeling off the shirt, peering at the hole that went from front to back of the girls' right shoulder.

Ani Jangchub couldn't help but notice the child's nipples looked like the tiny pinkish brown lotus buds on the Temple altar cloths.

"A clean wound, fortunately." Jetsunma dipped the rags into the cobalt stoneware cup that steamed with the blessing pill of healing herbs. Her long face showed relief. "I can treat this easily. I was afraid I might have to send for Zangpo Rinpoche. This can wait until he arrives tomorrow for the empowerment at the peak of the moon."

"Yes, Jetsunma." Ani Jangchub tossed the end of her robe over her left shoulder. She shivered, the situation, the cool room, and thoughts of the stern but kind Rinpoche affecting her. She felt afraid of the way Jetsunma and the high lamas seemed always to know what she was thinking.

Jetsunma spooned a few drops of tea into the child's mouth. She moaned and stirred a bit, but did not come to. Jetsunma fashioned a bandage from dry cotton swatches Ani Jangchub pulled from her bundle of healing supplies, and bound the bandage with a long strip of red cloth that she wound across the young girl's shoulder and chest after applying generous daubs of herbal tea followed by a dark, sticky salve.

"The girl is in shock, but she'll come around. You can help by putting drops of tea in her mouth, like so."

Jetsunma pushed the girl's chin up, dripping a few drops of tea under her tongue with a spoon.

"Just do that every few minutes. I'm going to see Pema in the kitchen. She'll send word to Rinpoche that we have a visitor and ask him for more herbs . . . You have a question, Ani?"

The nun nodded, her eyes wide with curiosity. She'd been bursting with questions since she found the girl. "How did she get here? Is she a demon? Or a dakini?"

Jetsunma tilted her head away, suppressing a giggle. "No child, she is a precious human like you. As for how she got here, well, I think Rinpoche can answer that question best. I have heard of such visitations, but this is the first I have seen. Rinpoche knows exactly what to do."

"Is she from space?" Ani Jangchub imitated her superior, placing drops of tea in the girl's mouth.

"No, not exactly, but she made her way through space. She may have begun her journey through the bardos and returned to Earth. Her aspirations, or the prayers of another, brought her here."

"How?"

Jetsunma regarded Ani Jangchub with a somber face. "I will answer your questions after Rinpoche arrives," she gently scolded. Although her accomplishments matched Zangpo Rinpoche's, Jetsunma had a deep reverence for him and always deferred to his immutable wisdom. "For now, keep her warm and dry and try to get some liquid into her."

The little nun drooped, a wildflower losing its bloom.

The corners of Jetsunma's eyes crinkled upward. She laughed when Ani Jangchub's rosy lips rounded with unasked questions.

"I will say this. It is an auspicious day." The nunnery will benefit from this child's presence and it will benefit her."

"Joy of the Triple Gem?"

Jetsunma nodded. "Wish-fulfilling jewel," she sang, launching into one of the lineage prayers. Voices rang out from the neighboring room, joining the revered nun in harmonic prayer. She disappeared down the wide hall.

"Oh." Ani Jangchub started when she sat gingerly at the edge of Jetsunma's bed and the child's eyes flew unexpectedly open in a flash of blue-green, a color she imagined the sea would be, though she had only seen it in pictures. Ani spoke to the child in soft Tibetan as though soothing a baby. The girl responded like a dear baby, her chubby cheeks taking on just the barest hint of color in the warmth of compassion and the cozy bed. The little one pulled her lips into the briefest of smiles, and serenely joined her hands together over her chest. Ani's eyes widened and she returned the girl's greeting. People from outside Asia did not always know this custom.

"I want the bad people to stop chasing my mama."

Ani stared at her. The girl said a few more words in what sounded like English, but she didn't understand the language. She'd heard Geshe-la interpret Rinpoche's teachings in English at Losar, the New Year, for some Christian nuns the year before. They'd traveled to Tibet from Canada, a rare treat for the remote nunnery.

As Ani Jangchub drew her prayer beads from her neck, the scent of sandalwood emanated from them. She placed them in the little girl's hand. The girl closed her hand around the strand of beads, a little golden lotus clenched tight.

"Om mani padme hung," the little nun said in a singsong voice.

"Om ma-nay pe-may hoong." The child's voice rang from the bed in a clear tone like a Tibetan bell.

Ani smiled. "Yes, that's right, you'll do puja with me soon."

The sunset-haired girl managed another wan smile in response. She said nothing, but her knowing eyes told Ani Jangchub she understood that everything was as it should be.

The little one's life work had just begun. "May all mother beings find refuge," Ani Jangchub murmured, smiling again as a bubble dissolved in the tea of the cobalt-glazed cup.

ACKNOWLEDGMENTS

Many hugs to my children and grandchildren, who endured frequent promises over many years that this manuscript was nearly finished.

Hugs and gratitude to my brothers Michael Robinson and Scott Robinson, and to my parents Richard and Elizabeth Robinson for supporting me in writing-related endeavors.

Clarissa Yeo, thank you for the wicked cool cover design!

Many thanks to the Stasis critique group in Prescott, Arizona for their patience and critiques: Tom A. Wright, John J. Rust, Michelle Pariza Wacek, Collette Ward, Marian Powell, Andrew Draper, Geri Davis, Doug Beach, Denise DiPietro, Greg Young, Joe DiBuduo, Nancy Owen Nelson, and Agnes Franz.

A tip of the hat to Professional Writers of Prescott (PWP), SCBWI-AZ and SCBWI-OC, and to all the amazing writing and editing members who share their passion and expertise with others.

Cheers to the prompt writers group in the Inland Empire, CA, for allowing me to share and learn: Kathryn Wilkens, Barbara Unsworth, Marie Griffiths, Ro Woodruff, Pamella Bowen, Sue Andrews, and Jeanine Miranda. You ladies rock!

Heartfelt thanks to supportive reading, writing, and artistic friends for their feedback, encouragement, and support: Brent Logan, Arlene Eisenbise, Leslie and Chris Hoy, Samantha Dillard, Kate Shannon, Delena Epstein, Math Bird, and Spencer Jones. There are many other writers and artists too numerous to mention that I admire and connect with on Facebook, Twitter, Google+, GoodReads, Pinterest, Tumblr, and other social media, and I follow you all with fond interest.

An extra thank you, Joe DiBuduo, for beta reading and author photo; to Amber Polo for her last-minute advice, for her nifty interviews, and for sharing her book marketing expertise; and to CA Brown and Carl Hitchens for their ever-present humor, their inspiring work, and a spot of advice on this project as well. Phil Perisich, you don't have anything directly to do with this book, but you're always there in the background with your entertaining thoughts, travel itineraries, and film critiques.

My heartfelt thanks also to Susan Lang, the founding director of the Hassayampa Institute of Creative Writing at Yavapai College, Prescott, Arizona. HICW was a wonderful initiation into writing conferences and where I first shared my pre-novel short story version of HoD in August 1999. Special thanks to Reed Schonfeldt for making it possible to attend. My first two writing teachers at HICW, Mary Sojourner and Brady Udall, still inspire me with their ongoing work and support of other writers.

I'm also grateful to the Aberystwyth University Postgraduate Creative Writing Program in Wales, where I was humbled and inspired and pushed from the nest by my talented professors, Jem Poster, Matthew Francis, and Tiffany Atkinson, and challenged and inspired by my fellow students during the 2009-2010 academic year. May all continue to write and prosper!

Thanks a million to Avaton and Vikki T., editor and secretary extraordinaire of Cosmic Awareness Communications in Olympia, Washington, and the many interpreters of Cosmic Awareness, including current interpreter Will Berlinghof, and to Reverend Robert Hanzel of Tucson, AZ, for their steadfast commitment to the Cosmic Awareness channel that provided a wealth of info for story detail.

Luminous gratitude to the precious lamas and lay teachers of the Drikung Kagyu lineage of Tibetan Buddhism, who nurture the seed of enlightenment in all beings, and the many bodhisattvas around the globe who aspire to realize the Buddha mind.

I'm grateful to Starstone Lit clients. We have journeyed together with words and ideas and we have grown.

I also offer my deepest gratitude to political and social activists everywhere who sacrifice their own comfort and well-being so that others may experience harmony and happiness.

KATE ROBINSON
August 2014

AKA @katerwriter, KATE ROBINSON promises to always dance

with absurdity and paradox. She began her literary career writing bad poetry at age ten. After working as a grocery clerk, nursing assistant and home health aide, city bus driver, museum aide, a variety of office assistant positions, and K-12 substitute teacher, all while studying (BA 1999, MA 2010) and raising a family, scribbling looked like a suitable diversion. Now she whacks words for Starstone Editorial and Tootie-Do Press amidst the saguaro forests of the mystical Sonoran Desert.

TooTIE-Do PRESS
Quirky speculative fiction with a romantic twist.

::: FORTHCOMING
Valentine's Day 2015

Cryonic Man: A Paranormal Affair by Joe DiBuduo
ISBN-13: 978-0692381281

What happens when the world's first Cryonic Man finds he shares body and mind with "Blood Countess" Erzsébet Báthory?

:::

Chapter 1

I bit down hard on the cold steel barrel of the Colt .38 to hold it steady in my trembling hands. A big eater, I never dreamed gun oil would end up on the menu. The bitter tang almost made me laugh through clenched teeth.

My finger tightened on the trigger. I shut my eyes, drew the hammer back, and pictured Emily's face for the last time.

Would I hear the gunpowder explode before my lights went out? Terrified, my body went numb as I imagined the bullet tearing through my brain.

Click.

The sound sent me sprawling across the bed.

I checked the cylinders. There were .38 slugs in five of the six chambers. How could I forget that I always left a chamber empty? Maybe my subconscious mind wanted me to play a little Russian roulette, give me an unexpected thrill.

I made sure a slug was under the firing pin, put the barrel back into my mouth, and bit down hard again.

Before I closed my eyes, I saw a reflection of Emily's portrait over the bed in the dresser mirror. Her face seemed to float above me like a disembodied spirit, her eyes accusing me of cowardliness.

I yanked the pistol from my mouth and shouted, "I'm no coward, Emily. I'm doing this to make it easier for you."

I shook with anger, but the reprieve gave me time to consider. It wouldn't be too damn pleasant for Emily to find me in the bedroom with my head blown off. Maybe I should leave a note and take myself out somewhere else. Yeah, that was it; leave a note so she'd understand. Emily would blame herself if I didn't tell her why I did it. I set the gun on the bedside table and tried to imagine what to say.

Dear Emily.

No, I couldn't say Dear Emily, I'm going to kill myself.

To Whom It May Concern, I killed myself because . . .

That didn't sound right, either.

What words might explain why a tough guy like me would commit suicide? How could I describe my lifelong fear, not of dying, but of becoming helpless? People on their way out, lying in bed, unable to wipe their own ass. I always swore that wouldn't be me and figured if I became helpless, I'd find a way to end it all, *quick*.

As I opened the nightstand drawer where Emily kept pen and paper, the perfume of her stationery drifted up along with warm memories of her. They say a dying man's life flashes through his mind and I grasped at my visions like a drowning man.

I crumpled a pillow under my head and tried to enjoy the memories while I worked up the courage to write a note and pull the trigger again.

TOOTIE-DO PRESS

Quirky speculative fiction with a romantic twist.

::: FORTHCOMING
Halloween 2017

The Contest and Other Stories
Short fiction by Joe DiBuduo and Kate Robinson

BW interior ISBN: 978-0692973684
Full color interior ISBN: 978-0692962213

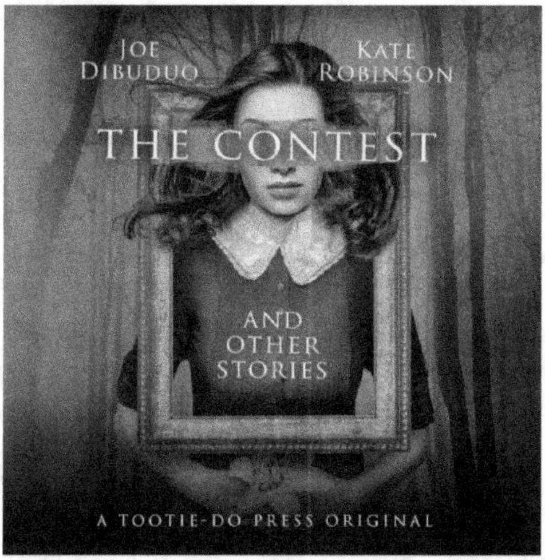

"Love the atmosphere and story narration. . . vivid and gripping . . . The frame narrative is more compelling than expected . . . has hints of beat literature, and the story arc about an art magazine is interesting."

–PekoeBlaze

EXCERPT

1

A Lonely Death

As my cab arrived at Fairhaven Cemetery, I spied a lone Catholic priest standing by my Uncle John's coffin, a study in black and white. Heavy snowflakes fell in swirling eddies like confetti from heaven over the monuments scored with epitaphs for mothers and daughters, fathers and sons, husbands and wives, all long dead and in some cases, long forgotten. Soon the snow would blanket one and all for the long winter's slumber.

I exited the cab reluctantly and pulled my collar up to stop the snow determined to swirl down my neck. As surprised by my presence as I was by his, the priest locked eyes with me for nearly a minute as though fishing for my soul, then bowed his head to read a blessing for my recently departed uncle from a battered prayer book. When he finished praying, he nodded at me and turned to walk toward the street into the blowing snow, a raven-like figure bobbing through the storm. Two workmen, gravediggers, emerged from the flurries on a pathway beyond the open grave and when they arrived, they lowered the casket into the ground. I threw a clod of dirt onto Uncle's coffin, startled by the finality of the hollow thump as it met the polished wood. But the clod soon whitened and disappeared under the falling snow as the workmen began to shovel in syncopated rhythms from a low pile of icy, moist earth beside the grave.

I walked away and waved the cab on so I could stroll alone through the storm toward my office at First Fiduciary Savings. When I arrived, I lay my damp overcoat across a meeting table near my desk and grabbed a cup of steaming coffee from the employee's lounge. I tried to concentrate on the never-ending stack of paperwork filling my inbox, still shivering twenty minutes later. The phone jangled suddenly, startling me even though my secretary picked it up at her desk outside my door. "Line two, Mr. Rizzo," Ruth said over the intercom.

"Peter John Rizzo," a clipped voice demanded when I answered.

"Speaking."

"Are you nephew to John Rizzo of Brooklyn, New York?"

"Who wants to know?"

"Harold O'Neill, attorney at law, calling the nephew of John Rizzo, called Peter John Rizzo. Am I speaking to the aforementioned nephew or not?"

What kind of person would actually talk like this? "Yes, John Rizzo is my uncle, and my name is Peter John Rizzo."

"I'm very sorry for your loss," O'Neill said tersely. "The reading of John Rizzo's last will and testament is at half-past three at my office tomorrow. 211 Broad St."

Without warning, Mr. O'Neill hung up and left me to sift through my thoughts.

I had trouble attending to my work because I still couldn't believe Uncle John was gone. Granted, I'd not seen him for years, but I never thought about losing him permanently. My eyes brimmed with tears, but I held back the storm by taking deep breaths. Shuffling blindly through the papers on my desk, I could only think about him. Because he and Aunt Millie had no children of their own to grieve for them, I'd made the trip to the cemetery. I had little knowledge of Uncle's social life and concluded he must have been a loner after Aunt Millie's death. I'd expected to see my father present, supposing that in the face of death he would drop his bitterness about his only brother. That I carried his brother's middle name probably didn't help the situation any–I had no clue why Mother insisted upon naming me after both Father and Uncle John. I remember well how he snorted every time he heard my middle name when I was a kid. Father hadn't cared to remember his estranged brother at all.

I was the only person present again the next afternoon in the tastefully appointed conference room at the law office of Harrison, Shearer and O'Neill.

"To my nephew, Peter John Rizzo, I leave my entire estate," Harold O'Neill solemnly read from the legal-sized sheaf of papers he pulled from a dark leather binder embossed with gold lettering.

Uncle John's entire estate consisted of "Classic Art Exposé," a bi-weekly magazine with art, and sometimes literature, as the main content, located in an old warehouse in New York City, plus seven hundred dollars in cash. I felt touched he'd thought of me, but I didn't have any interest in running his magazine because of my position at the bank and my need to placate my father.

O'Neill looked over his narrow reading glasses at me. "Peter John Rizzo, it's my duty to make certain you're aware that this bequest is conditional."

"Oh? What kind of conditions could Uncle John possibly place on a barely functioning publishing business and seven hundred dollars? I earn enough working for my father to buy and sell magazines like his anytime I want." After I spoke, I bit my lip, not liking the smarmy rich-boy declaration.

"I know you probably expected more, but your uncle went into debt to pay your university expenses."

"Wait a minute—I had a scholarship that paid for everything."

"Surely you did. But who do you think the donor was?"

My jaw nearly hit the floor. "Why did he do that if he couldn't afford it?"

"I'm not certain. Perhaps he wanted to annoy your father. . ." Mr. O'Neill said, speculating with feigned interest. "Here's the note for the loan he took out to pay for your scholarship." He handed me an itemized statement of loan payments and corresponding interest typewritten on a bank's letterhead.

Why would Uncle John go into debt just to annoy my father? I remember how proud he was that I showed the same inclination toward the arts that he had. I believed he wanted me to follow my heart. He knew how my father always manipulated people to do exactly what he wanted. My uncle wanted me to be free of that trait, and I suspect he may have been a bit envious of my father's wealth as well. To Father, my university tuition and living expenses were small change.

"Uncle John owned the magazine for years. Maybe he really could afford it," I stubbornly insisted.

"He chose to publish exactly what he wanted, not always what was best for the magazine. The business is breaking even right now, but Mr. Rizzo's notes are due in in eighteen months. Unfortunately, he took out a second mortgage to pay for the scholarship as well as a loan to keep the magazine afloat. One of his conditions is that you increase the circulation from ten thousand to forty thousand. By accomplishing that, you'll have enough cash flow to meet his expenses."

Who, What, When, Where, Why and *How* streamed through my mind and I barely heard the financial details. Uncle John had paid for my education—my feelings were in turmoil. Why didn't he tell me? Did my mother know? I knew I'd never figure out the answers. Now that Uncle was dead, I couldn't even thank him.

"Your uncle felt you could easily meet this stipulation. He always said how clever you are, and he was proud of that."

I still couldn't say anything. It had been almost thirteen years since my uncle and I had communicated. Though we both loved the arts, I wondered where he got the idea I am clever.

"The condition attached to this stipulation is that if you can't increase the circulation prior to the due date of his notes, then you're to forfeit all assets to his creditors, and you must donate seven hundred dollars to the Artists' Benevolent Society. But if you do meet his stipulations, you can do whatever you desire with the business. Likely he wanted you to gain experience in his field and still be able to sell the magazine if you choose."

Uncle John couldn't increase circulation in the last thirteen years and he wanted me to quadruple it in a year and a half? Why bother? He had no children and no other relative need assume his debts. Why not donate the seven hundred dollars to the Artists' Benevolent Society and let the magazine go? But something nagged at me, maybe my sense of decency. After all, I loved Uncle John and he'd miraculously paid for my education. I had made it through and now had an opportunity to try my hand at using my education to pay for my education . . .

"Can I have time to think about this?"

Mr. O'Neill nodded as he scooped my uncle's will into the binder. "You have thirty days to make a decision."

I went home and asked my father pointblank if Uncle John had paid for my schooling.

He scowled at the thought. "You're not deaf, are you? I've told you many times that your stupid uncle never did anything right in his life. He lived on dreams. He thought when you received your journalism degree that you'd work with him at the magazine and save his ass with your abilities. How could he possibly afford to pay for a scholarship?"

My mother, quietly threading a needle across the room, lowered her embroidery hoop and cast him a disapproving look, as if to say *how cruel to speak of your recently departed brother that way.*

I admitted I'd attended Uncle John's lonely burial and that I was considering taking the helm of the magazine.

"You know I'm counting on you to stay aboard at the bank. I envision a distinguished line of Rizzo men heading it in perpetuity. . . I'm getting on in years and you're the only son I have." His anger gave way to a rare heartbroken look.

Father's reply didn't surprise me. Seeing him distraught, I almost succumbed to his passive-aggressive behavior. But my mother's quiet disdain made me reconsider. After all, I had thirty days to make a final decision.

I announced at breakfast the next morning that I would quit my job at the bank and take over the magazine. Father reacted with his usual vigor and jumped up from his chair. "John has been borrowing for years to keep the magazine afloat. I approved the second mortgage on his run-down dump of a building. I'm going to buy every note he has and close the rag down. You'll be back begging for work," he shouted, waving his fork with a bit of egg still attached.

I turned my back and raced from the dining room, flinging the front door open to the sputtering of new threats from my father.

My mother watched me from the dining room. She nodded once as I looked back, then bit her lip and lowered her eyes as I pushed the screen door open and let it slam behind me.

When I stepped from the cab in Brooklyn with one small suitcase to stand before the magazine's office the next morning, I wasn't surprised to find it in a rundown part of town. A large sign on top of the dilapidated one-story brick building had the magazine's name spelled out in faded and peeling red letters: CLASSIC ART EXPOSÉ. My Aunt Millie had created the magazine logo and she also wrote features for it. She'd worked with Uncle John on the magazine layout as well, along with his assistant, Jason. Aunt Millie concentrated upon analyzing literature and writing about the concerns of the local literary community. The word "classic" in the title was a misnomer, as they actually criticized nearly any genre of art. They critiqued or interviewed any deceased or living artist they thought worthy of praise or criticism.

After Aunt Millie died two years ago, Uncle John worked overtime and delegated some of her work to Jason, hoping I'd step in to help him out after I graduated, according to my father. To everyone's surprise the magazine managed to do fairly well, the readership holding while other magazines rose and fell, dwarfed by the giants Life, Saturday Evening Post, and other household names, and surpassed as well by more highbrow art magazines.

As I entered the building, I heard my father's angry words echo in my head again, but I shook them off, determined to follow my heart. No one appeared at the receptionist's desk, so I made myself comfortable in a well-worn chair in the front lobby. I found out why the magazine's numbers held steady as I thumbed through the collection of old issues held in a sagging bookcase. The modest success of the magazine was due to the fact that Uncle John's and Aunt Millie's readers, mostly artists themselves, relished their critiques. Classic Art Exposé was a combination of the New York Times and the National Enquirer of the art and literary world, and my uncle's "exposés"–his features of little-known facts about artists–were of particular interest. His final issue's cover story "Did Picasso's foot fetish influence his painting?" discussed Picasso's obsession with feet and how easily his fetish could have influenced all his work., to the outrage of some Picasso devotees. These controversial or investigative features helped to keep
the magazine's circulation steady.

I knew it would be difficult but not entirely impossible to quadruple the circulation inside eighteen months and to pay off the debt Uncle John had acquired. My savings were substantial for someone my age because of working with my father, but just a fraction of the notes due. I was familiar with analyzing art and in particular, literature because of my schooling in English and journalism, and I obviously understood financial undertakings because of my banking experience, but I had no clue how to run a publishing business. I was no longer a figurehead executive vice-president of a respected banking institution but the editor-in-chief of a quirky art magazine. Standing at the helm of a magazine wasn't exactly like steering a bank . . .

TOOTIE-DO PRESS

LOS ANGELES
REDWOOD HIGHWAY 101
SAN DIEGO
AJO

www.ingramcontent.com/pod-product-compliance
Lightning Source LLC
Chambersburg PA
CBHW070557300726
48975CB00006B/1623
* 9 7 9 8 2 1 8 0 5 3 0 0 0 *